SCENT OF ROSES

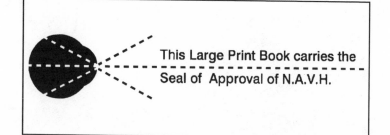

This Large Print Book carries the
Seal of Approval of N.A.V.H.

SCENT OF ROSES

KAT MARTIN

THORNDIKE PRESS

An imprint of Thomson Gale, a part of The Thomson Corporation

THOMSON

GALE

Detroit • New York • San Francisco • New Haven, Conn. • Waterville, Maine • London

LIBRARY OF CONGRESS CATALOGING-IN-PUBLICATION DATA

Martin, Kat.
  Scent of roses / by Kat Martin.
    p. cm.
  ISBN-13: 978-0-7862-9197-7 (hardcover : alk. paper)
  ISBN-10: 0-7862-9197-4 (hardcover : alk. paper)
  1. Divorced women — Fiction. 2. Family counselors — Fiction. 3. Large type books. I. Title.
PS3563.A7246S34 2007
813'.54—dc22
                                              2006030922

Published in 2007 by arrangement with Harlequin Books S.A.

Printed in the United States of America on permanent paper
10 9 8 7 6 5 4 3 2 1

PROLOGUE

She awakened with a start, her eyes coming sharply into focus, ears straining toward the odd sound that had pulled her from a deep but restless sleep.

There. There it was again, a strange, distant sort of creaking, like one of the floorboards under the carpet in the living room. She shifted on the pillow, trying to hear, but the sound had changed, become a peculiar moaning that sounded like the wind but could not be. Outside the house, the air was hot and still, the summer night densely black and quiet. She listened for the familiar chirp of crickets in the nearby field but they were oddly silent.

The sounds came again, an ominous creak, then a groan unlike anything she had heard in the house before. She sat up in bed, her heart pounding, easing herself slowly back against the headboard, her gaze locked on the door as she tried to decide whether to wake her husband. But Miguel had to go to work early and his days were long and exhausting. Whatever she had heard was surely her imagination.

Her ears strained into the silence, listening, listening. But the sound did not come again. She reminded herself to breathe, took a calming breath, and noticed an eerie thickening of the atmosphere in the bedroom. Maria found herself inhaling more deeply, working to suck air into her lungs as if a heavy weight pressed down on her chest. Her heartbeat quickened even more, thudding heavily now, each beat swelling beneath her breastbone.

Madre de Dios, *what is wrong?*

She dragged in another labored breath, drawing the thick air into her lungs and slowly forcing it out. She told herself to stay calm. *It is nothing . . . only a trick of the mind. Nothing but the hot, moonless night and the silence.* She inhaled again. Out and then in, deep labored breaths that should have steadied her but did nothing to ease her growing fear.

That was when she smelled it. The faint scent of roses. The odor drifted toward her, wrapped itself around her, began to press in

on her. It grew as dense as the air, turning thick and heavy, cloying, sickeningly sweet. The fields around the house bloomed with roses nearly half the year, but the scent was soft and light, a pleasing fragrance, nothing at all like the sticky smell that hung in the air: the scent of flowers, which had died and begun to decay.

The bile rose in her throat and Maria whimpered. Her hand shook as she reached for her husband, sleeping peacefully beside her. She paused, knowing once he woke up he would have a hard time returning to sleep, knowing how badly he needed his rest. Still, silently, she willed him to awaken.

Her gaze skipped frantically around the room, searching for the source of the noises and the smell, unsure what she might find, but there was nothing there. Nothing that could explain the terror that continued to well inside her, swelling with each frantic beat of her heart.

She swallowed past the fear clogging her throat and reached for Miguel, but just then the rose scent began to fade. The pressure on her chest began to ease and little by little, the air in the room slowly thinned to normal. She took a deep, cleansing breath and released it, then another and another. Outside the window, the familiar chirp of crickets reached her ears and she sagged against the headboard.

It was nothing, after all. Just the hot, dry night and her imagination. Miguel would have been angry. He would have accused her of behaving like a child.

Unconsciously her hand came to rest on her stomach. She was no longer a child. She was nineteen years old and carrying a child of her own.

She looked over at her husband and wished she could sleep as deeply as he. But her eyes remained open, her ears alert. She told herself that she was no longer afraid.

But she knew that for the rest of the night she would not sleep.

ONE

Elizabeth Conners sat behind her desk at the Family Psychology Clinic. The office was comfortably furnished, with an oak desk and chair, a couple of four-drawer oak file cabinets, two oak side chairs and a sofa upholstered in dark green fabric sitting against one wall.

Oak-framed pictures of the town in the early nineteen hundreds decorated the interior and a green-glass lamp sat on the edge of her desk, giving the place a casual, old-fashioned appearance. The office was neat and orderly. With the number of cases she handled, it was imperative she be well organized.

Elizabeth glanced at the stack of manila files on her desk, each one a case she was currently working. For the past two years, she had been an employee of the small, privately owned clinic in San Pico, California. Elizabeth had been born in the town,

9

mainly an agricultural community, situated near the southwest end of the San Joaquin Valley.

She had graduated from San Pico High, then gotten a partial scholarship to help pay her way through college. She had majored in psychology at UCLA, earning a master's in social work, making extra money with a part-time job as a waitress, as she had done in high school.

Two years ago, she had returned to her hometown, a quiet place of refuge where her father and sister lived, though her dad had died last year and her sister had married and moved away. Elizabeth had come to recover from a messy divorce, and the quiet life away from the city had helped bring her out of the depression she had suffered after her marriage to Brian Logan had fallen apart.

In contrast to the hustle of busy Santa Ana, where she had been working, San Pico was a city of around thirty thousand people, of which half the population was now Hispanic. Elizabeth's family had been among the original founders back in 1907, farmers and dairymen back then. During her childhood, her father and mother had owned a small neighborhood market, Conner's Grocery, but after her mother had died, her father had sold the business and retired, and Elizabeth had gone off to school.

She reached for the file on top of the stack on her desk, preparing herself for her upcoming session that evening with the Mendoza family, conducted in their home. The file contained a history of drinking and family violence that included an incident of child abuse, but the violence seemed to have lessened in the months the family had been in counseling.

Elizabeth fervently believed the sessions were helping family members learn to deal with each other in ways that did not include physical violence.

Leaning over the file, she tucked an annoying strand of dark auburn hair behind an ear and continued to scan the file. Like all of the Conners, she was dark-haired, slenderly built and a little taller than average. But unlike her sister, she had been blessed with the clear blue eyes of her mother.

Which meant that every time she looked in the mirror, she thought of Grace Conners and missed her.

Her mother had died a painful death from cancer when Elizabeth was just fifteen. They had been extremely close and the difficult months of caring for, then losing her had taken its toll. Elizabeth's blue eyes were her mother's legacy, but the memories they stirred were so painful that sometimes, instead of a blessing, her best feature seemed more of a curse.

Elizabeth sighed as she reached the end of the report, closed the file and leaned back in her chair. She had never expected to return to her hometown, which was flat and dusty and most of the year far too hot.

But sometimes fate had different notions and here she was, in a rented apartment on Cherry Street, doing the kind of work she had been trained for, and though she didn't particularly like living in the homely little town, at least she felt good about her job.

She was thinking about her upcoming session that night when a soft knock sounded at the door. She looked up to see one of the boys she counseled walk into the room. Raul Perez was seventeen years old, on work leave from juvenile detention, to which he'd been sentenced for the second time. Belligerent, surly and difficult, he was also smart and caring and loyal to his friends and the people he loved, and especially to his beloved sister, Maria.

His concern for others was the reason Elizabeth had agreed to do his counseling sessions without a fee. Raul had potential. He could make something of himself if he was given the right motivation — if she could convince him that his life would never improve as long as he involved himself in alcohol and drugs.

Burglary had been the result, of course, as it often was with kids like Raul. They needed money to buy the drugs and they would do whatever it took to get them.

But Raul had been drug free for over a year and he had told her that he meant to stay that way. There was something in his intense black eyes that made Elizabeth believe it might be true.

"Raul. Come in." She smiled at him warmly. "It's good to see you."

"You are looking very well," he said, always extremely polite.

"Thank you." She thought that she did look good today, in crisp beige cotton slacks and a short-sleeved turquoise silk blouse, her shoulder-length auburn hair in loose waves around her face.

Raul sat down in one of the oak side chairs and Elizabeth sat down behind her desk. To begin the session, she started with a question about his part-time job at Sam Goodie's, janitorial and delivery work that would end when Ritchie Jenkins got back on his feet after crashing his motorcycle down at the end of Main Street. In another week, the job would be over and unless he found something else, he would be back in juvenile detention full-time.

"So, how do you like working at the store so far?"

He shrugged a pair of linebacker shoulders. "I like the music — except when they play country western." Raul was only about five foot ten, but he was stocky and muscular, big for his age since he was a child. He had glossy, straight black hair and dark skin, marred only by the tattoo of a skull on the back of one hand and his initials in blue under the skin beneath his left ear. The initials were a homemade job probably done in grammar school. She thought the skull must have been done during his last stay in juvenile hall.

Elizabeth looked at him and smiled. "I know you'll be out of work by the end of the week, but I have some very exciting news for you."

He studied her warily from his place across the desk. "What is it?"

"You've been accepted at Teen Vision."

"Teen Vision?"

"I mentioned it a couple of weeks ago, remember?"

He nodded, his eyes fixed on her face.

"Since the farm is a fairly new facility, they only have room for twenty-five kids so far, but a couple of openings have come up and your application was one of the ones they accepted."

"I didn't put in an application," he said darkly.

She kept the smile fixed on her face. "I know you didn't — I did. I mentioned the farm to you when you were here before. You seemed interested. I took it one step further and applied in your name."

He was frowning. That wasn't good. The students who participated in the residential program at Teen Vision were there of their own free will. If he didn't want to be involved, being there wouldn't do him the least bit of good.

"The term lasts one year. You have to be between the ages of fourteen and eighteen and you have to agree to stay the entire twelve months or they won't let you in."

"I'm out of detention for good in six more months."

"You need to change your life so that you can stay out."

Raul said nothing.

"You would start next week. While you're there, your room and board would be completely taken care of. They even pay a small stipend for the work you do on the farm."

Raul grunted. "I know how much farm workers make. That's the way my family earned their living."

"This is different than being a migratory worker, Raul. You told me yourself you liked farming, being out in the fresh air working the soil. You could learn a vocation while you're there and you could get your GED. When your year is up, you could find a full-time job in agriculture or whatever you decide you want to do, something that would eventually make you a decent living."

He seemed to mull that over. "I need to think about it."

"All right. But I don't think you can make any sort of decision until you go out there, take a look at the facility and meet some of the instructors. Would you be willing to do that, Raul?"

He sat back in his chair, his eyes still on her face. "I would like to see it."

"That's great. Just remember, a place like that requires a commitment. It's a place you go in order to change your life. You have to want to do that. You have to want to start over and make a new beginning."

Raul said nothing for several long moments and neither did Elizabeth, purposely giving him time to think.

"When could we go?"

She stood up from her chair. "Do you have to work this afternoon?"

He shook his head. "Not until tomorrow morning."

"Good." Elizabeth rounded the desk and moved past him toward the door. She smiled and pulled it open. "Then why don't we go right now?"

The Teen Vision farm sat on fifteen acres of flat, arid land fronting Highway 51 a few miles out of town. It was a fertile piece of ground donated by Harcourt Farms, the largest agricultural farming company in San Pico County.

Until four years ago, Fletcher Harcourt had run the farm. After a nearly fatal accident that damaged the family patriarch's brain and left him in a wheelchair, his oldest son, Carson, had taken over the twelve-thousand acre operation. He had taken control of the company and assumed his father's once-powerful position in the community. Carson was well liked and generous. The attractive white stucco dormitory and outbuildings that housed Teen Vision had undoubtedly been funded in part by

Carson's donations.

Elizabeth had met Carson Harcourt several times since her return to San Pico. He was tall, blond and attractive. At thirty-six, after several brief relationships, he remained unmarried, though with his considerable wealth and social position, he could certainly take his pick of the women in town.

She was thinking of Carson as she drove her nearly new, pearl-white Acura through the front gates of Teen Vision and was only mildly surprised to see the man's silver Mercedes sedan pulling out of the parking area. He stepped on the brake as he drove past her, bringing the car to a halt, swirling a cloud of dust around them. Carson rolled down his window as if he didn't notice and gave her the famous Harcourt smile.

"Well, Ms. Conners — what a nice surprise. Looks like I'm leaving at just the wrong time." Carson had always been friendly. She had sensed he might have an interest beyond just being social, but if he did, he had never pursued it.

"It's nice to see you, Carson." She tilted her head toward her passenger. "This is Raul Perez. I'm hoping he'll be one of the farm's new enrollees."

"Is that so?" Carson ducked his head to get a look at the boy. "They do some good

18

work here, son. You had better grab the chance while you've got it."

Raul said nothing, as Elizabeth could have guessed. With the money and power Carson Harcourt possessed, he represented everything the boy rebelled against.

"This place . . ." She glanced around, taking in the group of boys hoeing the fields, the two boys laughing as they poured grain into a trough to feed the farm's small herd of four white-faced Hereford cattle. "This was very generous of you, Carson."

He shrugged. "Harcourt Farms likes to give back to the community whenever it can."

"Still, you've really done something good here. Someone else might not have been so supportive."

He smiled and glanced out at the fields, then back to her again. "Listen, I've got to run. Got a meeting with some labor union guys in town." He ducked his head to look past her to the boy. "Good luck to you, son."

Raul just stared and inwardly Elizabeth sighed.

"One more thing," Carson said to her. "I've been meaning to call you. I wanted to talk to you about the Teen Vision Benefit on Saturday night. I was hoping you might go with me."

She was stunned. Carson had been friendly, but nothing more. Perhaps he had discovered her interest in Teen Vision. Though she had never actually been to the farm, she knew the wonderful work being done and believed strongly in the project.

She cast him an assessing glance. Since her divorce, she'd rarely dated. The dark days after she had discovered Brian's infidelity left her wary of men. Still, it might be fun to spend an evening with an intelligent, attractive man.

"I'd like that, Carson. Thank you for asking. It's black tie, as I recall."

He nodded. "I'll call you at your office, get directions to your house so I can pick you up."

"All right, that sounds good."

He smiled and waved, rolled up the window of his Mercedes and drove away. Elizabeth watched him a moment in the rearview mirror, then stepped on the accelerator and drove through the gate into one of the spaces in the dirt parking lot and turned off the engine.

"Well, we're here." She smiled at Raul, who was staring out the window toward the group of young men working in the fields. A distant tractor threw up a plume of dust while a cluster of dairy cows stood on a hill waiting for the evening round of milking to begin.

Looking nervous and younger than his seventeen years, Raul cracked the door on his side of the car and climbed out into the afternoon heat. In the area between the parking lot and the house, the director of Teen Vision, Sam Marston, walked toward them.

Sam was average in height and build, a man in his early forties rapidly going bald who had shaved the sparse hair off, giving him a modern, stylish appearance. He was a soft-spoken man, yet there was a sense of authority about him. He waved a greeting as he walked up to where they stood.

"Welcome to Teen Vision."

"Thank you." She had met Sam Marston when she first moved back to town, knew his remarkable work with delinquent boys. "I know your time is limited. I thought I could come back for an official tour later on."

He understood what she was saying. That she wanted him to spend this time with Raul. "You're welcome anytime," he said with a smile, then his attention shifted to the boy. "You must be Raul Perez."

"Yes, sir."

"I'm Sam Marston. Let me show you

around, and while we're at it, I'll tell you a little about Teen Vision." Ignoring Raul's look of alarm, Sam slapped a hand on the youth's wide back and nudged him forward, forcing Raul into step beside him.

Elizabeth watched them walk away and found herself smiling. She prayed Raul would give the place a chance, that the farm would be his salvation, as it had been for a number of other boys.

Walking over to stand in the shade of a fruit tree to watch the boys in the fields and wait for Sam, she saw another car, a dark brown Jeep Cherokee, drive through the gate and pull into the space next to hers.

A tall, lean man in faded jeans and a navy blue T-shirt climbed out from behind the wheel. He had very dark hair and darkly tanned skin, a nice wide set of shoulders, narrow hips and a flat stomach. As he walked toward her, she saw that the shirt carried the Teen Vision slogan, Only You Can Make Your Dreams Come True, printed in white letters on the front. A pair of solid-looking biceps bulged below the short sleeves of his T-shirt.

Still, somehow she couldn't imagine him working as a counselor on the farm. His haircut looked too expensive, his long strides too purposeful, almost aggressive.

Even the fit of his jeans spoke of style and money. Elizabeth studied him from beneath the tree and though he wore wraparound shades and she couldn't make out his face, there was something familiar about him.

She wondered where she might have seen him and thought that if she had, surely she would remember. He moved past her as if she weren't there, his gaze focused ahead, striding with purpose in the direction of the new barn under construction where several older boys were busily hammering nails. The dark-haired man walked up to them and started talking. A few minutes later, he strapped on a carpenter's belt and set to work.

Elizabeth watched him for a while, enjoying the efficiency of his movements, his obvious skill at what he was doing, and continued to wonder who he was. When Sam and Raul returned, she intended to ask, but when they arrived, the boy's face was glowing and his smile so radiant the moment slipped past.

"You're going to do it?" she said, beaming up at him.

He nodded. "Sam says he and one of the counselors will help me figure out what I am most suited to learn. He says I can do whatever I am most interested in."

"Oh, Raul, that's wonderful!" She wanted to reach over and hug him, but she needed to remain professional and that would probably just embarrass him. "I can't tell you how pleased I am."

"He can check in on Saturday," Sam said. "We'll help him fill out the forms and sign whatever paperwork is necessary." Technically he would still be in the foster care system until next year and the paperwork would have to pass through proper channels.

"That sounds great." Elizabeth turned to Raul. "I can bring you out here, if you like."

"*Sí*, that would be good." Raul rarely slipped into his native language, only when he was angry or nervous. Still, he was smiling. Sometimes nervous could be good.

"Your sister will be so pleased."

His smile broadened. "Maria will be happy for me. Miguel, I think, too."

"Yes, I think they will both be very happy you made this decision."

They said their farewells to Sam, who promised to give her a personal tour of the farm whenever she had time, and they started back to the car.

She was feeling extremely pleased with the way the afternoon had gone when she glanced at Raul and saw that his smile had faded.

"What is it, Raul?"

"I am nervous. I want to do this right."

"You will. You've got lots of people to help you."

Still, he didn't relax. She knew he was worried that he would somehow fail. It was the failures, she had learned, that most of these young Hispanics remembered and those failures shaped their lives. But Raul had a number of accomplishments as well. He had stayed drug-free for a year and now he had pledged a year of his life to Teen Vision.

"Will you be seeing your sister tonight? I know how excited she'll be."

Instead of a smile, Raul frowned. "I will stop by and tell her the news." He glanced in her direction. "I am worried about her."

"Why? She isn't having trouble with her pregnancy, I hope?" Though Maria was just nineteen, this was her second pregnancy. Last year, she had suffered a miscarriage. Elizabeth knew how much this baby meant to her and Miguel.

"It isn't the baby. It is something else. Maria won't say what." His black eyes came to rest on her face. "Maybe you could talk to her. If you did, maybe she would tell you what is wrong."

She didn't like the sound of that. Though Maria's husband was a stereotypical macho Hispanic, convinced the man was the undisputed head of the family, the couple seemed happy. She hoped they weren't having marital problems.

"I'd be glad to talk to her, Raul. Tell her to call me at the office and we'll set up a time."

"I will tell her. But I do not think she will call." Raul said no more.

As Elizabeth slid behind the wheel of the car, hissing at the heat of the red leather seat against her skin, she cast a last glance at the barn under construction. Only two sides of the building had been framed, but they were making good progress. She studied the group still hammering away, but the dark-haired man was gone.

Sitting in the passenger side, Raul snapped his seat belt in place and Elizabeth started the engine. As they drove back to town, the boy seemed miles away and she wondered if his thoughts were on the very different future he was about to undertake, or if he was worried about his sister.

Elizabeth made a mental note to stop by the little yellow house occupied by Miguel Santiago and his pretty young wife. She would speak to Maria, see what was wrong, find out if there was something she could do.

Two

The hour was late. The night black as ink, just a fingernail moon casting a thin ray of white into the darkness. The smell of newly mown hay hung in the air, along with the rich musk of freshly tilled soil. Inside the house, Maria Santiago snapped off the small TV that sat on a little wooden table against the wall of her sparsely furnished living room.

Though the house wasn't large, just two bedrooms and a bath, it was only four years old and solidly built, with yellow plaster walls outside and a simple asphalt tile roof. The house had been freshly painted just before they moved in and the beige carpet looked almost new.

Maria had loved the house from the moment she and Miguel had seen it. With its grassy backyard and zinnia-filled flower beds next to the porch out in front, it was the nicest place she had ever lived. Miguel loved it, too, and he was proud of being able to provide such a home for his wife and the baby that was soon to come.

Miguel wanted a child even more than Maria. Aside from Maria and Raul, he didn't have much family, at least not nearby. Most of Miguel's family lived in the San Joaquin Valley farther north, near Modesto. Maria's mother had died when she was fourteen, and she had never known her father. Her mother once told her he had left when Raul was born and no one had seen him since.

With her parents gone and no one to care for them, Maria and Raul had moved in with a couple named Hernandez, migratory workers who traveled the agricultural circuit. One of the jobs they had worked had been in the orchards, harvesting almonds for Harcourt Farms, and that was where Maria had met Miguel. She had been not quite fifteen, her brother only thirteen, and Miguel Santiago had been their salvation.

They had married the day of her fifteenth birthday and when the workers left for their next job, both she and Raul had stayed with Miguel on the farm. Though he earned barely enough to get by, there was plenty to eat, and Raul could go to school. He had attended faithfully for the entire first year, but being so far behind the other kids, in a short time he had rebelled and refused to go.

He had begun to stay out late, to hang around with a bad element. Eventually, he had gotten into trouble and been sent to a foster home. Finally, he'd wound up in juvenile hall. Recently, he had been released into a halfway house and soon would be living at Teen Vision.

It seemed a miracle had occurred.

Another had happened two months ago, when her husband had received a promotion to overseer — one of four on the farm. He had been given a raise and a house to live in as part of his higher salary.

It was a very nice house, Maria thought again as she untied the sash on her bathrobe and tossed it over a chair. Dressed in a short white nylon nightgown that fanned out over her growing belly, she walked toward the bed, wishing Miguel would get home. But he often worked late in the fields and she had mostly gotten used to it.

Except that lately, when he didn't get home and the hour grew late, Maria was afraid.

She flicked a glance at the bed, her gaze lighting on the comfortable queen-size mattress, bigger than any she had ever slept in before.

She ached to slide beneath the covers, to rest her head on one of the pillows and drift off to sleep. She was so very tired. Her back ached and her feet hurt. Surely tonight she would sleep and not wake up until Miguel came home. Surely, what had happened to her last week and the week before would not happen again tonight.

It was after midnight, the house completely quiet as she pulled back the pretty yellow quilt on top of the bed and lay down on the mattress, pulling the sheet up beneath her chin.

She could hear the crickets in the field and the gentle, rhythmic sound gave her comfort. The pillow felt soft beneath her head. Her long black hair, left unbound the way Miguel liked it, teased her cheek as she shifted on the mattress, and her eyes drifted closed.

For a while, she dozed peacefully, unaware of the eerie creaks and moans, of the subtle shift in the atmosphere. Then the air grew thicker, denser, and the soothing chirp of the crickets abruptly halted.

Maria's eyes snapped open. She was staring up at the ceiling and a heavy weight seemed to be pressing down on her chest.

She could hear the eerie moaning, the creaking that wasn't the wind. In the darkness of the bedroom, the sickening, suffocating smell of roses drifted into her nostrils and the bile rose in her throat.

The putrid smell enveloped her, seemed to force her down in the mattress, to suck the air from her lungs. She tried to sit up, but she couldn't move. She tried to cry out, but no sound came from her throat.

Oh, Madre de Dios! *Mother of God, protect me!*

Silently she began to pray, to beg the Virgin Mary to save her, to send the evil away.

She was so frightened! She didn't understand what was happening. She didn't know if what she felt was real or if she was losing her mind. Her mother had suffered a tumor that eventually killed her. Toward the end, she had raved and ranted and imagined things.

Was that what was happening to her?

She twisted on the bed and tried to sit up, but her body remained completely frozen, rigid on the sheet. Something shifted, seemed to invade her mind, to fill her thoughts until she could think of nothing but the words spinning round in her head.

They want your baby, a small voice whispered through her terror-filled brain. *They'll take your baby if you don't leave.*

Maria choked on a sob. Fresh horror filled her. She wanted Miguel, prayed he would come home and save her. Silently, she cried out for God to bring him home to her before it was too late.

But Miguel did not come.

Instead, the small voice began to fade into the silence as if it were never there and the heavy smell of roses drifted away in the darkness. For long moments, she lay there, afraid to move, afraid of what would happen if she did.

Maria swallowed, managed to drag in a shaky breath of air. She tried to lift her arms and found that her limbs responded, allowing her to shift on the bed. She lay there staring at the ceiling, inhaling sharp, deep breaths, her hands trembling. She was shaking all over, she realized, her heart pounding as if she had run a thousand miles.

Tentatively, she extended her legs. She moved her arms, crossed them over her chest to control the trembling, then shakily pushed herself upright in the bed. Long black hair fell over her shoulder, reaching nearly to her waist. She drew her legs up beneath her chin, pulled the nightgown down to cover them, and rested her chin on her knees.

It was a nightmare, she told herself. *The same dream you had before.*

Maria's eyes welled with tears. She pressed a hand against her mouth to muffle a sob and tried to convince herself it was true.

Zachary Harcourt opened the front door of the house that was once his home at Harcourt Farms. It was a big, white, two-story wood-framed house with porches both front and rear, an impressive house that had been built in the forties and remodeled and improved over the years.

The molded ceilings were high, to help with the heat, and expensive damask draperies hung at the windows. The floors were oak and always polished to a glossy sheen. Zach ignored the sharp ring of his work boots as he walked down the hall into the room that had been his father's study, a man's room, paneled in dark wood, with shelves lining the walls filled with gold-edged leather-bound books.

The big oak, rolltop desk where his father used to sit still dominated the study, but now his older brother, Carson, sat in an expensive leather chair.

"I see you still don't believe in knocking."

Carson turned toward him, one hand still resting on the paperwork on his desk. The enmity on his face was unmistakable. The same dislike was reflected in Zach's eyes as well.

The men were about the same height, almost six foot two, though Carson, two years older, was heavier through the chest and shoulders, built more like their father. He was blond and blue-eyed like his mother, while Zach, a half brother born on the wrong side of the blanket, was more leanly built, with the nearly black, slightly wavy hair that had belonged to Teresa Burgess, his father's long-time mistress.

It was said that Teresa carried a trace of Hispanic blood from a distant grandmother, but she had always denied it, and though Zach's skin was darker than Carson's, his cheekbones high and more sharply defined, he had no idea whether or not it was true.

One thing was certain. Zach had the same distinct gold-flecked brown eyes that stared back at him when he looked at his father, marking him clearly as Fletcher Harcourt's son and Carson's brother — much to Carson's chagrin.

"I don't need to knock," Zach said. "In case you've forgotten, which you usually do, this house still belongs to our father, which means it is mine as much as it is yours."

Carson made no reply. After the fall that had left Fletcher Harcourt's motor functions impaired and his memory distorted, Carson, the eldest son, had been made conservator of the farm and all of their father's affairs, including his health care. It had been an easy decision for the judge, since Zach was younger and had a prison record.

At twenty-one, Zach had spent two years in the California State Penitentiary at Avenal for manslaughter, convicted of a drunk-driving offense that had resulted in a man's death.

"What is it you want?" Carson asked.

"I want to know what's happening with the benefit. Knowing your penchant for getting things done, I assume everything is in order."

"Everything's under control, just like I said it would be. I told you I'd help raise money for this little project of yours and that's what I'm doing."

Two years ago, Zach had set aside his pride and come to Carson with the idea of establishing a boy's camp for teens with drug and alcohol problems. As a youth, he'd been one of those kids, always in trouble, always butting heads with his family and the law.

But the two years he'd spent in prison had changed his life and he wanted that to happen for other boys who weren't as lucky as he had been.

Not that he'd thought himself lucky at the time.

Back then, he'd been sullen and resentful, blaming everyone but himself for what had happened to him and what his life had become. Out of boredom and hoping to find a way of shortening his sentence, he had started to study law and discovered he seemed to have a knack for it. He had gotten his GED, taken the SAT's and passed with extremely high marks, then gone to Berkley and enrolled in Hastings Law School.

Impressed by the changes he was trying to make in his life, his father had helped him with the tuition, and combined with the money from his part-time job, Zach had managed to get through school, graduating in the top percentiles of his class. He had passed the bar exam with flying colors and Fletcher Harcourt had used his influence to get Zach's felony record expunged so that he could practice law.

Zach was now a successful lawyer with an

office in Westwood, an apartment overlooking the ocean in Pacific Palisades, a slick new 645 Ci BMW convertible and the Jeep he drove whenever he came up to the valley.

He was living the good life and he wanted to give something back for the success he had found. Until that day two years ago, he had never asked his brother for anything — had sworn he never would. Carson and his mother had made Zach's life miserable from the day his father had brought him home and announced plans to adopt him.

There was bad blood between them that would never go away, but Harcourt Farms belonged to Zach as much as Carson and though his brother had complete control, there was plenty of available land, and the location he had chosen for the site was exactly the perfect spot.

Zach remembered the day he had approached his brother, the amazement he had felt when Carson had so readily agreed to his proposal.

"Well, for once you've actually come up with a good idea," Carson had said from his chair at the rolltop desk.

"Then you're saying Harcourt Farms will donate the land?"

"That's right. I'll even help you raise the

money to get the project off the ground."

It had taken Zack several months before he realized his brother had once again neatly turned the tables. The project became Carson's — though it was mostly Zach's money that provided the funding — and the entire town was now in Carson's debt.

Zach no longer cared. With Carson as spokesman, the money continued pouring in, enough to keep the farm running and even enough to expand. The more boys who could be helped, the better, as far as Zach was concerned. Zach would gladly stay out of the picture if it meant helping those kids, and with Carson's name attached instead of his own, the upcoming benefit on Saturday night would likely be another success.

"I just wanted to check," Zach said, thinking of the black tie affair he wouldn't be attending. "Let me know if there's anything you need me to do." Instead, he would spend the weekend building the barn, working with the Teen Vision boys, something he had discovered he loved to do.

"You sure you don't want to come?" Carson asked, though Zach figured having the black sheep of the family in attendance was the last thing Carson wanted.

"No thanks. I wouldn't want to cramp your style."

"You could bring Lisa. I'll be taking Elizabeth Conners."

The name hit a cord in his memory bank. *Liz Conners.* She was four years his junior. Once, before he'd gone to prison, he'd been drunk and high and he had come on to her pretty hard outside the coffee shop where she had a part-time job after school. Liz had slapped his face — something no other woman had ever done — and he had never forgotten her.

"I thought she was married and living in Orange County someplace."

"She was. She's divorced now, moved back to town a couple of years ago."

"That so?" San Pico was the last place Zach would want to live. Coming up to visit his dad in the rest home and working on expanding the youth farm was the most he could manage. "Tell Liz I said hello."

Inwardly he smiled, thinking he was the last person Liz Conners would be happy to hear from. He'd kind of thought Liz was the sort of woman who'd be able to see through a man like his brother. Then again, there was no accounting for people's tastes.

Carson said no more, just returned to the stack of work on his desk. Zach left the study without a goodbye and headed for his car. He was surprised Carson knew he had been seeing Lisa Doyle and he didn't like it that he did. He didn't like Carson knowing anything about him. He didn't trust his half brother and never had.

Whatever Carson might think, Lisa wasn't really his type. But she liked hot, raunchy sex, no strings attached, and so did Zach, and they had been sleeping together off and on for years.

And he didn't have to worry about getting a motel room when he was in town and Lisa didn't have to worry about picking up some stranger in a bar when she wanted to get laid.

It was a good deal for both of them.

Elizabeth looked up at the sound of a knock at her door. The door swung wide and her boss, Dr. Michael James, stuck his head through the opening. Michael, just under six feet tall with sandy hair and hazel eyes, had a Ph.D. in psychology. He had opened the office five years ago. Elizabeth had been working for him for the past two. Michael was engaged to be married, but lately he seemed to be having second thoughts and Elizabeth wasn't sure he was going to go through with the wedding.

"How'd it go with Raul?" he asked, another of the young man's supporters. Raul had a way of endearing himself to people, though on the surface he seemed to do his best to achieve just the opposite.

"He's decided to enroll in the program."

"That's great. Now if he'll just stick to it."

"He was excited, I think. Of course, Sam could sell sour milk to cows."

"So you were impressed with the farm. I thought you would be."

"It's really coming along. Carson has done a wonderful job."

"Yes, he has. Though it seems to me everything he does is a bit self-serving. Lately, I heard a rumor he may be running for a seat in the state assembly."

"I don't know him very well, but he seems community-minded. Maybe he'd be good for the job."

"Maybe." Though Michael didn't seem completely convinced.

They spoke for a moment more, then Dr. James left the office and the phone rang. When Elizabeth picked it up, she recognized Raul Perez's voice.

"I am calling about my sister," he said simply. "I saw her this morning after Miguel went to work. She was very upset. She tries to hide it, but I know her too well. Something is wrong. Do you think you could stop by the house sometime today?"

"Actually, I've been meaning to get over there to see her. I'll stop by this afternoon. Will your sister be home?"

"I think so. I wish I knew what was wrong."

"I'll see if I can find out," Elizabeth promised and as she hung up the phone she wondered what it could be.

In a job where she dealt with family violence, drugs, robbery and even murder, it would take a great deal to surprise her.

THREE

It was after five o'clock, and the office was closed by the time Elizabeth was able to leave. She made the drive through town in the after-five traffic, nothing like the bumper-to-bumper, endless line of cars on the L.A. freeways she used to battle when she lived in Santa Ana, but enough to keep her stopped on Main Street through two sets of red lights.

Downtown San Pico was only ten blocks long, some of the store signs printed in Spanish. Miller's Dry Cleaners, perched on the corner, had a laundromat attached. There was a JC Penney catalog store, several clothing stores, and a couple of diners, including Marge's Café, where she had worked part-time in high school.

As she drove past the coffee shop, she could see the long Formica counter and pink vinyl booths inside. Even after twenty years, the place still did a brisk business.

Aside from The Ranch House, a steak and prime rib restaurant at the edge of town, it was the only decent place to eat.

A few straggly sycamore trees grew out of the sidewalks that lined the downtown streets but not many. There were a couple of gas stations, a Burger King, a McDonald's and a sleezy bar called The Roadhouse out where Highway 51 intersected Main Street. The biggest boon to the area had been the arrival two years ago of a Wal-Mart, built to service the town and several outlying farming communities.

Elizabeth continued down Main and turned onto the highway, heading for Harcourt Farms. The little yellow house where Maria and Miguel Santiago lived sat just off the road in an area of the farm that included three other overseers' houses, half a dozen farm laborer cottages, and the big, white, wood-frame, two-story owner's house, which sat some distance away.

Elizabeth's car bumped over a set of abandoned railroad tracks not far from the house. She pulled off the road into a spot next to the driveway and climbed out of the Acura.

She had saved for two years to get the down payment for the car and she loved it. With its red leather seats and wood-paneled interior, it made her feel younger just to sit behind the wheel. She had bought the car because she thought that at thirty, she shouldn't be feeling as old as she often did.

She walked along the cement sidewalk past a flowerbed blooming with red and yellow zinnias. Elizabeth knocked on the front door of the house, and a few minutes later, Maria Santiago pulled it open.

"Ms. Conners." She smiled. "What a nice surprise. It is good to see you. Please come in." Maria was a slender young woman, except for the protrusion of her belly and her ever-increasing breasts. Her long black hair was braided, as she often wore it, and hanging down her back.

"Thank you." Elizabeth walked into the house, which Maria kept immaculately clean. The girl, as neatly kept as the house, wore a pair of white, ankle-length pants and a loose-fitting blue-flowered blouse. Except for the tight lines around her mouth and the faint smudges beneath her eyes, she looked lovely.

"Miguel and I, we want to thank you for what you did for Raul. I have never seen him so excited, though of course, he tried not to show it." She frowned as a thought occurred. "He is not in more trouble? That is not the reason you are here?"

"No, of course not. This has nothing to do with Raul. Except that your brother is worried about you. Raul asked me to stop by."

"Why would he do that?"

"He thinks you are upset about something. He isn't sure what it is. He hoped that you might talk to me about it."

Maria glanced away. "My brother is imagining things. I am fine, as you can see."

She was pretty, with her big dark eyes and classic features, and more than six months pregnant. Elizabeth had come to know Maria and Miguel through her dealings with Raul and she liked them both, though Miguel's overly macho attitude could be irritating at times.

"It is hot outside," Maria said. "Would you like a glass of iced tea?"

"That sounds wonderful."

They sat down at a wooden table in the kitchen. Maria went over to the refrigerator and pulled out a plastic pitcher, then popped cubes from an ice tray into two tall glasses and filled them with chilled tea.

She set the glasses down on the table. "Would you like some sugar?"

"No, this is perfect just the way it is." Elizabeth sat down at the small round table covered by a flowered plastic tablecloth and took a sip of her tea.

Maria stirred sugar into hers, paying slightly more attention to the task than necessary, Elizabeth thought, wondering again what the problem could be. Raul was a shrewd young man. He wouldn't have called without good reason.

"It must be hard being alone all day this far from town," Elizabeth began cautiously.

"There is always work to do. Before it got so hot, I worked in my garden. Now, with the baby getting bigger, I cannot stay out in the sun for so long. But I have clothes to mend and food to prepare for Miguel. Since we moved into the house, he comes home for lunch. He works very hard. I like to make sure he has something good to eat."

"So the two of you are getting along all right?"

"*Sí.* We get along very well. My husband is a good man. He is a very good provider."

"I'm sure he is. Still, I imagine he often works late, which means you are home by yourself. Is that the reason you aren't sleeping well?" It was a risk. She was guessing and a wrong guess might bring the young woman's guard up even more.

"What . . . what makes you think I am not sleeping?"

"You look tired, Maria." Elizabeth reached

across the kitchen table and clasped the girl's hand. "What is it, Maria? Tell me what's wrong."

The girl shook her head and Elizabeth caught the sheen of tears. "I am not certain. Something is happening, but I do not know what it is."

"Something? Like what?"

"Something very bad, and I am afraid to tell Miguel." She drew her hand away. "I think . . . I think I might be getting sick like my mother."

Elizabeth frowned. "Your mother had a tumor, didn't she? Is that what you mean?"

"*Sí,* a tumor, yes. In her brain. Before she died, she started to see things that were not there, to hear voices calling out to her. I think maybe that is happening to me." Leaning over, she hugged her swollen belly and burst into tears.

Elizabeth sat back in her chair. It was possible, she supposed but there could be any number of explanations. "It's all right, Maria. You know I'll help you in any way I can. Tell me why you think you might have a tumor like your mother."

Maria looked up, her hand shaking as she brushed away the wetness on her cheeks. She took a deep breath and let it out slowly.

"In the night . . . when Miguel is working, sometimes I hear noises. They are very frightening sounds, creaking and groaning, moaning that sounds like the wind but the night is still. The air in the bedroom grows thick, and so heavy I can hardly breathe." She swallowed. "And then there is the smell."

"The smell?"

"*Sí*. Like roses, only so strong I think I will suffocate right there in the bed."

"San Pico is famous for its roses. They've been growing them here for more than forty years. Occasionally, you are bound to smell them." She clasped the young woman's hand once more, felt how cold it was, felt it trembling. "You're pregnant, Maria. When a woman is carrying a baby, sometimes her emotions get mixed up."

"They do?"

"Yes, sometimes they do."

Maria glanced away. "I am not sure what is happening. Sometimes . . . sometimes it seems real. Sometimes I think . . ."

"You think what, Maria?"

"That *mi casa es encantada.*"

Elizabeth spoke passable Spanish, had to in order to do her job. "You think your house is haunted? Surely you don't believe that."

Maria shook her head, fresh tears welling in her eyes. "I do not know what to believe. I only know that at night I am very afraid."

Frightened enough that she had been unable to sleep. "But you aren't saying that you've actually seen a ghost."

She shook her head. "I have not seen it. I have only heard its voice in my head."

"Listen to me, Maria. Your house is not haunted. There are no such things as ghosts."

"What about Jesus? Jesus came back from the dead. He is called the Holy Spirit."

Elizabeth leaned back in the chair. She had been doing social work since she graduated from college. She had dealt with hundreds of unusual problems, but this was a first.

"Jesus is different. He's the Son of God and he isn't haunting your house. Do you really believe there's a ghost in your bedroom?"

"There is a ghost — or I am going to die like my mother." She started to cry again.

Elizabeth rose from her chair. "No, you're not," she said firmly, stilling Maria's momentary lapse into tears. "You are not going to die. But just to make sure there isn't a tumor, I'm going to arrange for a visit to the clinic. Dr. Zumwalt can do a CAT scan.

If there's anything wrong, he'll be able to tell."

"We do not have the money for something like that."

"The county will take care of it, if Dr. Zumwalt thinks the test needs to be done."

"Will it hurt?"

"No. They just take a picture of the inside of your head."

Maria rose from her chair. "You must promise not to tell Miguel."

"I won't tell your husband. This is just between you and me." She could only imagine what Miguel Santiago would say if he found out his young wife had started to believe their house was haunted.

"We will go to the clinic tomorrow?"

"I'll have to make the arrangements. I'll call you as soon as I know the date and time, then I'll pick you up and take you there myself."

Maria managed an uneven smile. "Thank you."

"Raul is going to ask me if you're all right."

"Tell him I am fine."

Elizabeth sighed. "I'll tell him I'm taking you in for a checkup just to be sure you're okay."

She nodded and flicked a glance toward

the bedroom. "Tell him not to tell Miguel."

Carson Harcourt drove up in front of the two-story stucco fourplex on Cherry Street, climbed out of his Mercedes and started up the walkway to apartment B. The area was quiet, the neighborhood one of the safest in town. He was only a few minutes late and he figured, at any rate, Elizabeth wouldn't be ready when he got there.

Women never were.

A brisk rap on the door. He was surprised when a fully dressed Elizabeth Conners pulled it open.

Carson's gaze ran over her floor-length dark blue sequined gown and he found himself smiling. His spur-of-the-moment invitation to the benefit was nothing short of genius. He had noticed she was pretty, of course. He'd had a hunch, once she abandoned the boring but professional business suits she always wore, she would be far more than that.

"You look gorgeous," he said, meaning it. She was a little taller than average and slenderly built. As he assessed her curve-hugging gown, he saw that she had nice full breasts, smooth shoulders, a small waist and well-shaped hips.

I should have done this sooner, he chided himself.

"Thanks for the compliment. You look very dashing yourself, Carson."

He smiled. He'd always looked good in a tux. The black showed off his blond hair and blue eyes, and the single-button style set off the width of his shoulders. Too bad it was still so damned hot. He'd only been out of the air-conditioned car for a couple of minutes and already he was sweating inside the collar of his white pleated shirt.

"Let's get going. It'll be cooler in the car."

Elizabeth nodded and took his arm. Carson led her toward his silver Mercedes and settled her in the passenger seat. The air conditioner blasted full force the moment he turned the electronic key in the ignition. It had been a while since he'd had time for female companionship. As he glanced over at Elizabeth, he thought that maybe it was time for that to change. He would see how well they dealt together tonight.

The benefit was in full swing by the time they arrived. Carson led Elizabeth through the milling crowd, waving to a few friendly faces, heading toward the front of the room. He stopped at the no-host bar and ordered a glass of champagne for Elizabeth and a scotch-and-soda for himself. They made conversation with a few of the guests, Sam Marston, head of Teen Vision, Dr. and Mrs. Lionel Fox, one of the organizations biggest contributors, a couple of high school counselors.

"Elizabeth! I didn't realize you would be here!" It was Gwen Petersen. She was there with her husband, Jim, district manager for Wells Fargo Bank, and apparently she was a good friend of Elizabeth's.

"I hadn't planned to come until Carson was kind enough to invite me. I meant to call you. I've just been so busy."

Gwen's gaze swung from Elizabeth to Carson, lingered there a moment as if she were contemplating the two of them together, then she smiled.

"Well, what a nice idea." She was a petite woman with red hair and attractive features. She and her husband had a couple of little boys, if he recalled correctly, and he usually did.

Carson returned her smile. "I think it was a very good idea."

Gwen's gaze returned to her friend. "I'll call you the first of the week. We definitely need to have lunch."

Elizabeth nodded. "See you then."

It was nearly time to start the proceedings. Carson seated Elizabeth at the white-draped head table and took a seat beside her.

The room began to quiet as the last of the guests took their places at the tables. The benefit was being held in the banquet room of the Holiday Inn, where most local occasions took place.

Carson introduced Elizabeth to the other people seated at the front of the room, some of whom she knew, and they all conversed politely as dinner was served, the usual rubber chicken in some kind of dull brown gravy, lukewarm mashed potatoes and overcooked broccoli. Dessert followed, a decent chocolate mousse that managed to satisfy the holes in his appetite the scant meal had been unable to fill.

Then the speeches began. Sam Marston talked about the progress they were making at the youth farm. John Dillon, one of the high school counselors, spoke about the opportunities the farm provided for troubled teenage boys. Carson was introduced last and received a big round of applause.

He straightened his tuxedo jacket as he moved behind the podium. "Good evening, ladies and gentlemen. It's gratifying to see such a fantastic turnout for such a worthy cause." More applause. He'd always liked the sound of it. "Sam told you a little about the farm. Let me tell you a little about the boys enrolled in Teen Vision."

He began with a brief history of some of the youths who had graduated from the farm. By the time he had finished describing the tragedies suffered by some of the young men and how Teen Vision had changed their lives, the entire hall had fallen completely silent.

"You've all been generous in your contributions. I hope you'll continue to support the farm as you have in the past. Tonight we'll be accepting donations. Just take your checks over to the table next to the door and Mrs. Grayson will give you a receipt you can use for your income taxes."

Everyone applauded vigorously and Carson sat back down next to Elizabeth.

"You were wonderful," she said, her pretty blue eyes shining. "You really painted a picture of what those boys have suffered."

He shrugged his shoulders. "It's a very worthwhile project. I'm happy to help in any way I can."

She was looking up at him and smiling. He liked that in a woman, that she appreciated a man and let him know it. And he liked the way she looked in that dress, sexy yet classy. Not too overblown. With a little more money to spend on the suits she wore, she would even look good in those.

"The band is starting to play," he said. "Why don't we dance?"

Elizabeth smiled. "I'd love to." She rose from her chair and led the way to the dance floor. Carson watched the sway of her behind and smiled approvingly. Sexy but not too flashy, a good memory for names, he had discovered, and a decent conversationalist, as well.

Interesting.

A slow song began. He eased her into his arms and her hands slid up around his neck. They stepped into the music as if they had danced together a dozen times and he liked the way their bodies fit together.

"You're a very good dancer," she said.

"I try." He thought of the ballroom dance lessons his mother had insisted he take when he was a boy. The effort was paying off now, as she had promised, though at the time he had hated every minute. "I've always loved to dance."

"So have I." Elizabeth followed him easily, making him look even better than he usually did. Her waist was trim, her body firm beneath his hands. He had always found her attractive. He was surprised he had not given her more consideration before.

Then again, his political ambitions had

loomed further in the future. Recently, that had begun to change.

The song ended. Carson followed Elizabeth off the dance floor, then both of them came to a sudden halt as a dark-haired man stepped in their way.

"Well, look who's here," Carson drawled, staring into his brother's gold-flecked brown eyes. Times changed, but some things didn't. His feelings for Zach — or lack thereof — were one of them.

Elizabeth looked from Carson to the man standing toe-to-toe with him, dark-haired, dark-eyed. Unbelievably handsome. The realization hit her — she had seen this man at the barn. Though his face had been hidden behind a pair of wraparound sunglasses, it was the man she had seen working on the barn at Teen Vision. And now she knew why he had seemed so familiar.

"I thought you weren't coming," Carson said to him, an edge to his voice that hadn't been there before. Elizabeth knew why. The man standing in front of her was Carson's half brother.

"I changed my mind." Zachary Harcourt's gaze moved to her and he flashed a smile that looked incredibly white against his dark skin. "Hello, Liz."

Her whole body stiffened. "Hello, Zach. It's been a while." But not long enough, she thought, remembering the last time she had seen him, remembering how drunk and insulting he had been, his eyes dilated from whatever drug he had been using at the time. She'd been a senior in high school, working part-time at Marge's Café. "I didn't know you were back in San Pico."

"I'm not. Not officially. Though I gather you're living here now."

"I've been back for a couple of years." She didn't tell him she had seen him out at Teen Vision, but she silently questioned Carson's judgment in allowing a man like his brother around a group of impressionable teenage boys.

"Nice party," Zach said, glancing around at the women in formal gowns, the men in tuxedos. "If you like rubber chicken and a band whose usual gig is the veteran's hall."

"This is San Pico, not L.A," Carson said stiffly, reaching up to adjust his black bow tie. "We're here to raise money, in case you've forgotten."

"After that tear-jerking little speech you gave, how could I possibly forget? Nice job, by the way." Zach's tux looked expensive, Italian, judging from the fabric and cut, Armani or maybe Valentino, designers who

60

specialized in clothes for men with the lean, hard build of a fashion model.

She wondered where he got the kind of money to buy clothes like that and thought maybe he had moved up to selling drugs these days. At least he no longer had the dazed look of a user.

"Mrs. Grayson will be happy to take your check," Carson taunted.

Zach arched a sleek, nearly black eyebrow. "I'm sure she'd be willing to take yours, too."

Carson cast him a warning glance. There had never been any love lost between the two brothers. It looked like that hadn't changed. "You said you weren't coming. Why'd you change your mind?"

Those dark eyes strayed toward Elizabeth. "I figured it would give me a chance to say hello to a few old friends."

FOUR

Zach watched Liz Conners dancing again with his brother. She was better-looking than he remembered, a little taller, her figure nicely filled out. She hadn't forgotten him, that was for sure. Those pretty blue eyes looked cold as stone whenever she glanced in his direction, which wasn't all that often.

It was remembering those eyes that had persuaded him to come. He used to have the major hots for Elizabeth Conners, but she was too smart to give him a second glance. She'd been right to stay away from him. Besides going after anything in skirts, he was a loser on the fast track to nowhere. Zach had been curious tonight to see how much Liz Conners had changed.

Substantially, he thought as he studied her graceful movements on the dance floor. She was far more confident than she had been in high school, and even more attractive, yet she still seemed as easy to read. He could clearly read her dislike of him in every look she cast his way.

Zach almost smiled. His interest in Liz had irritated his brother, as he had been certain it would. Perhaps that was the real reason he had come. He wondered how long the two of them had been dating, how heavily involved they were. He wondered if Liz Conners was sleeping with his brother and was surprised to realize it bothered him to think that she was.

She laughed at something Carson said and he remembered that laugh from more than ten years ago when she had been working in the café. It was a feminine laugh, crystal clear and a whole lot warmer than her eyes.

Zach turned away from the dancing couple and started for the door. Curiosity had motivated him to come. He'd had to have his personal assistant stop by his apartment and pick up his tux, had to have it couriered to San Pico to get here in time for the benefit.

He had purposely arrived at the banquet late, missing dinner and all of the speeches except his brother's. Grudgingly he admitted Carson had done a good job. The donations would be even higher than he had hoped.

It galled him to be indebted in any way to his half brother, but when he thought of the kids at the farm it was worth it.

"Hey, handsome. I didn't know you were in town." Madeleine Fox stood in front of him, long manicured nails curled around his black satin lapel. She was red-haired these days and looked pretty good that way.

"I just came up for the weekend. I've got to be back in L.A. on Monday."

"That still leaves Sunday, right?"

"I'm working out at the farm."

He had dated Maddie in high school. She'd been the wildest thing in town. She was reformed now — mostly. Married to a doctor. But whenever she saw him, she always stopped to say hello, and the invitation was clear in her heavily made-up blue eyes.

She ran a finger down his lapel. "You get bored, you know how to find me." She had given him a note with her cell phone number on it when he had seen her at the gas station a couple of weeks ago.

"I'll keep that in mind." He managed to smile and started walking. The last thing he needed was to get involved with a married woman. His black sheep reputation still haunted him in San Pico. He did his best to keep a low profile and except for Lisa

64

Doyle, that included staying away from the town's women.

It was Tuesday before Elizabeth could arrange an appointment for Maria with Dr. Zumwalt at the San Pico Clinic. Zumwalt, a tall thin man with iron-gray hair, was a professional, no-nonsense sort of man who understood the young woman's fears, but refused to jump to conclusions.

Elizabeth sat next to Maria in his office, a comfortably furnished room with plain white walls covered with eight-by-ten gold-framed degrees and awards.

Zumwalt picked up the pen on his desk. "Before we go any further, Maria, I'd like to check a few things. To start with, I'd like to know if you've been seeing your gynecologist regularly."

"I go every three weeks to see her," Maria said.

"And your hormones are normal, nothing out of the ordinary as far as your blood tests are concerned?"

The black-haired girl shook her head. "Dr. Albright says I am doing very well."

"All right, then. Let's talk a little more about these hallucinations you've been having. You said you hear voices in your head. Is that correct?"

Maria nodded. "Just one voice, a very small voice. It is soft and high, sort of like a child."

"I see." He jotted something down on the sheet of paper on his clipboard. "And at times you say you feel as if you can't breathe."

She swallowed. "*Sí,* that is true."

"I don't think it's time yet to worry, Maria. There is a good chance this is merely a case of Anxiety Disorder. In some cases, the symptoms can become extremely severe. Then again, with your mother's history, it's best not to take chances. We'll do the CAT scan first. If we find the least suspicion that something might be wrong, we'll follow up with an MRI."

Twenty minutes later, wearing a white cotton gown she held closed in the back, Maria followed a uniformed nurse down the corridor to a room filled with machinery. Elizabeth waited outside while the technicians completed the CAT scan, warning Maria that it would be easier if she just lay there, relaxed and closed her eyes.

She didn't, of course, and lying there on the table, her hands started shaking and she began to tremble. With a look of concern and a few soothing words, the nurse slid her out of the machine, gave her a mild sedative, then waited for the medicine to take effect. The CAT scan was finally completed but the results wouldn't be in until next week.

As Elizabeth waited for Maria to dress and join her, the doctor approached her in the hall.

"While we're waiting for the results to come in, I think Maria should get some counseling. As I said, there is a very strong chance we are looking at Anxiety Disorder, or perhaps some form of paranoia. Perhaps Dr. James could spend a little time with her."

Elizabeth thought it was a good idea. "I'll speak to him about it. I'm sure he'll be happy to talk to her. You'll let us know the results of the test when they come in?"

"I'll have the nurse call your office."

"Thank you."

Maria rejoined them just then, dressed once more in slacks and a loose-fitting maternity top. She looked more troubled than ever.

"You mustn't worry, Maria," Elizabeth said. "The test is done and until we know the results, worrying won't do you a lick of good."

She sighed. "You are right. I will try not

to think about it, though it is not so easy to do."

"There is one more thing."

"What is that?"

"Dr. Zumwalt thinks you ought to get some counseling. It's possible you're suffering from some kind of stress that is causing these things to happen in your mind. I'm going to arrange for you to speak to Dr. James. Perhaps he can help you find out what is wrong."

Maria nodded, but Elizabeth could see she wasn't happy with the idea. It was one thing to have a brain tumor, quite another to think you might be suffering some form of mental illness.

"If we are finished, I would like to go home," Maria said. "Miguel will wonder where I am if I am not there when he comes in for lunch."

Watching Maria's nervousness beginning to build again, Elizabeth wondered if the problem might not have a great deal to do with the girl's domineering husband. If so, talking to him might help.

It wasn't going to happen. At least not yet. Elizabeth sighed as the two of them walked down the hall and out into the hot July sunshine.

■ ■ ■ ■

It was just before lunch when Elizabeth returned to the office, a paper bag containing a low-fat Subway sandwich and a Diet Coke gripped in one hand. She set the bag down on the desk just as her phone began to ring.

"Elizabeth? Hi, it's Carson. I just called to thank you for such an enjoyable evening."

"I enjoyed it, too, Carson."

"Good, then how about we do it again? I'm having a small dinner party at the house a week from this coming Saturday. Representatives from a nominating committee associated with the Republican Party. They'll be flying in with their wives. I thought you might enjoy meeting them. I know they'd like *you*."

So it was true. He was thinking of running for office. Elizabeth had never been interested in politics, aside from voting in the elections for whichever candidate she thought would do the best job. Still, it was a fairly high compliment to be included at such an event.

"That sounds like an interesting evening. I'm registered as an Independent. I hope that doesn't make a difference."

He laughed. It was a very deep, very masculine sound. "At least you're not a Democrat. I'll pick you up at 7:00 p.m."

Carson hung up and Elizabeth set the phone back down in its cradle. Carson was attractive and intelligent. They'd had a good time together at the benefit. But instead of Carson's image appearing in her mind, his brother's dark visage arose.

Zachary Harcourt had always been good-looking. At thirty-four, he looked even better than he had ten years ago. But there was something different about him now, something darker and harder. He was no longer a boy but a man, one who could take care of himself. He had been to prison, she knew, and it showed in the lines of his face.

She wondered again what he was doing out at Teen Vision and vowed to ask Carson about it the next time they were together.

It was Friday, the end of Raul's first week at Teen Vision. Elizabeth wanted to check on him and today she finally had time to take Sam up on his offer of a tour.

Parking her shiny, nearly new Acura in the dusty lot, she climbed out of the vehicle and started toward the main office building next to the dormitory. Sam must have seen her drive in. She had called ahead, so maybe he had been watching for her. He was grinning as he walked out the door, joining her before she'd gotten halfway to the office.

"I'm so glad you could come." He caught one of her hands between both of his and squeezed warmly.

"So am I. I should have come out a lot sooner."

"You didn't have a reason to be here. Not until Raul." He guided her back into the office and showed her around. "We have six full-time counselors. There are always at least two people on duty at any given time."

He showed her the desk each counselor was assigned, pointed out the tiny bathroom in case she should need it, showed her the small conference room with its faux wood, Formica-topped table and dark-blue padded chairs, a place the counselors could have private discussions with the boys. Then he led her outside.

"Raul is out in the pasture. He's got a nice way with the animals."

"He has a very gentle side, though he does his best not to show it."

He took her into the dormitory building, showed her the TV lounge, and one of the shared rooms upstairs. "Each boy has a certain amount of privacy, but we don't allow any locked doors and we have random room inspections a couple of times a day."

The third building housed the dining hall, the main gathering place for the group. The kitchen was all stainless steel, immaculately clean, and she saw two of the boys in there working.

"We have a full-time cook, but the boys do the cleanup and help with food preparation. We rotate the tasks, so each boy spends an equal amount of time and doesn't get too bored."

"You're doing a wonderful job here, Sam."

He smiled, seemed pleased. They headed out to where the new barn was being constructed and as she looked at the group of boys pounding nails, framing the third wall of the barn, her steps unconsciously began to slow.

"What's Zachary Harcourt doing out here? I can't believe it's a good idea to have a man like that around impressionable young boys." Her gaze locked on his tall frame, shirtless today, his body sinewy and hard, muscles rippling as he pounded in another nail.

Sam followed her gaze and started to laugh.

"Why is that funny? Zachary Harcourt spent two years in state prison for manslaughter. He was drunk and high and he killed a man. From the look of his expensive clothes, he's still involved in something illegal."

Sam was still grinning. "I take it you aren't too fond of Zach."

She thought about the day he had embarrassed her in front of the patrons in the café. How he had shoved her up against the wall outside and tried to kiss her. How he had run his hand up her leg, trying to get under her silly little pink uniform skirt. "Zachary Harcourt was never any good. I doubt that has changed."

The smile slid off Sam's face. "Why don't we walk over there in the shade? There are a few things about Teen Vision that you ought to know."

He led her in that direction, into the shade of a thick-trunked sycamore not far from the barn. "The Zachary Harcourt you knew years ago no longer exists. He died during those years he spent in prison. By the time he got out, another man had taken his place. That is the man you see working over there."

Her gaze swung in that direction. Zach's lean body glistened with sweat, outlining muscular ridges and valleys. He had amazingly wide shoulders that tapered to a narrow waist. A pair of worn jeans hung low on his hips and covered long legs undoubtedly as sinewy as the rest of him. She might not like Zach Harcourt, but she had to admit he had an incredibly beautiful body.

"Zach's been working here at least two weekends a month since the farm first started. He's dedicated to building Teen Vision. You see, Zachary is the man who founded it."

"What?"

"That's right. It's mostly supported now by donations, but in the beginning, Zach put up a great deal of his own money."

"But I thought Carson —"

"That's the way Zach wants it. Carson is a highly respected, very important man in San Pico. With his backing, Teen Vision has grown faster than it ever would have without his help."

She looked back at Zach, who had turned and seemed to be staring directly at her. For an instant, her breath caught. She quickly looked away. "How did Zachary Harcourt come up with that kind of money?"

"Not the way you're thinking. When Zach was in prison, he began to study law. He'll be the first to admit he did it in the hope of beating the system. But he discovered it intrigued him and he was good at it and it got him to thinking. By the time he got out of jail, he had made up his mind to change his life. He went to work, got his law degree from Hastings, and passed the bar exam. His father used his influence to help him get his conviction set aside. Zach's now a partner in Noble, Goldman and Harcourt in Westwood, a very prestigious law firm."

Elizabeth mulled over the information, barely able to believe it. She glanced back toward the barn and saw Zach Harcourt walking toward them with those same long-legged strides she had noticed before. His eyes were fixed on her face and she felt that same oddly breathless sensation she had felt before.

Zach paused in front of them and a slow smile appeared on his lean, dark face. "Ms. Conners. Welcome to Teen Vision."

She tried to keep her gaze on his but it drifted down to his sweat-covered chest. A wide thatch of curly dark hair stretched across it, arrowing down into the waistband of his faded jeans. He was powerfully built, lean and hard-muscled. She forced herself to ignore an unwanted tingle of awareness.

"Sorry," Zach said, following the line of her gaze. "I didn't realize we were going to have company. I'll go get my shirt."

Elizabeth fixed her eyes on his face. "Don't bother on my account. I've got to get going shortly. I just came by for a tour and to say hello to Raul."

Zach turned and looked out toward the pasture. "I'll go get him."

"I'll go," Sam said. "I want to talk to Pete for a minute and the two of them are together."

"Pete?" she repeated as Sam walked away.

"Pedro Ortega. He prefers to be called by his American name. He and Raul have struck up a tentative friendship."

"He's a good boy . . . Raul, I mean."

"Kind of surly. A little bit rough around the edges, but they all are when they first get here."

"Raul is different. He's special."

One of his dark eyebrows arched. "If he's won you over, he must be."

"What does that mean?"

"It means you were always smart and even back in high school you had a way of seeing people for what they really were. I know that from personal experience."

She felt the heat creeping into her face. "That was a long time ago."

"I owe you an apology for the way I behaved that day at the café. I wasn't a very nice person back then."

"But you are now?"

He smiled, a flash of white in his handsome face. "I like to think so."

"I like what you're doing for these boys."

"I was one of them once."

Her gaze lit on the tattoo on his left arm, a coiled snake with the words Born To Be Wild tattooed in red below the image.

"I thought about having it removed," he said. "But I left it there to remind myself how different my life might have turned out."

Elizabeth eyed him with suspicion. Zach talked a good game, but Carson didn't seem to trust him and she wasn't about to leap to conclusions.

"Here comes Raul," she said, relieved to see the boy walking toward them, thick-chested and broad-shouldered, as tall as Sam but weighing a good deal more. "It's been nice talking to you."

"I still owe you for that day at the café. Maybe sometime you'll let me make it up to you."

Not likely. "Sorry, I'm afraid my schedule is really full, but thanks for the offer."

Zach's mouth inched up at the corner. "I remember now what it was I liked about you, Elizabeth Conners. You're not afraid to tell it like it is."

Elizabeth made no reply. She'd been cautious in high school. After Brian, she was far more cautious now. Turning to Raul, she led him over to a picnic table in the shade of another tree and they sat down and started talking.

She was glad to see the boy, glad to hear the enthusiasm that remained in his voice. Only once did her mind stray from the conversation to the dark, mysterious man who had returned to his work on the barn.

FIVE

The results of Maria's CAT scan came in on Monday. A phone call from Dr. Zumwalt's office relayed the news that there was no sign of lesions, hemorrhaging, a tumor or any other abnormality. They could do more testing, of course, but the doctor strongly believed the problem was mental, not physical.

"So you'll call Mrs. Santiago with the news?" Elizabeth asked the office nurse. A perk of her job as a family counselor was cooperation from the medical community. She had wanted to know if there was a problem so that she could be there with Elizabeth if the results came back positive.

"I'll call her right away." The woman hung up the phone and Elizabeth breathed a sigh of relief. The feeling was short-lived. Whatever was wrong with Maria had not gone away. At least it appeared to be psychological, not physical. She hoped Dr. James would be able to help.

As soon as Michael's patient left the office, Elizabeth went in to see him. "No brain tumor," she said simply, having kept the doctor up to date on the Santiago girl's progress and gaining his agreement to help if necessary.

"I've got a cancellation this afternoon. See if she can come in around three o'clock."

"Thanks, Michael."

He raked a hand through his sandy hair. "I like the Santiagos. They're hardworking, really good people. I know it hasn't been easy for them."

Not for Maria, married at fifteen, or Raul, who'd been in and out of trouble for years. "No, it hasn't. I'll see if she can come in."

Driving her husband's battered old blue Ford pickup, Maria arrived that afternoon right on time. Elizabeth walked into the reception room to greet her and they sat down on the dark brown leather sofa. The area was small but cozy, with an overstuffed chair that matched the sofa, an oak coffee table and an end table with a shiny brass lamp. A stack of magazines sat on the coffee table: *Redbook, Better Homes and Gardens* and a couple of tattered issues of *Family Circle.*

"How are you feeling?" Elizabeth asked

Maria, who sat with her hand cupped protectively over her belly.

"I am fine, a little tired, is all." She looked pretty today, in pink slacks and a pink-striped maternity blouse, her black hair drawn back into a single long braid.

"Sleeping any better?"

Maria sighed. "If you are asking if I have heard any more voices, no, I have not. Besides, Miguel has been home in the evenings before it is time for bed."

"Well, at least you've been able to sleep. Let's see what Dr. James has to say about what's been going on."

Maria stood up from the sofa. "Will you . . . will you come in with me?"

"I think the doctor would rather talk to you alone."

"Please?"

Elizabeth looked up to see Michael James standing in the doorway.

"It's all right, Maria. If Ms. Conners is free, she is welcome to sit in for a while."

Maria cast a hopeful glance at Elizabeth, who nodded, and all three of them went into the doctor's office. The women sat down in front of his desk and Michael took a seat in the leather chair on the opposite side. He slid a pair of tortoiseshell reading glasses up on his nose and scanned the information in the manila folder on the desktop.

When he finished, he took the glasses off and set them down on his desk. "Let me start by saying that Ms. Conners has told me a little about what you've been experiencing, Maria. I'm sure it's been very disconcerting."

Maria glanced at Elizabeth and the doctor realized she didn't understand the word.

"I'm sure it's been extremely upsetting," he said. "Having an experience like that is bound to be difficult."

Maria nodded. "*Sí.* I have been very frightened." She gripped her hands tightly in front of her.

"Before we get into a more serious discussion, let's start with something simple. I have two brief tests I'd like to give you. Just answer each question honestly, yes or no, then we'll see where we are."

She nodded, seemed to brace herself. For the next fifteen minutes, the doctor asked questions from the first sheet of paper he picked up, questions that would reveal symptoms of depression.

"All right, Maria, here we go. For the past few weeks or months, have you been excessively worried about work, family or finances?"

Maria shook her head. "No. Miguel is doing very well at his job, and Raul, he is doing very good, too."

"Have you lost interest in the things you usually like to do?"

"No. I am very busy at home getting ready for the baby."

"Have you been feeling sad or hopeless?"

"No."

"Have you lost interest in sex?"

Soft color rose beneath the dark skin over her cheeks. "My husband, he is a very virile man, but with the baby coming . . ." She glanced away. "Still, I feel desire for him."

Elizabeth bit back a smile and Michael looked down at the paper. "Do you cry often?"

"A few times lately, but only because I am afraid."

Michael made notes on the paper. "Are you irritable and out of sorts with other people?"

"No, I do not think so."

"Do you spend time thinking about death or dying?"

Maria shook her head. "I think mostly about having my baby. The doctor says it is going to be a little boy."

Flicking a glance at Elizabeth, Dr. James set the questionnaire aside and picked up a second sheet of paper. "This is a test for Anxiety Disorder. Answer each question just as you did before."

Maria nodded, sat up a little straighter in her chair.

"Do you sometimes feel that things around you are strange, unreal, foggy or detached from you?"

"*Sí.* . . at night . . . when I am alone."

"Do you have a fear that you are dying or that something terrible is about to happen?"

"*Sí,* and I am very afraid."

"Do you have difficulty breathing? Or feel as if you are smothering?"

"That has happened to me . . . yes."

He made notes on the paper. "Do you suffer chest pains, light-headedness or dizzy spells, shaking or trembling?"

"*Sí,* but only when the fear comes."

"Have you experienced the sensation of your legs being rubbery or jellylike?"

"It was not quite that way. The last time the voices came, I could not move my legs. I could not move from the bed. I could not get away."

Dr. James frowned. "Have you experienced a skipping or racing heart?"

"Oh, *sí.* My heart, it goes so fast I think it will beat right through my chest."

The doctor set the paper aside and pulled off his reading glasses. "From the answers you've given, Mrs. Santiago, you have the classic symptoms of anxiety. What you're feeling isn't really happening. But stress is making it seem as if it is."

"Then the voices, they are not real?"

"No. But you mustn't be afraid. Once we discover what is causing the anxiety, the voices will go away."

Dr. James glanced at Elizabeth, who took her cue and rose from her chair. "Dr. James is going to help you, Maria. All you have to do is talk to him, tell him your fears, be honest about yourself and your past." Elizabeth squeezed the young woman's shoulder. "If you do that, it won't be long before you'll start to feel better."

Elizabeth left the doctor's office, closing the door softly behind her. It looked like Maria was definitely suffering from anxiety. Michael James was good. In time, he would discover the cause. Once the problem was out in the open, the symptoms would likely disappear.

Elizabeth returned to her office, relieved yet wondering what had set off the young woman's recent attacks.

Her marriage, perhaps. Miguel Santiago

was twenty-nine, ten years older than his wife.

He wasn't abusive, just domineering, and up until now, Maria hadn't seemed to mind. She had been raised to believe the husband was master of the household and it seemed their mutual understanding was working to make a successful marriage.

Now, based on what Elizabeth had heard in Michael's office, she was beginning to have her doubts.

"So what do you think I should wear?" The week was over. It was Saturday afternoon, hot, as usual in San Pico, the sun beating down through the bedroom windows in Elizabeth's Cherry Street apartment.

"The black cocktail dress," Gwen Petersen said, plopping down on the edge of the bed in front of the mirrored closet. "Definitely." The room was simply furnished, with an inexpensive walnut queen-size bedroom set she had purchased right after college, and not much on the walls.

Elizabeth had never planned to return to San Pico and in the two years she had been back, she'd done little to make the apartment feel like home.

"Carson's house is very elegant," Gwen continued, "and he'll have the dinner professionally catered. Jim and I attended a function there not too long ago. You'll definitely need to wear something nice."

Gwen studied the dresses laid out on the bed, a red chiffon with a full, flowing skirt, and a light blue silk sheath with a modest neckline and small cap sleeves, and a simple black silk sheath. "The black is perfect, classic yet sexy."

"That's kind of what I was thinking. I've always felt good when I wear it. I usually wear my mother's pearls with it."

"Perfect." Gwen got up from the bed, picking up the hanger with the black sheath on it, holding it up in front of Elizabeth. "It's a good thing you still fit into the clothes you brought with you from L.A. You sure couldn't find anything like this in San Pico."

The above-the-knee sheath dress was made of black silk crepe, with a draped neckline that dipped down low in back.

"I don't suppose you could, but you really don't need clothes like these very often here, either."

"True enough, but if you seriously start dating Carson Harcourt, you're going to need everything you've got and a whole lot more."

"I'm not seriously dating Carson. I hardly

know the man."

"It'd be nice, though, wouldn't it? If you two got together? Carson has plenty of money and he's well respected in the community. Around these parts, the man is considered quite a catch."

"Well, I'm not trying to catch Carson or any other man. I've had one husband. As far as I'm concerned, one was more than enough."

Gwen held the dress up in front of her and looked at herself in the mirror. The skirt was too long for Gwen's petite frame, but the black did wonders for her fair complexion and short red hair. "Not all men are like your ex, you know. Jim's a terrific husband."

"Yes, he is. Jim's one in ten thousand. Unfortunately, I don't have time to plough through another nine thousand nine hundred ninety-nine to find one like him."

Gwen laughed. "It isn't *that* bad. There are a lot of nice men out there."

"Maybe." Elizabeth walked over and took down a shoebox that held a pair of black fabric high heels. "I just haven't had much luck spotting them. Besides, not everyone needs a man in order to be happy. I've got my career. I've got friends like you and Jim. I have a perfectly acceptable life and that's the way I intend to keep it."

"What about kids? Surely you want children. Having babies is a very good reason to find a husband. Unless of course, you're one of those modern women who wants to get pregnant and raise a kid on her own."

"I'm not that modern, believe me."

And when she had first married her college sweetheart, Brian Logan, she had wanted children very badly. But Brian always said it was too soon. They needed to get their careers established. There wasn't enough money. He just wasn't ready to be a father.

In the end, they had divorced before she'd had a chance to get pregnant. Now at thirty, her biological clock rapidly ticking, she had returned to using her maiden name and immensely disliked the idea of falling under any man's thumb again. Which meant there was a very good chance she would never have a baby.

"I'd love to have children," Elizabeth said, "but not unless I stumble across the kind of man who is committed to the long haul. No more divorces. Not for me. And we both know men like that are few and far between. It just isn't worth the risk."

Gwen didn't argue. She knew Elizabeth's views on marriage and no amount of discussion was going to change them.

"Listen, I've got to run." Gwen snagged her purse off the walnut dresser. "Call me tomorrow and let me know how it went." She grinned. "I'm still holding out hope for you, Liz, whether you like it or not."

Elizabeth laughed. "I'll call. I promise. But don't get too excited. It's just a date, nothing more."

"Yeah, right. See ya." Gwen disappeared through the bedroom door and Elizabeth heard the front door close as she left the apartment. The women had known each other since high school. Since Elizabeth's return to San Pico, they had become even closer friends.

It was the only thing she really liked about the ugly little town. Nice people. Gwen Petersen was one of them. An image of Carson Harcourt, tall, blond and handsome, rose into her head. Carson seemed nice, too. She wasn't completely immune to the notion of having a man in her life. Tonight might prove interesting.

Six

Elizabeth crossed the living room to answer the knock at her door. Carson stood on the small front porch, looking casually elegant in a pair of summer-weight tan slacks and light blue shirt, a navy blue jacket draped over one arm.

"Ready?"

"Let me get my purse." She grabbed the black fabric bag that matched her high heels, locked the front door as they walked out, and Carson guided her down the walk to his silver Mercedes.

"You look terrific, by the way," he said as he opened the door and waited for her to slide into the passenger seat. "Great dress."

"I wasn't quite sure what to wear. Fortunately, I had a very nice wardrobe by the time I left L.A. My ex-husband was a stockbroker with big aspirations. He wanted his wife to project the right image."

"Most of the women from here drive

down to L.A. to go shopping."

Most of the women married to men with money, he meant. Elizabeth no longer cared about playing the role she had played as Brian's wife, though she had to admit she was glad she had the appropriate clothes to wear tonight.

The drive out of town to the farm didn't take long. Carson parked his car in an immaculate four-car garage, but took her around to the front door to go into the house. The big, white, wood-framed structure with its wide porch across the front looked impressive and well cared for from the highway. Now she saw that the interior had recently been remodeled: new paint, new drapes, new furniture, which was a comfortable mix of overstuffed sofas and Victorian antiques, the oak floors adding a sense of elegance and charm. The molded ceilings were high, and an antique chandelier hung from the ceiling in the entry.

The decorating had been professionally done, she was sure, probably a designer from L.A.

"It's lovely, Carson. Like something out of *Better Homes and Gardens* only more inviting."

"Thank you. I wanted a place that looked

good but didn't put people off."

He led her into one of two front parlors, where a bar had been set up. A member of the catering staff, a young man in black slacks and a starched white shirt, poured her a glass of chilled champagne, Schramsberg, a brand she recognized as coming from the Napa Valley, a fairly expensive California label.

They talked as Carson gave her a tour of the downstairs portion of the house, including his modernized kitchen where the catering staff was hard at work, then on to his wood-paneled study. By the time they returned to the parlor, a long black stretch limousine was pulling up in front of the house.

"Looks like they're here. Three of the couples flew in on a twin-engine Queen Aire. I hired a limo from Newhall to collect them. Another is bringing the Castenados up from L.A."

"I gather you have an airstrip here on the ranch."

He nodded. "It isn't big enough to handle a private jet, but it serves most other small planes very well."

"Do you fly yourself?"

"I thought about taking lessons, but I really don't have time."

They walked toward the foyer and Carson pulled open the leaded glass door, inviting his guests inside. The fourth couple arrived within minutes of the other three, the group varying in ages from thirty-five to sixty. Introductions were made all around, then Carson led his guests into the bar and drinks were served.

Elizabeth was glad she had worn the black dress. The other four women had on equally expensive outfits, two wore sequin-trimmed pants suits, one a knee-length, ivory dinner suit, another a simple black sheath similar to the one she had on.

They talked for a while, then Carson rested a proprietary hand on her shoulder. "If you ladies don't mind, there are a couple of items of business that need to be discussed before we go in to supper. It shouldn't take all that long."

He didn't wait for their approval, just turned and started walking, all four males in the group following him down the hall toward the study.

Elizabeth turned to the ladies, taking over the role of hostess. "Is this the first time you've been to San Pico?"

"None of us have ever been here," said one woman in a dinner suit, Maryann Hobson, who was married to a real estate developer in Orange County. "Though, of course, we've known Carson for quite some time."

"His home is lovely," one of the other women said, Mildred Castenado, a tall, statuesque Hispanic woman whose dark eyes seemed to take in every detail.

"Yes, it certainly is," Rebecca Meyers agreed. Her husband was the CEO of a big pharmaceuticals company and Becky, as she had asked to be called, seemed a bright intelligent woman. "I particularly like what they've done with the molded ceilings." Painting the walls a creamy beige and the moldings very white.

"Have you known Carson long?" the fourth woman asked, silver-gray hair, thin lips and tight lines around her mouth. She was the eldest of the women, Betty Simino, wife of the senior member of the group.

"We've been acquainted for several years," Elizabeth said, not liking the assessing look in the woman's pale blue eyes. "This is the first time I've been to his home. I agree with Mildred. The house is quite lovely."

"Carson used the designer I recommended," Mildred said proudly. "Anthony Bass. I think he did a marvelous job."

"Yes, he did."

The conversation went on in that vein,

light, mostly pleasant, with only an occasional foray by Mrs. Simino into the nature of Elizabeth's relationship with Carson, which, of course, didn't actually exist.

Elizabeth found herself glancing toward the study door, wondering when Carson would return. Praying it wouldn't be much longer.

Carson surveyed the men seated on the comfortable leather furniture in his study.

The leader, Walter Simino, Assistant Chairman of the California State Republican Party, set his Waterford tumbler of scotch down on the coffee table in front of the sofa.

"You know why we're here, Carson. The women are waiting and we've got supper ahead of us. I don't see any reason to pussyfoot around. We came here for one reason — to convince you to run for state assembly."

They had discussed the possibility at length, of course, and he had given the matter plenty of thought.

Carson leaned forward in his chair, his gaze going to each man in the group. "I'm extremely flattered. You all know that. But going into politics isn't a step to be taken lightly. It takes years of commitment, years of struggle and hardship."

"That's right, it does." This from Ted Meyers, CEO of McMillan Pharmaceutical Labs, a tall man with thinning brown hair. "But what we've got in mind would be worth the hard work and it might not take as long as you think."

"We're talking about more than just the assembly, Carson." Walter looked him straight in the face. "A man like you, with your reputation, you could win the assembly seat and in the next election, run for state senate. From there, with the right backing, you could make a run for a seat in Congress. You're the right age, Harcourt, only thirty-six years old. You've got the looks and the charisma, your background seems to be clean as a whistle, and you've got the kind of connections that can take a man all the way to the top."

He'd been thinking that same thing. He had connections that went back as far as his fraternity brothers at the USC. With the right moves, the right people behind him . . . A vision of the White House popped into his head, but he quickly shoved it away. It was way too soon to be thinking like that. Still, as Walter had said, there was no limit to how far he might go.

"There's just one thing." Paul Castenado

looked a little uneasy and Carson knew exactly his concern — the nemesis who had plagued him since he was a boy.

"My brother."

"That's right. We need Zachary on our team. It's no secret there's bad blood between you two. It wouldn't look good if your brother opposed your bid for office."

Carson worked to keep his voice even. "I can't guarantee what Zach will do. He's a wild card. He always has been."

"Maybe," Walter said. "Then again, maybe with the right motivation, we can convince him to our way of thinking. That's the reason I asked you to invite him here tonight."

And amazingly, Zach had agreed. Carson didn't like it. Not one bit. But the fact remained, the men were right. It didn't look good for a member of a candidate's family to oppose his bid for office. Even if he and Zach were only half brothers.

While the others waited, Ted Meyers disappeared out the door and a few minutes later, Zach walked into the study. Meyers closed the door behind them.

Walter pointed to an empty seat, but Zach sat down in a chair closer to the door.

"I'm here as requested," Zach said. "What can I do for you, gentlemen?" His brother's deep voice held the slightly mocking tone Carson had always despised.

"Thanks for coming, Zach." Charles Hobson's smile was friendly. Hobson was a big-money real estate developer in Orange County who was fairly well acquainted with Carson's brother. Through his legal work, Zach knew a lot of important people in Southern California. "Let me introduce you to the group, then we'll tell you what it is we've got in mind."

What they had in mind, Zach discovered a few minutes later, was to win his support for his brother with promises of future paybacks. A quid pro quo kind of deal. Zach would agree to back his brother's bid for a seat in the assembly and in return, Carson would use his influence to help Zach get a judgeship in L.A. County. The money wouldn't be nearly as good as what he made now, but that kind of power was worth a lot.

Or at least that's what Walter Simino and the rest of the committee believed. And the fact was, with a judgeship he could do a lot of good.

"Once Carson's elected," Simono said, "he'll garner a great deal of influence. If your brother were to run again when his term came to an end, maybe pick up a seat in the state senate, his power would be even greater. He could be a tremendous help to you, Zach. Who knows, maybe sometime in the future, even a seat on the California Supreme Court might not be out of the question."

They were tossing out a powerful lure. Not that he believed it would actually happen. As the conversation progressed, Zach mostly kept silent. As he listened, he kept thinking of his brother running for political office. He had heard rumors, but he'd never asked Carson about them. Now that he knew those rumors were true, somehow it didn't surprise him.

Even here, as Carson sat across the room, he wore a politician's smile.

The conversation reached a pause and Zach rose from his chair. "I think I've heard enough. To be honest with you, there is nothing any of you or Carson could offer me that would be of the slightest interest, not even the idea of a judgeship. In regard to his campaign, I won't promise my support."

His brother's jaw faintly tightened.

"On the other hand, I won't do anything that could hurt him. I won't take part in anything that might be construed as opposition to his bid for office and I won't endorse anyone else. That is the best I can do. Have a good evening, gentlemen."

He turned and headed for the study door.

"What about supper?" Carson asked, amazed, it seemed, that he was leaving.

"No, thanks. But it's hot as hell out there. If you don't mind, I'll have a drink on my way out." He left the study and made his way back to the parlor. As he had walked into the house, he had spotted Liz Conners near the bar, speaking to the wives of the men in the study.

Curiosity led him in that direction. Curiosity, he told himself, nothing more.

Ignoring the women, he walked straight over to the bar. "Diet Coke with a lime," he said to the young man pouring drinks.

"Coming right up." The bartender poured the drink and set the crystal highball glass down on the bar. Zach picked it up and took a swallow, his gaze on Liz Conners. There was a break in the women's conversation and Liz walked off by herself. He made his way over to where she stood.

"Zachary Harcourt . . . I have to say, I'm a little surprised to see you here."

"Why is that? You don't think I'm the political type?"

"Actually, no."

"Then you'd be right. As a matter of fact, I'll be leaving in just a few minutes. I thought I'd come over and say hello before I took off."

Her gaze moved over his face as if she was trying to figure him out. A dark auburn eyebrow went up as she noticed the drink in his hand.

"Diet soda," he explained. "I do have a drink on occasion, just not when I'm driving. I was never an addict or an alcoholic. I was just stupid."

"So you really have reformed."

"For the most part. I hope I'm never as dull as my brother."

Her mouth tightened for an instant. She had a pretty mouth, he thought, full lips softly curved, colored a nice shade of pink.

"You don't think much of each other, do you?" She looked great tonight, even classier than she had that night at the banquet. He wondered how a psychology counselor afforded such expensive clothes. Then again, maybe his brother bought them for her.

"I try my best not to think of Carson at all. Speaking of whom, are you two an item?"

She took a sip of her champagne. "You mean are we seeing each other?"

"I mean, are you involved with him? Are

the two of you sleeping together?"

Liz stiffened as he had figured she would. He was testing her, he knew. Still for some odd reason, he really wanted to hear the answer.

"You know, Zach, I don't think you've changed as much as you'd like to believe."

In some ways, he supposed it was true. "Maybe not." He drank some of his Diet Coke. "So you aren't going to tell me?"

"My relationship with your brother is none of your business."

He looked away, trying not to imagine Liz Conners in Carson's bed.

"We're friends," she finally conceded. "We barely even know each other."

Zach found himself smiling. "No kidding."

"Look, Zach. I know you and your brother don't get along. Maybe paying attention to me is your way of goading him, I don't know, but —"

"My interest in you has nothing to do with Carson," he said, surprised to discover it was true. "I just . . . I don't know. I always thought you were different somehow. I guess I wanted to know if you still were."

"So am I?"

From the corner of his eye, he saw his brother and the rest of the men returning to the room. "I don't know." He took a long drink of his Diet Coke and set the glass down on the bar. "You'll enjoy the supper. Carson brings in some of the best chefs in L.A."

Turning, he started toward the parlor door. For an instant, he thought Liz Conners watched him as he walked away, but it was probably his imagination.

Elizabeth pulled her gaze from Zach Harcourt's tall, lean figure as he disappeared out of the room. She could still feel a faint buzz of electricity from their brief encounter. He had a way of getting to her, of challenging her, and at the same time looking at her as if he found her incredibly attractive. It annoyed her. And it intrigued her.

Zach Harcourt might no longer have a problem with drugs and alcohol, but he was just as irritating, just as overbearing as he'd been as a boy.

Still, she couldn't deny she found him attractive. There was something about him, something dark and mysterious that appealed to her in a sexual way. Women always seemed to like bad boys. Apparently, in some primal way, she did, too.

Carson walked up to her just then and her gaze swung to his. He must have noticed where she had been looking because his mouth seemed a little bit tight.

"I hope my brother wasn't bothering you. He can be fairly obnoxious at times."

She thought of that day outside Marge's Café. "I thought he was supposed to be a changed man."

"Zach's a lawyer. What can I say?"

She laughed at that. Lawyers never seemed to be anyone's favorite people. She wondered if Zach was a good one. He seemed a little too outspoken, a little too caustic for a job that often required a good deal of finesse.

"Dinner's ready," Caron said. "Why don't we lead the way into the dining room?"

"Good idea, I'm starving." Elizabeth smiled, determined not to spare another thought for Zachary Harcourt.

An hour later, it still hadn't worked.

SEVEN

The evening finally came to a close, thank God. Though Elizabeth had mostly enjoyed herself, her role as unofficial hostess had convinced her being a politician's wife had to be a devil of a job.

Since Carson had drunk wine with dinner and an after-dinner cordial, once the limo returned its passengers to the airstrip, he had the long black Cadillac drive Elizabeth home. Carson escorted her, walking her up to the door of her apartment. She thought about inviting him in, but the evening had been long and tiring and she didn't think he was any more interested in continuing the night than she was.

"Thank you, Carson, for another enjoyable evening."

"I'm the one who ought to thank you. You were wonderful, Elizabeth. You put everyone at ease and kept the women entertained while we had our meeting. I couldn't have done it without you."

She figured he had hosted dozens of parties on his own, but it sounded nice when he said it. "I thought everything went very well. I think your guests had a good time, too."

He smiled. "I hope so." Leaning down, he very lightly kissed her. Carson deepened the kiss and Elizabeth kissed him back, sliding her arms around his neck, a little surprised she felt only a mildly pleasant sensation. Carson was a good-looking man. Still, when he let her go and backed away, she wasn't sorry.

"I'll call you," Carson said.

Elizabeth just nodded. "Good night."

Carson stood on the porch as Elizabeth went inside and closed the door. She thought of his kiss and wondered at her reaction. There was such a thing as chemistry between two people and it didn't seem to be there with Carson.

Elizabeth thought of the irritating conversation she'd had with his brother, remembered the way Zach had looked at her — as if the heat in those dark eyes could burn right through her dress — and ignored the fluttery feeling in the pit of her stomach.

Crickets chirped in the warm summer air

and stars glittered like miniature diamonds in the black night sky. Zach couldn't see them in L.A. He supposed there was at least one good thing about the dusty little town of San Pico.

Making his way up on the porch, Zach used his key to open the door to the sprawling ranch house that belonged to Lisa Doyle. It was built in one of the better sections of town, three bedrooms, brick trim, shake roof, nicely landscaped, with a pool in the backyard. She had weaseled it out of her ex-husband in a nasty divorce settlement. Second time around for Lisa, who always seemed to come out on top when the dust finally settled.

A good reason to stay single, Zach thought.

The living room was dark when he walked in, though it wasn't really that late. She'd be waiting in the bedroom, he knew. She had a sexual appetite far beyond most women, which was something he couldn't complain about, except that when it came to men she was not all that discriminating. Which didn't say much for him.

As he stripped off his sport coat on the way to the bedroom door, it occurred to him that he didn't really want to be here tonight. The thought had occurred to him last week, as well, but tonight, for some odd reason, the notion rang with a clarity it somehow hadn't before.

Still, he had told Lisa he'd be in town and he had no real reason not to join her. Besides, his brief encounter with Liz Conners had left him itching for a hot round of sex and it was certain he wouldn't be getting it from Liz.

"I thought you'd never get here," Lisa said as he stepped through the bedroom door. "I'm horny as hell, lover. I need a good fuck. How about you?"

She was wearing red thong panties and nothing else and she walked straight up to him. She pulled his head down for a kiss and he kissed her back. Her hand gripped his crotch through his slacks and she rubbed till he got hard.

Still, he couldn't seem to really get turned on. He couldn't seem to get his mind wrapped around the thought of another bout of meaningless sex. He told himself that was exactly the way he liked it — no strings, no involvement.

But even as she led him over to the bed and stripped off the rest of his clothes, his thoughts strayed back to Liz Conners, how pretty she'd looked tonight, how sexy she was, yet exactly the opposite of Lisa. He shook his head, shoving the image away, and tried to concentrate on the gorgeous blonde with the big green eyes and luscious body standing right in front of him.

Oddly, it wasn't that easy.

Lisa could drive a man crazy with the tricks she knew, but Zach knew them all by now and the allure had long since faded.

Why am I here? he asked himself, but this time couldn't come up with a satisfactory answer.

"What's the matter, lover? Too tired?" Naked, he stood next to the bed. Lisa opened one of the foil wrapped packages on the beside table, rolled the condom onto his erection with amazing skill, then shoved him down on the mattress and climbed on top of him. "That's all right. I'm perfectly willing to do the work."

And so he let her. There didn't seem much else he could do and though he was a far different man than he had been before, he was still no saint. Zach closed his eyes and let Lisa work her magic. She brought them both to a powerful climax, but when she started in on him again, he rolled away.

"I need some sleep, Lisa. Sorry."

Lisa muttered a nasty word and curled on her side away from him. Zach lay there in bed, but as tired as he was, he couldn't fall asleep.

On Saturday morning, Zach drove out to Teen Vision. The barn was really coming along and just looking at how well their hard work was paying off made him itch to strap on his carpenter's belt and start hammering nails again.

The boys were already at work, had been since early that morning. The fifteen-acre youth farm grew a variety of crops that took a lot of effort to maintain. Peaches, apricots, oranges, lemons, almonds and pistachios were cultivated in the orchard. There were five acres of alfalfa to help feed the cattle.

The boys kept a large vegetable garden and grew enough corn to sell in local grocery stores. They raised chickens, had four cows in their dairy, along with four white-faced cattle they raised for meat. The farm was nearly self-sufficient, and the boy's successful operation of such a place gave them a great deal of pride.

Along with their daily chores, they attended a variety of classes, a number dealing with information on the consequences of drug and alcohol abuse. Zach lectured on those subjects several times a year and discovered that being honest about his past gave him a special rapport with the boys.

After his last session, Raul Perez had stayed after class to talk to him. He wanted to know if Zach believed Raul might be able to get into college after he got his GED.

"I think you'd have a very good chance, Raul. It would take a lot of hard work, but anything's possible. I can tell you that first hand."

Raul smiled. It was obvious the idea of hard work didn't bother him. Zach thought that Liz Conners might be right about the kid. There did seem to be something special about him, though Zach couldn't quite nail down what it was.

As he got out of the Jeep, he spotted the boy walking through the pasture, a big tough-looking kid, hard-edged until you dug a little deeper. Then you saw the same kind of need Zach had felt as a boy, the longing to have someone care about you.

Zach knew the kid had no father and lost his mother just as he entered his teens. His sister and her husband were the only family Raul had.

Zach had parents. Sort of. But Teresa Burgess, his mother, had been too busy keeping Fletcher Carson happy — at least in the beginning — to worry much about her son. Zach had been nine when his parents had ended their longtime relationship and his father had demanded custody of his son.

Teresa had agreed — for a price. She'd sold him like a hunk of meat for a new car and the title to the small house Fletcher had provided for her and Zach. His father had taken him home to live in the big house on Harcourt Farms, but instead of a blessing, it was the beginning of a life in hell.

Zach continued walking, heading for the maintenance shed to retrieve his carpenter's belt, and Raul started walking his way.

"Need some help?" the boy asked.

"I thought you were feeding the cattle."

"Already done. The dairy cows, too. I'm pretty good with a hammer."

He was pretty good at everything around the farm, Zach had noticed. And he actually seemed to enjoy the hard work.

"All right, good. The more help we've got, the quicker we get this thing finished. Sam wants to get the alfalfa under cover by the time summer's over."

"Sounds like a good idea." Following Zach into the shed, Raul retrieved another belt, nails and a hammer, and they started toward the barn. For a moment, Raul's steps slowed, his gaze going over the fields to the bright patches of color on the other side.

"What is it?"

"The roses. They are so beautiful this time of year."

Six hundred and forty acres of lush, Harcourt Farms roses bloomed in the fields that began at the edge of the property belonging to Teen Vision. From the air, the ground was awash with an incredible array of yellow, flame, red, pink, white and a spread of variegated blossoms. From May through September, when the breeze blew across the fields, the soft scent of roses filled the air.

Zach had always loved the fragrance. Maybe there were two good things about San Pico.

EIGHT

Maria couldn't sleep. Miguel was working late again and the house felt oddly empty. She had made a few women friends since she had lived at Harcourt Farms but most of them moved on when the workers headed off for their next job. Her best friend was a girl named Isabel Flores, who worked for Mr. Harcourt and lived in the big house on the farm. Though she was only a few years older than Maria, she was Mr. Harcourt's housekeeper. She took care of his house . . . and other of his personal needs.

Isabel had told her that she liked working there, that Mr. Harcourt took very good care of her. She didn't mind his occasional visits to her bed. In fact, she enjoyed them. And she was careful, she said. Though she had to confess her sin at church on Sunday mornings, she took birth control pills so she wouldn't get pregnant with his child.

Propped against the headboard in bed,

Maria considered getting dressed again and going over to see Isabel tonight. She would tell her best friend what had been happening to her, talk to her about the tests she had taken, the sessions she'd had with Dr. James. But it was really too late for a visit and Miguel would be home soon.

At least she hoped he would be. She thought about returning to the living room to watch a little more TV, but she was tired. When she had returned from her session with Dr. James, she had worked in the vegetable garden, and the heat had exhausted her even more than she had been already. Now it was late and she was sleepy.

She settled lower in the bed, pulling the sheet up beneath her chin, telling herself that now that she understood more about what was happening to her, the dream would not come again. She closed her eyes and tried to fall asleep, but the minutes ticked past and sleep remained elusive.

Instead, she waited, listening for the sound of Miguel's work boots on the steps outside the back door. More minutes passed. Slowly, her eyelids began to droop. Her body relaxed against the mattress and she slipped into sleep.

It was the cold that awakened her, an icy chill that seeped into her bones like death in a crypt. Even this late, it was almost ninety degrees outside. How could it be so cold in the bedroom? Her teeth began to chatter. She pulled the sheet up over her, reached down for the thin yellow quilt, folded across the foot of the bed.

Her fingers wrapped around the fabric tightly. For the first time, she noticed the sounds . . . the eerie moaning, the creak and groan like someone walking on the boards in the living room. The fragrance of roses drifted toward her. The odor thickened, grew more dense, turned harsh and cloying, filling her nostrils, burning her throat.

She swallowed, sat there in the bed afraid to move, her fingers frozen around the top of the quilt. Her gaze drifted there, down to the foot of the bed, and her whole body tightened. There was something there, a cloudy, milky image she could see through but not clearly, something with the vague shape of a person.

They'll take your baby if you don't leave. They'll kill your baby.

Maria whimpered. *Dios mio!* Gooseflesh rose over her skin and her hand started shaking, her knuckles going pale as she gripped the quilt.

They'll take your baby. They'll kill your baby if you don't leave.

She closed her eyes but the image remained, frozen there, behind her quivering eyelids. A child, maybe eight or nine years old, hovering, floating above the floor at the foot of the bed, a little girl, she thought from the sound of the voice, but she couldn't be sure.

It is not real, she told herself, repeating what Dr. James had said. *It is only in your mind.*

She whispered a silent prayer, told herself to will the image away, and kept her eyes tightly closed for as long as she dared. She repeated the prayer, whispering frantically to the Blessed Virgin, and when she opened her eyes, she saw that her prayer had been answered.

The eerie sounds slowly melted into silence. Little by little, the harsh smell faded, turning softer, no longer strong, but delicate, almost soothing. The icy chill was gone from the room and the temperature returned to normal.

But her heart still frantically pounded, slamming against her ribs, and her hands felt clammy, her mouth bone-dry. She shifted fearfully on the bed as another sound reached her ears, a familiar shuffling on the back porch stairs, then the smooth glide of the key sliding into the lock.

Miguel was home.

Maria closed her eyes and bit down on her trembling lips, determined not to weep.

Michael James sat behind his desk, listening to the wild tale told by the young Hispanic woman sitting across from him. He had seen Maria Santiago twice this week, but neither of the sessions had proved particularly successful.

"I saw it, Dr. James. Last night, I saw the ghost. *Un espectro.* I am not imagining it. I saw it with my own two eyes."

"It wasn't a ghost, Maria. There is no such thing. What happened is that you suffered an anxiety attack. It's not uncommon. A lot of people at some time in their lives have experienced panic attacks. Normally, I'd have something prescribed for you, a mild dose of Xanax to help you relax along with some Ambien to help you sleep, but with the baby so far along —"

"I do not need your drugs! There is a ghost in my house and all of the foolish questions you keep asking me are not going to make it go away!"

He kept his voice steady and calm. "There

are reasons for the questions, Maria. We're working to explore your past. We need to discover if something happened to you during your childhood, something that might not seem important, but is. In cases like these —"

"No! You ask about my father. Did he love me? Did I love him? I tell you he left when I was two years old. You ask about my mother. I tell you she loved me and Raul. We had no money and life was hard, but it was not so bad. You tell me I must be worried, feeling this thing you call stress, but I am saying that Miguel and me, we are excited about the baby. Until all of this started, I have never been so happy. You say that I am afraid of something I don't understand and you are right!"

Her hand clenched into a fist in her lap. "There is a ghost in my house and it is telling me to leave. It is warning me that someone is going to kill my baby!"

Michael took a long, deep breath and released it slowly. "There. Perhaps you have just hit on the answer to your problem. You're worried about losing the child. You've lost a baby before. Perhaps fear for the child you carry is what's causing your anxiety."

Maria stood up from her chair. He could

see that she was trembling. "You don't believe me. I knew that you would not." She turned and started walking toward the door, her belly making her sway a little as she moved.

Michael stood up behind his desk. "Maria, wait a minute. We need to talk about this."

She just kept walking, making her way across the small reception area, over to the desk. Michael got up and followed her through the door.

"I wish to speak to Ms. Conners. Tell her . . . tell her Maria Santiago would like to see her."

"She's just finishing a session," the receptionist, Terry Lane, told her. "She should be opening her door any minute."

"Fine. I will wait." She sat down heavily on the sofa, her back broomstick straight, chin thrust out.

It was only an instant later that Elizabeth's door opened and a blond woman and a teenaged girl walked out of the office. Elizabeth followed them into the reception area.

"All right, then. I'll see you both next week."

The woman, about forty with frazzled blond hair, just nodded. She motioned for her daughter to leave and both of them headed for the door.

Elizabeth's gaze lit on Maria, standing next to Terry's desk. Michael stood patiently waiting.

"Mrs. Santiago would like to talk to you," Terry told her. Terry was young, in her twenties, with short, spiky blond hair. She had only been working at the clinic for a couple of weeks, and Michael could see she was a bit unnerved.

"That's right, Elizabeth," Michael said from his open doorway. "Maria has something she wants to tell you."

Elizabeth flicked him a glance, caught his silent appeal for help. Sometimes it was difficult to win a patient's trust and obviously Maria trusted Elizabeth, not him. Michael had considered advising Elizabeth to counsel the girl, but anxiety was more his field of expertise, and they were afraid Elizabeth's relationship with Maria was too close for her to be completely objective.

Elizabeth smiled at Maria. "I've got a few extra minutes. I'll be happy to help in any way I can."

"Why don't we all go back into my office?" Michael suggested, then waited as the women filed past him into the room. They sat down in chairs on the opposite side of his desk, Elizabeth assessing the girl with obvious concern.

"Tell her, Maria. Tell Ms. Conners the story you told me."

"It is not a story," Maria said defensively. *"Mi casa es encantada."*

Elizabeth's blue eyes widened, though she kept her features carefully bland. "I thought we discussed this before, Maria. Surely you don't really believe your house is haunted."

"But I do. There *es un espectro.* Last night I saw it."

"Last night you saw a ghost?"

"*Sí,* that is right. It was small . . . like a child. It sounded like a little girl, but I could not tell for sure. The air was freezing cold and I heard the noises. And there was that same sickening-sweet smell. I am not making it up."

Elizabeth flicked Michael a glance and seemed to consider her reply. "If you are that convinced something happened, then perhaps there is another explanation. Maybe the house is just getting older, making different noises than you're used to. Maybe the smell is something that has died under the house."

"I would like to believe it is something like that, but I do not. I only know that something terrible is happening and I am afraid."

Elizabeth said nothing more and neither did Michael. In all his numerous cases, he had never had to deal with a ghost, but he could see that Maria was truly afraid.

"Perhaps I should speak to Miguel," Elizabeth suggested. "He could investigate, see what might be causing you all of this worry."

Maria's eyes widened in panic. "You must not tell my husband. Miguel will not understand. He will think I am being childish. That is what he says whenever we disagree."

Michael leaned across his desk. "Listen, Maria, you can't go on like this. You need to talk to your husband. I need to speak to him, as well."

Maria shot up from her chair. "No! You think to ask him the same stupid questions you asked me. Well, nothing he says will make any difference. You are wrong about this — both of you. And I am not imagining things."

Whirling away, she moved clumsily toward the door.

"Maria!" Elizabeth went after her and Michael let them go. There was nothing more he could do — not until the girl was

a long line of rooms filled with the elderly. The place was very nice, compared to the kind of rest homes he had read about. No more than two occupants to a room, some of them private, like his father's. After the terrible fall Fletcher Harcourt had suffered, he'd been brought to Willow Glen to recover as soon as he'd been released from the hospital.

Zach had wanted him to have in-home nursing so that he could live in his own house, but Carson believed he should stay in the nursing home where he could receive more professional care. Since Carson was the eldest, according to provisions in their father's will, he was named conservator of all of Fletcher Harcourt's holdings, including the farm and any decisions to do with his health care.

Zach had argued, but Carson had the final say, and their dad had stayed in the home.

Just one more thing to dislike about his brother.

Zach made his way along the hall, glancing into the rooms along the way, until he came to C-14 in the west wing. He recognized the woman walking out of a room just a few doors down and paused there in the hall.

"Hello, Liz."

She looked up at the sound of her name, came to an abrupt stop in front of him.

"Zachary . . ." She looked back over her shoulder. "You're here to see your father?"

He nodded. "I come by whenever I'm in town. What about you?"

"I'm doing a teaching series for the nursing staff."

"Subject?"

"Geriatric Psychology. Basically, it involves teaching techniques to deal with the elderly."

"Sounds useful."

"Every little bit helps." She turned toward the open door. "I knew your father was in here. I hope he's doing all right."

"His condition stays pretty much the same. His legs don't work quite right. There's some kind of problem getting signals from the brain. He doesn't talk much. When he does, he remembers bits and pieces from the past, which he gets mixed up with the present. Nothing about the accident or much about things that have happened since then."

"I heard about the accident when it happened. He took a fall down the stairs, right? My dad was still alive back then and my sister still lived here. She and her husband moved to San Francisco in March."

"Tracy, isn't it?"

She nodded. "Tracy's a couple years younger." She looked past him through the doorway to the form on the bed, lying beneath the sheets. "Such a terrible waste. Your father always seemed such a vital man."

"He could be a real bastard at times. But mostly he was good to me. I owe him a lot. More than I could ever repay."

"Is there . . . is there any chance he'll get better?"

He looked at the man on the bed. "The doctors still hold out hope for him. They say technology is always improving. They say there's work being done that might allow them to operate, remove the bits of bone that are pressing into his brain. I keep hoping. All of us do."

Liz looked at him, studying him as if he were a specimen under a glass. "You're a surprising man, Zach. You're here to see your father. Sam says you founded Teen Vision. You've conquered your drug and alcohol problems and you're a successful lawyer. You're also rude and overbearing and irritating as hell. I can't seem to figure you out."

Zach grinned. "It's encouraging to know you're trying. Why don't we go out to dinner and you can have another go at it?"

"I told you —"

"Yeah, I know. You're busy."

For a moment, she glanced away. "Look, I'd better get going. I've got a lot to do back at my office." She turned and started walking.

"Liz?"

She stopped, slowly turned to face him.

"If you won't go to out dinner with me, how about lunch?"

She didn't answer for so long his palms began to sweat. *Jesus.* The last time a woman did that to him he was in high school.

"When?" she asked and his heart kicked up just like it used to back then.

"How about today? It's already eleven o'clock. You've got to eat and so do I. We can meet at noon, after I've had a little time to spend with my father."

"All right, but if you say Marge's, the deal is off."

He laughed. "I was thinking The Ranch House. They've got a pretty decent lunch menu."

"Fine. I'll meet you at The Ranch House at one." She started walking again.

"One is fine. One is great. I'll see you there." Zach watched her turn the corner and disappear out of sight. She looked different today, all business in a simple coral suit with a plain white, open-collared blouse.

He dried his damp palms on his slacks, his heartbeat once more under control. It was crazy. Women didn't make him nervous. If anything, it was the other way around. Maybe it was some weird psychological hang-up left over from the big-time brush-off she had given him in high school.

Must be, he told himself. Still, he planned to meet her, and as he walked into his father's room, it bothered him to realize how much he was looking forward to it.

NINE

Elizabeth shoved through the door of The Ranch House at exactly 1:00 p.m. She was always on time. Her schedule was too tight not to be. Besides, she'd always felt being late was rude.

Surprisingly, Zach was already there, sitting on a bench in the foyer, not pulling the I'm-such-a-busy-guy-I-can-barely-squeeze-you-in routine that a lot of attorneys seemed to do. He looked good. Too darned good. He was fit and trim, his skin tanned from serious hard work instead of a tanning bed. He had thick, nearly black hair that waved just a little and a face as handsome as sin.

He dressed well — a short-sleeved yellow oxford cloth shirt with light beige slacks and Italian loafers. He looked great in his clothes, sophisticated as she had never imagined the ruffian in studded black leather she had known in high school would ever manage.

And yet something of that hard-edged youth remained. It was there in the line of his jaw, the faint curl of his lip, the slightly arrogant set of his shoulders. It seemed to make him all the more attractive.

Which was exactly the reason if she'd had a way to call him she would have cancelled.

"Right on time," Zach said, coming to his feet the moment he saw her. "I wasn't sure you would actually show up."

"I wouldn't have, if I'd had your cell number. I would have cancelled. This is crazy, Zach. What are we doing here? You and I have nothing in common. I have no idea why you asked me to lunch."

Elizabeth could hardly believe she'd agreed to meet him. Zachary Harcourt was the last person she wanted to spend time with. To say nothing of the fact she'd been seeing his brother. Carson would be furious if he found out she had met Zach for lunch. Though she didn't really owe the man any particular loyalty, at least not yet, somehow she felt guilty.

"I asked you to lunch because I don't like eating alone. And we have lots of things in common."

A short, overweight hostess appeared just then, ending her reply. The woman jerked a pair of menus out of the holder next to the cash register. "Two of you?"

Zach nodded.

"This way." The woman started walking and they followed her through the dining room, which was done in a western motif with cattle brands etched into the trim around the windows and doors. At a wooden table, Zach pulled out one of the low captain's chairs for Elizabeth, then took a seat himself.

"So what exactly is it that we have in common?" Elizabeth took a drink of ice water the hostess brought to the table.

"For one thing, we both have an interest in helping kids improve their lives." Zach spread his paper napkin across his lap. "And then there's the fact that we both hate politics."

"What? That's crazy. How do you know I hate politics?"

"Come on, Liz. Admit you were bored Saturday night. I could tell the moment I saw you."

"I wasn't bored. I was just . . . I didn't know any of the guests very well, that's all."

"If you had, you would have been even more bored."

She wasn't sure whether to be angry or amused. The latter won out and her lips faintly curved. "If you hate politics so much, what were you doing out there that night?"

Zach opened his menu but didn't start to read. Beneath the edge of his shirtsleeve, a pair of very nice biceps bunched.

"Walter Simino and his cronies were trying to bribe me — figuratively speaking — into supporting my brother's campaign, assuming there is one. I told them to shove it."

She fiddled with her menu, trying not to think of the way he had looked that day at Teen Vision, naked to the waist, hammering away on the barn, the muscles across his back stretching and tightening whenever he moved. "So if Carson runs, you intend to side with the opposition?"

"I didn't say that. I told them I'd stay neutral."

"Why?"

"Why, what?"

"You don't like your brother. It's unlikely you'd ever vote for him. Why did you agree to stay neutral?"

Zach breathed a sigh. His eyes were interesting, she thought, not just brown, but with tiny gold flecks in the irises that seemed to glow when he looked at her.

"To tell you the truth, I'm not exactly sure why I agreed. Maybe trying to hurt him that way just seemed too petty. Maybe I felt I owed it to my father. Besides, I'm too busy to get involved one way or another."

The waitress appeared at the table, ready to take their orders. With only a quick glance at the menus, both of them ordered hamburgers and fries, though Elizabeth generally nibbled at the side dish, knowing how fattening it was.

"So what kind of law do you practice?" she asked as the waitress left and they waited for their meal to arrive.

"Mostly personal injury."

"You're an ambulance chaser? I never would have guessed."

Zach laughed, the sound deep and easy, rolling over her like ripples in a stream. Dammit, she wished she weren't so aware of him. But even when she'd been a senior in high school working at the café, she had noticed him whenever he came in. Zach was four years older, one of the best-looking boys in town. Just watching him walk through the door made something flutter in the pit of her stomach. But Zach was always in trouble, always hanging around with a bad element. Even then, she had thought it was a pity.

"Actually, we specialize in small class-action suits. We don't do big mass torts. We prefer to handle a manageable number of clients at one time. Currently, we're working on a pharmaceuticals case involving a drug called Themoziamine. Normally, we don't go after the pharmaceutical companies. That's just not our thing, but this came to us through one of our former clients and involves only a limited number of people."

"What was the problem?"

"The drug causes brain damage in certain individuals — a higher than acceptable percentage, we believe. We're trying to get it taken off the market."

"Sounds interesting."

"We're the good guys, as far as I'm concerned. A couple years back our firm worked on a case involving three-wheeled vehicles. Nearly fifty thousand people a year were being injured, a lot of them being paralyzed or killed riding the damned things. We were able to prove the company knew the risk factor, even set money aside for settlements in their annual budget in the amount needed to cover them. The jury wasn't happy to find that out, and eventually we were able to get them taken out of production."

"I remember that case. As I recall, the settlement was huge."

"Over two hundred and fifty million."

"Wow, no wonder you can afford Armani."

He grinned. God, he had the whitest teeth . . . or maybe it was just that his face was so darkly tanned. "If you noticed, I guess it was worth it."

Oh, she'd noticed, all right. At the moment, she was noticing how great he looked just sitting there, and she wanted to kick herself for it.

The waitress arrived, providing a timely diversion. She set their hamburger platters down on a placemat decorated with cattle brands around the edge, and the aroma of freshly grilled meat rose up, making her stomach growl.

Zach didn't seem to notice. "So what about you?" Wrapping long, tapered fingers around the hamburger, he picked it up in both hands. "You're a social worker, right?"

"Independent family counselor."

"Okay, so are you working on any interesting cases?"

He took a big bite of his burger and she watched the muscles in his neck move up and down. He might be good-looking, but there was nothing the least bit effeminate about Zachary Harcourt. Every move he made screamed masculine and virile, and Elizabeth found herself shifting in her chair.

She picked up her knife and cut her hamburger in half just to give herself something to do. "Actually, I'm working on one of the most interesting cases I've ever been involved with — a young woman who believes she's being visited by a ghost."

He nodded as if that was no big deal, swallowed a large bite of burger. "Maria Santiago. The doctors think she's crazy. I heard about that."

"You know Maria? She told you about the ghost?"

"I know her brother, remember? We've been talking some lately. The subject of his sister came up. Apparently Maria told Raul about her ghost, and about her sessions with Dr. James."

Elizabeth sat up straighter. "Well, Michael certainly doesn't think she's crazy. He thinks she's suffering from anxiety, and so do I."

"Michael?"

"He's my boss at the clinic."

"Just boss or something else?"

A surge of anger rolled through her. "Why are you so fixated on my love life? Every time I see you, you're trying to find out who I'm sleeping with."

He set the last of his hamburger down on his plate. "So who *are* you sleeping with?"

"None of your damned business!" Tossing down her napkin, Elizabeth shoved back her chair and stood up.

Zach stood up, too. "Wait a minute. I'm sorry, okay? I just wanted to know if you were involved with anyone."

"Well, I'm not. Now are you happy?"

He grinned. "Yeah, I am."

They stood there until people started to stare and she had no choice but to sit back down.

"Where were we?" he asked. "Aside from the fact you're celibate at the moment."

The man was outrageous! She had no idea why she found herself biting back a smile. "We were talking about Maria Santiago, and I've already said more than I should."

"She isn't your patient, is she?"

"Well, no. Not officially. She asked me to sit in on her session with Dr. James as a friend."

"Then there isn't a problem. Eat your French fries. They're getting cold."

She picked one up and dipped it into the ketchup she had poured on her plate. "Maria refuses to see Dr. James again."

"I think I can understand that." Zach oversalted his fries, then picked one up, tossed it into his mouth, and chewed with obvious relish. "According to Raul, Maria made him promise not to tell her husband what's been going on in the house, but the girl is convinced the ghost is real."

"Why did Raul tell you all this?"

Zach shrugged. "Like I said, we've been talking. I come up a lot on the weekends. We're trying to get the barn built, you know? Working with the boys gives me a chance to get to know them, try to encourage them. I teach a class on drug and alcohol abuse. I talk about my past and how it's possible to change your life if you want to bad enough. By the way, I think you're right about Raul. He seems like a really good kid."

"And he told you about his sister?"

He nodded, swallowed a bite of ketchup-and-oversalted French fry. "Yeah. He's really worried about her."

"What did he say about the ghost?"

"He says he believes her. That's the reason he talked to me about it. He knows I'm a lawyer. Raul wanted me to speak to my brother, see if there was somewhere else Miguel and Maria could live."

"I don't believe this. She actually wants to move out of the house?"

"Apparently so. Whatever's going on, there's no way my brother's going to inconvenience himself because one of his farm workers believes in ghosts."

A shadow passed over the table. Elizabeth

glanced up as a tall blond man approached, and the guilt she'd felt earlier rose up again.

"Well, speak of the devil," Zach said, his expression going hard.

Carson stopped beside her chair and there wasn't the least hint of a smile on his face. "I thought you had more sense," he said, bringing a flush to her cheeks.

Zach shoved to his feet, one hand unconsciously fisting. "Leave her alone, Carson."

If Elizabeth had ever needed evidence the man had been in prison she saw it now in his face. Hard, cold, dangerous. Even lethal was a word that came to mind.

"She needed to talk to me about one of her cases," Zach said, "a boy at Teen Vision. That's why she agreed to come to lunch."

Carson's disapproving gaze swung to her. "That right?"

Elizabeth didn't flinch, though it wasn't that easy to do. "It doesn't matter why I'm here. I can to go to lunch with anyone I want, Carson. Even your brother. Just because we've been out a couple of times doesn't give you any say in what I do."

Carson's jaw tightened.

Zach seemed surprised she hadn't gone along with the half-truth he had invented to give her an easy out. She didn't need his protection. She didn't really care what Carson thought.

Carson forced a smile. "I suppose that's true." His gaze fixed on Zach. "How's Lisa?" A sarcastic edge crept into his voice, and Zach's eyes darkened in warning.

"I wouldn't know. I haven't seen her since I left town last week."

"If I happen to run into her, I'll tell her you said hello." Carson walked away and Elizabeth's gaze swung to Zach.

"Lisa?"

"Lisa Doyle. We see each other sometimes when I come up on the weekends."

Lisa Doyle. The name leached the blood from her face. She knew Lisa Doyle. Their enmity went back a long way. "You're seeing Lisa Doyle?"

"Not exactly. We're not really involved, if that's what you mean."

Elizabeth rose shakily from her chair, her stomach twisted into a knot. "Not really involved? You mean you're just screwing her. Why am I not surprised?" He was Zachary Harcourt, after all. When he was young, he had used women like Kleenex and tossed them away. She wasn't about to be treated like one of them.

Opening her purse, she took out her wallet and tossed enough bills on the table to pay for her lunch and a tip.

Zach snatched up the bills and stood up. He thrust the money in her direction. "I invited you to lunch and dammit, I don't answer to Lisa any more than you answer to Carson."

"I'm not sleeping with Carson." Ignoring his outstretched hand, she turned and started walking, but Zach caught her arm.

"Look, I didn't handle this right. It was a spur-of-the-moment invitation. I didn't think it would matter. I'm sorry."

She looked at him and something twisted inside her. "Funny thing is, so am I."

She shouldn't have let it bother her. So what if Zach was seeing someone? She'd been dating Carson, hadn't she? And it was only a friendly lunch.

But Zach had been pressing her for a date for the past two weeks and he hadn't mentioned that he was involved with someone. That it was Lisa Doyle, the woman who had destroyed her marriage, made her stomach roll with nausea.

Her hands tightened on the steering wheel as she drove back to the office, a memory stirring of the weekend she and Brian had come back to San Pico three years ago to attend her high school class reunion. He'd insisted she go, perhaps because they had been having problems in their marriage. Brian was always working late, even on the weekends, and Elizabeth had begun to grow suspicious.

That night had been glorious, seeing old friends, Brian more solicitous that he had been in months. She had been talking to Gwen and her husband, dancing with some of the guys she'd known in high school. She didn't even notice when Brian slipped away.

Then the band had taken a break and she couldn't seem to find him. He'd had a lot to drink and she was worried about him driving the car back to her sister's house where they were staying. More and more concerned, she walked out in the parking lot in search of him. That's when she spotted the Lexus — and saw that it was moving, rocking back and forth on its springs.

As she started toward the car, Elizabeth's legs were shaking, her heart pounding. Dread clogged her throat at what she might find.

The car was parked beneath a big overhead light in the parking lot. When she reached it, she could see two people crammed into the deep cream leather backseat — Brian and Lisa Doyle, one of the most popular girls in Elizabeth's class.

Brian's pants were down around his knees, Lisa's skirt shoved up to her waist.

For several seconds Elizabeth just stared. She could hear the slap of bodies, the moans and grunts of sex.

"That's it, baby," Brian said. "Come for me."

A whimper caught in Elizabeth's throat. She turned and started running back toward the cafeteria where the reunion was being held. He'd heard her high heels hitting the pavement because the car door swung open.

"Elizabeth!" Brian's voice reached her. "Elizabeth, wait!"

But she just kept running, pushing her way inside the entry, heading for the women's bathroom. She wanted to hide, desperately needed time to recover herself, to try to figure out what to do.

In the end, Gwen came in to get her, helped her wipe her tearstained face and repair her makeup. Apparently Brian had made up some story of a misunderstanding and Gwen did her best to pretend she believed it. But Elizabeth knew the truth. Brian had been cheating all along, just as she had suspected. Their marriage was over.

And the image of her husband screwing Lisa Doyle in the backseat of their car was forever burned into her brain.

The afternoon slid away. Zach returned to the hospital to spend a bit more time with his father, who seemed to be a little more lucid than usual. Zach pushed his wheelchair out onto the covered patio and they sat in the shade, absorbing the heat and listening to the water splashing in the fountain. Zach got him talking about the old days on the farm, the older man smiling with pleasure at the distant memories that only occasionally returned.

He talked until he grew sleepy, then the nurse came out, chided Zach for tiring him and pushed the wheelchair back inside the building.

Zach thought it was probably good for his father and didn't regret the hours they had shared, something that had never happened when he was a boy.

As he left the rest home, the sun was setting behind the low range of hills to the west, casting the sky into deep shades of pink, orange and blue. The long day was nearly over. Driving down the highway, he thought of his disastrous lunch with Liz earlier that day.

Zach swore softly. If he had ever felt like getting drunk, tonight was the night. He wouldn't, of course. He'd been down that ugly road and he never intended to go there again.

He shouldn't have done it, shouldn't have pressed Liz for a date when he was still seeing Lisa. He wasn't sure why he had. Hell, he hadn't really believed she would accept. And for chrissake, it was only lunch!

He had always admired her honesty. He should have been honest with her. Damn!

Zach took a deep, steadying breath. From the start, there had been some kind of spark between them. Liz might not want to admit it, but it was there just the same. He had seen it in her pretty blue eyes whenever she looked at him — though she did her best to ignore it. And he had screwed it up.

He could still remember how pale she had gone when Carson had said Lisa's name, the son of a bitch. There was something going on there, Zach figured, something between Elizabeth and Lisa that Carson knew about and Zach didn't.

It didn't matter, he told himself. It was just a lunch date, probably wouldn't have gone any further anyway.

Still, he was done seeing Lisa. Whatever attraction he had felt for her had been fading for some time. He hadn't wanted to sleep with her last week, couldn't wait to leave the following morning and had gotten a room at the Holiday Inn instead of going back that night.

He'd talk to her tomorrow, tell her their arrangement was over. He didn't figure she'd be too upset. She had a string of admirers a block long waiting in the wings. Zach knew she saw some of them when he wasn't around, just as he dated whomever he wanted in L.A.

Nothing serious. Just women he met and enjoyed. They knew where he was coming from. Just like Lisa. For as far back as he could remember, Zach had always been a loner. Hell, his nickname in high school had been the Lone Wolf.

He didn't like people getting too close, didn't like letting his guard down enough to let them. If he did, something always seemed to go wrong. Better to keep his distance, play it safe. With Lisa that had been easy.

With Liz, he didn't think it would be.

Hell, maybe it was good things had turned out the way they had. Better for everyone all around.

At least that was what he told himself as he steered his Jeep along the highway that evening, slowing as he reached the gate to Teen Vision, meaning to have supper with the counselors and the boys.

He did that sometimes. Though visiting hours and phone calls were strictly limited, as the organization's founder he had special privileges. It gave him a chance to talk to the kids, try to encourage them.

He parked in the dirt lot, got out and closed the door, then pressed the lock button on his key fob and headed across the parking lot.

Sam Marston met him before he reached the dining hall.

"Zach! I'm glad you're here."

"What's up?"

"It's the Perez boy. He's skipped. If he's not back in a couple of hours, I'll have to turn him in."

Raul was out of juvenile detention but still under strict rules of supervision and those did not include leaving the premises without special permission.

"What happened?"

"According to his friend, Pete Ortega, he made his usual Friday night call to his sister then headed back up to his room. Pete said he seemed upset about something and a little while later, he turned up missing."

"Keep your cell phone handy. I'll call you if I find him." Zach went back to his Jeep and cranked up the engine. A few minutes later, he was rolling along the highway toward the section of Harcourt Farms that contained the workers' cottages, the overseers' houses and the main farmhouse.

Zach had a very strong hunch Raul had gone to see his sister.

TEN

Elizabeth pulled into the driveway of the Santiago home and parked next to the single car garage. As soon as she cracked open the car door, she was hit by a wave of evening heat. The town was furnace-hot this time of year, the ground as hard as pavement except for the irrigated agricultural land that provided most of the jobs in the area.

She glanced at her surroundings, at the perfectly spaced walnut trees in the orchard behind this section of the farm, the endless rows of cotton stretching for miles along the road. The heat worked miracles on produce, but it was hell on the people forced to endure it five months out of the year.

Ignoring the perspiration beginning to dampen the back of her neck, she started toward the narrow cement walkway leading to the small, yellow stucco house.

Maria had called her at home, which she had never done before. Elizabeth was careful of the people she gave her home number to, but in the two years she had been working with Raul, somehow Maria and her brother had become people she particularly cared about, and she was determined to help them.

She thought of the young woman's frantic phone call.

"I am sorry to bother you at home," Maria had said, an edge of panic in her voice, "but I did not know what else to do."

"It's all right, Maria. What is it? What's happened?"

"It is Raul. He called me as he usually does on Friday and I mentioned that Miguel was going to be working all night. He asked me if I was afraid to stay alone and I told him I was. I wish I had lied, but he would have known if I did. He said he was coming over to stay with me until Miguel got home. I tried to talk him out of it, but he would not listen. He is on his way here now."

Elizabeth sighed into the receiver. Leaving the youth farm would have dire consequences for Raul. "Once he gets there, just keep him there. I'll be over as quickly as I can."

Elizabeth hung up the phone, grabbed her

purse and car keys, and headed out the door. If Raul was caught AWOL from Teen Vision, he'd be sent back to juvenile hall. Neither Maria nor Elizabeth wanted that to happen.

She was out of the car and walking up the sidewalk when a dark brown Jeep Cherokee pulled up next to her car. Her mouth thinned as Zachary Harcourt got out and closed the driver-side door. Annoyance warred with a funny little tug in the pit of her stomach.

He caught up with her at the bottom of the front porch steps. "I gather we're both here for the same reason."

"I suppose so. Raul?"

He nodded.

"I'm not sure he's here yet. I take it he's not at the farm."

"He was earlier. Turned up missing just after supper."

She glanced in that direction, but the youth farm was too far away to see. "Maria called to tell me he was coming. I was afraid if he left he'd get caught."

"Sam's closing his eyes to this for the moment. But I've got to get Raul back before Sam's patience wears out. Let's go see if he's in there."

Elizabeth didn't move. "There's no need

for you to trouble yourself. If he's there, I can bring him out to the farm."

"Sorry. This is my problem as much as yours. Let's go."

He didn't give her time to argue, just started up the steps of the little front porch and she fell in beside him. She wanted him to leave, to tell him he didn't need to interrupt his evening with Lisa, but like it or not, he had a point. Raul was missing from Teen Vision and that made it Zach's problem as well as her own.

He firmly rapped on the door and a few seconds later, Maria pulled it open. Her eyes widened when she saw a man she didn't know standing next to Elizabeth.

"It's all right," Elizabeth said. "This is Zachary Harcourt. He's come to take Raul back to the farm."

Maria looked around, uncertain if she should admit her brother was inside.

"Raul isn't in trouble," Zach told her. "Not yet. That's why I'm here — to make sure he gets back before he is."

Maria opened the door and stepped out of their way. "He is here."

Zach waited for Elizabeth to go in ahead of him and as soon as she walked into the living room, she spotted Raul on the sofa. He shot to his feet the moment he saw

them, and Elizabeth recognized the belligerent look on his face. She had seen it before
and seeing it now did not bode well for
Raul.

"My sister is frightened. I am not leaving
her alone in this house."

Zach spoke before she had the chance. "If
you don't go back with me tonight, Raul,
they'll return you to juvenile detention. You
can't protect your sister while you're locked
up in there."

The boy's black eyes darted from Zach to
Elizabeth and she could read the turmoil
there. "I have to stay. She is my sister and
she is afraid."

"You cannot stay!" Maria practically
shouted. "This is the chance you have been
waiting for. You must go back before it is
too late!"

Raul just shook his head.

Elizabeth glanced between the two sib-
lings, focused her attention on the brother.
"It's all right, Raul. I'll stay with Maria." As
the words spilled out, it occurred to her that
perhaps it was a good idea. When nothing
happened in the house tonight, maybe the
girl would concede the possibility that her
ghost might not exist and return to her sessions with Dr. James. "If it's all right with
Maria."

"You do not need to stay," Maria said. "I am fine here by myself."

"Your brother is afraid you'll be frightened. If I'm here, you won't be."

Maria swallowed, glanced nervously toward the open bedroom door. "I called my friend, Isabel, but she was . . . expecting company tonight. I shouldn't have told Raul."

"It isn't a problem for me to stay, Maria. Really."

Raul stared at her and all his bravado deflated like a pin-pricked balloon. "You would stay?"

"I think it's a good idea, don't you?" She managed a smile. "Maybe I'll see Maria's ghost."

Maria looked up at her and hope sparked in her jet-black eyes. "*Sí,* maybe you will see her. Then you will not think I am crazy."

"I don't think you're crazy and neither does Dr. James." She caught herself before she launched into another fruitless discussion about anxiety. "But if I happen to see your ghost, of course it would make a difference."

Maria turned to Zach. "Do you believe in ghosts?"

The edge of his mouth faintly curved. "I suppose I would if I saw one."

Very diplomatic, Elizabeth thought with a trace of humor. Maybe he really did have the finesse it took to make a good lawyer.

"Maybe Ms. Conners will see one tonight," Maria said.

His mouth curved even more. Such a sexy mouth. Something warm and completely unwanted slid into the pit of her stomach.

"Perhaps she will." Zach looked over at Raul. "I think it's time for us to go."

The boy hung his head and nodded.

"Go get in the car. I'll be right there."

"I am sorry for the trouble I caused."

"It's all right. You were trying to take care of your family. I can understand that. We just need to work things out so that you won't have to do it again." Raul headed for the door, and Zach cast a meaningful glance at Elizabeth. "Can I speak to you for a moment?"

She would rather he just left, but he had work to do just as she did. By the time she joined him on the porch, Raul was sitting in the passenger side of the Jeep. Zach reached over and closed the front door behind her. His arm brushed hers, and a little tremor of awareness went through her.

"You need to get Maria to tell her husband what's going on. Once he understands what's happening, they can work it out so she's not alone."

"I've tried. She won't do it. He's not exactly the understanding type, if you know what I mean. He's ten years older, one of those macho types. Maria doesn't think he'll believe her and it'll only make him mad at her."

"Then you're going to have to do it. It isn't fair to Raul to carry this burden by himself. At any rate, I don't know what other choice you have — aside from staying over every time her husband goes out of town."

"Fortunately, that doesn't happen very often. But you're right. He ought to be told." She turned, trying to think of a way to approach Miguel, and felt Zach's hand on her arm, turning her to face him.

"About this afternoon . . . I was wrong. I should have been more honest. I apologize for what happened."

Her mouth tightened. She drew her arm away, trying to ignore the heat of his fingers that remained. "Doesn't matter. Like you said, it was only lunch."

"Yeah, only lunch."

She started to turn away, but Zach's deep voice stopped her.

"It's over with Lisa. I'm not going to see her anymore."

"Why not?"

"Let's just say she's not my type."

She took hold of the doorknob.

"I just wanted you to know," Zach said.

Elizabeth turned the knob and pushed open the door. "Well, now I know." She walked inside and closed the door.

Zach drove Raul back to Teen Vision.

"Thanks, Zach." Raul cracked open his door as Zach turned off the engine in the parking lot. "I really appreciate what you did for me tonight."

"Sam did it, not me. But I'll tell you, Raul, those breaks come few and far between. Don't expect another one."

He nodded. "Do you . . . think you might talk to your brother about the house?"

That was a joke. Like talking to Carson would do an ounce of good. "Let's just see how Ms. Conners does in the house tonight. Maybe she can help Maria figure out what's going on." If anything really was, which he sincerely doubted.

Still, with the crazy stuff that happened in the world today, anything seemed possible.

"I like Ms. Conners."

A memory of her standing next to him on the porch sent a ripple of heat into his groin. It was crazy. Every time he saw her, his attraction to her grew. "So do I."

Unfortunately, she's never been too keen on me.

"I hope she sees the ghost."

Zach grinned. "So do I." He could imagine the look on Liz Conner's face if there actually was a ghost.

"You'd better get going," he said. "Sam is already worried enough." Which was true, though Zach had phoned as soon as they'd gotten in the car to tell Sam he was bringing Raul back to the farm.

Raul nodded and climbed out of the car. "See you tomorrow."

"I'll be here." Zach restarted the engine. "I'll expect to see you, hammer in hand."

Raul smiled for the first time that night. Then his smile slowly faded and Zach figured his earlier concern for his sister had returned.

Maybe Liz's being there would help. Zach hoped so.

Though he didn't think it likely she would see Maria's ghost.

"I'll sleep in here on the couch," Elizabeth said to Maria, who, now that Elizabeth had agreed to stay, worried that the accommodations wouldn't be good enough. Earlier, Maria had insisted on fixing her some-

161

thing to eat, which was fine by Elizabeth, who discovered she was ravenously hungry. She hadn't finished her meal with Zach at The Ranch House and been too busy to get anything since.

After a delicious dinner of leftover *chile verde,* homemade tortillas and Spanish rice — and an agreement that from now on Maria should call her Elizabeth — they retired to the living room to settle in for the night.

"You could take the bed," Maria said, "but I do not have an extra pair of clean sheets."

"The couch is fine. It actually looks pretty comfortable."

Maria studied the brown, overstuffed sofa and bit her lip. "There are two bedrooms but the other one is empty. We are saving to buy a crib for the baby, but we don't have enough money yet. I have a very nice quilt that belonged to my mother. I will put it over the sofa. And you can borrow one of my nightgowns."

Elizabeth changed out of the khaki pants and sleeveless yellow blouse she'd been wearing when Maria had phoned, into the ankle-length pink nylon nightgown the younger woman loaned her. They were about the same height so the length wasn't a problem, and it wasn't so sheer her modesty was at stake.

"It is too tight for me right now," Maria said a bit shyly. "But soon I will be able to wear it again."

"I know you must be excited with the baby so close."

"*Sí*. I cannot wait to have a child of my own. That is why I am so afraid. The ghost . . . she said they will kill my baby if I stay."

Elizabeth walked over and lightly touched Maria's shoulder. The young woman had also changed into a nightgown, her feet bare beneath the hem, which fluttered in the current of air coming from the room air conditioner in the window. There was only one unit in the house. Even with the machine running full-blast, the house was on the warm side of comfortable.

Certainly it couldn't account for the awful chill Maria had mentioned.

"You mustn't worry, Maria. Everything's going to be fine." They sat down on the sofa together and Maria used the TV tuner to flip through the few channels they received on the little thirteen-inch TV sitting on a table against the wall.

"Not much on," Elizabeth said. "It's getting late, anyway. Why don't we just go to bed?"

Maria yawned and nodded. "That is a good idea." She turned toward the bedroom and started walking but her steps slowed as she approached the open door.

Sensing the young woman's nervousness, Elizabeth walked up beside her and peered into the room. "I've got an idea. There's a comfortable-looking chair in the corner. I'm not really sleepy yet. Why don't I sit in here for a while, until you fall asleep? Maybe I'll see the ghost."

Not much chance of that, but her presence would probably put the girl at ease enough to sleep.

"Oh, *sí,* that is a very good idea. Perhaps she will come. You are sure you would not mind?"

"Not at all."

Maria yawned again as she slid between the sheets. In the thin stream of moonlight slanting in through the window, Elizabeth noticed how exhausted the young woman looked. The shadows beneath her eyes seemed even more pronounced, the hollows in her cheeks sunken a little deeper. Maria closed her eyes and it didn't take long until she was deeply asleep.

Sitting in the chair, Elizabeth waited a while, not wanting to wake her, feeling a little bit groggy herself. She rested her head against the upholstered back and didn't realize she had fallen asleep until an odd sound penetrated her conscious.

It was an eerie sort of creaking, probably just the house settling a little, she figured. It came a second time, more distinctly than before, and her heart kicked up. Footsteps on the floor in the living room! Her pulse increased another notch. Someone was in the house!

The door leading into the living room stood open. Easing out of her chair, she crept silently in that direction, wishing she had some sort of weapon. She flattened herself against the wall, then eased forward until she could peer into the other room. There was no lamp on, but enough light seeped in through the break in the curtains to see that no one was there.

Her heart was clattering, slamming against her ribs. Maybe whoever it was had gone into the kitchen or other bedroom. She thought of waking Maria, but she was beginning to think she had only imagined the sound. Still, she needed to know for sure.

As quietly as possible, she checked the little bathroom next to the bedroom, then made her way into the living room, crossed to the second bedroom, and opened the door. Again, the room appeared empty. She checked the closet. Nothing. Then she went into the kitchen.

The back door was locked. The front door as well. There wasn't a soul in the house. No one but her and Maria. She breathed a sigh of relief. It was only her imagination.

Amazing what the power of suggestion could do!

Feeling like a fool, she decided it was time she actually went to bed and started toward the sofa in the living room. She had taken only a couple of steps when the wind began to howl, the oddest sort of low, pain-filled moaning she had ever heard. It seeped beneath the door, seemed to slither over the windowsill. Goose bumps rose on her skin and a chill slid down her spine.

Taking a breath to slow her heartbeat, determined not to make a fool of herself again, she walked over to the window and pulled back the curtains. The night was dark, just a sliver of moon, and not a leaf on the chinaberry tree in the yard was moving. Not a branch, not a flower in the beds beside the front porch.

She opened the front door and looked out. The hot, dry night air crept into the living room, but there wasn't a hint of breeze to propel it.

Elizabeth closed the door with an unsteady hand and turned the lock, securing the place once more. The moaning had stopped. But the eerie feeling it left in the house remained. The air conditioner hummed quietly in the living room window. She turned back toward the bedroom, walked the short distance to the door.

Maria was still asleep, lying on her back in the middle of the bed, the plain white sheet drawn up beneath her chin. It was comfortable where Elizabeth stood, but the minute she stepped through the door of the bedroom, she felt a chill so cold, so viciously freezing, her breath caught in her lungs. She gasped, began to breathe faster, trying to get enough air. She moistened her lips, which were freezing cold and rapidly turning numb.

Dear God, what was happening?

She started to shiver, wrapped her arms around herself as her gaze frantically scanned the room, looking for some explanation. She turned toward the bed, saw Maria moving restlessly beneath the sheet, curled now into a ball against the icy chill, her eyes twitching beneath her quivering eyelids.

Elizabeth tried to control the fear gnawing at her insides, bit down on her trembling lip as her teeth began to chatter. Her heartbeat roared. She tried to tell herself that no one was there in the house and she was safe. But something unexplainable was happening. Something frightening.

And she was afraid.

For the first time, she understood why Maria had been so frightened. Understood that this wasn't just happening in the young woman's mind.

The chill moved away from the bed, away from where she stood shaking next to the nightstand, but it seemed to Elizabeth that the cold remained there in the room, hovering like an invisible force somewhere near the corner.

A fresh rush of fear slid through her. She thought again of waking Maria, but she couldn't seem to make herself move.

Then she noticed the smell. Thick and heavy. Sickeningly sweet. A cloying odor that only vaguely mimicked the scent of roses. It felt sticky on her skin, sticky in her throat as she breathed in the fetid air. Her chest squeezed, clamped down, and suffocating feeling overwhelmed her.

Her gaze shot to the bed. Maria had awakened. She was lying there on her back, her eyes wide-open, a trembling hand at her throat as she stared at Elizabeth in terror.

She made a whimpering sound, and it was the catalyst Elizabeth needed to force herself to move.

The instant she did, she felt the change. The air began to thin and she could breathe more easily. The temperature in the bedroom slowly began to return to normal. The smell disappeared as if it had never been there, leaving only the faintest trace of rose perfume. By the time she reached the bed, even that had faded.

"Maria! Maria are you all right?"

The girl's eyes filled with tears. "Did . . . did you see her?"

"No. I didn't see anything, but —"

"She was here. I know she was."

"Maria," she said gently, sitting down beside her on the bed. "Something happened here tonight. I heard the noises. I felt the chill. Something is going on and I admit it was frightening, but I don't believe it has anything to do with a ghost."

"I tell you she was here."

"Did you see her?" she asked gently.

"No. I have only seen her once. But I could feel her. She was here. She came again to warn me."

Elizabeth managed a smile. "I'm glad I was here tonight. Now I understand your fears and I think at least part of what is happening is real. We just need to find out what's going on."

Maria looked up at her, her face pale in a faint ray of moonlight streaming in through the part in the curtains. "What do you mean?"

Elizabeth reached over and turned on the lamp beside the bed. The soft glow dispelled the last remnants of whatever had been in the room.

"You live on a farm. There are animals and plants all around you. They use fertilizers in the soil and spray the air with chemicals and pesticides. Perhaps something was done to the house. Maybe they put something in the ground before the house was built. I'll speak to Mr. Harcourt, see if he knows what it might be. We'll figure this out, Maria. It'll just take a little time."

"I want to move away. I don't want to stay here."

"We'll work this out, I promise. In the meantime, I'm going to speak to Miguel."

Her eyes flew wide and she opened her mouth to protest.

"I won't mention the ghost. I'll just tell him what happened while I was here tonight. I'll tell him you're frightened and that I was frightened, too. I'll ask him to make sure you aren't left here alone at night."

"If there is something wrong with the house, why does it not happen in the daytime?"

Good question. "Maybe it does, but in the daytime, you're too busy to notice. Does this happen every night or just once in a while?"

"Just once in a while. But each night I am afraid it will happen again."

"But it doesn't happen when Miguel is here?"

"Sometimes he is here, but he does not wake up."

"Well, maybe he's just too tired to notice." Elizabeth released a breath into the now quiet house. "I suppose we should try to get some sleep."

Maria nodded. "*Sí,* I guess we should." She stared at the rumpled white sheets on the bed. "Only I am no longer sleepy."

Elizabeth followed her gaze, thinking of the frightening things that had happened in the room. "Neither am I. Why don't we see what's on TV?"

ELEVEN

Elizabeth left the house early the following morning. It was Saturday. She went home and changed into shorts and Reeboks, went into her second bedroom, which served as an office and an exercise room, and climbed on the stationary bike. She then did fifty sit-ups, used the free weights, then climbed on the treadmill.

She liked to stay in shape. Her job was mentally stressful and exercising seemed to help. The apartment complex also had a pool and she swam whenever she got the chance. As soon as she had showered, she fixed herself something to eat, then, seeing how bare the cupboards were getting, decided to do some grocery shopping.

Later in the afternoon, she planned to speak to Miguel. She called Maria to be sure she was all right and ask what time would be good for her to stop by.

At five o'clock, she left her apartment and

headed down Highway 51. Miguel was standing at the living room window when she crossed the abandoned tracks and pulled up in the driveway, a lean, black-haired man without an ounce of extra flesh beneath his weathered, brown, suntanned skin. At twenty-nine, with his heavily lashed dark eyes and strong jaw, he was handsome. He was also the kind of man who believed he was always right, especially when the person who disagreed with him was a woman.

"I do not understand any of this," Miguel said once Elizabeth finished telling him her tale. "You and Maria — both of you think something is wrong with the house, but that cannot be. This is a good house. My wife is lucky to live in a house as fine as this one."

Elizabeth kept the smile fixed on her face. "It's a very good house, Miguel. That's the reason we need to find out what's wrong with it."

"Nothing is wrong with it! You and my wife . . . I think there is something wrong with you!"

This wasn't going to work. She wished she had never mentioned the house. She would have been better off to approach the problem from an entirely different angle. Then again, knowing Miguel, there probably wasn't any good way to approach the problem.

"Maria loves this place as much as you do," she said. "It's just that there may be a few things that need to be fixed. Sometimes it makes noises that frighten her. She has the baby to think of, and when you aren't home at night, she's afraid."

"She is a child. It is time she grew up."

Damn, she was making a mess of this. "What I'm trying to say, Miguel, is that Maria feels . . . she feels safe when you're here with her. She knows that you can protect her. I thought maybe you could find someone to stay with her on the nights you won't be home until late."

Miguel said a word in Spanish she couldn't quite make out and didn't want to. In the course of her job, the Spanish she had learned in high school and college had become a second language. She couldn't imagine working in the area without it.

"I will take care of my wife as I always have. You do not need to worry."

Elizabeth forced herself to smile. "Thank you, Miguel. I knew you would understand." *Understand?* The man had the understanding of a rabbit. Thank God she hadn't mentioned Maria's ghost.

She left the two of them standing at the

window in the living room, hoping Maria would not suffer for the attempt she had made to help. Whatever happened, she had promised the girl she would help her find out what was happening in the house and she meant to keep her word. First thing Monday morning, she would phone Carson Harcourt and ask if she could stop by and see him.

She called Carson from her office, but he didn't seem the least bit pleased to hear from her.

"I'm afraid I'm busy most of the day," he said brusquely. "What is it you need?"

"Look, Carson, I realize you're angry about my having lunch with Zach, but that has nothing to do with this. I need to talk you about something that's happening on the farm."

A momentary pause. "All right. I'll be working in my study most of the afternoon."

"Is two o'clock okay?"

"Fine. I'll see you then." He hung up the phone and Elizabeth waited for the regret to set in. It was obvious Carson wouldn't be asking her out again. She ought to be unhappy. But the plain truth was she wasn't attracted to Carson Harcourt and never would be. This would have happened sooner or later. It was far better that it happened now.

She had three counseling sessions lined up that Monday morning. At nine o'clock, Geraldine Hickman and her daughter, Carol; followed an hour later by ten-year-old Nina Mendoza; then an appointment with Richard Long, a member of her rage counseling group.

Mrs. Hickman and her daughter were there at Mrs. Hickman's insistence, having discovered her twelve-year-old was having sex with a number of boys at school.

"Mark paid for my ticket to the matinee," Carol explained to her mother during the session. "How else was I supposed to repay him?"

It made Elizabeth sick to think how little these young girls valued themselves — their bodies worth no more than a ticket to the movies.

Nina Mendoza's sessions were paid for by the county. The entire family went into counseling after the police were called to their home for the third time in a row. Emilio Mendoza had been arrested for drunk and disorderly conduct and resisting arrest. Later, it was discovered he had also given his youngest daughter, eight at the time, a beating severe enough for a trip to the emergency room for not eating all of the food on her plate.

Nina was removed to foster care, but she was returned to her family now, and all of them were beginning to understand that violence didn't have to be a way of life.

Elizabeth's final appointment of the morning was with a forty-two-year-old man named Richard Long. Richard was there at the court's insistence, a local attorney who had battered his wife on so many occasions it was either get counseling or lose his license to practice law and spend time in jail.

Richard was also ordered to attend the Thursday night group session that either she or Michael conducted, but so far, the man just seemed to be marking time. Elizabeth wondered if there was the slightest chance he would ever change.

With the morning over, she left the office at noon, grabbed a quick sandwich for lunch, ran a couple of errands, then went out to see Carson at Harcourt Farms. The housekeeper, a young Hispanic girl, showed her in.

"Señor Harcourt is expecting you. He is working in his study. If you will please follow me."

She was pretty, Elizabeth thought, perhaps

twenty-one or two, with a curvy figure that even her plain black slacks and white blouse couldn't hide. She smiled as they reached the study then silently slipped away.

Working at his desk, Carson stood up as Elizabeth walked into the room.

"Hello, Elizabeth."

"Hello, Carson. Thank you for seeing me."

"Have a seat. What can I do for you?"

Letting his abrupt manner set the tone, she walked over to the chair next to his roll-top desk and sat down while Carson returned to his seat.

"I spent Friday night with Maria Santiago. Something odd is happening in the Santiago house. I was hoping you might be able to help me figure out what it is."

For the next twenty minutes, she explained about the odd happenings in the house and her suspicion that something was wrong with the construction or the pipes or maybe the ground underneath.

"This is a farm, after all," she said. "Maybe the soil was polluted by something before the house was built. That might account for the smell, at least. What I'd like to do, if you don't mind, is bring in someone to take a look at the place, see what we might be able to discover."

Carson rose from his chair, giving him the

advantage. She wanted to stand up, too, but forced herself to remain in her seat.

"Actually, I do mind. I mind a great deal. Miguel Santiago is the youngest overseer on the farm. He was given that job ahead of several other well-qualified workers. The house you're discussing is only four years old and there is absolutely nothing wrong with it."

"I spent a night in that house, Carson. Something was definitely wrong."

"The girl is young. She has a vivid imagination. Whatever she told you influenced what you thought happened that night. That's all there is to it."

She held on to her temper, knowing it would only make things worse if she got angry. "Then perhaps there's another solution."

"And that would be . . . ?"

"Maybe there's somewhere else they could live. Another house in the complex, or somewhere not too far away."

His face began to redden. "There are four overseers' houses in the compound and four overseers working on the farm. All of the houses are occupied and I am not about to rent a place somewhere else because Santiago's wife is pregnant and imagining things. Besides, I want my foremen here,

179

close by if they're needed."

It was a good argument. A twelve-thousand acre farm required good management. He needed his foremen nearby to handle the numerous problems that came up. Still, she hadn't been imagining things that night at the Santiago's house. And she was beginning to understand Maria's frustration at not being believed.

Elizabeth stood up to leave. "Well, that's it then. Thank you for your time."

"Sorry I couldn't be more help."

"I understand your position."

His blue eyes fixed on her face. "Do you? I don't think so." He was no longer talking about the farm, she knew, but her lunch date with his brother. "I had hopes for us, Elizabeth. I can't believe you're letting Zach use you the way he is. I thought you were smarter than that."

"What are you talking about?"

"It's obvious, isn't it? He saw me with you that night at the benefit. He realized I had an interest in you and now he is trying to destroy it. That's the way Zach is. He's been jealous of me all his life. He'll do anything he can to hurt me."

She smoothed a wrinkle on the front of her skirt. "He isn't going to oppose your run for office. That must mean something."

"Maybe he won't. Then again, you never know what Zach is going to do."

She mulled that over, wondering if Carson might not be right. In his youth, Zach had been wild and unpredictable. There was a good chance he still was.

"I'd better get going. As I said, thanks for your time."

"Think about what I said, Elizabeth. If you decide I'm right about Zach, give me a call. I'd still like to see you. But not as long as my brother and I are in some sort of competition."

She opened her mouth to tell him there was no competition, that she wasn't the least bit interested in Zach. Then she realized she was even less interested in Carson, so instead she simply nodded. "I'll give it some thought."

She left the study and made her way out to the car, hissing in a breath as she slid across the burning red leather seat. Sticking her key in the ignition, she started the car.

Carson wasn't going to help, she thought as the engine roared to life. But that didn't mean she couldn't find a way around him. Carson wasn't the only Harcourt who had a say in what happened at Harcourt Farms. She decided she would phone Sam Marston and get Zach's number in L.A. The notion of calling Zach sat like a stone in her stomach, but she had to find out what was happening in the house and somehow put a stop to it.

It was Thursday before Elizabeth managed to get hold of Zach. Their last conversation hadn't ended that pleasantly, but in truth, she *had* overreacted at the news of his involvement with Lisa. It was, after all, only lunch. And he had apologized, rather sincerely, she thought.

Still, she wasn't sure quite how to approach him. As she dialed the number for Noble, Goldman and Harcourt that Sam had given her, she decided her best strategy would be to use Carson's refusal as leverage to gain his brother's agreement to help.

She almost smiled. They wanted to play games. Well, she could play a few herself.

The operator passed her through to Zach's office and a moment later, she heard his deep voice on the line.

"Liz? I can't believe this is really you."

"I need to talk to you, Zach."

"Something earthshaking must have happened for you to be calling me here." She heard the shift in his voice. "It isn't Raul? Something hasn't happened to the boy?"

"No, it's nothing like that. Well, at least

this only indirectly concerns Raul. It's about Maria . . . about the Santiago's house."

"My God, don't tell me you actually saw a ghost!"

She laughed. "No, of course not. But . . ."

"Go on."

"But something odd did happen that night. Something very odd. And more than a little bit frightening." She had his attention now. Sensing victory might lie ahead, she went on to tell him about the noises and the smell, the terrible cold and her difficulty breathing.

"One thing is fairly certain — I don't think Maria is suffering from anxiety. I don't think what's happening has anything to do with a ghost, but there is definitely something wrong with that house."

She told him how she had gone to see Carson to try to find out if there was a problem with the construction or maybe something else, but he had refused to allow her to bring anyone in to examine the place.

"He was adamant about it," she said, hoping to goad him in the direction she wanted. "I don't understand it." She paused. "Of course, there is always the possibility he was just paying me back for having lunch with you."

She could feel the sudden tension on the

line. As a game strategy, she had just scored one big point.

"I'm not sure how I can help, but I'll be up there tomorrow afternoon." He cleared his throat. "What do you say we have dinner and discuss it?"

Her hand tightened on the phone. Score one for his side. "I don't think that's a good idea."

"I'm not seeing Lisa anymore. I told you that and I meant it."

"I believe you, but —"

"If you're afraid Carson will object —"

"I don't give a damn about Carson."

She could almost see him smile. "I like hearing those words. So we're on for supper?"

If it were anyone else, she would agree, but this was Zachary Harcourt. And if they went to The Ranch House again, the gossip would be all over town. "I don't know, I . . ."

"We'll drive over to Mason. No one will have to know you're out with the town bad boy."

She found herself smiling. He was certainly that. "All right, we'll have dinner. What time?"

"I'll pick you up at seven."

She gave him the address to her apartment and hung up the phone, feeling as if she had lost the first skirmish. Still, she was determined to win the war. Tomorrow she would find a way to convince Zach Harcourt to help her uncover the answers to the problems in the house.

TWELVE

Zach knocked on her apartment door promptly at seven o'clock. Apparently that was another thing they had in common — they were both punctual people.

In concession to the hundred-degree heat, typical for this time of year, Elizabeth wore an apricot sundress with a slim skirt, wide straps and a wide, matching belt, along with a pair of white, high-heeled, open-toed sandals. As she pulled the brush one more time through her shoulder-length, dark auburn hair, she told herself the extra care she had taken with her appearance had nothing to do with Zachary Harcourt.

"Looks like you're ready," he said from her doorstep, looking cool and attractive in a short-sleeved pale blue shirt and lightweight tan slacks. His gaze went over her from head to foot, the gold in his eyes heating up in a slightly different way than it had before.

She assessed that look. "Depends on what I'm getting ready for."

Zach laughed. "Not much more than dinner, I don't imagine."

Reaching down, she plucked her white leather bag off the coffee table, slung the gold chain over her shoulder and started for the door.

"Nice car," she said as they reached the end of the sidewalk, admiring the flashy black BMW convertible pulled up at the curb.

"Thought I'd drive this instead of the Jeep, since I'm trying to impress you. Is it working?" He held open the passenger door and she slid into the black leather seat, which was still cool from the air-conditioning.

"I like nice cars, so yes. Especially since you were wise enough to leave the top up."

"I wanted to impress you, not fry you alive." Zach closed her door, rounded the car and slid in behind the wheel.

"So how many cars *do* you have?" she asked as the engine roared to life.

"Just two. I've got a Harley, though, and I just bought a thirty-foot sailboat."

One of her eyebrows arched. "Well, you know what they say — the difference between men and boys is the price of their toys."

"Ouch."

They drove along the two-lane highway toward Mason, a slightly bigger farming town thirty miles away. He glanced over at her. "I like the things money can buy, I freely admit it. But I'm not driven to own them like some people are."

She thought about the money he'd donated to Teen Vision and figured maybe that was true. He could have bought a lot more toys if he had kept the money for himself.

"I like nice things, too," she agreed, "but not enough to sacrifice my happiness for them."

For several seconds, he looked her way. "You're talking about your marriage."

"Brian always wanted the best. Expensive cars, designer clothes. He wanted me to have them, too. He was generous that way, though I think he was mostly motivated by the image he wanted to project."

"What happened?"

"I wasn't enough for him. It's as simple as that." She gazed out the window, her mind shifting to the past. "Three years ago, we came up to San Pico for my class reunion. I caught him, as you lawyers would say, in flagrante delicto in the backseat of our car with Lisa Doyle."

Zach's jaw tightened. "No wonder you freaked out when Carson mentioned her name."

"I probably shouldn't have told you. But you can see why she isn't my favorite person. Not that it was entirely her fault."

"Lisa's all for Lisa. She makes no secret about it."

"But you apparently enjoyed her company."

"I enjoyed the sex. We used each other. That's about all there was to it."

All there was to it? She couldn't imagine using a man for sex, as Lisa apparently had. "So why did you end it?"

"Because I was tired of feeling nothing. I taught myself that, to go through life feeling nothing, letting nothing in. For a while, Lisa was my perfect woman. We saw each other and anyone else we felt like. There were no strings attached. There was also nothing there when I woke up next to her in the morning."

Elizabeth said nothing more. She liked that he was being so honest, or at least seemed to be. The old Zach would have rattled off some phony line then laughed when she ignored it.

They reached the town of Mason, the

county seat of San Pico County. It was just another valley town only bigger, with a Target *and* a Wal-Mart, and a few more restaurants.

Zach pulled into the parking lot of a place called The Captain's Table. According to the sign, the restaurant specialized in seafood, which she had learned never to order in the valley because it was so hot and the fish came from too far away.

They went in and got settled in a nice private booth. For an instant his gaze touched her face and the gold in his dark eyes seemed to glitter. Zach looked away.

"I've never been here, have you?"

She shook her head. "I don't come to Mason very often." But it looked as if the restaurant had been there a while, the red leather booths a little worn, the carpet a little faded. Still, the red glass candles glowing in the middle of the table gave it a nice kind of old-fashioned intimacy.

They made easy conversation until the waitress finished taking their order, then Zach turned the discussion in the direction she was there for.

"All right, you came out with me tonight so we could talk about the Santiago house. But I have to warn you in advance, I'm not sure I can help."

Hoping he could, she told him in detail about the eerie night she had spent in the house. "It was really frightening, Zach. The strange noises, the cold, that god-awful heavy rose smell. It got so bad, I almost couldn't breathe. It happened to Maria, too. It scared us both, I can tell you. I can't imagine what could cause those kinds of things to happen."

"To tell you the truth, neither can I. On the phone you mentioned getting someone out there to look at the place. I gather you think they might find some rational explanation?"

"Surely there is one. I don't believe in ghosts."

"I don't, either. Except for ghosts from our past, of course. Those always seem to haunt us."

She cast him a sideways glance. "You aren't talking about that day at Marge's, are you?"

He smiled. "Not really. But as long as it's taken to get you to go out with me, I could be."

Her lips lightly curved. "This isn't really a date. We're here to talk business."

"Oh, that's right. For a minute there, I forgot."

Elizabeth fought a smile then fiddled with

191

the red cloth napkin in her lap. She looked up at him, found him watching her with those unusual golden brown eyes. "Does your past haunt you, Zach?"

He gazed off toward the window, but the red velvet curtains were closed, blocking the last glow of twilight.

"I suppose in a way it does. I lived in the fanciest house in San Pico, but my life was hell. I wasn't welcome there. No matter what my father demanded of my mother and brother, they hated me from the moment they found out I existed. My father couldn't change that. Carson and Constance did everything in their power to make my life miserable, and my father was rarely home to do anything about it."

"No wonder you got into trouble." She remembered it well, the trial in the summer after her senior year, the sentence Zachary Harcourt received for vehicular assault and negligent homicide. It had been the talk of the tiny town for weeks.

Zach's mouth edged up and a little shimmer of awareness went through her. God, he had the sexiest mouth.

"I can't really blame what happened on my parents. It was pure stupidity on my part. I guess I wanted my father's attention. But the worse I behaved, the less I saw of him. We didn't get to be friends until I got out of prison. He was there for me then. As far as I'm concerned, none of the rest of it matters."

"We all make mistakes, I suppose. We just do the best we can."

"That's what I tell the kids at Teen Vision. We all make mistakes. The trick is to figure out what you're doing wrong and stop doing it. Turn your life in a different direction."

Their food arrived, prime rib for Elizabeth, lobster for Zach, and they relaxed and enjoyed their meals. Well, *relaxed* wasn't exactly the word. She was too aware of him to actually relax. Instead, she found herself watching him, noticing things about him, the long, tapered fingers, the graceful way he moved, how easily he smiled. She couldn't remember ever being so conscious of a man.

And he was interesting, she discovered, well-read, and a good listener. She was attracted to him even more than she had feared.

Which meant he was trouble, plain and simple.

She didn't want to like Zach Harcourt. She knew too much about his past to trust him. After Brian, she didn't trust any man, not completely.

At least, not enough to let down her guard.

Still, by the end of the evening, she felt easier in his company, a little less tense but no less aware of him. They were on the road, heading back to her apartment by the time she got around to the subject they had left unfinished in the restaurant.

"So what do you think about the house? Will you give me your approval for someone to come in and inspect it?"

"I would if I could. But my brother controls the farm. He has since my father's accident. As the oldest son, Carson was named conservator of the estate in my father's will. He's in charge of the ranch and my father's medical care."

"So Carson has complete control. You're an attorney. Why didn't you go to court, make him give you some kind of say?"

"Because I don't give a damn about the farm and never have. Carson can shove the place as far as I'm concerned. I do worry about my father, though. My brother and I never seem to see eye to eye on Dad's health care."

Elizabeth settled deeper into the car seat. Outside the window, rows and rows of cotton rolled by, the white, open bolls of fiber the only thing visible in the darkness.

"I'll tell you what I'll do," Zach said. "You call someone to come out and look at the house. If Carson finds out, you can tell him I said it was okay." He grinned, a flash of white as bright as the cotton bolls out in the fields. "Nothing I like better than pissing him off, anyway."

Elizabeth straightened in her seat, wondering if Carson were right and goading his brother was the reason Zach had been pursuing her. "That's probably not a good idea."

"Where Carson's concerned, nothing is ever a good idea, but, hey — you want to know what's going on in the house, don't you? Well, this is the way to find out."

It wasn't exactly on the up-and-up, but then this was Zachary Harcourt talking. He might have changed in some ways but it was obvious he was still a little reckless. She found herself smiling. In a way, she was glad he hadn't changed completely.

He cast her a sideways glance. "What are you smiling about?"

Her cheeks went hot. She hoped he couldn't see them in the darkness inside the car. "Nothing. I was just . . . I was thinking you were right. I promised to help Maria. And if you're willing to take the blame —

hey, that's okay with me."

He grinned. He did that a lot, she noticed, and it looked really good on him. "That's my girl."

"First thing Monday, I'll call and make the arrangements."

"Like I said, it's not that big a deal. Odds are Carson will never have a clue."

Zach drove through town, rounded the corner onto Cherry Street, and pulled his sporty black convertible up to the curb. He walked her up to the door of her apartment and she wondered if he would expect a good-night kiss.

"Thanks, Zach. I really appreciate what you're doing."

He tipped his head toward the door. "Aren't you going to invite me in for a drink?"

"I thought you said you didn't drink."

"I said I don't drink *much.* And never when I'm driving. Besides, I was thinking of a cup of coffee."

She knew she shouldn't. But it was Friday night and she rarely went out and so far Zach had been a perfect gentleman.

A thought she found oddly annoying.

She doubted Zach would behave this way with Lisa Doyle. Apparently, she didn't have as much sex appeal as Lisa had.

"All right, come on in. I'll make us a pot of decaf. That way we'll be able to sleep."

Zach's eyes found hers and her breath caught. There was nothing gentlemanly in the hot look he gave her. It was blatantly sexual, almost scorching. Sleep, it said, was the last thing on his mind.

Her stomach contracted. Now that they were there in her apartment, their business concluded, his manner seemed to have changed.

She swallowed. As she thought back over the evening, she had noticed that same look several times, but his gaze had quickly been shuttered and she figured she had imagined it.

"Decaf sounds good," he said, his eyes still on her face.

Turning away, she went into the kitchen. She was surprised when Zach followed.

"Nice place." He looked around at the bare tile countertops, just a toaster and a can opener; the small round wooden table with nothing but salt and pepper shakers in the middle.

"Nice and clean, you mean." She pulled a can of decaf down from the cupboard. "I keep meaning to decorate the place, but I can't seem to get my mind wrapped around the fact I'm back here in San Pico. When I was in high school, all I ever thought about was leaving."

"Why'd you come back?" He was standing right behind her, so close she could feel his breath against the nape of her neck. Her nerves kicked in. As she reached for the bag of coffee, she tried to keep her hand from shaking.

"I needed a place to recover from my divorce. My dad was here, my sister. Now Dad's gone and my sister's moved away. If it weren't for my job, I don't think I'd still be here."

He moved a little closer. "I'm glad you are."

The air snagged in her lungs. He settled both hands on her hips and slowly turned her to face him.

"What . . . what are you doing?"

"What I've been wanting to do all evening — getting ready to kiss you. I just hope you don't slap me as hard as you did that day outside Marge's."

She looked up at him, saw the heat in his eyes he no longer tried to hide. For the first time, it occurred to her that she had been wanting him to look at her that way all evening. "I won't slap you."

"Thank God," he said an instant before he bent his head and kissed her thoroughly.

It was an incredible kiss, his mouth like hot, damp silk. It burned across her lips, taking and taking, making her catch fire along with him. She could feel his heat, his hunger. She knew now it had been there all along.

Zach kissed her and kissed her, deep, penetrating kisses, hot, drugging kisses that made her insides turn to mush and her knees wobble. He backed her up against the table, trapping her as if he thought she might try to escape, and kissed her some more. Elizabeth looped her arms around his neck and slid the tips of her fingers into his thick dark hair.

His tongue was in her mouth and she could taste the maleness of him. No man had ever kissed her this way, as if he couldn't get enough, as if he needed to kiss her as much as he needed to breathe. Her nipples tightened, throbbed inside the cups of her white lace push-up bra.

"You drive me crazy," he said against the side of her neck. "I can't stop thinking about you." Her head fell back and he began to rain kisses along her throat and over her shoulders.

"This is insane," she whispered, but she was talking to herself and not to Zach.

She felt his hands on her breasts, cupping

them over the fabric, gently kneading. "I want to make love to you. There's nothing insane about that."

She shook her head, knew she should pull away. But she wanted to feel the heat, the fire, just for a few minutes more. She tried not to think of Lisa Doyle, of the women he had in L.A. She tried not to remember what Carson had said, *I can't believe you're letting Zach use you this way.*

She heard the buzz of her zipper, felt his hands slide inside her bra to cup her breasts. Desire roared through her. Heat tugged low in her belly, speared out through her limbs. She had to stop him. This was happening way too fast. She wasn't Lisa Doyle. She didn't do one-night stands.

He nibbled the lobe of an ear. "God, you taste so good."

She swallowed, tried to move away, but his fingers were tugging on her nipple, his hands testing the size and shape of her breasts, making them swell into his palms.

She hadn't been with anyone since Brian. It was only natural, she told herself, to be excited by the touch of a man.

But this wasn't just any man, this was Zachary Harcourt and she didn't trust him. Couldn't afford to trust him.

He unfastened her belt and tossed it away,

buzzed the zipper the rest of the way down over her hips. He started to slide the dress off her shoulders, but Elizabeth caught his hand.

"I can't do this."

He kissed the side of her neck. "Why not? We're both adults. We can do whatever we please."

She stepped a little away, took a deep breath and looked him straight in the face. "Carson says . . . he says you're just using me to get to him."

Zach's jaw hardened. He caught her hand, pressed it against his erection. He was big and hard. He thickened even more at her touch. "Carson has nothing to do with this."

"I'm not like Lisa."

"No, you were never like Lisa."

"Zach, please."

There must have been something in her tone, something that made him understand that she was fighting not just him but herself.

With a sigh, he reached behind her and zipped up her dress. "I'm sorry. I didn't mean to rush you. It's just . . ."

Her hands trembled as she adjusted her clothes. "Just what?"

"I've wanted you from the moment I saw you that day at Teen Vision. I've made myself go slow. I wanted to give you a chance to get to know me. I've tried to be patient, Liz. I'm not a patient man."

She fumbled for something to say, her heart racing madly. "No one calls me Liz anymore."

"Why not?"

"Brian didn't like it. He thought Elizabeth sounded more sophisticated."

He leaned down and very softly kissed her. "They're just names for different facets of the same person. I think Liz is your sensual side." He kissed her softly and she trembled. "You haven't done this a lot, have you?"

She shook her head. "I had a boyfriend before Brian. That's all."

"And since then?"

She looked away. "I don't think I can handle a man like you, Zach. You've been with dozens of women. I don't have that kind of experience."

He caught her chin, forcing her to look at him. "You said you weren't like Lisa and you're right. But a real woman doesn't need to use sexual tricks to satisfy a man. I'm hotter for you right now than I was when I was inside Lisa Doyle."

She flushed. Zach was a virile, sensual man and he made no bones about it.

"Besides, I could teach you those things.

Whatever you want to learn. We could do anything you can imagine."

Her stomach clenched. *Anything you can imagine.* She had never thought of herself as a sexual woman and yet those words made a soft ache throb deep in her womb. "I — I need to think about this, Zach. You and I, we're different people — especially when it comes to sex. I — I'm just not that brave."

He dragged her against him and started to kiss her again, his tongue sliding deep inside her mouth. Her body tightened, trembled. His hand found the hem of her skirt and he shoved it up till it rode at her waist. He palmed her sex over her white lace panties. She was wet. And she was hot. She couldn't remember ever being so hot.

"I think you're brave enough," Zach said, sliding his hand inside her panties. "You just don't know it."

She gasped as he caressed her, stroked her, caught her moan in his mouth. She was on the edge of climax when he stopped kissing her and pulled his hand away, eased her skirt back into place. He stepped back a little, leaving her trembling with desire, aching to have him inside her.

"I want you, Liz. I'm crazy to have you. But not for any other reason except that

I'm attracted to you in a way I haven't been to a woman in years. I want to see you again tomorrow night."

She wildly shook her head.

"All right. Next week then. I'll give you some time, if that's what you need."

"I . . . I don't know, Zach."

"Yes, you do, Liz. You know what you need and so do I. I'll see you next week." Turning away from her, he walked out of the kitchen, crossed the living room, and pulled open the door.

At the echo of it closing behind him, Elizabeth sank down in one of the kitchen chairs. As a game player, she was certainly no match for Zachary Harcourt.

Then again, maybe he wasn't playing a game. Maybe he wanted exactly what he said. Maybe he just wanted her.

Her body pulsed at the heady thought.

It was insane, of course, and yet, why shouldn't she consider it? Zach said he wanted her. After tonight, it was clear how much she wanted him. She had always been careful where men were concerned, never done anything wild or reckless.

And where had it gotten her?

Married to Brian Logan, who had cheated on her nearly every day.

Maybe for once she ought to do something

daring. Maybe she ought to explore her very limited sexual education with Zach.

She had a week to think about it.

Surely by then she would come to her senses.

THIRTEEN

The Integrity Home Inspection truck arrived at the Santiago house on Tuesday morning after Miguel had left for work in the fields. Elizabeth met them at the property, left them there for the three hours they would be working, then returned when it was time for them to leave.

"What did you find?" she asked Wiley Malone, the owner of the company. He and two of his employees had been hired to make a thorough inspection of the home. She would have to pay the cost herself, but the price he had quoted hadn't been all that bad.

"Good solid house," Wiley said, a burly man in coveralls with thinning, gray hair. "No leaks, no problems with the plumbing. Walls have good insulation."

"What about under the house? Did you find anything in the crawl space?" The house sat about three feet off the ground, supported by a concrete perimeter foundation, with wooden floors beneath the carpet.

Malone grinned. He had very large teeth. "Found some fat black widow spiders. Sprayed 'em for you — no charge. Didn't smell anything unusual, though, just a little mold and musty-smellin' dirt. If you're worried about the soil, I'd get Higgins Consulting out here to take a sample. They look for contamination, environment problems. Maybe they can find something."

"Thank you, Mr. Malone."

"It's just Wiley, and you're welcome." The men collected their gear — ladders, flashlights and toolboxes — and headed over to the truck they had come in. Elizabeth watched them drive away, then turned to see Maria standing on the porch.

"What did those men find?"

"They said the house was sound."

Maria nodded resolutely. "I did not think they would find anything wrong."

"We still need to check the soil under the house, see if there is some sort of environmental pollution. I'll call the company today."

"They will not find anything, either."

Elizabeth sighed. "So you want me to believe there is actually a ghost in the house."

"What if there is?"

"I'll call the soil company. Once we see what they find out, we can go from there."

But Higgins Consulting didn't find anything wrong with the soil, certainly nothing that would explain the noises, or the cold or the sickening smell.

Or the hazy vision Maria claimed to have seen.

Frustrated and worried, Elizabeth was busy working at the office when Zach called. She dragged a curl of heavy auburn hair out of the way and pressed the receiver against her ear.

"You busy? It's Zach."

"Hello, Zach." Her fingers tightened around the phone at the familiar deep tones of his voice. "I'm always busy, but I'm not with a client right now."

"I just called to see how you were, and how it went with the house inspectors."

"I'm fine. The house is fine, too, unfortunately. I had Integrity Home Inspection and Higgins Consulting both take a very thorough look, and neither of them found a damned thing. In fact, they said the place was in very good condition."

"I suppose something that obvious would have been too easy."

"I suppose. Luckily, I don't think Carson

knows they were there."

"Lucky for one of us, at least."

She chuckled.

"Listen, after I left San Pico on Sunday, I did a little research."

"Yeah, what kind of research?"

"Research on ghosts. Guess what?"

"I'm not sure I want to know."

"What you felt that night is called a cold spot. It's a commonly reported phenomenon in houses that are supposedly haunted."

"I don't believe this. Are you seriously thinking there may be a ghost in the house?"

"I'm just telling you what I found out. I thought you might be interested."

She rubbed the bridge of her nose, feeling the beginning of a headache. "Considering I haven't got a single clue what else could be wrong, I suppose I am."

"Listen, I'll be up there on Friday. I'll leave as soon I can get away from work. I'd like to take you out on Friday night."

"Zach, I really don't think —"

"I know, I know. I didn't mean to let things get so out of hand last weekend. It just sort of happened."

That was an understatement. She had been thinking of nothing but sex with Zach all week. The more she tried not to, the worse the obsession seemed to get.

"We'll just go out," he said. "Go to the show or something, get a pizza, maybe. You don't even have to invite me in when I bring you home. What do you think?"

Was this really Zach Harcourt? He'd been pushy back in his youth, determined to have his way. Then again, maybe he was just as determined now, in a slightly different manner. Whatever the truth, she wanted to see him even though she knew she shouldn't.

"All right, I suppose going to the show would be safe enough."

"Hey, is the old drive-in theater on Crest Lane still open?"

"What?"

"Just kidding."

She smiled into the phone. "You are an evil man. What time?"

She could hear him chuckling. "Movie probably starts at seven. Pick something out for us to see and I'll try to be there by six. I'll call if I get tied up in traffic."

Elizabeth hung up the phone just as the intercom buzzed.

"Your next appointment is here," the receptionist, Terry Lane, told her.

"Send her in." Elizabeth straightened the jacket of her cream linen suit, determined to force her mind back to work and not wonder if she'd been a fool to agree to another date with Zach.

The intercom buzzed on Zach's big glass-topped desk and his secretary's voice filled the room. "You've got a call, Zach. It's your brother."

So much for Carson not finding out. He pushed the speaker button instead of picking up the receiver just to keep a little distance between them.

"Carson. Good of you to call."

"My ass. What the hell do you think you're doing?"

"I don't know. Why don't you tell me?"

"Fine, I will. You told Elizabeth Conners she could bring people in to inspect the Santiago house. You had no right to do that, Zach."

"So what if I did? What the hell do you care? They didn't find anything wrong with the place. In fact they said it was in great condition. You ought to be ecstatic."

Silence on the end of the phone. "I don't like it, that's all. I told her no, so she ran to you. You don't have squat to say about anything on the farm."

"It was no big deal, all right? You're not out a dime. Liz is happy, and maybe Maria

Santiago will be able to sleep a little easier."

"I still don't like it. Keep your nose out of Harcourt Farms business."

"I've never tried to interfere in your decisions, Carson. But remember one thing. I'm a lawyer and a good one. If I wanted some say in running that place, I'd find a way to get it."

"Don't threaten me, Zach."

"That's a fact, Carson, not a threat. Fortunately, for you, I don't want a damned thing to do with the farm. I never have. Just make sure you're putting Dad's share of the profits in his account and I'm a happy man."

Carson grunted in reply and hung up the phone and Zach's thoughts returned to where they had been before his brother's call. Liz Conners.

She'd agreed to go out with him again. In a way, he was surprised. He'd damned near scared her away, pressing her so hard to get her to go to bed with him. He hadn't meant to. He'd had a feeling Liz was inexperienced when it came to sex and she was already skittish where he was concerned. Somehow he'd just lost control.

It didn't happen often and the fact it had happened with Liz just showed how much he wanted her.

And she wanted him, he now knew. Liz

was one hot lady. She just didn't know it. Zach couldn't think of anything he would rather do than awaken the sexuality he had sensed in her as far back as her senior year in high school. Still, he had meant what he said. He wouldn't press her, not again. Liz was a woman worth waiting for.

Silently, he vowed that this time when he saw her, he would take things slow and easy, be careful not to frighten her away.

Maria phoned Elizabeth at the office early Friday morning. Terry had not yet arrived and the front desk was empty, so Elizabeth picked up the phone. She recognized Maria's voice, though it sounded high-pitched and shaky, the woman very near the edge of hysteria.

"Elizabeth, *Dios mio,* thank God, you are there."

"Take it easy, Maria. What's wrong?"

"She . . . she came again last night. The ghost. She was there in my house."

Elizabeth ignored a faint shiver as she remembered the frightening night she had spent in the little yellow house. Still, there couldn't be a ghost. She didn't believe in ghosts. "Was Miguel there when she came?"

"He was sleeping. I tried to wake him, but I couldn't. It was the same as before, only I could see her better. She said that I should leave the house. She said that if I stayed they would . . . they would kill my baby."

"Maria, listen to me. We're going to figure this out."

Maria started crying. "Señor Harcourt, he is sending all of the overseers to the County Farm Implement Show up in Tulare. Miguel will be gone for two nights. I am supposed to stay with Lupe Garcia. She is Chico's wife, another of the other overseers. I do not want to go. They all think I am loco, that I am behaving like a child." She started sobbing into the phone.

"Don't cry, Maria, please. What nights will Miguel be gone?"

"Tomorrow night and Sunday."

"All right, then. You have a place to go for those two nights and in the meantime . . . In the meantime, I'm going to try to find out what is happening in the house."

Maria's breath hitched. "You are not . . . you are not thinking to stay there yourself?"

The notion had only been swimming around in her head. Now it seemed like a good idea. *Sort of.*

"Yes, I am. I'm going to find out what's happening. I think this is the best way to do it."

"But you should not stay there alone. It is not safe."

"I'm not afraid of ghosts, Maria. I'll be fine."

"I do not think —"

"Someone has to do this. We have to figure out what's going on."

Maria's voice trembled. "You are right, but still I am frightened."

"Everything's going to be all right." Elizabeth hung up the phone, beginning to formulate a plan.

Tomorrow morning, she would go over and see Maria, make arrangements to get a key so she could get into the house that night. She owned a gun. With the kind of work she did, she even had a permit to carry, though she had never done it. Tomorrow night, she would take the gun with her just in case. Perhaps someone was playing a terrible joke, or maybe whoever it was meant to hurt the family living in the house. If they came while she was there, she might need the gun to defend herself.

Or maybe something had been wired into the walls and the inspectors had somehow missed it. If someone was there, manipulating the eerie happenings, she would be ready.

She worked hard all day, her mind skipping from her client appointments to the task she had set for herself tomorrow night. In a way, she was excited. Maybe there really was a ghost!

She laughed at the notion. Something was going on, but she doubted the place was haunted.

At five o'clock she finished up for the day and left the office. Her thoughts were on Zach now, on the evening ahead. All week she had tried not to think of him and rarely been successful. She had tried to imagine herself as the femme fatale Zach believed her to be but couldn't seem to conjure the image.

Still, by the time six o'clock rolled around, she was restless and growing more so by the moment. She had picked out a movie for them to see, but discovered she was no longer in the mood. When Zach called to tell her he was going to be half an hour late, she found herself prowling the apartment thinking about him, remembering the way he had kissed her, touched her, remembering the promise he had made.

I could teach you those things. Whatever you want to learn. We could do anything you can imagine.

Her stomach contracted. Desire slipped through her and her nipples tightened. It was ridiculous.

Wasn't it?

Then again, she was a woman just like any other. She had the same wants and needs.

By the time Zach knocked on the door, her breasts were tingling, her skin sensitive in a way she had never experienced before. Her hand trembled as she reached out to open the door.

"Hello, Zach." Her voice sounded husky and unfamiliar, as if it came from a different woman.

Zach's warm brown eyes instantly darkened. He must have some sort of mating instinct, she thought, an ability to read exactly what she was thinking.

"Hello, Liz." His gaze slid down to the sleeveless scoop-neck top she wore and he noticed her nipples were pebbled into little peaks. "You've been thinking about me."

She looked up at him, saw the glittering heat in the gold of his eyes. She should have been embarrassed but she wasn't. "Yes," she said softly. "I have."

For several seconds, Zach just stood there, looking like a man at war with himself. "I've been thinking about you, too," he said, and then he hauled her into his arms.

Damn, he'd planned to be on his best

behavior tonight, been determined to control the throbbing sexual need he felt whenever he saw her. Then he had stepped through the door, looked into those pretty blue eyes and read the need she no longer tried to hide.

Christ, he wanted her, wanted to be inside her so much he ached with it. Instead he kissed her. Kissed her and kissed her, ravaging her lips, taking her with his tongue, filling her mouth as he longed to fill her body. She was slim, yet beautifully curved, a womanly figure that perfectly fit his taller frame. He reached beneath her pale blue, short cotton skirt and cupped her bottom in his hands, pulling her closer, into the vee of his crotch, letting her feel how hard he was for her.

Her slim hands dug into his shoulders and he felt her tremble. He was wildly aroused. He wanted to rip off her clothes, wanted to drag her down on the carpet and bury himself inside her. He clamped down on his control, determined not to let it get away from him as it had before. Liz wasn't fighting him, wasn't resisting, and yet he was determined that if she made the least attempt to stop, he would let her.

This wasn't supposed to be happening. But God, he was glad it was.

He trailed kisses along her jaw. "I want you so much," he whispered against the side of her neck. Waves of burnished dark hair brushed his cheek and his groin tightened. "I can't remember wanting anyone so badly."

"I want you, too, Zach."

He took a deep breath, fighting to remain in control, but the feel of her breasts pillowing against his chest made it nearly impossible to do. Feeling no resistance to another penetrating kiss, he lifted her into his arms and carried her across the living room to the bedroom, set her on her feet beside the queen-size bed.

His mouth settled softly over hers. He loved kissing her, loved the way she tasted, the slickness of her tongue over his, the little ripples of pleasure that moved through her body whenever he deepened the kiss. Catching the hem of her sleeveless knit top, he drew it off over her head, then pressed soft kisses along her throat and shoulders.

She was wearing the same kind of lacy white bra she had been wearing before, sweet but incredibly sexy. He popped the catch, drew the straps off her shoulders, then gave himself a moment to enjoy the sight of her lovely bare breasts.

He didn't take too long. He knew this was

difficult for her. Any minute he expected her to bolt from the bedroom. He palmed her breasts, circled the nipples with his thumb, tugged on the ends, pinched lightly, then replaced his hands with his mouth.

The creamy texture of her skin made an ache throb in his groin and he fought to stifle a groan.

"Zachary . . ."

"Easy, baby." He suckled the fullness, bit the ends, then returned to exploring her mouth. He could feel her trembling, feel her heart pounding nearly as hard as his own.

He unzipped her skirt and eased it over her hips, let it fall into a puddle at her feet. Her toes were painted a pretty pale pink, and he liked the feminine way they looked peeking out of her open-toed, high-heeled sandals. She was wearing a tiny pair of lacy, white thong underwear, he saw, and another jolt of heat rocked through him.

"Did you wear those for me?" he asked, palming her sex, feeling the heat there, making her tremble.

"No, I . . . maybe I . . . yes, I suppose I must have."

She hadn't meant to do this, he figured. Or if she had, the decision had been subconscious. He knelt in front of her, blew on the folds of her sex through the panties, pressed his mouth there, his tongue against the fabric, dampening it and giving him even better access to the soft flesh beneath.

He thought of stripping the panties away and taking her with his tongue, but she was a novice at the game of pleasure and he didn't want to frighten her.

"Zachary . . . ?"

Hearing the faint note of uncertainty in her voice, he moved up her body, tasting her breasts again, kissing her until she relaxed once more.

She reached for the buttons on his shirt, her courage apparently returning. "I want to touch you," she said. "The way you touched me. I want to see you naked."

Zach kissed her. "I want that, too."

She unfastened the last few buttons, her hands shaking, then eased the garment off his shoulders and tossed it over a chair in the corner. He kicked off his loafers as she unbuckled his belt and unzipped his fly, hesitated only an instant, then shoved his pants down his legs to the floor.

He stepped out of them and took off the rest of his clothes, his eyes on her face as she studied his erection.

"I hope I can . . . handle all of that."

He gave her a reassuring smile. "Don't

worry, I'll be there to help."

She reached out and touched the tattoo on his arm. "Born to be wild." She looked up at him, desire clear in her eyes. "Make love to me, Zach."

She didn't have to ask him twice. Lifting her up, he settled her in the middle of the bed, took care of protection, then came down slowly on top of her. He kissed her, slid his hands down her body until he found her softness and began to stroke her. She was incredibly wet and slick and it made him want her even more.

"Zach, please . . ."

"Soon, love." But not until he had her on the edge of climax, until she was close to screaming. He liked sex and he was good at it. He wanted to be good for Liz.

He stroked her slowly, skillfully, kissed her breasts, her throat, her lips. He increased the rhythm and she arched up off the bed, made a soft little pleading sound in her throat.

"Zach, please . . . I need . . . I need . . ."

"I've got exactly what you need, baby." And then he was parting her legs, fitting himself between them, sliding his erection into her softness.

Liz arched upward, driving him deeper still, burying him all the way to the hilt. He groaned at the feel of her gloving him so sweetly, heard her soft little mewling sounds of pleasure. Her nails dug into his back, and she trembled beneath him.

"Oh, God, oh, God, Zach, you feel so good."

"Easy." Out and then in, deep, rhythmic strokes, giving her as much of himself as he knew how, but the pleasure was beginning to overwhelm him and he was afraid he would lose control. *Not yet,* he told himself. *Not until she's ready. Just hang on just a little longer.*

He surged deeply again, and sweat popped out on his forehead. Faster, deeper, harder. Sweet Jesus! He couldn't take much more.

He was clinging to his last thread of control when he heard her cry out his name, felt her body tighten sweetly around him. She slipped into a powerful climax, and Zach let himself go.

He reached his own, earth-shattering release and wondered why it seemed so different with Liz.

FOURTEEN

It was an hour later that Elizabeth finally left the bed. Zach ordered Chinese takeout from the Great China Restaurant, and she went to answer the door in her bathrobe, since he refused to let her get dressed.

"No way," he had said, shaking his head. "I've got plans for you tonight and clothes aren't part of those plans."

Elizabeth laughed, determined that just this one night, she would be the siren Zach seemed to believe she was. Tomorrow would bring a return of sanity, she was sure, but just for this one night . . .

They made love again before they fell asleep and again before dawn. Bright sun poked through the curtains far too soon, and Elizabeth awakened to find herself sprawled over Zach's chest, groggy and pleasantly sated.

But the light of day was upon her now, the knowledge that what had happened last night couldn't possibly continue. She had known that from the start, known that this was just a fling, a wild night to remember. He was Zachary Harcourt, the town bad boy, and no matter how much he had changed, there were things about him that hadn't.

His affair with Lisa Doyle proved that.

Zach liked women, used them, left them. He always had.

Elizabeth wasn't about to risk her heart with a man like that, no matter how much she enjoyed him in bed.

She eased away from him, slipped quietly into the bathroom to shower and dress for the day. As the water pounded against her skin, easing the unfamiliar soreness between her legs, she heard the doorknob rattle, then his softly muttered curse.

He wanted to join her in the shower, but she wasn't about to let him, no matter how tempting the notion might be. The water was washing away the scent of him, the evidence of his possession, and in its place, the solid, practical woman she had been before was emerging.

She dried herself, toweled her hair, leaving it to dry in soft curls around her face, put on a little makeup and left the bathroom. The smell of fresh coffee brewing in the kitchen pulled her in that direction. Zach was standing there shirtless, wearing just his slacks and no shoes, and the sight of all that bare, hard-muscled flesh sent a surge of heat pulsing through her.

Elizabeth ignored it. "You can use the shower, if you like before you leave."

One of his dark eyebrows went up. He surveyed her no-nonsense khaki slacks and loose-fitting white cotton blouse.

"I noticed there's a swimming pool out back. I was thinking we might take a swim then maybe drive over to Mason a little later and catch a movie or something, but it looks like you're having morning-after regrets."

She shook her head. "No regrets. Last night was great, Zach. Incredible. It's just . . ."

"Just that you don't intend for it to happen again. The question is, why not?"

She accepted the cup of coffee he handed her. "You know why not. Because you're you and I'm me. I've got my career and you've got yours. You live in L.A. I live in San Pico. To put it simply, we're two very different people."

"That's right. You're a woman and I'm a man. That's about as different as it gets."

She was afraid he'd be stubborn. "All right, I'll spell it out for you. I don't want to risk getting involved with you, Zach."

Zach opened his mouth to argue, then closed it again and walked over to the window, shoving his hands into the pocket of his slacks along the way. He stared outside for several long moments, then turned back to her.

"Maybe you're right. As much as I'm attracted to you, I'm not looking for a long-term relationship. I'm a loner. I always have been. I like my life the way it is."

"No strings. No involvement."

"Yeah, that's about it." But there was something in his eyes . . . something that said maybe he wasn't so sure.

It didn't matter. She knew the risk he posed and after Brian, she didn't have that kind of courage.

Zach refilled his coffee cup, took a slow sip as he studied her over the rim. "Even if you're right, we've still got the weekend. I don't see why we can't enjoy ourselves until it's over."

Elizabeth shook her head. "Better to end things cleanly. Besides, I've got plans for tonight."

He took another sip of coffee and she saw that his eyes had darkened. "That so?"

"Yes."

"Tell me you don't have a date with my brother."

She laughed. She couldn't help it. "Of course not. I'm spending the night at Maria's."

"Miguel's going out of town again?"

She nodded. "Maria's staying with one of the other overseers' wives. I figured with them away, I'd have a chance to really see what's going on."

Zach frowned. Setting his cup down on the counter, he strode toward her. "You aren't saying you plan to spend the night there by yourself?"

"I think it's a good idea. I'll be able to do a little investigating, maybe figure things out."

"What if what's going on in that house is some kind of sick joke? What if there's someone behind it, someone who doesn't care who gets hurt?"

"I've got a gun. A thirty-eight revolver. I'm going to take it with me."

"Yeah? Well, what if there really is a ghost? You can't kill a ghost with a gun."

"That's ridiculous."

"Maybe it is, maybe not. Lately, I've been doing a lot of research on the subject. According to the stuff I've read, there are things called malevolent spirits. They can do some pretty bad stuff, and you sure as hell can't stop them with a gun."

"I don't believe in ghosts."

"Neither do I, but that doesn't change the fact you might be putting yourself in danger."

"I'm going, Zach. That's all there is to it."

"Fine, then I'm going with you."

She took an unconscious step backward. "No way."

Zach gave her a ruthless half smile. "Either I go with you or I call my brother and tell him what you're up to. What's it going to be?"

"Blackmail's illegal, Zach. I thought you'd become a law-abiding citizen."

"Sometimes you have to make your own laws. If you're going, I'm going, Liz. You might as well accept it."

A sound of frustration slipped out. She didn't want him to go. He posed too big a temptation. But he was determined, and perhaps she was a little relieved. "You're as big a bully now as you were twelve years ago."

Zach had the nerve to grin. "I guess in some ways I am."

Elizabeth gave a sigh of resignation. "All right, you can come. But I expect you to behave yourself."

"No seduction, you mean." He nodded, not the least surprised to have gotten his way. "I can handle it if you can. What time are you going over there?"

She flushed at the comment, since she was the one who had seduced him last night. "I figured about nine o'clock. I don't think anything's ever happened before dark."

"Fine. I'll meet you there at nine. In the meantime, I've got a room at the Holiday Inn. Believe it or not, I didn't plan to make love to you last night. If you need to get hold of me before that, I'll be out at Teen Vision working on the barn. I'll see you tonight."

Zach finished dressing and left the apartment, and Elizabeth wandered into the living room to watch him drive away. She was determined not to get involved with him. She just wished she wasn't so glad she would be seeing him again that night.

Elizabeth picked up the key to Maria's house that afternoon.

"I'll be back about nine," Elizabeth told her. "Zachary Harcourt will be staying here with me so you don't have to worry."

Maria looked relieved. "That is good. The bed is freshly made so you will have a clean place to sleep and Mr. Zach can sleep on the sofa. I hope the ghost comes. Then you will know I am telling the truth."

"I guess we'll see."

With the key to the house in her purse, Elizabeth returned to her apartment. She worked out for a while in her exercise room, stretching the sore muscles from having sex with Zach the night before.

Her cheeks warmed at the memory of his hot kisses and intimate caresses. No question, Zach Harcourt knew how to make love. Which was exactly the reason she wanted no more part of him. He was too damned sexy, too damned good a lover. A man like Zach could make a woman fall head over heels and she couldn't afford for that to happen.

She did a couple more sit-ups, twisting to touch her knees with her elbows, then spent some time on the treadmill. She was glad Zach had been honest. He didn't want a permanent relationship anymore than she did. Better they part now, before someone — namely her — got hurt.

Determined to stop thinking about him, she showered and dressed in a pair of jeans and a pale blue cotton blouse, then went in and made herself supper: fish sticks and salad. A cup of fat-free chocolate pudding served as dessert. A quick glance at the clock and she picked up her purse and headed for the carport behind her apartment.

It was still hot outside, even this time of evening, but at least the sun was going down, the intense, burning rays fading into a steady dry heat.

Zach's car wasn't at the Santiago house when she turned off the highway a little bit early and pulled up next to the single car garage. Making her way up the front walk, she used the key to let herself in, then went over and turned on the little TV in the living room, just to have some noise in the house.

She'd also brought a paperback novel to read, doubting the "ghost" would appear as long as the television was on. Once Zach arrived, she'd turn it off so the house would be quiet.

He arrived right on time, nine o'clock straight up, and came in carrying a couple of plastic bags full of groceries.

"I thought we might get hungry," he said, pulling a bag of chips and a couple of cans of Diet Coke out of the bag and setting them down on the coffee table. A sack of trail mix and a couple of candy bars came out next. "I'm not big on junk food. This is just in case of emergency."

He looked at her and smiled, and she saw that once again his gaze was carefully guarded. He wanted her still. A little frisson of heat ran through her, but she quickly tamped it down. She was there on a mission and she meant to see it done.

"How did it go out at the farm?" she asked, opting for a safe subject as she took a seat on the sofa.

"Great. We'll have the barn finished before fall sets in." Zach sat down beside her, not too close, she noticed.

"What will you do once it's complete?"

"You mean will I still come up to San Pico? I'll come up to see my dad, but not as often. Not unless . . ." He shook his head. "You want some chips?"

"No, thanks." She looked over at the little TV, the sound so low she could barely hear it. "I think we should turn off the television. No respectable ghost would appear while we're watching *Saturday Night Live*."

He smiled. "I suppose not. I brought some work to do. I figured I'd better keep my mind on something besides making love to you."

Her cheeks flushed as she pressed the off button on the front of the set. So did other parts of her body. "I brought a book. At least we can keep ourselves entertained."

His gaze ran over her, letting her feel it head to foot, and hot sparks glittered in his eyes. "I can think of a lot more interesting things we could do, but I guess that's not going to happen."

"I guess it isn't." Much to her regret. Pulling the paperback out of her purse, a romantic suspense she wouldn't have brought if she'd remembered how steamy the sex scenes were, she turned to the page she'd left off. She would skip the juicy parts, she vowed, and settled in to read.

They sat in surprisingly companionable silence, Elizabeth absorbed in her book, Zach poring over the pages of a legal brief he was working on.

It was getting late. Elizabeth yawned, shifted on the sofa. She checked her watch, saw that it was nearly midnight. Flicking a glance to where Zach leaned back against the sofa, she saw that his eyes were closed, his thick dark lashes fanned out against his cheek. His long legs stretched in front of him and his head rested on the back of the couch. He was sound asleep, and Elizabeth realized she was equally sleepy.

Yawning, she made her way as quietly as possible into the bedroom. As far as she knew, the vision — assuming there was one — had never appeared anywhere except this room. She lay down on the bed, still fully dressed, plumped the pillow behind her head, and closed her eyes. As tired as she was, it didn't take long to fall asleep.

She wasn't sure how long she slept or what awakened her. When she opened her eyes, the first thing she noticed was how still the room had grown, or at least if felt still and close, the air thicker than it should have been. An odd creak came from the living room, the same sound she had heard the first time she stayed in the house. A few seconds later, the wind began its eerie moaning. She wanted to rush to the window to see if the noise was real, though she was fairly sure it wasn't.

She wondered if Zach could hear it. She cast a glance toward the living room and saw that he was sitting up very straight on the sofa. He could hear it, too, she thought with some relief. At least, she wasn't imagining things.

Her pulse beat a little faster as the air thickened even more. She could see Zach on the sofa, his head cocked toward another, different sound rising in the distance, the eerie wail of a train whistle, screaming into the blackness of the night. She could hear the ding, ding, ding of the warning bell at the crossing, then the locomotive roaring down the track through the cotton fields on the other side of the highway.

The track crossed the road just north of the house and the place shuddered as the train drew near. But the tracks had been abandoned for years. She wasn't even sure the rails were still there.

A chill swept through her as Zach turned to look out the window, but Elizabeth's attention swung in another direction. Something cold had crept into the bedroom, something so dense and chilling she couldn't seem to move. She sat frozen on the bed, her heart beating as if it were trying to escape through her ribs. Something was there — she could feel it — and an icy fear began to well inside her. The dense air made it hard to breathe, hard to think, and her mind seemed cloudy, her thoughts far away.

A faint sound reached her, a voice so soft, the words so faintly spoken, she couldn't be sure she had heard them.

"I . . . want . . . my . . . mama. Please . . . I want . . . my . . . mama."

Her heart clutched, speeded up even more. The chill was pervasive now, filling the room, stretching into every corner. Her gaze went to Zach who perched on the edge of the sofa, completely alert, waiting to see what would happen next. The atmosphere in the bedroom shifted. The chill remained, but with it now came the cloying scent of roses.

The smell was unbearably heavy, dense and putrid, a sickening odor that made the bile rise in her throat.

"Mama . . .? Mama are you there? Please . . . I want my mama."

The fear inside her swelled. Her gaze shot to the living room in search of Zach and it must have shone in her eyes. She saw him get to his feet and start moving toward the open bedroom door. Then something caught her eye. A faint, translucent light began to appear at the foot of the bed, a wavering, eerie glow barely visible in the room. But Elizabeth was certain it was there, and a strangled sound of fear came from her throat.

Zach stood in the doorway, his feet braced apart, and the minute he heard the sound, he started toward her, his strides long and angry.

"That's it! That's enough!" Storming into the bedroom, he came straight to the bed, sat down on the edge and pulled her into his arms.

"Oh, God, Zach!"

"Easy, baby, it's over. Everything's all

right. You're safe now." He glanced around the room, searching every corner. "Whatever it was is gone."

She trembled wildly and Zach's arms tightened around her. Burying her face against his shoulder, she started to cry. The tears were coming and she wasn't exactly sure why. She just knew she would be forever grateful that he was there with her tonight.

"Hush," he said softly. Reaching over, he turned on the lamp on the bedside table, the soft glow warming the room, dispelling the last of her fear. "It's over."

Elizabeth swallowed and nodded, dragged in a shaky breath of air. "I'm sorry. I don't . . . don't know what happened. I didn't mean to fall apart that way."

"Don't be sorry. That was the scariest thing I've ever seen."

She closed her eyes, took another calming breath and swung her legs to the edge of the bed, fighting to compose herself.

"Stay here," Zach said. "I want to check outside. I'll only be gone a minute." He headed for the front door, turning on a lamp as he passed, and left to make a search of the perimeter of the house. A minute seemed like an hour. Again and again, her mind kept replaying the terrifying sounds and the awful smell, the whisper of a little girl's voice. When Zach returned a few minutes later, Elizabeth met him at the front door.

"I checked outside." He walked back inside the living room and closed the door. Elizabeth looked at the closed portal longingly, wishing it were time to leave.

"I looked under the house, checked the garage. Nothing. You know how to get into the attic?"

"Probably through one of the closets." She went in to look for an opening in the Santiago's bedroom closet while Zach went to search the second bedroom.

"It's in here!" he called out. She followed him in, the room lit by the ceiling light he'd turned on, watched him shove back the attic cover in the closet and haul himself up with those impressive biceps of his.

"See anything up there?"

"Not a damned thing but a lot of dust." He lowered himself back down and dropped to the floor, brushing off his hands.

"Okay, you didn't find anything," she said as they returned to the living room, "but you did hear the noises and feel the cold. You noticed the smell, right?"

He nodded. "I heard the train too."

"That didn't happen before."

He tipped his head toward the window. "There's an abandoned track just down the road, but it hasn't been used for years. And there's no warning bell, Liz. The line was completely dismantled."

She fought down a shiver. "I know. I hope to God you didn't see a train when you looked out the window."

The edge of his mouth tipped up. "No train. But I sure as hell heard one."

A fresh chill moved along her spine. "Did you see the light at the foot of the bed?"

"I thought I saw something. I'm not sure what it was."

"Whatever it was, it was eerie. And there was something else, Zach. I heard this voice. It was very faint, so I don't think you would have noticed, but I'm sure I heard it. It sounded like a little girl."

"That's what Maria claims she heard. What did the voice have to say?"

"She said, 'I want my mama. Please . . . I want my mama.' It sounded like she was about to cry."

Zach caught her hand, gave it a reassuring squeeze. "Maybe this is some kind of elaborate hoax, but I don't think so."

"Then you believe . . . you think the house is haunted?"

"I don't know what to believe. But the

only way we're going to figure this out is to start thinking outside the box. Either something in the house is affecting our minds . . . or the things that are happening are real."

"How do we find out which it is?"

"Since we haven't found any kind of foreign substance or anything that might affect our brains, let's assume this is all really happening. I'll do some more research. If there really is a ghost, we need to find out who it is."

"Oh, my God, I never thought of that." She shook her head. "Of course, my experience with this kind of thing is sorely limited."

"Maria thinks she saw a little girl. You both heard a little girl's voice. We need to find out if a child died in the house."

It was a chilling thought, and yet Zach was right. They had to start thinking outside the box. "The house is only four years old. Something like that should be easy enough to find out. I'll have Maria ask around. I'm sure a number of the workers have been here that long."

"Sounds like a good place to start," he said.

"What do you think I should tell Maria about tonight?"

"Tell her we're still working on figuring things out. And tell her whatever happens, not to spend the night here alone."

Ignoring a feeling of unease, Elizabeth turned to survey her surroundings. The living room was quiet, everything in its place. Lamplight shined through the open bedroom door and the window air conditioner hummed away. The house felt completely normal again, not the least bit frightening. Still . . .

"Do you think we need to stay here the rest of the night?"

"Stay? Are you kidding?" Zach gripped her hand and started tugging her toward the door. "Not on your life."

Elizabeth smiled and pulled away. "Give me a minute to straighten the bedroom and turn off the lights and we'll leave."

Zach nodded, started refilling the grocery bag with the goodies he had brought while Elizabeth straightened the quilt on the bed. A few minutes later they had locked the front door and were standing outside the house, looking back at it.

"It's a cute little house," she said, surveying the yellow stucco walls with the sparkling white trim.

"Yeah, it's great — unless you try to sleep in there."

Zach walked her over to the car. "I'll call you if I find out anything useful."

"I'll do the same."

He started to turn away, but Elizabeth caught his arm. "I owe you an apology, Zach. I'm glad you were here tonight. I don't know what I'd have done if I'd been here alone."

He ran a finger along her cheek. "You're pretty damned tough, lady. You probably would have been just fine, but I'm glad I was here just the same."

He bent his head and very softly kissed her. "I know you're probably right about us. But, God, I wish you weren't."

So do I, Elizabeth thought as she slid into the seat of her car and Zach closed the door. She ignored the little pinch in her heart as she started the engine and drove away. Zach's BMW followed her protectively all the way back to her apartment.

He didn't drive away until she was safely inside.

Elizabeth told herself she was glad he hadn't asked to come in.

FIFTEEN

Knowing Maria would be worried, Elizabeth phoned her at Mrs. Garcia's after church on Sunday morning. Maria had given her the number and it was obvious she had been waiting for the call.

"*Dios mio*, I have been so worried! Are you all right?" She lowered her voice to a whisper. "Did you see the ghost?"

"I'm fine, and no, I didn't see her. I think I heard her, though. At least I heard something." *To say the least.* But she didn't want to frighten Maria any more than she was already. "It sounded like a little girl."

"*Sí*, that is her!"

"I want you to do me a favor. I want you to ask around, find out if sometime before you moved in a child died in the house. If there is a ghost — and I'm not saying there is — we need to find out who she is."

"*Sí, sí*, I will try to find out what I can.

Thank you, Elizabeth. Thank you so much."

"We'll figure this out, Maria. Try not to worry."

"I will call you." Maria hung up the phone and Elizabeth sighed. The wheels were in motion. Surely something would turn up.

It was late in the afternoon when Zach called. She clamped down on the little thrill she felt at the sound of his voice.

"I'm out at Teen Vision. I've been using one of their computers to access the Internet."

"Find anything interesting?"

"You won't believe the stuff I've found."

She adjusted the phone against her ear. "What kind of stuff?"

"Well, I thought I'd start with the basics. I went to Google and typed in *ghosts.* There are over two million sites on the Internet that deal with ghosts. On one site alone, fifteen hundred people have sent in stories of personal encounters they supposedly had with one or more ghosts."

"I figured there'd be a lot of information on the subject. Still, it's pretty amazing when you think about it."

"Yeah. So I guess we aren't the only ones crazy enough to think there might actually be a ghost in that house."

"Maybe not, but you've got to wonder if any of those stories are really true."

"I'm sure some of them are purely fiction. But the quantity alone is staggering. And most of these people actually believe they saw something supernatural."

"What about ghost hunters? Did you see anything about them on the Net?"

"Sure did. When I typed in the words *ghost* and *research,* more than two hundred thousand sites popped up, all sorts of groups involved in researching the existence of ghosts. Listen, I'm going to print some of this stuff and bring it over. We can go over it and figure out our next move."

"Our?"

"In case you've forgotten, I was in that house with you last night. It's not an evening I'll soon forget. Like it or not, I'm involved in this, too. Besides, the house is on my father's property. I may not be involved in the day-to-day business of running Harcourt Farms, but as long as my dad's still alive, I feel a certain obligation to keep an eye on the place."

"I can certainly understand that."

"I've got a couple of things to do here, then I'm on my way." Zach hung up the phone and a half hour later, she heard his knock at the door. A little frisson of awareness went through her as she turned the knob to let him in and he brushed past her into the living room. No matter how many times she saw him, she couldn't quite get over how handsome he was, or the way his presence seemed to fill a room.

"Hi," she said.

"Hi." He smiled, his dark gaze lingering a moment on her face. She tried to read his thoughts, but his expression was carefully guarded.

He held up a manila folder stuffed with papers. "I pulled this off the Internet. I figured we could go over it, but on my way over here, I remembered you saying you had a computer in the apartment."

She nodded. "I use the second bedroom for an office."

He followed her in, heading for the desk in the corner where her computer was set up, checking out her exercise equipment along the way. "No wonder you look so good naked."

Her gaze flew to his face and she saw that he was grinning.

"Sorry, I couldn't resist. What I meant was, it's obvious you take care of yourself. I think that's really important. I do so much legal work sitting at my desk, I try to get as much exercise as I can. We've got a gym in my office building in Westwood. I try to get in there at least three times a week."

It shows, she thought, remembering his lean, hard-muscled body when they had been in bed. Her cheeks burned at the memory and Elizabeth glanced away, hoping Zach wouldn't see.

"Why don't you sit at the desk," he said, "since you're familiar with the machine." He waited while Elizabeth sat down in the chair, then took a seat in the chair next to hers.

Elizabeth flipped on the computer, moved the mouse to the icon for Internet Explorer, brought up Google.com and typed the word *ghosts* in the search box. A few seconds later, she was staring at pages of Web sites that all dealt with spirit phenomenon.

"Just prowl around a little," Zach said. "I think you'll find it interesting."

She started clicking away, a little surprised to discover how many people were seriously involved in the study of hunting ghosts. Apparently, Maria Santiago was just one of millions who believed in spirits. She scrolled down another page, surveying the dozens and dozens of sites, clicking on one that looked interesting now and then. *Shadow-*

lands; Ghosts and Hauntings; History and Hauntings; All about Ghosts; Ghosts Online; Photos of Ghosts and Apparitions. The list seemed endless.

She clicked on one of the sites that claimed to have actual photos. White spots and eerie distortions — some even looking like transparent faces, but with the way film could be manipulated today, the evidence wasn't convincing. Still, as Zach had said, millions of people seemed to believe ghosts actually existed.

"Check this out." Leaning over, his hand covered hers on the mouse, moved it up, returned to the search engine, and typed in *ghost research.*

Aware of the heat of his touch and the loss she felt when he pulled away, she read the list on the screen in front of her. As he stood behind her, his chest brushed lightly against her shoulder and a tremor of warmth slid into her stomach. Elizabeth ignored it and started to read the sites on the page.

American Ghost Society; Ghost Research Foundation; GhostLabs Research Society; Toronto Ghost and Hauntings Research Society; Paranormal Investigative Research and Information Training. She clicked on one of the groups, skimmed some of the information.

She clicked on another and another. "These people are deadly serious — pardon the pun."

Zach laughed.

"Look at this. They not only believe in ghosts, they go out and try to prove they really exist."

"Yeah. And check out the equipment they use." Zach punched up a site. "Digital cameras, 35mm cameras, video cameras, audio recorders, electromagnetic field detectors, temperature sensing equipment."

Her eyes widened at the long paragraphs under each item naming the different brands and models of the various equipment available. "Unbelievable."

"After reading some of this stuff," Zach said, "believing in ghosts doesn't seem nearly as far-fetched as it did before."

"I guess not." But Elizabeth still wasn't convinced. She turned to look at Zach, found his eyes once more on her face. For an instant, she saw the heat, the hunger, then he looked away. She ignored the sudden pounding of her heart and the clutch in her stomach.

"What . . . what do you think we should do?"

Zach cleared his throat and returned to the business at hand. "Well, according to most of these sites, we need to research the history of the house."

"Which Maria is trying to help us do."

"Right. And if a little girl did die there, it would validate Maria's vision and the voice you think you heard."

"At least we'd have something."

But when Maria called on Tuesday, she grimly reported that as far as the workers knew, neither a child nor anyone else had ever died in the house.

"Thanks for trying, Maria. You didn't . . . haven't had any more visits?"

"Not since she came before."

"That's good to hear. I was thinking, maybe if you told your doctor you were having trouble sleeping, he might give you something that would help."

"*Sí,* I was thinking that, too. At night I worry that she will come and I am too afraid to sleep."

"You mustn't get discouraged. I'm still working on this and so is Zachary Harcourt." Though he was back at work in L.A. "We'll let you know as soon as we find something."

The moment Maria hung up, Elizabeth dialed Zach's office number. His secretary rang her right through, which made her wonder if Zach had left instructions she be given special treatment. It was ridiculous to hope that he had.

"Sorry to bother you," she said when she heard his deep voice, "but I thought you'd want to know. Maria called. She says, as near as she can find out, there hasn't been any sort of death in the house, a child or anyone else."

Zach sighed. "I really didn't think there had been. I haven't spent much time on the farm since I left San Pico, but I figured I would have heard if something like that had happened."

"So we're back where we started."

"Not exactly. I didn't want to mention this — not until we heard from Maria. I was hoping the answer might be simpler."

"What is it?"

"There was another house in the same location before the new one was built. I remember it being there when I was a kid. The place wasn't worth fixing. My dad had it torn down to make room for the new house he wanted to build."

A shiver raced down her spine. She'd been reading up on ghosts, soaking up information from the sites on the Net. Houses might change. People might change, but for a ghost, time was eternal.

"What you're saying is that a child might have died in the old house. Which means it could have happened years ago."

" 'Fraid so."

"What's our next move?"

"I've got a couple of ideas. I've been asking around, talking to some people I know. They think I should call someone, an expert on this kind of thing."

"Who — Ghostbusters?"

"Sort of. There's a woman . . . a friend of a friend. Her name is Tansy Trevillian. She's got a good reputation, as far as I can tell. She's supposed to be what they call a sensitive."

"Let me guess . . . for a nice fat fee, she'll come up and do a séance — talk to the ghosts in the house and tell them to leave."

He chuckled into the phone. "Actually, all she wants are her expenses, meaning gas and meals. She'll meet us there whenever it's convenient . . . that is, if you're interested."

"If she did come, I imagine she would have to come at night."

"That's what she said."

"So how do we get rid of Maria and Miguel?"

"Good question. Maybe Maria can come

up with something."

"Maybe. She wants this resolved even more than we do. Will you be coming up this weekend?"

He paused for an instant. "I figured I would."

"If I can manage to get the two of them out of the house, I'll call and you can set up the meeting with the Trevillian woman."

"Sounds good. I just hope you don't hold it against me if this turns out to be a crazy idea."

"Any idea is better than no idea, which is exactly what I have at the moment."

"Let me know," Zach said and hung up the phone.

After catching a quick bite at Marge's Café, Elizabeth spent a frustrating afternoon of seeing semicooperative patients, including Geraldine Hickman's daughter, who still couldn't quite believe that a date did not automatically include having sex; and the attorney, Richard Long, who was pissed at his wife for some imagined crime and proud of himself for not knocking the crap out of her.

"She never does what I tell her. You can't blame me for getting angry."

Elizabeth sighed. "Marriage is supposed

to be a partnership, Richard. Do you really believe that because you're Jennifer's husband you should have complete control of her life?"

"I pay the bills, don't I? I work my ass off so she can buy expensive clothes and drive around in a fancy car. And does she appreciate it? Hell, no."

Elizabeth wanted to ask him, if he was so disgusted with his wife, why he didn't just get a divorce? But Jennifer Long was pretty and sexy. Richard didn't want to divorce her — he just wanted her to submit to him, totally and completely. The real question was, why didn't Jennifer divorce Richard? But Elizabeth knew the man had destroyed the woman's self esteem to the point where she didn't believe she could make it on her own.

Elizabeth wished Jennifer sat on her couch instead of Richard.

It was nearly five o'clock before she got a chance to phone Maria. She was a little uneasy about mentioning the "sensitive" Zach had told her about, but Maria seemed nonplussed.

"You think this woman — Señora Trevillian — you think she will be able to see the ghost?"

"I have no idea. I don't think these people

actually see them. I think she's supposed to be able to sense their presence, though. I thought it might be worth a try."

"Oh, *sí*. If she can come on Saturday night, I will get Miguel to take me out. He is off on Sunday so he can sleep late. I am too fat to dance, but I like to listen to the music."

"That would be great, Maria." Elizabeth thought of the young Hispanic woman, too far along in her pregnancy to enjoy an evening of nightclubbing on the town, but desperate to resolve her frightening situation. Maybe Tansy Trevillian would make a discovery that would make Maria's sacrifice worthwhile. Elizabeth hoped so, but she had her doubts.

Zach worked on his Themoziamine case until late Thursday night, then returned to work early Friday morning. At two o'clock in the afternoon, he left his Westwood office, his suitcase already packed and loaded into the trunk of his car. He had a stop to make before he took off for San Pico.

Pulling onto the 405 Freeway, he slogged along in the heavy Friday traffic, heading for Culver City, then took the Washington Boulevard exit and headed east. His mother's apartment was on Wilson, a side street on the south side of the road.

Though Zach didn't see his mother all that often, he tried to stop by whenever he could. Years ago, after Teresa and Fletcher Harcourt had gone their separate ways and Zach was living in the house at Harcourt Farms, his mother had gotten married. The marriage had ended in divorce and a few years later, she had married again.

Teresa had always liked men. Her current husband, Harry Goodman, was a beefy car salesman who worked at Miller Toyota just down Washington Boulevard. Harry took up most of Teresa's time and that was the way she wanted it.

Zach wasn't sure why he felt the need to see her today, but here he was, pulling up next to the curb in front of her two-story, gray stucco apartment building. Carrying a two-pound bag of her favorite coffee beans, he climbed the stairs to the second floor, and knocked on her apartment door. A few seconds later, his mother pulled it open.

"Zachary — come on in." She took his hand and pulled him forward, closing the door behind them. "I was surprised when you called this morning."

"I was thinking about you. I haven't stopped by in a while."

She gave him a brief hug — something she had only lately begun to do — then stepped away, a woman in her early fifties who still wore her shoulder-length black hair loose around her shoulders, still wore her skirts above her knees, though she was at least thirty pounds overweight. When she smiled, she remained attractive, but she was rapidly losing her looks, which bothered her immensely, since she had pretty much survived the years by being a sexy, desirable woman.

"You usually like to get out of town early on Fridays," she said. "You're not going up to San Pico?"

"I'm going. I just thought I'd stop by before I left town." He handed her the bag of coffee. He usually brought her some little gift or gave her some pocket money. He sent her a monthly check to help cover her bills, but the extra was just for her.

He tapped the bag of coffee. "I figured you'd be running out of the good stuff by now."

She opened the sack and inhaled deeply, let out a contented sigh. "Costa Rica Royale. My favorite. Thank you, honey."

She led him into the kitchen to brew a pot, lit up a cigarette, and they sat down at the kitchen table. Teresa drank coffee and smoked all day. As a kid, he had hated the smell of stale cigarette smoke and still did. He'd tried to get her to quit, but he didn't think she ever would.

She inhaled deeply, let the smoke trail out slowly. "You look a little tired today. Everything all right?"

The question took him by surprise. Teresa had never been much of a mother. While other kid's mothers baked cookies and attended PTA, Teresa enjoyed San Pico's limited nightlife. And satisfied Fletcher Harcourt's demands, which came before everything else.

"Everything's fine. I've just been working hard lately, is all."

"Well, then, let's have a cup of coffee and I'll tell you about the party down the block that Harry and I went to last night."

They chatted for a while, saying nothing much really, Zach mostly listening, since Teresa generally did the majority of the talking.

Half an hour later, as he wove his car back into the vicious L.A. traffic, heading north to San Pico, he wondered again why he'd felt the urge to see her. As a boy, he had yearned for her love and attention, ached for the love of his parents but never really got it. Over the years, he had taught himself to live without that kind of emotional attachment. He had learned to take care of himself, learned to make the most of life without ever letting anyone get too close.

Lately, he had begun to understand that the distance he put between himself and others was a defense mechanism, a way of protecting himself. He didn't want to need anyone the way he had as a boy.

Perhaps he had gone to see Teresa to remind himself of the painful life he had lived before he had learned to guard his emotions, to rely only on himself. Before he had learned how much it hurt to care when the other person didn't, or at least not nearly as much. Maybe he had needed the reminder.

As usual, getting out of the city was murder, the clogged freeways putting him even more on edge than he was when he left the office. But it wasn't just the traffic. He was heading back to San Pico. A week ago, he had spent the night in Liz Conner's bed and he wanted to be there again. He wanted to sample more of the passion he had aroused in her. Even more than that, he just wanted to be with her.

And it scared the hell out of him.

Zach steered the BMW through an opening between two cars, accelerating into a break in the traffic that allowed him to make a little headway. Earlier in the week, Liz had called to say she had spoken to Maria and that Saturday night Maria would keep Miguel occupied so they could spend time in the house.

Liz had been all business, her voice cool on the line, yet he could sense the tension she tried to hide. He wondered if she might be remembering how good they were together, remembering the hot night they had shared. As soon as the car neared the summit and started down the Grapevine into the San Joaquin Valley, Zach dialed her home number.

Tansy Trevillian had agreed to make the trip to San Pico tomorrow night. He just needed to call Liz and confirm that everything was ready. One quick call, he told himself, strictly business.

"Hello." The single word, spoken in that softly feminine voice, had the power to make him go hard.

"It's Zach. I just wanted to check in, make sure everything is set for tomorrow night."

"So far, everything looks good. Maria thinks she can keep Miguel away until at least midnight."

"Good. Great."

"You said she'd be there about dark so I

guess I'll see you then." She sounded way too eager to hang up the phone and a thread of irritation slipped through him.

His hands tightened around the wheel. "You sound busy. Got a hot date?"

Her voice flattened out. "No."

"Why not? You're a beautiful woman. I'm surprised every man in town isn't trying to get you into bed."

"The only man who's been trying is you, Zach. I guess the rest have figured out I'm not interested."

"Maybe. And maybe you're living in a town full of idiots. I want to see you, Liz." He hadn't meant to say it. The words just seemed to pop out of his mouth.

"I told you before, Zach, it's not a good idea."

"Maybe it is. How can we know for sure unless we try it and see?"

A momentary pause. "Are you sure you're not just looking for someone to fill in for Lisa?"

"Yes, I'm sure. I've been thinking about you all week. I'll be in town in less than an hour. I want to come over and see you."

"Please, Zach, don't push this thing. I made a mistake last week, all right? I don't know exactly how it happened, but I don't want it to happen again."

"Dammit, Liz!"

"I've got to go, Zach. I'll see you tomorrow night." Liz hung up and Zach swore softly. He tossed his cell phone into the passenger seat and raked a hand through his hair. Liz was determined to stay away from him — and she was probably right. He wasn't the kind of guy a woman should get involved with. He was too much of a loner, his single lifestyle too much a part of him. Liz deserved better than a brief affair with a guy like him.

Zach thought of his mother and Fletcher Harcourt and how they had mostly ignored him. He thought of Fletcher's late wife, Constance, and how she had made him feel like the dirt beneath her expensive high heels.

Then there was Carson, who had bullied him until he'd gotten tough enough to fight back. Carson hadn't stopped his harassment, just changed his tactics to ridicule and ostracism. Over the years, Zach had built a wall around his emotions, a wall that existed today.

After Liz's experience with her good-for-nothing husband, she had built a wall, too.

Maybe she was right to keep herself safely locked behind it.

But having done exactly that for as long

as he could remember, Zach was no longer
so sure.

Sixteen

On Saturday night, Elizabeth left her apartment just before dark. She was nervous. She had never met what Zach called a "sensitive." She didn't know if the woman was for real or a complete and utter fraud. She had no idea what might happen tonight in the house.

And Zach would be there. Since his phone call last night, he had been constantly in her thoughts. As soon as she'd heard his voice, she had wanted to see him, so badly it hurt.

Zachary Harcourt attracted her in a way no man ever had. She had never craved a man, never lusted after one, never ached for a man the way she did Zach.

It was frightening.

And impossible.

Zach was Zach, a dedicated bachelor who enjoyed the single life, a man used to sleeping with dozens of women. He hadn't bothered to deny it. She doubted he had ever been seriously involved with a woman and he probably never would be.

But Elizabeth wasn't that way. If she let down her guard, her attraction to Zach would grow. She might even fall in love with him. She knew it could happen. Every time she saw him, she felt the tremendous pull between them. Zach Harcourt wasn't a man she could chance falling in love with. If she did, he would only break her heart.

Elizabeth thought of her marriage and remembered the crushing despair she had felt at her husband's betrayal. Brian had taken the love she had offered and little by little destroyed it. She couldn't go through that again. She didn't think she would survive it.

As she drove down the road toward the little yellow house, Elizabeth steeled herself. No matter what Zach said, no matter how much she wanted him, she wasn't going to let him sway her.

Her purpose once more clear, she focused her attention on the strip of blacktop in the headlights in front of her. It was very dark tonight, the moon hidden behind a dense layer of clouds, its faint rays breaking through only now and then. A summer storm was moving in from the west. She could smell the ozone in the air, see the faint glow of lightning over the barren, far-distant hills.

Elizabeth dimmed her headlights as she neared the house, then pulled off the road onto the gravel driveway. Spotting Zach's silhouette behind the wheel of his car, she pulled up next to the black convertible and turned off the engine. Zach got out and started toward her as she climbed out of the car.

"Hi," he said softly, his dark eyes on her face. She could see the golden flecks in them and something else, something that made her chest ache.

"Hello, Zach."

He glanced away, took a slow breath, and when he turned to face her, the look was gone. "Tansy isn't here yet, but she called me on my cell and said she was on her way."

Elizabeth nodded. "I guess we can wait on the porch."

"Good idea. After what happened last week, I'm not in any rush to go in."

They sat down on the front porch steps. Zach was wearing a pair of worn Levi's and a V-neck, pullover shirt. He looked good. Too good. She wanted to reach out and touch him. She wanted to kiss him. She wanted to have him inside her.

"You keep looking at me that way and I won't be responsible for my actions."

She flushed. It was one thing to lust after a man, another altogether to get caught doing it. She fiddled with a strand of dark auburn hair, looped a thick curl behind her ear. "I wonder when she'll get here."

Zach gazed off down the highway. "Headlights coming. Maybe that's her."

Fortunately for Elizabeth, who was growing more and more nervous with Zach so near, it was. Both of them got up from the step and Zach walked over to greet her as her car pulled in and she turned off the engine.

Tansy Trevillian was nothing at all as Elizabeth had imagined. Instead of some dilapidated, flower-painted Volkswagen van, she was driving a white Pontiac Grand Prix, and she wasn't wearing a long, flowing paisley dress. In her simple beige slacks and pink-and-beige print blouse, her brown hair cut short and smartly styled, she looked more like a businesswoman than the lost-in-time hippy Elizabeth had more than half expected.

Zach stepped back as she got out of her car, then walked the petite woman over for introductions. "Liz, meet Tansy Trevillian."

The woman, probably no more than a few

years older than Elizabeth, gave her a smile. "It's a pleasure to meet you, Liz."

Elizabeth didn't correct the shortened name. She was beginning to get used to it. In high school, lots of her friends had called her Liz. "Same here."

Tansy stuck out a small hand and Elizabeth shook it, the handshake firm, the woman's smile warm.

"Thanks for coming," Elizabeth said.

Tansy turned toward the house and her smile slowly faded. "Zach hasn't told me much. Just that the people who live here have been having some problems. We find it works better that way, knowing as little as possible. People like us are susceptible to suggestion just like anyone else."

" 'People like us?' " Elizabeth repeated.

"Sensitives. Psychics. Clairvoyants. People with those kinds of gifts."

Or curses, Elizabeth thought.

Tansy's gaze slowly scanned the fifteen-acre compound that formed the main living area of the ranch. As the clouds parted and a portion of the moon broke through, she studied the distant set of overseers' houses, the workers' cottages and the big, two-story ranch house on the opposite side of the compound some distance away. Though the night was warm, Tansy wrapped her arms around herself to control a shiver.

"What is it?" Zach asked.

Tansy's gaze scanned the row of houses in the distance. "There's something here. I can feel it." She turned, fixed her attention on the yellow stucco house. "Something dark and evil."

Elizabeth's heart slammed into gear. "You can feel something clear out here in the open?"

Tansy's eyes returned to the other houses perched on the wide, flat, barren piece of ground. "It's everywhere around here. I've never felt anything quite like it."

A shudder climbed Elizabeth's spine. She didn't feel anything and yet the pale hue of Tansy Trevillian's face said she was telling the truth. No one said a word, just stood in the darkness waiting. Tansy shivered again, then faintly shook herself, as if she fought to return from the place she had been.

"Let's go inside." She started walking toward the door. Zach flicked a glance at Elizabeth and fell in step beside her. They followed the woman up the steps and Elizabeth used the key Maria had given her to open the front door. Zach entered first, took a quick look around, then held the door open for the women. Tansy took a single step into the living room and froze.

Her face looked even paler than it had before, and Elizabeth noticed that she trembled.

"You can feel it in here?" Zach asked softly.

Tansy nodded. "It's stronger in here. I can hardly catch my breath."

"Why don't you sit down?" Elizabeth suggested. "I'll get you a drink of water."

Tansy didn't respond. Instead, she started walking, her eyes fixed straight ahead. The living room curtains were open, the room dimly lit by the few, thin, shadowy streamers of moonlight creeping into the room. As if in a trance, Tansy headed straight for the master bedroom, her gaze fixed ahead, her hands shaking. She stopped at the foot of the bed.

"Something terrible happened in this house." She stood there, statue-still, as if she had crossed some line into another world. For several minutes, no one moved. Elizabeth's heart thumped, hard and fast, and her stomach was tied in knots. Though she felt none of the things she had experienced in the house before, Tansy must have sensed them. Crossing herself, she began to whisper some kind of prayer.

As the last words drifted away, she looked up, her eyes still unfocused, eerily glazed and oddly distant.

"Do you know what happened here?" Zach asked softly.

Still staring, Tansy swallowed. "Death. A brutal, horrible death." She looked at Zach, her eyes big and round in her small, feminine face. "And the evil that caused it still exists here."

Elizabeth's palms began to sweat. Her heart, already clattering loudly, jerked into a higher gear. She wasn't feeling any of the things she'd felt before, yet it wasn't hard to believe that Tansy Trevillian might be sensing something fearful in the house.

"What else can you tell us?" Zach pressed.

Tansy shook her head, glossy short brown hair falling over her ears. "It's all jumbled together. I can't get a fix on anything specific. I just know something terrible happened. And evil was the cause." She turned toward the door and started walking. "I can't stay here any longer. I'm sorry."

Walking out of the bedroom, she crossed the living room and went out the front door. Elizabeth, with Zach close beside her, followed the woman out into the yard.

"I'm sorry I couldn't be more help," Tansy said as she reached her car. "Too much has happened. There are too many layers, one overlapping the other." She pulled open the door. "They're in danger . . . the people who live in the house."

Elizabeth swallowed. She could almost hear the small, high-pitched voice she had heard in the bedroom. "What . . . what should we do?"

Tansy looked back at the house. "Find out what happened here. Perhaps then you will know what to do about the house."

Zach held the car door while Tansy slid behind the wheel.

"Thank you for coming," he said. "You've got my card. Send your bill to my office."

Tansy shook her head again. "Not this time. This one's on me." Snapping her seat belt in place, she started the engine. Pulling the car out onto the highway, she accelerated off down the road, driving a little faster than she should have.

Elizabeth moved toward Zach, wondering at his thoughts, as another set of headlights turned into the driveway. It was an old blue Ford pickup, and recognizing the face of the driver, she muttered a dirty word.

"Looks like the kids are home from the dance a little early," Zach said dryly.

"Looks like. And if that scowl on Miguel's face is a clue, he isn't happy to see us."

As Tansy's taillights disappeared down the highway, Miguel jumped down from the driver's seat of his pickup and marched toward them. Maria struggled to get down from the passenger side of the truck and hurried as best she could in the direction of the group in front of the house.

"I tried to keep him away," she said, looking as if she had been crying. "He was afraid I was getting too tired. I am sorry."

"It's all right, Maria," Elizabeth said. "It's time Miguel knew the truth."

"Truth," he growled. "What truth? That you believe there is a ghost in my house?"

Elizabeth's gaze swung to Maria. "You told him?"

"I thought he might listen. I should have known he would not."

"You believe there is a ghost because my pregnant wife says so? She is a child. And she is frightened to be having a baby. That is all there is to it, and I forbid you to encourage any more of her crazy notions."

Maria started crying, and Miguel turned his wrath in her direction. "Get in the house! You will not speak of this again — do you hear me?"

Maria took a shaky breath and wiped at the tears on her cheeks. "I am sorry," she whispered to Elizabeth.

"Go!"

Maria hurried away, not looking back, and

Miguel fixed Elizabeth with a glare. "You are no longer welcome in this house."

"Take it easy, Miguel," Zach said, stepping a little in front of her. "Something's going on here — whether you believe it or not — and your wife is frightened. We're only trying to help."

"You want to help? Then leave us alone!" He stalked up the front porch steps, walked inside and slammed the door.

Elizabeth felt Zach's arm go around her. As much as she knew she shouldn't, she found herself leaning against him.

"He isn't a bad husband," she said. "He's just old-fashioned."

"Someone needs to take him down a peg or two."

She noticed the set of Zach's jaw and realized he wouldn't hesitate to confront Miguel Santiago — or anyone else who posed a threat to people he cared about. It was an oddly comforting thought.

"This has really been hard on Maria," she said. "Now Miguel is angry, just as she was afraid he would be. We've got to find a way to help her."

"We'll figure something out."

She glanced back at the house, thinking of Tansy Trevillian. "It sounded pretty far-

fetched . . . all that talk about evil, but still
. . ."

"Yeah, I know what you mean." Zach led her over to her car and waited while she slid behind the wheel. "We need to talk about this."

She nodded. "I know. I'd invite you over to my place, but I don't think . . ."

"I already know what you think. How about we go to Biff's and I'll buy you a cup of coffee? Worst brew in the county, but at least they're open. Not many choices in this town."

Biff's was a restaurant/bar on Main Street. The limited menu, basically frozen fried chicken and pizza, was lousy, the employees surly. She couldn't figure out how the place stayed open but it had been there for years.

"All right, Biff's is good."

"I'll follow you down there."

She nodded and started her car.

There wasn't much going on in town as they drove along Main Street, but there rarely was, even on Saturday night. The high school kids mostly took their dates to Mason, where there was a six-theater cinema and, being a farming community, the rest of the town's residents went to bed early, even on Saturday night. Except, of course, for the beer-drinking crowd, which hung around the Top Hat Bar, on a side street a few blocks away.

Elizabeth parallel parked in a space just down from Biff's front door, and Zach parked his BMW in the space behind her. She hadn't been in the restaurant — to use the term loosely — since she had returned to San Pico, but she found it hadn't changed. Worn linoleum, a pool table in the back of the narrow room, a long bar where patrons could eat or drink and a row of wooden tables along the wall.

Zach led her over to a table, then went up to the bar and ordered a couple of cups of coffee.

"Sorry, this is the leaded version," he said as he set the white china mug down in front of her. "They don't believe in decaf at Biff's."

"That's all right. After what happened tonight, I could use a bracer."

Zach smile. "Maybe I should have ordered you a whiskey."

Elizabeth ignored what that grin did to her. "Maybe you should have." But if she had a shot of alcohol and lost even a few of her inhibitions, she would invite Zach back to her apartment, back into her bed, and she didn't want to do that.

"So . . . what do we do next?" she asked.

Picking up the little metal pitcher on the table, she poured a good dose of cream into her thick black coffee.

"Tansy says we need to find out what happened in the house, which we've already started to do — unfortunately, without much success. I guess we'll just have to try harder."

"What else can we do?"

"I'll talk to a few of the workers on the farm, see if anyone has been around long enough to remember any of the people who lived in the old house before it was torn down." He took a sip of his coffee, then grimaced at the bitter taste. "The place was there a lot of years, though. As far back as I can remember. I imagine quite a few tenants have lived there at one time or another."

"After you mentioned it, I remembered seeing it there when I was a kid. I just never paid that much attention."

"It wasn't much to look at, an old, gray, wood-framed house with a big front porch."

"It didn't make much of an impression. I remember it had white wooden shutters at the windows, and by the time I was in high school, it was pretty run-down."

He nodded. "The problem is finding out who lived there."

"More importantly, we need to know if anyone died in the house, particularly a child."

"According to the stuff on the Net, violence is usually part of the equation, or a sudden, unexpected death, like an accident or something. Of course, there's no way to know if it's true."

"No, but it's something to keep in mind."

Zach took a sip of his coffee then set the cup back down on the table. "I'll find out as much as I can. I'm not exactly welcome out at the farm, but I'll try talking to Carson."

"That ought to be interesting. You going to tell your brother you're trying to find a ghost?"

"Not hardly. I'm going to tell him I'm interested in the history of the farm." He took another sip of the bitter brew. "I'll tell him I have someone interested in writing a book on the area. Carson will jump through hoops for a little publicity."

Elizabeth stirred more cream into her mug, trying to disguise the taste. "I really appreciate your help with this, Zach. This isn't exactly my area of expertise."

"Mine either."

They spent the next half hour planning their strategy. Since the house sat on ground owned by Harcourt Farms, there were no separate ownership records to search. Public utility companies seemed the most promising avenue — if their records went back far enough and the company could be convinced to share them.

Harcourt Farms provided its overseers with a house and water, Zach told her, but the phone was paid by the tenants, as were the gas and electric bills. Elizabeth planned to speak to the telephone and utility companies to see what she could find out.

She decided to use Zach's story that someone wanted to do a history of the farm. Of course, their best hope was that Carson might have some sort of record of who had lived there, or that the longtime employees on the farm might remember something useful.

It was getting late by the time their plan was set. Elizabeth had managed to finish several cups of the too-strong coffee, leaving her wide-awake. So was Zach, she discovered as he walked her to her car, then leaned down and gave her a soft, incredibly sexy kiss.

She didn't resist. It just felt too good.

"Let me come home with you." He kissed her again, a deep, thorough kiss that turned her insides to butter. "We're good together,

Liz. Let's see where this thing takes us."

She leaned toward him, tempted. Oh, so, tempted. Instead, she pressed her fingertips against his lips to stop his seductive words.

"I wish I could, Zach. You'll never know how much. But I just can't take the risk."

He stared at her for several long seconds, then cupped her face between his hands and kissed her deeply. Knowing she shouldn't, she let him.

"I could persuade you, Liz. You know I could."

She looked into those hot dark eyes and knew he was right. "I know you could. I'm asking you not to."

Zach said something beneath his breath and stepped away from her, raking a hand through his short dark hair. "I wish things could be different."

"I wish I were more like Lisa."

Zach reached toward her, cupped her cheek with his hand. "I wouldn't want that. I like you just the way you are. I wouldn't change a thing." A last soft kiss and he took her arm, led her around to the driver's side door of her car, then waited as she settled inside.

"I'll keep you posted," he said when she rolled down her window. "You do the same."

"I will. Good night, Zach."

"Good night, baby."

She watched him in the mirror as she drove away, saw his headlights appear behind her as he followed to make sure she safely reached her house, and wondered if she had made the right decision.

SEVENTEEN

Carson Harcourt sat in his study, poring over the production records for the month. It took a moment for the light knock on his door to penetrate his thoughts. When he looked up, he saw his housekeeper, Isabel Flores, standing in the open doorway.

"I am sorry to bother you, Señor Harcourt, but your brother just drove up in front of the house. I thought you would want to know."

"I appreciate that. Thank you, Isabel." Carson watched her walk off down the hall, hips swaying, full breasts jiggling, and thought how smart he had been to hire her. She was wise enough to treat him with respect whenever she was working in the house, and she knew how to please him in bed.

His groin tightened. He'd been busy lately, getting ready for the lettuce harvest. He'd also been working with Walter Simino, preparing to launch his campaign for the assembly, which he would begin in early spring, starting with a big barbecue to announce his candidacy. With so much on his mind, he could use a little sexual relief and Isabel managed that quite nicely.

And since she was in the country without a green card, he didn't have to worry about her giving him any trouble. Carson made a mental note to pay the girl a visit tonight.

He was smiling as he looked up to see his brother walk through the door. The smile instantly faded.

"Well, look who's here. What brings you out from under your rock, today, Zach?"

Zach's expression remained bland. After years of goading, he had taught himself incredible control. Only the faint tick of a muscle along his jaw said Carson's jibe had been effective.

"Something came up. I thought you might be interested."

"Really. Something like what?"

"A guy called me a couple of days ago. He was working on a book about agriculture in the San Joaquin Valley. He was interested in Harcourt Farms. He thought I might be able to help him with some of the history."

"You're right, that is interesting. Are you sure this isn't going to have some kind of negative slant?"

"He's just concerned with the history."

"Have him give me a call. I'll see what I can do."

"He wanted me to talk to some of the longtime workers, see what they might remember about the place in the old days. I figured you wouldn't have time. I told him I'd give it a try, see what I could turn up."

The last thing Carson wanted was to spend time with his farm workers. That's why he hired overseers.

"I told him I'd talk to you about it," Zach continued. "I figure once he gets the basics, he'll want to talk to you about the other aspects of the farming operation."

Now that was more like it. He wouldn't mind having something written about him and the success of Harcourt Farms, as long as it had a positive ring. Let Zach do the unpleasant legwork.

Still, there was something in his half brother's manner that bothered him. Zach was never much good at lying. Carson wondered how he managed to earn those fat legal fees he got in L.A.

"All right, go ahead. Stiles hasn't been here that long. He probably wouldn't do you any good." Lester Stiles was foreman of Harcourt Farms, Carson's right-hand man.

"Mariano Nunez has probably been working here the longest. He lives in the third house down the row."

"Yeah, I remember him. He ran the orchard crew back when I was in high school. I remember he was my boss when I worked the shaker in the almond harvest."

"Maybe the old man can tell you something of interest. And tell your guy — what did you say his name was?"

Zach glanced away, a sure sign he wasn't being completely honest. "Steven Baines."

"Tell Baines to call me. I'll set aside some time for an interview."

Zach just nodded. "Great. Thanks. You wouldn't have any kind of list, would you? Something that might tell the names of the people who worked here over the years?"

Carson eyed Zach warily. He didn't like the direction this conversation was going. "No. Why would you need a list?"

Zach shrugged, but his shoulders looked tense. "I just thought it might be useful, jog some memories. At any rate, the next time I talk to him, I'll tell Baines to give you a call."

Carson watched his brother walk out of the study, more certain than ever that something was going on. He'd find out what. He practically ran San Pico. People told him whatever he wanted to know. Well, he wanted to know what Zach was up to and it wouldn't take him long to find out.

Carson picked up the phone.

Zach left the house and headed for the workers' compound. He still had a bad taste in his mouth from his conversation with Carson. He hated to ask the bastard for anything. He just hoped the result would be worth it.

It was Sunday, a day off for a number of people on the farm so there were more people than usual around the housing area. Zach spent the morning talking to some of the longtime workers, and the head overseer, Mariano Nunez, a weathered old Mexican who had been employed by Harcourt Farms for more than thirty years.

"I remember the old gray house," the old man said. "I had friends who lived there . . . the Espinozas. Juan Espinoza came up with me from Mexico."

The old man remembered a couple of other residents who had lived in the wood-framed house over the years. The Rodriquez family had been the only other residents of the new yellow house besides the Santiagos. The last resident of the gray house, a man named Axel Whitman, had lived alone for a number of years. Zach wrote down all of the names Mariano could remember, but he didn't know where any of them had gone after they left the farm.

Juan Espinoza and his family had lived there the longest, Mariano told him, then moved to a farming community near Fresno, where Juan had later died. As far as the old man could recall, no one had ever died in the house, at least not in the thirty years he had lived on the farm.

Zach didn't see the foreman, Les Stiles, anywhere around but he wouldn't talk to the man if he did. Stiles kissed Carson's ass, big-time. Odds were, he wouldn't know anything useful and asking him questions might make Carson suspicious.

Zach thought about calling Liz with the morning's unhelpful information, but decided against it. He needed to go out to Teen Vision, see how things were coming along with the barn.

Maybe instead of calling, he'd stop by her house before he drove back to L.A.

Raul Perez hung up the phone in the hall outside his dorm room. He had called his sister, but Maria was away at the grocery store, so he had talked to Miguel instead. It wasn't a pleasant conversation. His brother-in-law had ranted and raved, furious at

Maria, angry at her friend, Elizabeth Conners, and the brother of the man who owned Harcourt Farms.

"Your sister thinks there is a ghost in the house. She is acting completely crazy. I cannot believe it!"

"Maybe there is a ghost," Raul said softly.

"*Por Dios,* if you believe that, you are as crazy as she is! If there is a ghost, why have I not seen it? Why is it just your sister?"

It was a very good question, one Raul had pondered himself. "I don't know. Maybe there is a ghost, maybe there isn't, but Maria is afraid."

"She doesn't have to be afraid. Not as long as I am here to protect her. On visiting day, I will bring her out to see you. Talk to her, tell her she is being foolish. Maybe she will listen to you."

Raul nodded, though Miguel could not see. "I will do my best." Raul hung up the phone, and unconsciously his hand clenched into a fist. His sister was frightened. He didn't know what was happening to her, but something was wrong and he was powerless to help her.

He started down the dormitory stairs to join his roommate, Pete Ortega, in the mess hall, his stomach rumbling, reminding him it was time for lunch though his appetite wasn't nearly as big as it had been before he'd talked to Miguel.

"Raul! Wait up!"

Turning, he saw Zachary Harcourt hurrying to catch up with him, heading in the same direction he was.

"Hi, Zach."

"Hey, kid. Good to see you." The dark-haired man looked into his face and Raul's smile faded. "What's the matter? You look like your dog just died."

Raul sighed. "It's my sister. I talked to Miguel this morning."

"Damn. Then I guess you know I'm not exactly on his good list and neither is Ms. Conners."

"He said you were out at the house last night, looking for the ghost."

"Not exactly, but close enough."

"Did you see it?"

Zach shook his head. "I don't know if what's happening out there is real or not, but something's going on and we're going to find out what it is. Once we do, your sister won't have to be afraid."

"I am worried about her. I wish I could be there to help her."

Zach stopped walking and caught Raul's arm. "Listen, Raul. I'm not exactly sure how I got in the middle of this mess, but now that I am, I'm not going to abandon you or your sister. I'm not quitting until the problem is resolved. I give you my word on that."

Raul felt a wave of relief so strong something burned behind his eyes. "Thank you."

Zach clapped him on the back. "You just keep doing as well as you have been. That's all the thanks I need."

Raul just nodded. His throat felt too tight to speak.

"Come on," Zach said, his hand back on Raul's shoulder, steering him toward the mess hall. "I'm starving. Let's get something to eat."

Raul let him lead the way, determined not to worry about his sister. Zachary Harcourt had given his word. Raul just prayed he would keep it.

Zach pulled down his visor against the glare of the late afternoon sun. He should have been driving the opposite direction, heading east down the highway toward Interstate 5, on his way back to his Pacific Palisades apartment, getting ready for a long day at the office tomorrow. They were starting to take depositions on the Themoziamine case this week and he needed to be prepared.

Instead, he was driving down Main Street, turning onto Cherry Avenue, pulling up in front of Liz's apartment building. He'd only stay a minute, he told himself, just long enough to fill her in on his unsuccessful morning at Harcourt Farms.

Shoving the gearshift into Park, he turned off the engine, then hesitated only a moment before opening the door into the pervasive afternoon heat and climbing out of the car. Making his way to apartment B, he knocked on Liz's front door, and a few minutes later, she pulled it open.

"Zach! What are you doing here?"

His mind went completely blank. She was standing there in a little orange bikini that showed every luscious curve of her body. Her glorious dark auburn hair was wet and she was drying it with a beach towel, obviously having just come in from the pool. His body stirred to life and he went rock hard.

He cleared his throat but didn't look away. "I know I should have called. I just decided at the last minute to stop by. I wanted to tell you what happened when I went out to see my brother."

Noticing the greedy way he was devouring her with his eyes, she wrapped the beach towel around her hips and tied it in a knot.

Damn, she was sexy. He wasn't sure exactly what she had that made her different from other women he had known, but she sure as hell had something.

"Come on in." She stepped back smiling, inviting him in, and he walked into the living room and closed the door behind him. "Give me a minute to put on some dry clothes."

His gaze slid over her breasts, barely covered by the tiny cups of her bathing suit top, and his body tightened. "Don't bother on my account."

Liz's smile deepened, until her glance caught on the thick ridge at the front of his Levi's and something shifted in her pretty blue eyes. "I'll be right back," she said, her voice a little huskier than before.

She started to turn away, but Zach caught her hand and tugged her around to face him. He hadn't meant to do it, but when her eyes widened in surprise and her lips parted, he hauled her into his arms and claimed her mouth.

Her hands came up to his chest and for an instant he thought she meant to push him away, then he felt her tongue slide over his as she kissed him back and every cell in his body caught fire.

Christ, he wanted her. His fingers closed around the towel and he untied the knot she had made, let the damp material puddle on the floor. Her orange bikini was wet, clinging to the cheeks of her bottom, and he cupped them, kneaded the firm round flesh, and heard her soft moan.

He glanced toward the window and saw that the curtains were mostly drawn, slid a hand into her thick, wet hair, and deepened the kiss. The sides of her swimsuit bottom fastened with tiny orange bows. He pulled one and then the other, jerked the wisp of fabric away and tossed it into a corner. The top went next, exposing those full, rose-tipped breasts. He suckled each one and she began to tremble.

"Zachary . . . ?"

He could hear the uncertainty in her voice, tinged heavily with desire. He refused to give her time to think, time to withdraw from him again. Instead, he backed her up against the wall and unbuttoned the fly of his jeans. He was hard as granite as he urged her legs apart and began to stroke her. The plump softness was slick and wet and he realized she was as ready as he.

"I want you so damned much," he said, kissing the side of her neck, then taking her mouth again. Positioning himself at the entrance to her passage, he lifted her a little and drove himself home.

■ ■ ■ ■

Elizabeth bit back a sob. Zach was here and he was inside her, exactly where she wanted him to be. She was shaking, her body trembling at the feel of him, at the heavy length filling her, heating her from the inside out. He hooked her legs around his waist and pressed his mouth against the side of her neck, and the warm slickness of his tongue spread goosebumps over her skin.

There was something wildly erotic about being naked while Zach remained fully clothed. She could feel the roughness of his jeans against her thighs, the brush of the buttons on his shirt against her breasts. As he surged inside her, she worked those buttons frantically, then pulled the fabric apart and pressed her breasts against his chest.

She could feel his heartbeat, feel the lean muscles expanding and contracting. Tightening her hold around his neck, she settled her mouth over his for a deep, penetrating kiss and heard him groan.

He gripped her bottom as he filled her again, gliding in and then out, thrusting deeply, his heavy strokes lifting her onto her toes, impaling her again and again. God, she wanted this, wanted him. Every place he touched her seemed to burn.

"Zachary . . ." There was no uncertainty now. She knew what she wanted, what her body wanted, and she gave into it, let the heat and need wash over her, let her desire for him blot out everything around her.

Zach lifted her, wrapped her legs around his waist, and drove into her again, deep pounding strokes that filled her with pleasure. Her body shook and her pulse hammered. She had never felt like this, never felt as if each moment he claimed a bigger part of her.

It was frightening, terrifying, and yet she was powerless to stop it.

Zach drove into her again, his hands gripping her bottom, holding her in place to receive each of his thrusts. Fresh waves of pleasure washed through her, and a deep, pulsing need. She hovered on the edge of climax, her body desperate for release, yet not wanting the sensations to end.

She felt the warmth of Zach's mouth against her ear, the whorl of his tongue. "Come for me, Liz."

And the wave tore free. She was flying, spinning through the stars, drenched in sensations so sweet she never wanted them to end. Zach followed her to release and the tension in his muscles, the fierceness of his climax, sent her into fresh spasms of pleasure.

Zach gently kissed her, then set her back down on her feet. His eyes found hers and his expression grew concerned.

"I didn't come here for this, I swear. I just . . . I saw you standing there and you looked so damned beautiful . . . and I wanted you . . . so damned much." He blew out a breath, raked a hand through his hair. Reaching down, he picked up her towel and handed it over. "Where you're concerned, my usual self-control seems to go right out the window."

Elizabeth wrapped the towel around her, covering her body from breast to thigh, tucked the fabric in at the top. "I could have stopped you."

"Yes."

"I wanted you, too, Zach."

He reached out and touched her cheek. "There's nothing wrong with two people wanting each other."

She looked away from him, trying not to feel regret for what they had done. "I don't suppose there is."

"Let me spend the night."

She started shaking her head. "I don't think —"

"You don't think it's a good idea."

"And you do?"

He sighed heavily. "I'm not sure. There's something going on here, Liz. And it's more than just sexual attraction. I feel it and so do you."

"Whatever we might be feeling — it doesn't change the way things are."

"Maybe it does. Why don't we wait and see?"

She walked away from him, away from the heat that had returned to his eyes and the look she had seen there before. She told herself not to imagine it was yearning. Whatever it was, it didn't change what he was, didn't change the fact that he had always been a loner and always would be. Didn't lessen the awful risk she would be taking if she allowed herself to get more deeply involved with him.

"I need to go change," she said, wanting to put some distance between them. "I'll be right back."

Zach just nodded, reading her thoughts, a look of resignation on his face.

Elizabeth returned a few minutes later, dressed in a pair of tan shorts and a crisp white blouse, her resolve back in place. No matter how much she desired him, she couldn't take the risk.

She walked past him toward the kitchen.

"I made a pitcher of iced tea just before you got here. Would you like a glass?"

He nodded. "Sounds good."

She noticed he had straightened his clothes and combed his hair. He looked as good as he had when he'd walked through the door and it bothered her to realize she wanted him again.

She busied herself dropping ice cubes into glasses and filling them with tea. Setting the glasses down on the kitchen table along with a spoon, she shoved the sugar bowl over to Zach's side of the table.

His eyes remained on her face. "It's fine the way it is." He picked up the icy glass and took a long swallow, and she watched the long muscles moving in his throat.

"Did you get a chance to talk to your brother?" she asked, determined not to think of sex with Zach.

"Actually, that's the reason I stopped by. I talked to Carson. Unfortunately, he says there isn't any list of former tenants. I also talked to some of the workers. Mariano Nunez has been there the longest. He remembered most of the families who lived in the house while he was there. I wrote them down."

He pulled a piece of paper out of his pocket and tossed it down on the table.

"But the old man had no idea where to find them. He says as far as he knows, no one ever died in either the old house or the new one."

"That leads us nowhere."

"We've still got the utility companies. You'll take a stab at them tomorrow?"

She nodded. "I can get away from work for an hour or so, I think. I'll see if I can dig up any information."

"You haven't eaten supper, have you?"

"No, but . . . Look, Zach —"

"We could order some more Chinese — or maybe a pizza, sit around and watch a little TV."

"Or you could go back to your world and I could stay here in mine."

"We could do that. I don't want to."

She looked at him, looked into those intense golden brown eyes, and her heart clenched. "I don't want to, either."

She couldn't believe she'd said it. Now that she had, she realized it was true, and that it didn't really matter anymore. She was already in way over her head. Whatever happened, she was going to get hurt.

In the meantime, she had Zach. She would enjoy the time they had together.

She set her glass of tea down on the table, walked up and slid her arms around his neck, kissed him full on the mouth.

"Let's order something later," she whispered against his ear. "I can think of something a whole lot better to do than eat."

Zach grinned and kissed the side of her neck. "We'll have to see about that." Lifting her up in his arms, he carried her into the bedroom.

Eighteen

Zach set the alarm for four o'clock the next morning, but awoke before the buzzer went off. Snuggled spoon-fashion against him, Elizabeth felt him stir, felt his morning arousal and moved to take him inside her. He made love to her slowly, until they both peaked, then he kissed the side of her neck and left her lying drowsily in bed while he showered and dressed to leave.

At this time of morning, without the usual traffic, it should take less than two hours to drive back to L.A., but Zach would need time to change clothes, and he had told her he had work to do before his first meeting.

"Call me this afternoon," he said as he walked to where she lay in bed. "Let me know what you find out from the utility companies."

She mumbled something unintelligible, then gave him a sleepy smile. "I will."

Zach bent down and kissed her. "Don't forget."

"I won't."

"Talk to you soon, love."

The endearment rolled over her, making her smile again. Plumping her pillow, she snuggled down under the sheet and went back to sleep.

The alarm went off again at 6:00 a.m. Elizabeth showered and dressed for the day, the ridiculous smile still on her face. It remained there even when she walked through the back door of the office humming some silly tune, and apparently her boss noticed.

"My, you're certainly cheerful today," Michael said. "You must have had an exceptionally good weekend."

She blushed. She couldn't help it.

Michael took in the high color in her cheeks and smiled. "Never mind. I don't think I want to know." He poured her a cup of coffee from the pot in the tiny kitchen that served as lunch room and lounge and handed it over.

"What about you?" Elizabeth doctored the brew with cream, then sat down next to him at the tiny kitchen table. "You and Barbara set a date yet?"

Michael's thick, sandy brows drew slightly

together. "Not yet. I don't see any reason to rush."

"Neither do I. Especially if you still have any doubts."

"I don't have any doubts. It's just that marriage is a really big step."

She thought of Brian and what a disaster that had been, then thought of Zach and tried to imagine him in the role of husband but couldn't make the image appear. "A very big step," she agreed, not feeling nearly as chipper as she had when she'd walked through the door. She wasn't quite sure why, since she certainly didn't want to get married again and especially not to Zach.

She spent the morning with clients. There was a gap in her schedule after her first two appointments, which gave her some time before lunch. Grabbing her purse on the way out the door, she headed off to So Cal Edison, the first stop on her list.

"May I help you?" A blond woman wearing an array of heavy imitation gold jewelry and too much makeup sat at the information desk.

"Yes, thank you, I'd appreciate that. My name is Elizabeth Conners. I'm a counselor at the Family Psychology Clinic. I'm helping someone with a research project that involves the history of San Pico, in particular the agricultural history of certain farms in the community. I was hoping you might be able to help me document the chain of residents who may have lived in one of the workers' houses in the compound at Harcourt Farms."

Clearly impressed with the words *research* and *history,* the woman's blond eyebrows drew together. The pencil in her hand tapped briskly on the top of the desk.

"Have you tried city hall? They have all the records of homeowners in the area."

"Unfortunately, the house is occupied by tenants. The only records would be phone or utility company records."

"I see." Turning to the computer screen in front of her, the woman — Janet was the name on the plastic tag on her right shoulder — began to type in letters. "Do you have an address for the property?"

"It's 20543 Route 51, San Pico."

The letters on the keyboard clattered. "I don't know how much this will help. Our service records only go back ten years."

Elizabeth felt a stab of disappointment.

"Currently, the gas and electric service is listed in the name of a Miguel Santiago."

"That's right. Can you give me the names of the people who lived in the house before the Santiagos moved in?" Zach had given her the names Mariano Nunez had mentioned. She might as well verify as much as she could.

"I'm not really supposed to do this," Janet said, but continued to page down on the screen. "Looks like the Santiagos just moved in a couple of months ago. Before that, it was someone named Rodriquez. There's a gap here a few years back of about ten months. Looks like the house was empty."

"The house that was there before was torn down and this one built in its place."

The blond woman nodded. "That would explain it. I'll print the list back as far as it goes."

Elizabeth waited as the sheet printed out. Mariano had remembered the tenants in the house back almost thirty years but he didn't remember anyone dying there. She wished the So Cal list went back further.

Elizabeth accepted the printout the woman handed her. "Thank you very much."

Scanning the page, she recognized one of the names on Zach's list, Bob Rodgers, apparently not Hispanic like most of the men who worked on the farm. But then neither was the current foreman, Lester Stiles, and a number of other employees. Aside from

Rodgers, the only other occupant of the old wood-framed house in the last ten years was named De La Cruz, also mentioned on Zach's list.

Elizabeth folded the paper, thanked the woman again, and headed out the door.

Next stop, Ma Bell.

Unfortunately, she had even less success there than she had at So Cal Ed. Even though they had been cooperative and their list went back a total of fifteen years, no new names showed up. If there was a ghost, it must be someone who had died before Mariano Nunez arrived at the farm thirty years ago.

Elizabeth thought of Maria and how frightened she was, and by the time she got back to the office, her mood was grim.

Having promised to phone Zach with whatever news she had gleaned, she dialed his office number. As before, his secretary put her call straight through.

Zach picked up the phone and started to smile the moment he heard Elizabeth's voice. "Hi, baby."

"I hate to bother you, Zach. I know you're busy, but I promised I would call."

"You're not bothering me. What'd you find out?"

"Nothing. That's why I hated to call."

"I'm glad you did. I'm up to my ass in alligators here. It's nice to hear a friendly voice."

"What are we going to do, Zach? I feel so sorry for Maria. I wish I knew how to help her, but this ghost thing is way out of my league."

"I know what you mean. But as I was driving back this morning — trying not to think how sexy you looked lying there in bed — I got an idea."

"What is it?"

"It occurred to me we haven't tried the obvious. Mariano was fairly certain no one died in the house during the years he's worked on the farm — which covers about thirty years — so if there was a death, it probably happened further back in time. San Pico is a pretty small town, even smaller thirty or forty years ago. According to most of the info, ghosts usually result from a violent, or sudden, unexpected death, right?"

"Right."

"Maybe there's something about it in the newspaper."

"Zach, you're a genius! Why didn't we think of this sooner?"

"Like you said, ghost-hunting is kind of

uncharted territory."

"I'll go down to the *Newspress* as soon as I get a chance. I think they keep the old papers on microfiche or something. I'll see what I can dig up."

Zach laughed. "Now there's a pun. I'll go online, try to see if I can find something useful. It's a long shot, but you never know."

"Good idea."

"If we don't find anything in the paper, I'm going to try talking to my father. He doesn't remember anything that happened after his fall, but sometimes his mind can be fairly sharp when he talks about the past."

"You think that's a good idea?"

"To tell you the truth, I think he likes to reminisce about the good ol' days. He would have been a kid in the forties, when the gray house was first built. Maybe he'll remember something about the people who lived there as he grew up."

"It's definitely worth a try. I gotta run. My next client just walked in."

"Let me know if you come up with anything."

"I will."

"I'll see you Friday."

There was a pause on the other end of the

line. "See you Friday."

Zach hung up and realized his stomach was clenching. He'd been gripping the phone, inwardly praying Liz hadn't changed her mind again and would refuse to see him this weekend. He took a deep breath and forced himself to relax. He had never known a woman who affected him the way Liz did.

He thought about the girl she had been in high school, determinedly independent, refusing to give in to peer pressure like other girls her age. Her mother had died from cancer when she was fifteen, and talk was, it had been a slow, agonizing death. Afterward, her dad's small grocery store had gone straight down-hill and he had finally been forced to file bankruptcy. Liz had gone to work at Marge's Café, the place he'd first noticed her.

She was smart. He figured she might have gotten some kind of scholarship, but likely still had to work to put herself through college. He admired her for the grit it must have taken. She had always been the kind of person who cared about others, undoubtedly the reason she had gone into family counseling.

Zach sighed and leaned back in his chair. He was getting in way too deep and he knew it. The little voice in his head was telling him to run before it was too late.

But his heart was saying something else. Something he had never heard before. *Take a chance. Just this once.*

Just thinking about it made his stomach clench harder.

With her busy schedule, Elizabeth didn't make it down to the San Pico *Newspress* until Wednesday afternoon. Zach had told her he thought the house had been built some time in the nineteen forties, so she asked the clerk at the counter if she could look at newspapers dating back to that time.

She planned to scan the headlines. In a town the size of San Pico, any sort of violent crime would have been frontpage news.

A gray-haired woman, slightly pudgy, wearing a pair of silver reading glasses on a chain around her neck, stood behind the counter.

"May I help you?"

Elizabeth told her she wanted to look at old newspaper records and the woman motioned for her to come through the low wooden gate into the working area of the office, then led her into a room at the rear of the redbrick building, fairly new since the town had been growing and newspaper readership along with it.

"Going back the last five years, every-thing's on computer," the woman said proudly. "We're getting very modern here. Unfortunately, before that, you'll still be dealing with microfiche. The machines are on the table against the wall."

Elizabeth turned in that direction, saw two clunky old microfiche readers with big screens and buttons on the side to run the film from reel to reel.

"You know how to run one?"

"I think so, yes. I used machines like these to do research when I was in college."

"The film's in boxes in those metal file drawers." The woman pointed to a tall cabinet that held four, legal-size drawers. "The label tells which years each roll of film covers. Every copy of the paper ever printed is in those files. Let me know if you need any help."

The woman walked away and Elizabeth set to work, starting in the early nineteen forties, looking for any sort of violent crime that might have happened in the house or anywhere on Harcourt Farms. It was a long, tedious job that took the entire afternoon. She was just finishing up when the clerk returned at closing.

She sighed as she got up from her chair. If

she had time, she could come back and check the police blotter, which showed anything reported by the police, but for that many years, the undertaking would be huge.

She was exhausted and discouraged when she left the building. Most of the violence in San Pico seemed to center around family disputes or arguments in local bars, and as far as she could tell, none of them had resulted in a death at Harcourt Farms. She'd looked for suicides and found a number, but none that had happened on the farm.

Later that evening, she phoned Zach at his apartment, figuring he would be home from work by now, but got his answering machine instead. She couldn't help wondering if he was out on a date, then shoved the unwanted thought away. She watched TV for a while and resisted the urge to phone him again before she went to bed.

She didn't want to be disappointed.

It was six o'clock the next morning when the phone on Elizabeth's nightstand began to ring, rousing her from a restless sleep. An instant later, her alarm clock went off. Groggy, she shut off the alarm and fumbled for the phone, immediately recognizing the woman's voice on the other end of the line.

"Maria? Is that you?"

She was crying. Elizabeth couldn't make out her words.

"It's all right, Maria. Just take a deep breath and try to calm down. I want you to start at the beginning and tell me what's wrong."

Maria made a strangled sound into the phone as she gulped back tears. "I saw her. Last night in my bedroom. The little girl. She was there, standing at the foot of my bed." A sob escaped. She dragged in a choking breath of air.

"All right, let's just take this slowly. You're all right now, aren't you? You're feeling all okay?"

"*Sí, sí.* I am feeling all right."

"That's good. Was Miguel there with you last night?"

"*Sí,* he was there."

"Did he see the little girl, too?"

"I do not know. I think he saw something. He woke up right after I did. I tried to talk to him after it was over, but he only got angry and walked out of the bedroom. He slept on the sofa, then before the sun came up, he went to work."

"Listen, Maria. I'm coming out there. We'll talk about this and you can tell me what you saw."

"Miguel will not like it if you come."

Elizabeth chewed her lip. She didn't want to cause Maria more trouble. "Did he take the car?"

"No, he is working in the fields."

"Do you feel well enough to drive?"

"*Sí,* I can drive."

"Come down to my office. I'll meet you there in an hour."

"I will come."

Maria arrived out in front of the building just as Elizabeth opened the back door to the office and walked in. She heard the rap on the front door and hurried to open it.

"Maria! Here, let me help you." Elizabeth wrapped an arm around the younger woman's shoulders, barely recognizing the trembling, pale-faced girl who stumbled into the room. "It's going to be all right. We're going to figure this out."

"The ghost . . . she is trying to warn me. She says they are going to kill my baby."

Elizabeth led Maria into her office and settled her on the dark green sofa. "What else did she say? Do you have any idea who she is trying to warn you about?"

Maria shook her head. "She kept asking for her mother. 'I want my mama. Please . . . I want my mama.' It sounded like she was crying. It made me feel so sad."

Elizabeth shivered, remembering the small voice she had heard the frightening night she had spent in the house. "What did she look like?"

Maria took the Kleenex Elizabeth handed her and dabbed at the tears in her eyes. "She was very pretty . . . like an angel . . . with long blond curls and big blue eyes. She was all dressed up like she was going to a party."

Elizabeth sat down beside her on the sofa. "Could you see what she was wearing?"

Maria wiped away a tear. "A little white gathered skirt with a pink ruffled bib. I do not remember what you call it. Pin something, I think."

"Pinafore? Is that what you mean?"

"*Sí,* that is it, I think."

It seemed impossible. A ghost in a party dress. "How old would you say she was?"

"Eight or nine. Not more, I do not think. She had on a pair of shiny black shoes."

Elizabeth reached over and gently grasped Maria's hand. "I think you should move out of the house, Maria. Whether there really is a ghost or not isn't important. You're frightened and that isn't good for the baby."

Maria started crying again. "I want to move out but there is nowhere for me to go, and Miguel . . . I have never seen him this way. He says this is all in my head. He gets angry if I say anything about the house. If I leave, I am afraid he will not want me back."

"Miguel loves you. Surely —"

"My husband is a very proud man. He says he does not believe in ghosts and I am acting like a child."

"You could stay with me until the baby comes."

"I cannot do that. I am Miguel's wife and a wife should stay with her husband."

"What about the baby? You need to think of your unborn child."

Maria stiffened. "I must stay with Miguel." She gave up a shuddering breath. "I should have taken the sleeping pills Dr. Zumwalt gave me."

Elizabeth got up from the sofa and paced over to her desk. She wished there was something she could say. Letting Maria stay with her at the apartment wouldn't be a problem, but the woman losing her husband would be. She couldn't force the girl to leave her home. And as long as Miguel was convinced his wife was imagining things, there was no chance he would let her go without a fight.

They needed some kind of proof that something was going on, something beyond the word of a self-proclaimed "sensitive" like Tansy Trevillian or a pregnant young wife.

By the time Maria prepared to leave the office an hour later, she was feeling a little better, a little more hopeful.

"You aren't alone in this," Elizabeth said as she walked the girl out to her battered Ford truck. "Zachary Harcourt is coming up this weekend to speak to his father. Maybe he can help us figure out what happened in the house."

Assuming something actually had.

Assuming Fletcher Harcourt's mind would be clear enough for him to remember.

"What will we do then?"

Good question. "I'm not really sure, but at least we'll have more to go on that we have now." Elizabeth squeezed the girl's hand. "Call me if you need anything, anything at all."

But even if Maria called, Elizabeth wasn't sure she could find a way to help.

NINETEEN

Carson Harcourt leaned back in his expensive black leather desk chair. The morning paper sat neatly folded on a corner of his rolltop desk, read hours ago when he had first come into his office. A farmer's day started early and Carson always had work to do.

He'd been busy going over a list of pesticide invoices, products used in the rose fields, when the telephone rang. He had recognized his foreman's voice on the other end of the line and listened with growing fury as the man made his report.

"Keep an eye on them," he told Lester Stiles. "And keep me posted. I'll call if I need you." Clenching his jaw, he slammed the receiver down in its cradle.

"Goddamn, I knew it!" His fist crashed down on the top of his desk, the sound echoing through the open door out into the hallway. Carson didn't care. He'd been certain his half brother had been up to no good the last time he had come out to the farm. As soon as Zach had left the house, Carson had phoned Les Stiles and asked him to nose around, see if he could find out what Zach was up to.

Spending his nights in Elizabeth Conners's bed, Stiles had discovered, which by now Carson could have guessed.

Zach had a way with women. Always had. Carson had falsely believed that Elizabeth would be able to see beyond the flashy cars and designer clothes, the smooth lines and sex appeal. He had hoped she would be interested in a man with a future, a man who had opportunity and power within his grasp.

Apparently Elizabeth was no different from the other women Zach had charmed, just another Lisa Doyle.

It didn't matter. What mattered was discovering what the two of them were up to. And Stiles was the man for the job.

Les Stiles had been working for Carson just under four years. Before that, he'd been in the Rangers, then spent time in South America doing some kind of mercenary work. But he'd been born in San Pico, raised on one of the big farms in the area, and four years ago, tired of the life he'd been leading, he had returned.

He had answered an ad for the foreman's job at Harcourt Farms, and Carson had hired him. Over the years, the job had grown into something more than just supervising work on the farm. Stiles did whatever Carson needed him to do, no matter what it took. He didn't ask questions and he was compensated well for his loyalty and competence.

Stiles had told him that whatever Zach was involved in had something to do with the Santiago family and the house they were living in, and that meant it had something to do with Harcourt Farms.

Carson ground his jaw, silently cursing his half brother. Zach had been a thorn in his side since the day his father had brought the sullen, dark-haired boy home and announced that Zach was his son.

Fletcher Harcourt had made it legal, adopting Zach, giving him a room of his own in the main house and enrolling him in school as Carson's brother. Even now it set Carson's teeth on edge to think of the gall it had taken and the hurt it had caused his mother for the old man to bring home his bastard son.

His mother was dead now. Carson figured Zach had helped send her to an early grave.

His thoughts returned to his conversation with Lester Stiles. Stiles had tailed Zach all last weekend, then kept an eye on Elizabeth through the week. According to his foreman, Elizabeth had been dredging up old utility company records, trying to find out who had lived in the Santiago house over the years. Zach had asked the same question last weekend when he had been out at the farm.

Johnny Mayer, a friend of Stiles who owned the FoodMart out on Highway 51, had told him about a woman who had stopped to ask directions to the compound at Harcourt Farms. She had mentioned that she was in town to help the people who lived in one of the houses — supposedly some kind of psychic or something.

"I think this has something to do with a ghost," Stiles had laughed. "Can you believe it?"

Carson wasn't laughing. Whatever their reasons, they had no business digging into Harcourt Farms affairs. And Carson intended to put a stop to it — once and for all.

Elizabeth got a call from Zach on Friday afternoon saying he wouldn't be arriving in San Pico until late.

"I've got an afternoon appointment with the attorneys for Themoziamine. It's going to take us a while. And the traffic's always bad on Friday night."

Elizabeth's fingers tightened around the phone. "I . . . um . . . tried to call you Wednesday night, but you weren't home."

"Why didn't you leave a message?"

"I figured you were . . . I thought you were probably . . ."

"Probably what, Liz?"

"Out on a date."

Silence fell on the other end of the line. "I've never even thought about going out with someone else, not since I started seeing you."

"You don't owe me anything, Zach. I didn't mean for it to sound as if you did."

"Are you dating other people?"

She swallowed, thought about lying. "No."

"Then neither am I."

"Okay." The relief she felt made her dizzy. It was a very bad sign. "I guess I'll see you tonight."

"Count on it."

She waited for him to end the call but he didn't.

"Why did you call me on Wednesday?"

"I wanted to tell you I didn't find anything in the papers. I can try the police blotter but it's going to take a lot of time and I don't really think I'll find anything useful."

"I was really hoping you would."

"Maria called me yesterday morning. She saw the ghost, Zach. Up close and personal. A little blond girl. I'll tell you about it when you get here. She was really scared, Zach."

Zach blew a breath into the phone. "I'm going out to see my dad first thing in the morning. Maybe he'll remember something."

"I hope so. Maria looks terrible. I'm really getting worried about her, and the baby." She hoped Maria wasn't alone in the house tonight.

"Just hang in there. We'll come up with something. I'll be there as soon as I can."

Zach arrived even later than he had expected, but Elizabeth waited up for him. She hadn't imagined he would stride through the door and sweep her into his arms, carry her into the bedroom and make passionate love to her, but he did.

She smiled as she padded into the kitchen at nearly midnight to fix them a snack while they talked about Maria and what she claimed to have seen in the house.

"If the ghost really is a little girl with blond hair and blue eyes," she said, "that eliminates a number of children who lived in the house over the years."

"Unless this has nothing to do with a child who actually lived there."

"What do you mean?"

"Maybe she was a friend of someone who lived there."

Elizabeth blew out a breath. "I hadn't thought of that. For the present, let's just stick with the theory we have."

"Yeah, this is all hard pretty hard to swallow in the first place. Let's not complicate matters unless we have to."

They snacked on cold roast beef Elizabeth made into sandwiches while she filled him in on her failed efforts to discover the secrets of the house. Sometime during the night, they made love again. Still, neither of them slept very well.

Elizabeth worried about Maria and what might be happening to her in the house, and Zach worried about Raul and whether the boy would do something crazy if he found out his sister was in trouble.

He brought up the possibility as they dressed the next morning to drive over to Willow Glen to see his father.

"I hope she keeps her brother out of this," Zach said, pulling a short-sleeved, yellow knit shirt over his head.

"I know she'll do her best. She's very protective of Raul. And she wants very badly for him to succeed."

"They seem to mean a lot to each other." There was something in his face, something that looked strangely like envy.

"I guess that isn't the way it was with you and Carson."

A disgusted sound came from his throat. "Carson hated my guts from the moment he laid eyes on me."

"How old were you?"

"Eight, the day I moved in. Carson was ten."

"Ten. That's pretty young to start hating people. How do you feel about him? Do you hate him, too?"

Zach shook his head. "Not really. Hating someone takes too much energy. Besides, I guess I always felt a little sorry for him."

"You felt sorry for Carson? Why?"

"Because my father expected so much of him. Carson never seemed to come up to scratch, no matter how hard he tried. Me, my father mostly ignored."

"Until you got out of prison."

"Yeah. I don't know exactly what happened. Maybe he figured he was partly to blame. When he found out I was serious about turning my life around, he did everything in his power to help me."

"Which probably didn't please Carson."

Zach grinned. "Yeah, he was about as pleased as a boll weevil with a crop duster overhead."

"Carson seems to have done a good job running the farm."

"I think he has. The place means everything to him. In a way I think he's glad the old man is out of the picture."

Elizabeth said nothing to that. Since Fletcher Harcourt's accident, Carson had become the power behind Harcourt Farms. Running the multimillion dollar farming operation gave him a position of prestige and influence most men would envy, though Zach didn't seem to want any part of the business.

"Are you ready?" he asked.

"Let me get my purse." She grabbed her straw bag off the coffee table, and they headed out the door. Zach was driving his Cherokee today, she saw, and Elizabeth tossed him a smile.

"I guess you aren't trying to impress me anymore."

Zach gave her a wicked grin. "I was hoping you were already duly impressed."

Thinking of his skillful lovemaking, Elizabeth laughed. "I suppose I am."

She waited while Zach opened the door then slid onto the brown leather seat. They rode in silence out to Willow Glen, and she could tell that Zach was getting more and more nervous.

"You don't have to go in," he said. "You can wait out in the lobby, if you want. I never know what to expect when I see him. Sometimes he seems almost normal, other times he can hardly speak. There are times he gets mad and throws things. Sometimes he'll remember the past and think it's the present. You just never know."

"You said the doctors believe there's something pressing on parts of his brain."

He nodded. "When he fell down the stairs, small bits of bone chipped off the inside of his skull. If there was a way to remove them, his speech would improve, his motor skills as well, and more of his memory would probably return. He could live a fairly normal life."

Zach didn't say more, just wheeled into the parking lot and turned off the engine. Once they were inside the building, he led her down the hall toward his father's room. "Like I said, you don't have to go in."

"I was out here teaching once a week up for a couple of months. It gave me a fairly good idea what goes on in a place like this."

They kept on walking, stopping just out-side Fletcher Harcourt's room. One of the staff doctors passed along the corridor about the same time.

"Hello, Zach."

"Hi, Dr. Kenner. How's he doing?"

"You're here at a very good time. He's having one of his more lucid periods."

"Great." He turned to Elizabeth. "I'll let him know I'm here and that I've brought a friend."

She nodded.

"By the way," the doctor said, "Dr. Mar-vin wants to talk to you. He's planning to call your office on Monday morning."

"Dr. Marvin's the neurologist who's been handling Dad's case," he told Elizabeth, then returned his attention to Kenner. "Do you know why he's calling?"

"I'm not sure. Something about some new, experimental surgery. He was pretty excited about it. That's all I know."

"Thanks, Doc." Kenner waved and con-tinued down the corridor.

"I wonder what's up," Zach said.

"Maybe they've found a way to help your dad."

"I don't want to get my hopes up, but, man, that would sure be terrific."

Zach stepped quietly into the room, said

something to his father, then motioned for her to join him.

"Dad, this is a friend of mine, Elizabeth Conners."

Fletcher Harcourt nodded. "Pleased."

"Hello, Mr. Harcourt." She smiled, and he managed a partial smile in return. Even sitting in a wheelchair, he was an impressive man, tall, heavy through the chest and shoulders, with iron-gray hair and the same gold-flecked brown eyes as Zach. The lines of his face were strong, weathered by years of outdoor work, but the four years since his accident had taken their toll.

The muscles in his throat had begun to sag, as well as the skin along his jaw. And yet she could see that he had been handsome. At sixty-seven he was still an attractive man.

"Liz came to talk to you about the farm," Zach said gently. "She's interested in the history of the place. She thought you might be able to help."

He stirred in the wheelchair, seemed to sit up a little straighter. Though his speech was slow and a little bit slurred, his mind seemed to clear as they began to discuss the farm, Zach easing his father into memories of the past.

"Do you remember the old house, Dad?

The overseers' cottage you tore down so you could build a new one in its place?"

"I tore it . . . down?" He slowly shook his head. "I never . . . tore any of the workers' houses . . . down."

Zach flicked a glance her way. "I guess you were just thinking about it. Place must have been there since you were a kid."

"You're talking . . . about the old gray, wooden house . . . the one my dad built. Been there as long as I can . . . recall."

"That's the one. Do you remember any of the families who lived in the house? Way back, I mean."

Amazingly, Fletcher Harcourt launched into a lengthy discussion of one family after another, most of them non-Hispanic back in the early days of the farm, which might be important, Elizabeth thought, since the vision of the child Maria believed she had seen had blond hair and blue eyes.

Talking slowly, the old man continued his discussion of the past. Back forty or fifty years ago, men worked for the same employer for long periods of time so there were fewer names than she would have thought.

Using the small notepad she carried in her purse, Elizabeth wrote down each of the names he mentioned, then asked a little about each family. He had been too young in the forties to remember anything useful, but as they moved through the fifties and sixties, a few more memories surfaced.

"Let me see . . . there was a man . . . Martinez . . . Hector Martinez . . . that was his name. Had a wife. I think her name . . . was Consuela. Had to fire him. Got real . . . belligerent toward the end. Wife was . . . pregnant. Hated to . . . do it."

Elizabeth's ears perked up. "His wife was pregnant?"

He nodded. "Moved to Fresno . . . last I heard."

She flicked a glance at Zach, who was thinking the same thing she was. No one but Maria had been troubled by the ghost — at least that anyone knew of. If the Martinezes were still in Fresno, maybe they could find them. Maybe Consuela had also seen the ghost. Maybe there was some connection to the fact that the women were pregnant.

"Do you remember, Mr. Harcourt, if any of the other women who lived in the house were going to have a baby?"

Fletcher's heavy gray eyebrows drew together. "Long time back. Can't . . . recall. Seems like Espinoza's wife. Think she lost it . . . though."

A chill went down her spine. *They're going*

to kill your baby. They'll take your baby if you don't leave.

Elizabeth swallowed. Juan Espinoza was Mariano Nunez's friend. Elizabeth made a note to find out if the man remembered anything about Espinoza's wife having a miscarriage or if losing an unborn child had happened to any of the other women who had lived in the house.

Fletcher looked up at Zach and frowned. She could see they had tired him.

"You behavin' yerself, boy? Stayin' out of trouble? You aren't getting drunk? Aren't smokin' that damned weed again, are you?"

Zach just shook his head. "No, Dad."

Fletcher flicked a glance toward Elizabeth. "Looks like you got a nice girl there, for a change. You see you treat her proper." He pinned Zach with a glare. "And tell your mama I'll be over to see her in a day or so. Soon as I get outta this damned place."

Zach's voice faltered. "I'll tell her." He tipped his head toward the door and Elizabeth started in that direction. "We gotta go, Dad. You take care of yourself." Zach reached down and squeezed the old man's shoulder before he headed for the door.

Behind them Fletcher grumbled something Elizabeth couldn't hear.

"Connie!" he shouted. "Get your ass in

here, woman. And bring that good-for-nothing son of yours with you. I gotta bone to pick with him."

Zach said nothing as they headed down the hall, but his face looked grim. It was obvious seeing his father that way bothered him greatly.

Elizabeth reached over and took his hand. "Maybe Dr. Marvin will have good news."

"Maybe."

But she could see he didn't really believe it.

TWENTY

Zach's expression remained closed as Elizabeth waited for him to slide the key into the ignition and start the Jeep. It was roasting hot inside the car, the pavement surrounded by ripples of heat. She could feel perspiration collecting between her breasts and was glad he rolled down the windows as they drove out of the parking lot.

As she studied his profile, she noticed that the muscles were taut across the bones in his cheeks.

"Your father didn't mean to upset you," Elizabeth said gently. "He was remembering something that happened a long time ago."

"I know. It's just . . . it brings back memories, things I try not to think about too much."

"Prison, you mean?"

He nodded. "I talk to the boys about it. I try to make them understand that there are other choices they can make."

"Was it really bad, Zach?"

He cast her a look, then pulled the Jeep into the other lane to pass a produce truck plodding along the road. "Not as bad for me as it was for some of the other guys. I'd been hanging around with a pretty bad element for the past couple of years. By the time I went inside, I knew how to take care of myself. And living on the farm, I spoke Spanish like a native. I got in a fight with one of the Mexican gang members in my cell block. The guy was a real pit bull but I came out the winner. Another guy in the gang considered I did him a favor and from then on I never had a problem."

He kept his eyes fixed ahead, but his jaw was set as if he were seeing the past instead of the highway.

"What happened that night, Zach? The night of the accident?"

He sighed into the quiet inside the car. "To tell you the truth, I'm not really sure. I was so damned drunk and high I can't remember much of anything that happened that night."

"I know it was the summer I graduated from high school," she said. "The accident was all over the local news."

"I'd been hanging out at The Roadhouse

a lot that summer. They had a really rough crowd and I fit right in. That night I was drinking with a couple of my so-called buddies. I smoked some dope, got good and high, and started drinking straight shots of tequila. The last thing I remember was arguing with my brother."

"Carson was there that night?"

He nodded. "He and Jake Benson came out there to get me. My father sent them. Jake was his foreman back then. I remember Carson telling me to get my ass in the car, that he'd drive me home in my car and Jake could follow us in Carson's car. I wouldn't do it. I said I wasn't ready to go."

"Your brother left you there?"

"I wouldn't go with him. What other choice did he have?"

"So how did you wind up driving home when you were that drunk?"

"That's the worst part. I don't know. It wasn't something I usually did. Carson and Jake drove off and I passed out in the parking lot. That's pretty much the last thing I remember. I've got a hazy memory of getting into my car, but I'm not really sure it's real. When I woke up, I was slumped over the wheel, blood running down my forehead and three of my ribs broken. I'd hit another car head-on. The driver was dead and it looked like I was the guy who killed him."

Elizabeth frowned. "What do you mean, 'it looked like you were the guy'?"

Zach's glance slid away. "Like I said, I'm not really sure. I refused to plead guilty at the hearing. I have a vague memory of getting into the car, but every time I think of it, I see myself climbing into the passenger seat, not the driver's side."

Elizabeth's eyes widened. "You don't think you were the one driving the car that night?"

"I might be wrong. It's possible."

"But if you're right, you went to prison for something you didn't do."

His hands tightened on the wheel. "Whether it was my fault or not, that wreck changed my life. If I hadn't gone to prison — if I hadn't realized the bad stretch of road I was heading down — God only knows what would have happened to me. Of course, I didn't feel that way the first year I spent in jail."

Elizabeth studied his lean, handsome profile. "If you weren't driving that night, who do you think might have been behind the wheel?"

Zach just shook his head.

She stared at him hard. "You don't think it was Carson, do you?"

For several seconds he didn't reply. "If it was, I don't remember. And I'm sure as hell not going to accuse another man of something like that when I was so drunk and stoned I was half out of my head."

"What did Jake Benson say?"

"He said they never went back to The Roadhouse."

"And you believed him?"

"I didn't have much choice."

Elizabeth said nothing. It took a lot of courage to accept responsibly for a crime you might not have committed. More and more, she was coming to admire Zachary Harcourt. She didn't want to. The more she liked him, the more it was going to hurt when their affair was over.

Elizabeth watched the flat landscape passing by outside the car window, the fields of Harcourt Farms cotton stretching row after row toward the horizon. Farther along the highway, swatches of bloodred roses formed a scarlet slash in the distance.

As Zach drove back to her apartment, she couldn't help wondering if Carson Harcourt was really the kind of guy who would let an innocent man go to prison.

Elizabeth and Zach were just finishing a breakfast of French toast and bacon the next morning when someone started hammering on Elizabeth's front door.

Pulling the sash on her pale blue terry-cloth robe a little tighter, she padded into the living room to open the door. She was surprised to find Carson Harcourt standing on the other side of the threshold.

"Good morning. May I come in?" It was a polite request that didn't match the hard look in his eyes and he didn't wait for permission. His glance swung from her to Zach, who strode in from the kitchen barefoot, wearing only a pair of jeans and a shirt he didn't bother to button.

Zach stopped in front of him. "Well, here's a surprise. What's the occasion, Carson?"

"The *occasion* is that since you are no longer to be found at the local Holiday Inn — or in residence with your last paramour — I came to speak to you here."

Zach's features hardened. "You should learn to think of women as ladies, Carson, you'd have a lot better luck."

"What I think is my business, not yours — which is the reason I'm here."

"Go on."

"I want you and Elizabeth to stop snooping into Harcourt Farms business. Whatever it is you're trying to find out, it's none of your concern."

"There's no law against researching public records," Zach said calmly, hiding the same surprise Elizabeth was feeling that Carson had somehow found out.

"That's right, there isn't." Carson's mouth curved but it wasn't really a smile. "And there's no law against firing an incompetent employee. Stay out of farm business — both of you — or Santiago and his wife will find themselves out on the street."

Zach stiffened. He was every bit as tall as Carson, but leaner, his muscles harder, more defined. Still, Carson was a formidable opponent. While Zach had a past in San Pico, Carson had power and influence. Carson might be able to cause trouble for his brother, as well as the Santiagos. Elizabeth's stomach tightened at the thought.

"Mrs. Santiago is frightened," Zach tried to explain. "She's afraid for her unborn child and to tell you the truth, I think she has every reason to be afraid."

"What the hell are you talking about?"

Elizabeth stepped forward. "Things have been happening in the house . . . things that can't be explained. Zach and I stayed there most of one night and it was terrifying. I know it's hard to believe, but . . ."

"But what?"

"There's something there," Zach said. "We're trying to find out what it is. If you would cooperate —"

"Forget it. I'm not about to encourage any of this. There is nothing the least bit wrong with that house. In fact, the inspectors thought it was in very good condition — you told me that yourself. Now I'm telling you — stay out of Harcourt business. If you don't, it's going to be the Santiagos who suffer."

Turning on his heel, Carson stormed out the door, leaving them standing there staring after him. The door slammed so hard the sound reverberated through the whole apartment.

"Sometimes I actually do hate him," Zach said darkly.

"If he does fire Miguel, the family will really be in trouble. Jobs are hard to find, especially one that pays well and includes housing, and they've got a baby on the way. What are we going to do?"

Zach paced over to the window. "I promised Raul I'd do whatever it took to help him and his sister. I'm not going to break my word." He turned to face her. "We're going to do exactly what we've been doing. We'll just be more careful about it."

"How do you think he found out?"

"Carson's got a long reach in this town. We'll have to find a way to get around it. I'll get word to Mariano Nunez. I've got to go back to L.A. tonight, but I'll try to set up a meeting as soon as possible."

"You think he'll show up?"

He nodded. "There's a little cantina he and his friends hang out in at the edge of town. I can get him to meet me there. I'll find out if Espinoza's wife had a miscarriage and if he knows of any other women in the old house who lost their unborn children. In the meantime, I want you to go back to the newspaper and run that list of names."

They had a fairly complete list now. It would make the research a lot easier. "There's an alphabetical index of names found in each paper," she said. "I'll call my office in the morning and have Terry cancel my appointments. I want to go over to the paper first thing." She glanced up. "What if Carson finds out?"

A muscle tightened along Zach's jaw. "If he wants to play hardball, two can play the game. They've got a strong farm union in this town. Even Carson doesn't like going up against those guys. He tries to fire Miguel without cause, and I'll have the union all over him. Carson likes things to run nice and smooth. Problems with the union are the last thing he wants."

"I hope you're right." She walked to where he stood at the window. Outside, two little boys played kickball on the lawn in front of the apartment building. She wondered if she'd ever have a child of her own. What kind of a father would Zachary Harcourt make? She thought of him with the kids at Teen Vision and the amazing thought struck that he would probably make a good one.

She took a breath, her chest suddenly tight. Unfortunately, Zach wasn't the type of guy to make the kind of long-term commitment it took to raise a child.

She turned away from the window, walked over to the sofa. "I wish I could call Maria, make sure she's all right, but Miguel wouldn't like it, and I don't want to cause her any more trouble."

Zach moved behind her, slid his arms around her waist and pulled her back against him. "We're doing the best we can. Maybe something will turn up tomorrow."

Elizabeth hoped so.

She wasn't sure what kind of danger Maria and her baby might be facing, but whenever she thought of the night she had spent in the house, she believed, soul deep, that danger was real.

Elizabeth left her office early Monday morning, drove down Main, then turned onto Fifth Street, heading for the redbrick newspaper building three blocks away.

She was thinking about the list she carried in her purse when she glanced in the rearview mirror and noticed another car turning the corner, a dark green pickup she had seen several times before. The day she had gone to So Cal Edison, she had noticed the truck two cars behind her. She remembered because another car had turned sharply in front of the truck and there had nearly been a collision, would have been if the driver of the truck hadn't fiercely blown his horn.

The pickup was there again today, three cars back. She passed the entrance to the newspaper office and instead of turning in, kept on going. She pulled through the drive-thru at McDonald's, ordered coffee and an egg McMuffin, then turned back onto Main and turned into the parking lot behind her office.

As she parked the car in one of the empty spaces, she saw the truck drive slowly past. She didn't recognize the occupant, a large man in a short-sleeved, checkered shirt wearing a battered straw cowboy hat.

Was he following her?

Surely not. She was just getting paranoid.

Still, she didn't want Carson to know what she was up to. She didn't want to risk Miguel's job.

Walking into her office, she made a couple of phone calls then went through a few of her client files. When a half hour had passed, she walked out the front door and made her way the few blocks over to the newspaper office.

The pickup was nowhere in sight. She just hoped the lady at the front desk wasn't somehow in touch with Carson.

"I'd like to do a little more work with the microfiche," she said to the gray-haired woman.

"Help yourself." The woman continued to type away on her computer. "You know where everything is."

"Yes. Thank you." Elizabeth made her way back to the room with the file cabinets and microfiche readers. She had already checked the names on Mariano's list, but now she had Fletcher Harcourt's more extensive list, which went a lot farther back.

As she moved through the years, starting clear back in the late nineteen fifties, she saw a couple of names that matched the ones in her notepad. Same name, different people, as it turned out. After she had pulled the actual newspaper article, she'd discovered that none were occupants of the house.

Another name appeared. A guy named Vincent Malloy that Fletcher Harcourt had mentioned living there in the early sixties was arrested for drunk and disorderly conduct. In nineteen sixty-five, a man named Ricardo Lopez was killed in a car wreck on Highway 51.

Elizabeth sighed and returned to the master index for the next ten years, comparing the names on her list to the names on the microfiche. It was eleven o'clock straight up, the morning slipping away when another of the names in her notebook appeared.

Consuela Martinez. Below it, listed alphabetically, the name of her husband, Hector, also appeared. The index covered the decade of the nineteen seventies, which, according to Zach's father, didn't match the time frame the Martinezes had occupied the house. But the older man's memory was hardly reliable.

Elizabeth blinked as her eye ran down the sheet of microfiche and she saw the two names listed half a dozen times.

Returning again to the file cabinet, she

plucked out the roll of microfiche that covered the earliest newspaper article containing Hector and Consuela Martinez's names, September 15, 1972. The reel hummed and slowed as she searched for that date then found it. It took a while to locate the article, which was halfway down the page. Her heart nearly stopped when she saw it.

Fresno Couple Arrested For Murder.

Her pulse began to drum. She hurriedly scanned the article, then read it again. By the time she had finished, her heart was beating wildly, her mouth cotton dry.

According to the article, the Fresno couple that had resided for a brief time in San Pico, had been arrested for the kidnap and brutal slaying of a twelve-year-old girl. The child had been sexually abused before her death, and according to the article, both the man and his wife had been charged with the murder, which had taken place in their home.

Stunned, Elizabeth sat back in her chair. Though the crime had happened in Fresno, not in the house at Harcourt Farms, the violence of the act, the fact that the murder had happened in the couple's home and that the victim had been a child, simply could not be ignored.

For the next half hour, Elizabeth found, read and printed every article in the San Pico newspaper that mentioned the Martinez couple. Since at the time they were no longer residents of the area, the coverage was slim, with only sketchy information on the girl who had been killed and few actual details of the crime.

There was an item in the paper before the upcoming trial, then another when the couple was convicted of the murder. The most prominent article was headlined Hector Martinez Sentenced to Death. Because of the brutal nature of the crime, the jury had recommended the death penalty and the judge had agreed. Martinez's wife was sentenced to life in prison without parole.

The last date listed on the index card was August 25, 1984, nearly twelve years after the couple was first arrested. It was a report in the *Newspress* printed the day after Hector Martinez was executed in the gas chamber in San Quentin State Penitentiary.

Tired but excited, Elizabeth picked up the material she had printed and left the office. The murder in Fresno might be completely unrelated. That the couple had once lived in the house in San Pico might simply be coincidence.

But something told Elizabeth she had just

stumbled onto the clue that could help them find the answers to the frightening occurrences happening in the Santiago house.

TWENTY-ONE

Sitting behind his desk, Zach listened as Elizabeth recounted the disturbing information she had dredged up at the newspaper office that morning. What she told him sent chills down his spine.

"I think this is important, Zach."

"So do I. I've got to finish out the day, but I'll be up there late tonight."

"Tonight? You're taking time off from work?"

"I'd pretty much already decided. I spoke to my partner, Jon Noble, this morning. He said he'd cover for me during the week. Then Dr. Marvin called. He wants to talk to me and Carson about a new surgical procedure. He's going to be up in San Pico on Wednesday to take another look at my dad. He wants to see both of us when he gets there."

"That's great, Zach. Maybe this is the chance you've been waiting for."

"I hope so. In the meantime, I need to speak to Mariano again. I can't forget the frightening things that happened to us that night in the house and I can't help thinking about Maria. We've got to find out what's going on. If Maria and her baby really are in danger, time is running out for them."

"She's eight months pregnant. This is a crucial time for her."

"Did any of the articles you read give a description of the girl?"

"No, they just gave her name, Holly Ives. But she was twelve, not eight or nine."

"We still need to know more about her. Tomorrow we'll drive up to Fresno, see what else we can find out."

"I'll clear my calendar."

Zach hung up the phone, wondering if the murdered girl might have had blond hair and blue eyes. From what he'd read, if seemed a stretch to think the apparition Maria had described was the girl murdered in Fresno, since her death took place more than a hundred miles away, but this was the first lead they'd had and they needed to look at any possible connection.

Zach checked his wristwatch. The hour was slipping toward closing. He had a couple more things to do before he'd be finished for the day, then he needed to go by his apartment to pack some clothes. He wasn't sure how long he was going to be in San Pico, but he'd made up his mind he wasn't going to leave until he had kept his word to Raul and his sister.

Until he somehow managed to solve the riddle of the terrifying happenings in the house.

It was just before five o'clock, nearly time for the day to end. Elizabeth walked her last client to the door then returned to her office to retrieve her purse and a couple of files she wanted to take home with her that night.

"I'll see you on Wednesday," she said to Terry, who was shutting down the computer on the receptionist's desk, getting ready to leave. As Elizabeth had promised, she had cleared her schedule for Tuesday, saying only that she was working on a case that involved some research in Fresno.

Terry stuck a pencil into her short, frosted-blond hair. It was moussed into a hi-tech style that looked surprisingly good on Terry. She was tall and athletically built, smart and a hard worker, an asset to their small office staff.

"Anything special you need me to do, just call," Terry said.

"I will. And I'll have my cell phone with me. Don't hesitate to call if a problem comes up."

Dr. James was already gone for the day. A couple of times, he had asked about Maria and her "ghost," but Elizabeth had merely said she had been trying to help the girl straighten things out. There was no way Michael was going to believe Maria Santiago had actually seen a ghost.

The truth was, Elizabeth had a hard time believing it herself.

She was walking over to lock the front door when the knob turned and a familiar, red-haired woman stepped into the waiting room.

"I was hoping I'd catch you before you left for the night," Gwen Petersen said with a smile.

"Your timing's perfect." Elizabeth returned her friend's smile. "I was just getting ready to leave." She flicked a glance at Terry. "I'll lock up. Have a good night and I'll see you on Wednesday."

Terry waved and headed out the back door.

"I'm glad you stopped by," Elizabeth said to Gwen. "I've been thinking about you all week. I've been meaning to phone. I just got so busy."

"Seems like everybody's been a little crazy lately. That's why I decided to see if I could catch you."

"How about a Diet Coke or something? There are usually some sodas in the fridge."

"Sounds great. It's really hot out there." Gwen followed Elizabeth into the little kitchen/lounge at the back of the office and settled herself at the tiny wooden table. Elizabeth opened the door of the fridge and pulled out a soda. She divided the contents, pouring the liquid into a couple of glasses, and then joined her friend at the table.

Gwen took a sip of her drink. "So you've been working hard lately?"

"I've been putting in some pretty long hours. Like I said, I meant to call but the time just slipped away."

"That happens sometimes." Gwen wasn't much for small talk. And looking at her now, there was something in her face that made Elizabeth wary.

"You don't usually come by the office. Is there something in particular on your mind?"

Gwen set her glass down on the table. "Actually there is." She ran a finger over the moisture on the outside of the glass, making abstract designs in the condensation. "Jim and I were having dinner out at The

Ranch House. On my way to the ladies' room, I ran into Lisa Doyle."

Elizabeth's lips curved in a smile that wasn't. "I'm sure she sends her best."

"Actually, I think she'd like to cut out your heart with a dull-edged knife."

"She already did that. Tell her she'll have to think of something else."

Gwen didn't smile. "Lisa says you're sleeping with Zachary Harcourt."

Elizabeth's hand shook as she reached for her glass, picked it up, and took a long drink of diet soda. "I don't think who I'm sleeping with is any of Lisa's business."

"It wouldn't be my business either if you weren't my best friend."

It was true. They rarely kept secrets from each other and this secret was a ten on the Richter scale. "Zach and I are working on a case together."

"Really. What kind of case?"

"Zach is heavily involved in Teen Vision. Most people don't know it, but he's actually the person who founded the place."

A sleek red eyebrow arched up. "I thought it was Carson's project."

"Apparently attaching Carson's name makes it easier for them to raise money. At any rate, Zach's helping one of the kids in the program. I'm trying to help the boy's sister. We thought working together might get better results."

"So it's just business. You aren't really involved with him."

Elizabeth glanced away. It was impossible to lie to Gwen. "We're seeing each other. Just on weekends, or whenever he's in town."

Gwen's eyes widened. "Oh, my God, then it's true. You're sleeping with Zachary Harcourt!"

Elizabeth shrugged, trying to appear nonchalant when that wasn't the least how she felt. "We're both adults. We can do whatever we want."

"Have you lost your mind?"

Elizabeth swallowed. The astonished look on Gwen's face reminded her that she had once felt exactly the same. Memories rushed back of the man Zach had been when she was in high school — wild, reckless, uncaring. Women meant nothing to him. He liked them easy and only for a night or two. He lived up to his high school nickname in a very predatory way.

"I mean, I can understand the attraction," Gwen went on, "any woman could — but that just makes getting involved with him even worse."

"It's not as bad as all that," Elizabeth

defended, trying to shake off the memories, trying to convince herself. "It's purely a physical thing. Neither of us is looking for a long-term relationship."

Gwen leaned toward her across the table. "Who are trying to kid, Liz? Zach or yourself? This is your best friend you're talking to. I've known you for years and we both know you aren't the kind of woman who goes in for casual sex."

Elizabeth glanced away. She didn't want to have this conversation. She didn't want to hear her own thoughts put into words. "For the most part, no, but this is different. It's been a long time since I've been sexually attracted to a man — and never the way I'm attracted to Zach. I wanted to know what it felt like — just this once. There's nothing wrong with that."

"Not there isn't. But in this case, there are other things to consider."

"Like what?"

"Like the fact that Zach's a loner and always will be. He was when we were kids and he still is. Lisa can handle a guy like that. Sex means nothing to her. You aren't that way."

No, she was nothing like Lisa. She had said those same words to Zach, but he had convinced her it didn't matter.

"I really like him, Gwen. He's nothing like he was back then. He cares about those boys at Teen Vision. When I'm with him, I feel like he cares about me."

"Maybe he does," Gwen said gently. "Maybe he cares a great deal. But in the end, he'll leave. That's the way he's always been, the way he always will be."

Elizabeth glanced away, her throat suddenly tight. "I know you're right. It could never work between us. But I'm not ready to give him up. Not yet. I wish I could, but I can't."

Gwen reached over and squeezed her hand. "The guy's a hunk, no question. Just don't let him in too deep. Don't let him break your heart."

Elizabeth made no reply. She had a very bad feeling it was already too late.

On his way into San Pico, Zach stopped by the little cantina, La Fiesta, at the edge of town on the off-chance Mariano Nunez might be there with some of his friends. For once luck was with him. The old man was on his way out as Zach walked in.

"Señor Harcourt," the overseer said with a friendly smile. "I did not expect to see you again so soon."

"I stopped on the chance you might be

here. I've got a couple more questions I was hoping you might answer. How 'bout I buy you a beer?"

The old man's smile widened and Zach noticed one of his bottom teeth was missing. "*Gracias, señor.* It is still hot outside."

Zach ordered a couple of Dos Equis and they sat down at one of the battered wooden tables at the back of the bar. The smell of green peppers and roasting meat drifted out from the kitchen at the back of the room.

"I thought maybe you could tell me a little more about the Espinoza family."

While Zach sipped his beer, Mariano talked easily about his friends, answering Zach's questions. Speaking partly in Spanish, he told Zach that Juan's wife had borne him a number of children over the years. Six, as he recalled, but none had arrived after the couple had moved into the old gray house.

"My father mentioned something about Señora Espinoza losing a child," Zach said, getting to the subject he had come to discuss. "Do you remember anything about that?"

Mariano frowned, the lines in his weathered face etching more deeply into his nut-brown skin. "*Sí,* I remember. She was carrying their seventh child when Juan got one of the overseer's jobs and moved his family into the house."

"What happened?"

Mariano shook his head, moving the long gray hair around his ears. "She got sick or something. She lost the child and they moved away a few months later. I was sorry to see them go."

"Do you recall what year it happened?"

"The family moved away in the fall of nineteen seventy-two. I remember because I had to help find a replacement for Juan. It was not an easy thing to do."

Zach took a swig of his beer and set the icy bottle back down on the table. He couldn't help wondering if Señora Espinoza had seen the ghost Maria claimed to have seen, if perhaps she had received the same dire warning and paid it no heed.

He shoved back his chair and came to his feet. "Thank you, Mariano. You've been a big help."

The old man grinned. "It is good to talk of old times."

Zach just nodded. Maybe it was good for Mariano, but the information he'd just received made Zach's insides churn.

Señora Espinoza had birthed six healthy children before she moved into the old gray house. She had lost the seventh baby and shortly after that, the family had moved away.

Perhaps it was only coincidence.

The knot in Zach's stomach told him it wasn't.

The drive through the San Joaquin Valley took a little over three hours. Fresno was a valley town much like the other small towns around it, flat and dusty, sprawling ever outward. Except that the city itself was bigger, with multistoried buildings downtown and several freeways spewing traffic from one end to the other, the surrounding farmland more likely planted with vineyards and orchards than cotton.

Leaning back in the passenger seat, Elizabeth watched the passing landscape with little thought to her surroundings. Her mind was on Zach and the conversation she'd had with Gwen at the office yesterday after work.

Though she had tried to ignore Gwen's warning and had succeeded somewhat when Zach had arrived last night, in the bright light of morning, her friend's ominous words sat in the back of her mind like a bitter lump of poison. As she looked over at Zach's handsome face, she couldn't help thinking of the Lone Wolf he had been and always would be.

She'd been a fool to get involved with him and she knew it, and the urge to run grew stronger by the moment. Or at least the desire to reconstruct the wall she had once put between them.

She would do it, she told herself, but not today. Today she needed Zach's help. She had a frightened young woman to protect and a murder to unravel. Perhaps today they would find the answer to the mystery of the house.

She shifted in her seat as the town of Fresno approached through the smaze, a local combination of smoke and haze hanging over the valley. Zach pulled the Jeep off the 99 Freeway and headed through town to E Street and the building that housed the *Fresno Bee.*

As always, it was hot, the late August heat permeating the car the instant the doors swung open in the parking lot. Neither of them spoke as they made their way inside the structure, up to the receptionist's desk.

"May I help you?" asked an older, heavy-set woman with at least two chins and a weary expression that said she was bored with the job she'd been doing for too many years.

"We need to look at your old newspaper files," Elizabeth told her, following the same approach she had used in San Pico.

The woman nodded, jiggling her chins. "I'll have someone come out and show you where to find the records."

The receptionist was helpful and the rest of the staff friendly. They spent the balance of the morning poring over old newspaper records, reading and printing every article they could find on Hector and Consuela Martinez, starting with the day the kidnapping of Holly Ives had been reported, the couple's arrest, the trial, and the twelve years that followed, until Hector's execution in 1984. One last small notice reported Consuela's death from cancer in 1995 during a life-sentence term in the women's prison in Chowchilla.

"Take a look at this." Elizabeth handed Zach a copy of the article she had just printed. "This was published the day after Holly was reported missing. It gives a detailed description of what she looked like."

Zach took the article and skimmed the words. "It says she had brown hair and hazel eyes."

Elizabeth nodded. "Which means she can't be the ghost Maria claims to have seen."

"Apparently not. To tell you the truth, I

didn't really think she would be. The age wasn't right and it happened too far away."

"I couldn't help hoping. I still think there's a connection."

"So do I." Zach skimmed a couple more articles, reading them in chronological order. "Here, look at this." He handed her a printout of the article he'd been reading, and a shudder rippled through her.

Body of Victim Found Buried in Basement. Her chest squeezed painfully. "Oh, my God, Zach. This is just so awful."

"Yeah, and the people who did it lived in the old gray house."

"Which sat on the same spot where the new house is built."

"No wonder the place is so scary."

She scanned another article. It went over the story again, listing the brutal details of the murder. She swallowed past the lump in her throat. "They tortured her, Zach. They tortured that poor young girl."

Zach took the printed page from her shaking hand. According to the article, Holly Ives had been brutally beaten, then raped and sodomized with various household items before being murdered. She had been strangled, then buried in a shallow grave in the basement of the house.

Elizabeth closed her eyes and drew in a

steadying breath. "This was easier when I didn't know all the awful details."

"There wasn't as much written about it in the *Newspress,* since the Martinezes were no longer living in San Pico."

Elizabeth looked down at the stack of printed pages. "I can't stand this, Zach. Even if Hector was the one who killed Holly, how could a woman sit by and watch her husband do something like that? How could she allow it to happen?"

Zach just shook his head, his eyes dark and hard. "I don't know." He set the page he was reading down on the top of the stack. "It looks like Holly Ives's death is unrelated to what's going on in the house."

"Not directly, at least."

"But I keep thinking that if Hector and Consuela Martinez kidnapped and murdered a child in Fresno, maybe they did the same thing a couple of years earlier — when they were living in the house at Harcourt Farms."

Elizabeth's stomach knotted. The notion had been nagging her, too. It made sense. Too much sense. "That's what I've been thinking."

"And maybe the reason no one can remember a child dying in the house is because no one knew."

She said nothing, the terrible notion squeezing painfully inside her. "All right, if that's what both of us are thinking, where do we go from here?"

"We'll need to speak to the Fresno PD, see if there's anyone still working in the department who might remember the case. If there is, maybe he can tell us something that isn't in the papers."

Elizabeth nodded, dreading the idea of hearing even more gruesome details of the young girl's murder. Then she thought of Maria and her baby and remembered the terrifying night she had spent in the house.

"Let's go," she said and started for the door.

Twenty-Two

"One of the worst cases I've ever seen." Detective Frank Arnold shook his head, his leonine mane of gray hair teasing the collar of his slightly frayed white shirt. "Happened over thirty years ago, but I remember it as clear as if it had been yesterday."

Arnold was in his early sixties, but not yet retired, still married to the job, still working long hours, his memory apparently as sharp as it was back then.

"We've read everything we could find in the newspapers," Elizabeth told him. "Can you tell us anything more about the case?"

"We're particularly interested in finding out if the Martinezes were suspects in any other homicides," Zach added.

The detective's head came up. "Funny you should mention that. I always had my suspicions there were, but neither of them ever confessed to any other murders and we were never able to connect them to any other missing persons."

"But you think it's possible," Zach pressed.

"Those two were as bad as they come. What they did to that girl —" He broke off, shaking his head. "The papers didn't print half the details. We didn't want the facts made public and we were trying to shield the parents as best we could."

"It said in the newspaper she was kidnapped from the mall," Elizabeth said.

"That's right. We never found out the exact details. Holly went shopping with a couple of her girlfriends. They got separated . . . you know how kids are. Her friends never saw her again."

"What did the Martinezes say?" Zach asked.

"They admitted to the murder but never gave up any of the details. We tried to play them against each other, but neither one of them ever said much. We figure Holly might have decided to go home early. Maybe the wife offered her a ride home or something. Consuela was five months pregnant at the time. She probably looked pretty harmless."

Elizabeth's eyes widened. "Consuela Martinez was pregnant when she murdered that girl?"

"That's right. Sick, isn't it? She never

made it to term, lost the kid while she was in jail. That was the hand of God at work if I ever saw it."

Elizabeth felt the blood leach out of her face. "She was pregnant, Zach."

"Yeah." He fixed his dark eyes on the detective. "We don't have any proof yet, but there's a chance the Martinezes may have murdered another girl when they were living in San Pico."

"Oh, yeah? You got a name?"

"Not yet. We've got a general description, that's about all." He gave the detective the description of the child Maria had seen, the blond hair and blue eyes, around eight or nine years old, the party dress she had been wearing. The detective made notes on his pad.

"How'd you come across this information?"

Zach took a deep breath. "So far, like I said, it's just speculation."

"Based on . . . ?"

Zach cast Elizabeth a desperate glance.

"We'd rather not say quite yet," she told the detective, "not until we have more to go on. But we'd really appreciate it if you'd take a look at your missing persons file from 1967 to 1971. Those are the years the Martinez couple lived in San Pico. If you run

370

across a child who fits the description Zach gave you, we'd really like to know."

"I'll take a look. Doesn't ring any bells, though. I'll let you know if I run across anything in those files."

Zach extended his hand. "Thanks, Detective. We appreciate your time."

They left the Fresno police department, Elizabeth exhausted and depressed.

"That was even more awful than I thought it would be," she said as Zach drove out of town.

"Yeah." He looked as tired and tense as she was feeling.

"We've got to tell Maria," she said.

"If we do, she's going to be even more frightened than she is already."

She sighed. "Maybe we should tell Miguel. If he knows a pair of brutal murderers lived in his house, maybe he'll move out."

"They didn't live in his house. They lived in another house that was in the same place, and it was over thirty years ago. Even if we tell him about the murder, I don't think it will convince him. He needs his job too badly."

"Maybe we should talk to your brother again."

He flicked her a disbelieving glance. "We need something more solid, something that will force Miguel to believe his wife's story and let her move out of the house. Better yet, something that will convince my brother to let them move."

"We need to find out if the Martinezes murdered another child while they were living in the old gray house."

"Yeah. One with blond hair and blue eyes."

"Then we've got to find out if a child who fits that description went missing somewhere around San Pico sometime between 1967 and 1971."

Zach turned to look at her. "You know this could all just be some weird coincidence."

"It could be. I don't think it is."

"Neither do I." Zach raked a hand through his hair. "I know a guy . . . a private investigator named Murphy. I'll give him a call as soon as we get back, put him to work on this and see what he can find out. In the meantime, we'll talk to the local police. Maybe they can help."

"Maybe we'll get lucky. In the meantime, don't forget tomorrow you've got an appointment with Dr. Marvin."

"I haven't forgotten. I'm supposed to be at Willow Glen at one o'clock."

She smiled for the first time that afternoon. "I'll be holding good thoughts for you."

"I was . . . um . . . kind of hoping you might go with me."

Surprised, she glanced at his profile, taking in his dark skin and lean, handsome features as he studied the road. "I could take a late lunch. It wouldn't be a problem."

Some of Zach's tension seemed to ease. "Thanks."

Elizabeth didn't say more. She thought of the things Gwen had said, but she couldn't seem to make them fit with the man who sat beside her, a man who seemed to need her, as Zach had just then.

She couldn't keep her hopes from rising. Maybe Gwen was wrong. Maybe Zach wasn't the loner he used to be.

Elizabeth knew it was dangerous thinking.

Zach spent the morning chasing down Ian Murphy, putting him to work on finding a missing girl who met the description of Maria's ghost, then he went over to the San Pico police department.

He was given the names of a couple of longtimers who had been in the department since the late nineteen sixties. They remembered the old gray house. Unfortunately, they also remembered Zachary Harcourt —

or at least the man he'd once been.

"Officer Collins?" Zach offered his hand to a tall man with a slight paunch and Collins reluctantly shook it. "Thanks for taking time to see me."

"No problem." He eyed Zach up and down, assessing the beige slacks, knit shirt and Italian loafers. "I guess you gave up black leather."

Zach forced himself to smile. "Yeah. Did that some time back."

"You know, we met before," Collins said. "Maybe you remember. I was there the night you were busted for negligent homicide."

Zach kept the smile fixed on his face, though it took a Herculean effort. "Actually, I don't remember a whole lot about that night. What little I do recall, I'm trying to forget."

The other man moved closer, gray-haired and iron-jawed, a sergeant named Drury, according to his badge. "Heard you were a big-time lawyer now. Fancy firm in L.A. somewhere."

"I'm a lawyer in Westwood. Whether I'm big-time depends on your definition."

"So what do you want to know?" the sergeant asked.

"I need to talk to you about a Hispanic

couple who used to live in a house on my father's farm. You might remember them — Hector and Consuela Martinez? They murdered a girl up in Fresno. Hector Martinez got the death penalty for it."

Both men seemed to stand a little straighter. "I remember that case," Officer Collins said. "Bad one. Most of us followed it pretty close, seein' as the two of 'em lived here in town a couple of years before it happened."

"That's why I'm here. I'm trying to find out if it's possible they might have committed another murder here in San Pico before the one in Fresno. I was hoping you might be able to take a look at the missing persons files, see if there were any young girls who came up missing in this area between 1967 and 1971."

"I can tell you right now there aren't any," Sgt. Drury said. "We checked our files real good when those two were arrested, checked this whole end of the San Joaquin Valley. Nothing turned up. No missing girls, no unsolved murders, nothing that might point to the Martinezes."

"How about the sheriff's office? The house they lived in was on the farm, which is in the county."

"The departments work together on stuff

like this. We traded information, came up with a big fat zero."

"I imagine it was harder to check the records back then."

"A whole lot harder," Collins agreed. "No computers back then, but we did our best."

"I don't think we missed anything," the sergeant said. "At least not around here."

"But they could have snatched someone in L.A."

"Like Officer Collins said, we didn't have the fancy computers we've got today. We mostly stuck with the San Joaquin Valley. So it's possible, I suppose. To tell you the truth, bad as those two were, I was surprised no other victims turned up."

"Well, thanks," Zach said, "I appreciate your help."

"No problem." Drury mustered a smile but it didn't reach his eyes, and the curve of his lips looked insincere.

Zach walked away, taking a deep breath as he headed down the hall, damned glad to be finished and out of there. He had more than enough bad memories of the place. He would be happy to get outside, even if it was over a hundred degrees.

Making his way to the front of the building, he stepped out into the heat. It was just after noon. He was meeting Elizabeth at

Willow Glen at one. He clung to that thought as he strode down the cement steps and crossed to where his Jeep sat waiting in the parking lot.

Elizabeth sat in the lobby of the Willow Glen Retirement Home. Expecting Zach to walk in, she stood up from the overstuffed sofa only to realize the man shoving through the front door was blond, not dark, his features handsome, but not the sort to make her heart thrum the way Zach's did.

"Elizabeth." Carson Harcourt came to a stop in front of her. "I guess I'm supposed to say it's good to see you. If circumstances were different, I'm sure it would be. I gather you're waiting for Zach."

"I'm here because Zach asked me to come."

Carson frowned, a little surprised it seemed. "I'm sure he'll be here any minute. We're both eager to hear what Dr. Marvin has to say."

"I hope the doctor's bringing good news."

Carson smiled. "We all do."

Zach walked in few minutes later. His jaw tightened when he saw her talking to his brother. Elizabeth gave him a reassuring smile and walked over to greet him. "I got here a few minutes early. So did Carson.

He's anxious to hear what the doctor has to say."

Zach flashed him a look. "Is Marvin here?"

Carson walked over to the receptionist station and the woman directed them into a conference room in the C wing, where the doctor would meet them as soon as he finished a brief visit with their father.

The room was empty, but as nicely decorated as the rest of Willow Glen, in shades of dark green and burgundy. They sat down at a long walnut conference table, Zach next to Elizabeth, Carson on the opposite side of the table.

Zach reached over and squeezed Elizabeth's hand. "Thanks for coming."

"I'm glad you asked me."

He smiled and something melted a little inside her. Where was the wall she had vowed to resurrect? Instead of pushing Zach away, she was letting him get even closer. She couldn't afford to let that happen but she couldn't seem to find a way to stop it.

She glanced his way, saw him stand up as the door swung open and the doctor walked in. Carson rose, as well. Two brothers. One dark, one fair. So completely different.

"Carson. Zachary. It's good to see you." Dr. Marvin was perhaps mid-forties, a thin man with sparse brown hair and wearing a suit instead of the white coat she had expected.

"This is Elizabeth Conners," Zach said, making the brief introduction. "She's a friend."

Dr. Marvin's smile looked sincere. "It's nice to meet you, Elizabeth."

The doctor sat down in the chair at the head of the table and both of the brothers sat back down. "I'm glad you all could come. The news I have to share is extremely exciting. It involves an incredible new surgical technique that has recently been brought to my attention."

"Exactly what sort of surgery are you talking about?" Carson asked.

"It's an extremely delicate laser technique for surgery in the brain. At this point, it's been successfully performed enough times that I believe it may be viable as a means of helping your father. Currently it's being performed by a handful of doctors, two of which I can personally recommend."

"Go on," Carson said, leaning back in his chair.

"The procedure uses a new type of biomedical, microlaser technology. The technique utilizes optical energy called photonics. It's an extremely accurate, far less invasive method that allows precise alterations of patient tissue inside the brain. This new technology allows the surgeon to remove tiny bits of foreign matter that have been embedded in the brain through some kind of trauma."

"Like a fall down the stairs," Zach said.

"Exactly. In your father's case, the technique would be used to remove the bits of bone currently lodged in the cerebrum and cerebellum. These tiny skull fragments are pressing on vital areas, causing much of his memory loss, as well as hampering his motor functions. Once the bone is removed and the pressure is released, there is a very good chance that in time he'll return almost completely to normal."

Zach's hand caught hers again. She saw that he was smiling. "That sounds terrific, Dr. Marvin."

"What's the down side?" Carson asked.

"The odds are about eighty percent that the surgery will be completely successful. There is a ten percent chance there will be no measurable improvement or perhaps it will be extremely minimal."

"And the other ten percent?"

"Any surgery is dangerous. In this case, there is a ten percent chance the surgery could be fatal."

Carson stood up from the table. "Ten percent is too much. There's no way I'm taking that kind of risk with my father's life."

Zach stood up, too. "What are you talking about? There's an eighty percent chance Dad could have his life back and only a ten percent chance he might die. There's no question the operation should be performed."

"He's doing all right the way he is. He's here at Willow Glen and he's happy. Any risk of dying is too great, as far as I'm concerned."

"He's existing here, Carson! That's all he's doing. Dad would want to do this and you know it!"

Carson's jaw tightened. "I'm his conservator. The decision is mine and I'm not willing to risk his life."

A flush rose under the bones in Zach's cheeks. "This is the chance we've been waiting for ever since the accident. There's no way I'm going to let you deny him the right to live a normal life again."

Dr. Marvin stood up from his chair at the end of the table. "Gentlemen, please. It looks as if you're going to need some time to discuss this. I've got a patient I need to see. I'll be back in Los Angeles in the morning. Call me if you have any questions I can answer." The doctor walked out of the conference room and the door swished closed behind him.

Carson stared at Zach, both men still on their feet. "Like I said, the decision is mine and I won't be responsible for causing my father's death."

Zach's jaw clenched. "This is bullshit, Carson. And if you think I'm going to sit by and do nothing, you're dead wrong. I realize you've gotten used to your position as head of Harcourt Farms. I've never contested your appointment as conservator and I've never interfered in any way in how you ran the farm, but this is Dad's life we're talking about. Dad deserves this chance and I'm going to see he gets it."

Carson planted his hands on the table and leaned toward Zach. "You do this and you'll wind up killing him." Carson gave Zach the coldest smile Elizabeth had ever seen. "Then again, maybe that's exactly what you want. With Dad out of the way, you'd inherit half of Harcourt Farms. You'd be able to sell your interest for a very sizeable fortune. According to the latest appraisal, the land and business are worth more than thirty-five million dollars. Maybe you're willing to kill in order to get your share."

Carson's expression went from cold to utterly chilling. "After all, you've done it before."

Zach started around the table toward his brother, his hand clenched into a fist. Elizabeth shot up from her chair and caught his arm.

"Let it go, Zach. Don't play his game. That's exactly what he wants you to do." She could feel Zach trembling, knew how hard he was fighting for control.

He took a deep breath and released it slowly. "This isn't over, Carson. Not by a long shot." Sliding an arm around her waist, he urged Elizabeth toward the door of the conference room, jerked it open, and guided her out into the hall.

As the door swished closed, she heard Carson curse.

"God, I wanted to hit him. If you hadn't been there . . ." Zach shook his head. They were sitting in the living room of her apartment, two chilled glasses of white wine on the coffee table in front of them. Though Zach rarely drank, the occasion seemed to call for a little soothing of nerves.

"You're an attorney," Elizabeth said. "You'll find a way to help your father get the operation."

"You bet I will. I'm calling my partner.

Carson will be served with papers by the end of the week. I'll sue for a change of conservator, either myself or someone appointed by the court who will approve the surgery."

"It won't be easy. Carson's a powerful man."

"So was my father. He's still got lots of friends in San Pico. Men in high places. If I'm lucky, some of them will feel the same way I do about Dad having this surgery. Maybe together we can pull this off."

But not everyone would agree with him, she knew. And Elizabeth was sure Carson would make Zach out to be the bad guy, the way he always had. A man willing to kill his own father to gain half interest in the multimillion dollar farming operation he had no control over now. She prayed Carson wouldn't be able to convince the town that Zach was the black sheep he had been as a youth. She hoped they wouldn't believe that a man like Zach, a man convicted of killing a man before, would do it again.

But Carson was a fierce opponent. Elizabeth worried that he might just succeed.

TWENTY-THREE

Elizabeth went back to the office after the meeting while Zach made phone calls from her apartment, including one to his partner, Jon Noble, in Westwood.

"I've got to tell him what's going on," he said, "get the wheels turning to put the lawsuit into motion." Zach was determined his father would get the surgery that could give him back his life.

By seven o'clock she was back in her apartment, work over for the day, at least for her. Though the sun still beat down relentlessly outside the window, Zach was full of restless energy, worried about his father, worried about Maria and her baby.

"Let's get out of here for a while," he suggested, "go get something to eat."

Elizabeth didn't really want to go out in the heat again but she could tell Zach needed a break. They decided on The Ranch House. If Gwen Petersen knew Elizabeth was seeing Zach, then Lisa Doyle had probably made sure the rest of the town knew, as well.

Still, Elizabeth didn't expect to run into the woman as they walked into the restaurant. Lisa was dressed in a tight-fitting red sundress so short it barely covered her very shapely behind, cut so low her bosom nearly exploded out the top.

With a smile fixed on her face, Lisa sauntered up to Zach in that sexy way of hers that made men go a little crazy. She flipped a strand of her long sun-streaked blond hair over one bare shoulder.

"Well, if it isn't the lovebirds. I heard you two were an item."

"News in San Pico always travels fast," Zach said.

Lisa looked over at Elizabeth and gave her that same phony smile. "Interesting combination, you and Zach. But somehow I never thought of you as the bad-boy type."

"I was the married type until you came along. I thought I'd try something different for a change."

Lisa laughed, a throaty, provocative sound. She ran a long, manicured nail along Zach's cheek where a five-o'clock shadow was beginning to darken his jaw. "When you get bored, honey, give me a call. You know how to find me."

Zach caught her hand and eased it away. "Don't count on it, Lisa."

She just laughed, as if she knew he'd be back. As if, after all, she was a far better lover than Elizabeth ever would be and it was only a matter of time.

All of Gwen's warnings rushed back into her head. Elizabeth suddenly felt sick to her stomach.

"Have a good time," Lisa said, waving at Zach over her shoulder, rejoining the man she had come with.

Elizabeth glanced over at Zach, whose jaw still looked hard. "I'm sorry. All of a sudden, I'm not feeling very well. Probably the heat, but I'm just not hungry anymore."

Zach nodded. Resting a hand on her waist, he ushered her back out the door. They didn't speak on the ride back to her apartment. Zach said nothing as she walked into the kitchen and poured herself another glass of wine.

She took a long, calming sip, but it did nothing to soothe her nerves. Her heart was still pumping, her stomach tied in knots.

Zach came up behind her, settled his hands on her shoulders and gently turned her to face him. "I'm sorry that happened. I shouldn't have taken you there. I know The

Ranch House is one of Lisa's favorite hang-outs."

"It doesn't matter. It would have happened sooner or later." She stepped away from him, out from under his touch. She wished she were anywhere but standing in her apartment just a few feet away from Zach.

"What it is, Liz? I know something's wrong."

"I told you, it's probably just the heat."

"That's bullshit. You're upset about running into Lisa, but it isn't just that. You've been acting strange since I got here last night. I could feel the ice field the minute I walked through the door."

Elizabeth shook her head, moving the shoulder-length dark auburn hair around her face. Something was definitely wrong and apparently Zach had noticed. She thought that he was a man who rarely missed much.

She took a sip of wine, hoping it would help clear her head. "I don't . . . I don't know, Zach. Things just seem to be spiraling out of control. Too much is happening. I can't handle everything that's going on and try to deal with my personal life as well."

A muscle jumped in his cheek. "Life happens. We have to deal with it. Eventually, all of this will pass and things will return to normal."

She dragged a shaky hand through her hair, shoving it back from her face. "I don't know what normal is anymore. Especially not where you're concerned." She looked up at him, willing him to understand. "I never should have gotten involved with you, Zach. I can't handle this kind of relationship. It's just not my style."

His eyes seemed to darken. "What kind of relationship do we have, Liz? Tell me, because I really don't know."

"Purely physical. That's what we agreed on, isn't it?"

"Is it?"

"It has to be. You know it and so do I."

"So what are you trying to say? You think we should stop seeing each other?"

"I don't . . . know. We're working together. We've made promises to Maria and Raul. And I desperately need your help."

Zach sighed. "Look, Liz, whatever happens between us, I'm not going to abandon you — or Maria and her brother. Maybe we shouldn't have gotten involved, but we did. Shit happens."

He paced over to the window, looked out for a moment, then turned and walked back. "I need to get back to L.A. Now that this problem with my father has come up, there are things I need to do. I was planning to leave in the morning, but maybe it would be better if I left tonight. That would give us both a chance to think."

She nodded, but her throat felt tight.

"I'll be in touch with Ian Murphy, the investigator I hired. I'll call you if I hear from him or if anything new comes up."

"When . . . will you be back?" she couldn't help asking, her insides trembling as she looked up at him. God, she was hurting already and he hadn't even left yet.

Zach reached out and gently touched her cheek. "I need time, too, Liz. If you want to know the truth, I'm just as confused as you are. I've never let myself get in this deep. I've never wanted to. Maybe if we take a little time, things will be clearer for both of us."

She nodded again, felt the sting of tears and prayed they wouldn't give her away.

Zach went into the bedroom and packed his things, then reappeared in the living room. "I'll call you," he said as he headed for the door, his leather overnight bag gripped in one dark hand. He reached for the knob, but never touched it. Instead he dropped the bag, turned and walked back to where she stood in front of the sofa. Framing her face between his hands, he bent and very gently kissed her.

"I'll be back," he said. "I'm not letting you give up on us so easily."

And then he was gone. Elizabeth sat down on the sofa and took another drink of wine. Maybe if she got good and drunk, she could forget about Zachary Harcourt. Maybe she could think clearly again, as she hadn't been able to do since she first met him.

But she didn't really think all the liquor in San Pico would do her any good. Not when her heart was hurting so badly.

Not when she had been stupid enough to let herself fall in love with him.

The Westwood offices of Noble, Goldman and Harcourt were hopping. The elaborate conference room with its long mahogany table and dozen high-backed chairs echoed with the sound of rustling papers and the low-pitched conversation of attorneys who represented Themoziamine. Half a dozen staff lawyers were prepared to meet with lawyers for the opposition.

In the expensively decorated reception room out front, the firm's usual clients waited on overstuffed sofas reading magazines like *Time, Newsweek* and *Architectural*

Digest. Business was booming. So much so, the partners were thinking about opening a branch in San Francisco. Jon Noble wanted Zach to run it, since he didn't have a family to move.

He had half made up his mind to do it. He loved the Bay Area and it would be a great place for his newly purchased sailboat. Maybe by Christmas he'd be ready to tackle the project.

At the moment, Zach just wished he were back in San Pico.

He blew out a breath. Irritated that his thoughts had strayed to Elizabeth again, he concentrated instead on the lawsuit he was preparing against his brother.

By the morning of the following day, the documents had been prepared and delivered to an attorney in Mason who had been hired to go over to the county courthouse and file them. A local process server had delivered the papers to Carson, who apparently swore a string of blue oaths at the young woman who brought them to his door.

Things were rolling. He was up to his neck in the business of being a lawyer, just the way he liked it. Last night he'd worked late into the evening, burying himself in work, then got up before sunrise and started all over again. He was determined not to think of Liz and how much he missed her, determined to keep his mind on business.

It was almost closing time Friday afternoon that he got a call on his cell from Raul.

"Señor Harcourt . . . Zach? I am sorry to bother you. I know how busy you are."

Zach's senses went on alert. "It's all right, Raul. It's good to hear from you."

Raul took a deep breath. Zach could hear the whisper of desperation as he released it into the phone. "It is my sister," he said simply and Zach's body tensed.

According to the teen, last night Raul received permission for a few hours leave from the farm and got an evening pass to have dinner with his sister and her husband.

Unfortunately, he and Miguel had gotten into a fight.

"One minute we were talking, the next we were yelling, calling each other names."

"Take it easy, Raul. Back up a little and tell me what happened."

"I do not know exactly. When I saw my sister, she looked like she was sick or something. Dark circles under her eyes . . . her face puffy and pale. I told Miguel I was worried about her. I asked if she had been sleeping all right, if she and the baby were okay. Miguel got angry . . . like I was blaming him or something. Then I asked him about the ghost. I should have kept quiet. I knew he didn't really believe there was a ghost."

"Tell me the rest."

"Miguel started shouting at Maria. I thought he was going to hit her. I shoved him away from her and that is how the fight got started."

"Are you okay?"

"*Sí.* It didn't last long. Miguel stormed out of the house, and a little while later, Maria drove me back to the farm."

"What did she say?"

"She is worried about Miguel. She says he is angry all the time. He yells at her for nothing. He stays out drinking and doesn't come home until late. It is not like him. He has never been this way before."

"Did you talk to her about the ghost?"

"Yes. She has been taking sleeping pills. Too many, I think. I tried to get her to move out of the house — just until the baby comes — but she will not leave Miguel."

Zach raked a hand through his hair. "I'll call Liz — Ms. Conners. I'll ask her to speak to Maria, make another try at convincing her to leave."

"Thank you, Zach."

"I'm glad you called, Raul. From what Sam Marston says, you're doing great in your studies. You're a hard worker and you never complain. And you're great with the other kids. He's proud of you and so am I."

"What about my sister?"

Zach's hand tightened around the phone. "If Ms. Conners can't convince Maria to leave, I'll come back up and talk to Miguel."

"He will not listen. He will just get angry."

"Yeah, well, you'd be surprised how convincing I can be." Zach broke the connection, thinking of Maria and her ghost, and the murdered girl in Fresno. He reached for the phone to call Liz, wishing he weren't so eager to hear her voice.

He had told her he needed time. Maybe he did. Mostly he had pulled back because he was afraid. What if Liz ended the relationship? Just the thought made him sick to his stomach. He didn't know how his feelings for her had grown so deep so fast, but they had.

He was crazy about her. He had broken his own rule and now he was in very serious trouble. But Liz wasn't sure of her feelings. Or if she was, she was even more afraid of them than he was.

He didn't know what to do. Apparently neither did she. But both of them had something more important to worry about than their own personal problems.

Taking a deep breath, he leaned back in his chair and dialed Liz's number.

All of the turmoil Elizabeth had felt when Zach left rushed back with brutal force when she heard his voice on the phone line in her office. She'd been doing her best not to think of him, trying to put her life back into perspective. But working together as they had been for nearly a month, it was almost impossible to do.

Zach kept the call brief and fairly impersonal, phoning to tell her about the fight between Miguel and Raul, and ask her to speak to Maria. If she heard a wistful note in his voice, it was only that she wanted to hear it so badly.

She didn't linger over the call. She knew how she felt about Zach — she was in love with him. But she was realistic enough to know that whatever Zach felt for her would be fleeting. Zach was a loner, a runner, a man who needed no one, and every hour she spent with him would only make losing him harder.

As soon as she hung up the phone, she dialed Maria's home number, praying Miguel would still be working in the fields.

Thankfully, a woman picked up the phone.

"Maria? It's Elizabeth. Can you talk?"

A tight sound came from Maria's throat. "I am so glad you called."

Worry trickled through her. "I would have called sooner. I didn't want to cause a problem with Miguel. Are you feeling all right? Is everything okay with the baby?"

"I am tired, is all. I am taking the sleeping pills at night, but no matter how much I sleep, I am tired just the same."

"Have you seen the doctor lately?"

"*Sí,* just three days ago. I was spotting a little, not much. He said I should stay off my feet, try to get more rest. He said the baby is doing all right."

"He was sure about that?"

"*Sí.*"

"Is there a chance we could talk? I mean in person? I'd really like to see you."

"I would like to see you, too. I was thinking to call. Miguel is gone two nights. Last night Isabel stayed with me — Isabel Flores. You remember her?"

"You said once that she was a friend."

"That is right. She lives in the big house here on the farm but she is busy a lot."

"Did anything happen last night? Did Isabel see the ghost?"

"No, I do not think so. The little girl . . . she does not come that often. I have not seen her for a while."

"Is Isabel staying with you tonight?"

"She was going to stay . . . but Señor Harcourt . . . he wishes to see her tonight."

"Señor Harcourt? Carson Harcourt?"

"*Sí.* Isabel is his housekeeper." There was something in Maria's voice, something she wasn't saying. Elizabeth remembered the attractive young Hispanic woman she had noticed several times the night of the party she had attended at Carson's house. Surely Carson wasn't involved with the girl. Then again, even if he was, they were both consenting adults.

Still, Carson was her employer, the man who paid her salary. Elizabeth couldn't help wondering if Isabel's duties included more than just taking care of his house.

"If Isabel can't stay, would you like to spend the night at my apartment?"

"*Gracias,* no. I cannot do that. Miguel might call and if he does, he will be worried if I am not here."

Miguel. The thing Elizabeth wanted most to talk to Maria about. "You can't stay there by yourself."

"I was hoping . . . I thought maybe you

might come and stay with me."

Elizabeth's stomach contracted. She knew things Maria didn't know. The articles she had read rose up in her mind, the sickening descriptions, the way the young girl in Fresno had been raped and tortured. How her body had been mutilated before she had been buried.

Elizabeth's mouth went dry. How could she spend another night in the house when she knew the truth about the people who had lived there?

Not there, she told herself. *It was a different house, a completely different time.*

Besides, how could she allow Maria to stay in the house if she were unwilling to do the same?

"Are you sure you won't stay with me?" she pressed. "We could make popcorn. I could bring home a video and we could watch it on TV."

"Miguel would not like it."

Elizabeth sighed, fighting an urge to kick Miguel. "All right, if that's the way you feel, then I guess I'll have to come out there." But sometime soon — whether or not Maria was afraid it might cause trouble — she had to talk to Miguel, somehow convince him that forcing his wife to stay in the house during these last important days of her pregnancy was harmful to her and their baby's health.

Relief sounded in Maria's voice. "You will come. That is good. Maybe you will see the ghost."

A shudder rolled down Elizabeth's spine. Maybe she would. If she did, what would it mean?

Elizabeth's chest tightened at the gruesome possibilities.

"I need to see you."

"Where are you?" Carson asked Stiles.

"Ten minutes away."

"I'll be here when you get here." Carson hung up the phone and a few minutes later, Isabel showed Les Stiles down the hall to his office. Carson thought about the plans he had for the girl that night and gave her a smile of reminder, which she warmly returned.

His smile slid away as Stiles walked in, hooked his beat-up straw cowboy hat on one of the brass hooks in the row next to the door, then sat down in the chair next to his desk.

"What is it?" Carson asked.

"I got a call from a friend this morning . . . fella named Collins, known him since way back when. A couple of days ago, your brother and the Conners woman made a trip to see the Fresno police. Then Zach went down to talk to the local PD. That's where Collins works."

Carson's insides tightened. "Zach and Elizabeth went to the police? What the hell's going on, Les?"

"According to Collins, they were asking questions about a girl who was murdered in Fresno. Seems like she was killed by a man and woman who lived in the old gray house here on the farm."

Carson leaned back in his chair. "For chrissake, those two lived here years ago. What the hell are they digging into something like that for?"

"You knew about the murder?"

"Not really, just rumors here and there. It happened just after I was born. The people who did it had been gone from the farm for several years when it happened. I guess there was something in the local paper back then. My grandfather was running the place in those days, but even years later, my dad never talked about it. I don't think he liked the idea that a couple of murderers had worked here on the farm."

"I wonder why Zach's digging into something like that?"

Good question. Carson swiveled his chair

toward Stiles. "I rarely have any idea what my half brother's up to, but in this case, I don't like it. In the spring, I'll be announcing my intention to run for political office. Having a solid reputation is one of my strong points. Zach would like nothing better than to see my name linked to some long-ago murder that didn't even happen in San Pico."

"Papers would prob'ly be all over it. It sure wouldn't do you any good."

"No, that kind of thing is never good."

"You want me to handle it?"

"I want both of them to stop digging into matters that don't concern them. Do what you have to in order to make that happen."

Stiles just nodded and shoved his big frame out of the chair. Grabbing his battered hat off the rack, he jammed it on his head, stepped out into the hall and closed the door.

Carson just sat there. *Goddammit!* Why did things always have to go wrong? He stood up and walked over to the window. The harvesters were moving through the rows, harvesting fat white bolls of cotton. Fields of roses still bloomed in the distance, but the season was coming to an end. Carson turned away from the window. For once, his mind was far from the farm.

Returning to his desk, he sank down heavily in his chair. *First the lawsuit, now this.* And just like before, it was all Zach's fault.

Carson's hand unconsciously fisted. He had to take charge, had to take control before it was too late. Silently he vowed he would do whatever he had to.

TWENTY-FOUR

Such a simple little house. Two bedrooms, one bath, sparsely furnished with second-hand furniture and inexpensive, sentimental knickknacks. Painted a soft shade of yellow with plain white trim, it looked almost friendly.

Elizabeth shivered as she climbed the front porch steps and knocked on the door, knowing the place wasn't friendly at all.

Maria pulled it open and a wide smile broke over her face. The moment Elizabeth stepped through the door, the young girl swept her into a hug, which was a little clumsy with the size of Maria's belly and the plastic bag of groceries hanging from Elizabeth's arm.

"Thank you for coming," the young woman said. "I am so glad to see you."

"I brought a few things." Elizabeth held up the bag. "And I ordered a pizza for supper. I hope that's okay. The delivery man ought to be here any minute."

"I love pizza! Miguel likes my cooking better, so we do not have it very often."

And they didn't have much money. It was the reason she'd ordered the food and brought some goodies for them to munch, some popcorn and a six-pack of Diet Coke, since Maria couldn't drink alcohol. Elizabeth would rather have had a bottle of wine — or better yet, a big bottle of tequila — something that would knock her out for the night so that she could forget about ghosts and murderers and maybe fall asleep.

They unpacked the goodies in the kitchen, put the Cokes in the fridge and set the popcorn out to pop later. Then the doorbell rang and the pizza man arrived, a young man wearing a Dave's Pizza apron and a little paper hat. Elizabeth paid the boy, and as soon as he was gone, they sat down to eat pepperoni pizza and drink soda at the little table in the kitchen.

It was getting dark outside, the early September days finally getting a little shorter.

"I am glad you are here," Maria said, flicking a glance toward the window where the light had begun to fade.

"Is it this way every night, Maria? When it starts to get dark, do you worry about what might happen in the house?"

The girl was standing at the kitchen counter. She finished the last of her Coke and set her empty glass and Elizabeth's down in the sink. "I try not to think about it. Mostly, I am all right . . . until we go to bed. Miguel is so tired he usually falls right to sleep. I take my pills and then I sleep, too, but even when I am sleeping, sometimes I see her."

"You wake up and see her, you mean?"

She shook her head. "She is there, sometimes, in my dreams, trying to warn me. And always she is so frightened."

"What do you think she's afraid of?"

Maria turned away from the sink and sat back down at the table. "I do not know. Whatever holds her here. And she is afraid for me and the baby."

An icy shiver ran down her spine. "We've done a lot of research, Maria, Zachary Harcourt and I. We found out things about the house — or at least the old house that was here before this one was built — some of them not so good. I think maybe you're the link, the fact that you're pregnant. I don't think the ghost has shown herself to very many people, but since you are here now, and you are going to have a baby, she has come."

"*Sí,* I think that, too. I think there is something that connects the ones she fears with my baby."

"More than one? Are you sure?"

She shrugged her shoulders. "It just seems that way."

"But you don't know who they are."

Maria shook her head. Elizabeth was tempted to tell her about the couple who had once lived in the old gray house, that a few years after they moved, the man and his wife had tortured and murdered a child in Fresno, that Consuela Martinez had been pregnant at the time of the murder and later had lost the baby.

Perhaps the information would convince Maria to leave. But if she refused, she would be even more terrified than she was already.

They watched TV for a while, switching through the three valley stations the television was able to receive.

There wasn't much on. As the evening settled in, they popped corn and ate it watching a *Seinfeld* rerun, then an old John Wayne western neither of them had seen. The national news came on at eleven, but it was the same depressing mayhem that was on every day. The local news followed, the big news in San Pico being the upcoming weeklong Rose Festival near the middle of September, which was less than two weeks away.

Sitting next to Elizabeth on the sofa, Maria yawned and her eyelids began to droop. They couldn't put it off any longer. It was time to go to bed.

Elizabeth nudged Maria. "Why don't you go to bed? It's getting late and the doctor says you need your sleep."

She nodded, pointed at the lightweight quilt folded neatly on the chair next to the sofa. A foam pillow covered with a fresh case sat on top. "If you need anything —"

"This is fine. I'm sure I'll sleep like a baby." That was a lie. She'd be lucky if she could relax enough to close her eyes.

Maria waddled heavily off toward the bedroom, and Elizabeth went over to check the front door. She turned the deadbolt, heard it click into place, went into the kitchen to be sure the back door was locked as well, then returned to the living room to put on the pair of pale blue nylon pajamas she had brought.

Maria's door stood open. Elizabeth didn't blame her for leaving it that way. She wondered whether the girl had taken her nightly sleeping pill, but didn't ask. Instead, she draped the quilt over the sofa, placed the pillow at the end, then sat down and tried to tell herself she was sleepy.

The window air conditioner hummed. Even in September San Pico was hot. She lay down on the sofa and let the white noise soothe her. Amazingly, she drifted off to sleep.

It was the creak of the floorboards beneath the carpet that awakened her. Her eyes cracked instantly open at the distinct groan she remembered from before, the sound of footsteps, someone moving carefully across the living room floor.

Her eyes searched the dim light in the room. For long seconds, she lay there, straining to hear. The sound came again, as if someone passed by the end of the sofa, but enough light filtered in through the curtains that she could see no one was there. She sat up slowly, peering into the darkness, her gaze swinging toward the open bedroom door.

The footsteps moved forward, as if they walked through the opening, and Elizabeth's heart clattered, thundered beneath her breastbone. Her hands shook as she drew back the quilt and quietly rose to her feet. Barefoot, she moved toward the bedroom door, her own steps silent on the carpet.

As she reached the opening, she saw that

Maria lay quietly sleeping, but even as she watched, the woman's breathing quickened and her eyes twitched wildly beneath her closed lids. Lying on her side, Maria drew her legs up toward her protruding stomach as if she tried to protect the precious life inside. She moved a little, began to shift restlessly under the sheet, and a soft moan seeped from her throat.

Elizabeth started toward her. She had taken a couple of steps into the room before the wind began to howl. The room seemed to grow darker, the faint thread of moonlight outside the window no longer able to penetrate the thin muslin curtains over the bed.

What felt like a strange electrical current filled the air, lifting the hair at the nape of her neck. Elizabeth stepped backward, pressing herself against the wall, her heart pounding, her mouth so dry her tongue felt glued to the roof of her mouth. Around her, the air in the room began to thicken and swell, and suddenly it was hard to breathe. A pale haze crept into the bedroom, a faint light that was there and yet wasn't. The wind moaned outside, a fierce, almost human keening, a tortured sound that conjured images of death and dying.

She forced herself to breathe, to drag deep

breaths into her lungs, and made herself look at the bed. Maria sat in the middle, her legs out in front of her, staring straight ahead. Her dark eyes were open and staring, the pupils wide but unseeing, and Elizabeth had the wild notion that she was still asleep.

The air grew even more dense, felt almost tangible against her skin, and Elizabeth recognized the faint scent of roses. The smell grew heavier, thicker, cloyingly sweet, a sickening odor that built and changed, turned even more repulsive, reminding her of rot and decay and making her stomach roll with nausea. The awful smell drifted into every nook and cranny, floated to the ceiling and oozed over the floor.

Then as quickly as it came, it faded.

Elizabeth's gaze shot to Maria, still sitting rigidly in the middle of the bed. Her lips began to move, and though Elizabeth couldn't make out the words, she saw that Maria's gaze was fixed firmly on something at the foot of the bed.

For the first time, Elizabeth felt a wave of real fear as the haze in the room began to move and swirl, began to condense, and she realized it was taking the form of a person.

She bit back a frightened sob at the sight of the small figure slowly taking shape, the image growing clearer and clearer, the figure of a little girl. She could see her now, the tiny black patent shoes, the full skirt gathered around her tiny waist, covered by her pretty pink pinafore. Her blond hair fell in waves around her face, down to her shoulders. Her skin was pale, completely translucent, and yet there was a hint of color in her cheeks.

Elizabeth could see her plainly and yet behind her — though her — Elizabeth could make out the bureau against the wall, the small porcelain lamp sitting at one end.

The child said nothing, at least no words that Elizabeth could hear, though she had the oddest sense that she was somehow speaking to Maria. The young woman started to shake, her body trembling almost uncontrollably.

Frightened for her and for the baby, Elizabeth started toward her. Terror struck as she realized that she could not move. Not a finger. Not even a toe. She was pressed against the door as if an invisible force held her paralyzed.

Elizabeth opened her mouth, but no sound came out, and the fear inside her swelled to immense proportions. Her gaze locked on the tiny, pale figure at the foot of the bed, and she watched in horror, frozen in place, her eyes darting from the child to Maria and back again.

Then the image slowly began to fade. In seconds, it was completely gone, along with the eerie haze in the room. Except for the hum of the air conditioner in the living room, the bedroom was utterly silent. Sitting in the middle of the bed, Maria blinked several times then looked up at her and burst into tears.

The sound jolted Elizabeth into action. Freed from the force that had held her immobile, her legs shaking, she released the breath she had been holding and rushed toward the bed.

"Maria!" Reaching out, afraid she would frighten the girl even more, Elizabeth gently caught her shoulder. "It's me, Elizabeth. Are you all right?"

The girl's head slowly turned. "Elizabeth?"

"Yes. I'm right here. I saw everything." Sitting down on the bed, she leaned toward Maria and the girl went into her arms. "It's all right. It's over." Maria clung to her fiercely, weeping against her shoulder.

"It's all right," she said again, though at that moment, nothing felt right at all.

"Elizabeth . . . something bad has happened. I am bleeding."

Elizabeth looked down, saw the bloodred stain spreading across the sheet. "Oh, my God!" Leaping up from the bed, she raced toward the phone in the living room. "Don't move!" she called behind her. "I'm getting help!"

She was shaking so hard, she was barely able to dial 911, fumbled once, then made herself slow down and do it correctly. Hurriedly, she told the operator that a young, pregnant woman was hemorrhaging and that she desperately needed an ambulance out at the workers' compound at Harcourt Farms. Though the operator wanted her to stay on the line, the cord wasn't long enough to reach the bedroom. Elizabeth left the receiver off the hook and hurried back to Maria.

"Just hang on," she said. "They're on their way."

But Maria wasn't looking at her. She was staring at the wall at the foot of the bed. Elizabeth followed her gaze and her eyes filled with horror.

Painted in slashes of crimson that matched the blood on the sheet was a message:

LEAVE — OR THEY WILL KILL YOU AND YOUR BABY.

Elizabeth started to tremble. It was a terrifying message that could no longer be ignored.

Zach shoved open the glass doors leading into the reception area of San Pico Community Hospital. A quick scan of the sterile interior said Elizabeth wasn't there.

"I'm looking for Maria Santiago," he told the woman behind the front counter. "She was just brought in a couple of hours ago. Can you tell me which room she's in?"

Peering through a pair of tortoiseshell half-glasses, the stocky woman gave him the room number and pointed him down the hall in that direction.

"Just follow the yellow line painted on the floor," she said. "It's past visiting hours, so I doubt they'll let you in, but at least the nurses can tell you how she's doing."

"Thank you." Zach made his way down the corridor, passing uniformed nurses, and doctors in pale green scrubs. He kept hoping he would run into Liz but he didn't see her, not until he pushed open the door to Maria's room and walked in.

Liz sat in a chair near the bed. Maria Santiago lay sleeping in the narrow bed, her face the same bone-bleached color as the sheet. With her black hair fanned out around her shoulders and her skin so pale, she looked more dead than alive, and guilt washed over him.

He should have done something, should have forced her to leave the house. He had promised Raul. And he had promised Liz.

She saw him then and came up out of her chair. Her beige slacks and print blouse were spotted with blood, her face nearly as pale as Maria's.

Walking toward him, she hooked a curl of burnished hair out of the way behind her ear and he noticed that her hand was trembling. He moved toward her, opened his arms, and she simply walked into them.

"I'm so glad you came," she said.

He gathered her close. "I wish I'd never left." He kissed the top of her head, aching for what she had been through, wishing he had been there when she needed him. "How's Maria doing?"

Liz glanced at the door and tipped her head in that direction, urging him out into the hall. Outside, they walked down to a small waiting area and sat down on one of the sofas.

He reached over and took hold of her hand, encouraging her to tell him more about what had happened.

Liz took a shaky breath and shook her head. "I thought she was going to die, Zach. If I hadn't been there, she might have."

He laced his fingers with hers, felt how cold her skin was.

"Maria's lost a lot of blood," she said, "but they were able to get the hemorrhaging stopped before the baby started to come. The doctor wants her to hold on as long as she can, give the baby as much time to grow as possible. He's ordered complete bed rest."

She looked up at him, her blue eyes suddenly fierce. "Whatever happens, I'm not letting her spend another night in that house."

"No," he said softly, tightening his hold on her hand. "She can't stay there any longer. I'll speak to Miguel." He glanced around, realizing for the first time the man should have been there. "Where is he?"

"Still in Modesto, I guess. The hospital called the motel where they were staying. Someone spoke to Mariano, but Miguel wasn't there."

"I'm sure he'll come as soon as he gets word."

"Raul was here until a few minutes ago. Sam Marston brought him over. He stayed until the doctor sent him home. He wouldn't leave until he was sure his sister was going to be all right."

"But they're pretty sure she will be."

She nodded. "Pretty sure. They'll transfer her to the County Hospital in Mason if she has to stay very long."

"How about you? Are you all right? Some of the things you told me on the phone . . . I'm not sure I would be."

She bit her bottom lip, and he saw that she was fighting back tears. "It was the most terrifying thing I've ever experienced, Zach, like some kind of horror movie. It started like before . . . like the time you were there, but this time it got worse. I couldn't move and neither could Maria. I suppose being so frightened is what brought on the hemorrhage, or at least that's the logical explanation."

"But you aren't sure that's really what happened."

She shook her head. "I'm not sure of anything anymore."

"What about the message you said appeared on the wall?"

She swallowed and glanced away. "The letters looked like they were written in blood. *Leave — or they will kill you and your baby.*" She shivered, crossed her arms over her chest against the cold air blowing down from the air conditioner.

"Maria saw it, too, I gather."

"She just sat there staring at it, sitting in the bed in all of that blood."

"What happened next?"

"I called 911, then I ran and got some towels. We used them to slow the bleeding. Then the ambulance pulled into the driveway and things got hectic. By the time the men ran into the bedroom, the message was gone."

"Gone? What do you mean, *gone?*"

"It disappeared, Zach. As if it had never been there. The wall was completely blank. It was the same freshly painted white it was before."

Zach raked a hand through his wavy dark hair. "None of this makes any sense."

"Not unless you believe in ghosts. I saw her, Zach. Long blond hair, big blue eyes, wearing a little pink pinafore. She was there at the foot of the bed — and I could see right through her."

A shudder whispered through her. He didn't believe in ghosts. Yet Maria's brush with death made it clear they couldn't ignore the things that were happening in the house any longer.

"I'll speak to Miguel as soon as he gets back to town. I'll tell him his wife is moving out, whether he likes it or not, and he had better give some thought to moving himself."

"What about Carson? If Miguel moves out, Carson will fire him."

Knowing it was true, Zach released a frustrated breath. And even if he went to the guys at the farm labor union, it might not do any good. "Maria has to leave. No question. I can try to talk to Carson, but I doubt he'll listen. So far, Miguel doesn't appear to be in any danger, so maybe it won't matter if he stays."

"Have you heard anything from that investigator you hired?"

"He's promised to call me tomorrow."

"I hope he finds something."

"So do I."

Twenty-Five

Elizabeth left the hospital sometime after two in the morning. Zach followed her back to her apartment to be sure she got home safely, but didn't come in. She had asked him if he needed a place to sleep, but he said he had called ahead and reserved a room at the Holiday Inn.

She wished she weren't so disappointed. More than anything, after the terrifying events of the night, she wanted to fall asleep in Zach's arms, to feel safe and secure, at least for a while. Perhaps he would have liked that, too.

But until they both knew what they wanted, until they could deal with their feelings, whatever they were, staying apart seemed the wisest course.

The clock in the kitchen read ten o'clock when the doorbell rang and Zach arrived at her apartment the following morning.

"Murphy called," he said as he walked

into the living room. "I figured you'd want to know what he had to say and there are some things we need to discuss."

"I'm glad you came." She just wished she weren't quite as glad as she was. "The coffee's on. You want a cup?"

"Sounds great." Following her into the kitchen, he sat down at the table while she poured him a mug of rich dark coffee. She placed the mug in front of him on the table, then sat down in a chair across from him.

"So what did Murphy have to say?"

"I told him we'd spoken to the police in Fresno and also the cops here in San Pico. Since the authorities don't believe the victim came from anywhere in the valley, he's been working his way south. He talked to the police in Santa Clarita then the authorities in the San Fernando Valley. He's using the description of the little girl Maria says she saw, the same one you gave me last night."

"Does he know we're looking for a ghost?"

Zach shook his head. "I saved that little surprise for later. I figured he might not turn up anything and if he didn't, it would probably be better if he never knew."

"But you said he called this morning."

Zach nodded. "About an hour ago." He took a sip of his coffee and gave up a sigh.

"Yesterday, Ian spoke to a friend of his in the FBI. Over the years, he's been involved in a number of missing person cases. I guess he's made some useful contacts. His friend spent the afternoon searching FBI cold case files, looking for children reported kidnapped in the years between 1967 and 1971."

"When the Martinezes lived in the old gray house."

"Exactly. It took a while, but believe it or not, the guy came up with the name of a missing child who fits the description. Murphy took the information and cross-checked it with a disappearance that was reported in the *L.A. Times,* the story of a little girl who went missing in September of 1969, blond, blue-eyed, nine years old. He hasn't got much of anything else — except that she was abducted right out of her own front yard."

"Oh, God."

"Yeah. Sounds a little like what happened to Holly Ives, doesn't it? Young girl taken brazenly in the middle of the day? Murphy doesn't know if this is the girl we're looking for, but he wants us to talk to one of the LAPD detectives who worked the case back then. He's retired now, living in the San

Fernando Valley. I thought we'd drive by the hospital and check on Maria, then head down to L.A."

Her pulse was racing. This was the first real break they'd had, the chance, at last, to find some answers. After last night, she was desperate for an explanation — any explanation — no matter how far-fetched it might seem.

"What about Miguel?"

"If he's back in town, we'll talk to him before we leave. Oh, and pack an overnight bag. Ian says we may be able to speak to the girl's parents, the mother, at any rate. She's working today, but she's usually home on Sundays."

Elizabeth nodded and headed for the bedroom. She packed a toothbrush and her cosmetics bag, a comb, hairbrush and a change of clothes. She didn't let her thoughts dwell on the notion that the trip might require an overnight stay. Zach had spent last night in a motel room; she could certainly do the same. And she knew he wouldn't press her to do something she didn't want to do.

They left the apartment half an hour later in Zach's black convertible.

"I wanted to get here in a hurry" was his explanation for driving the car instead of his Jeep. "The BMW's faster."

Which seemed to be true as he sped through town on the way to the hospital. As the car leaped away from a stoplight, Elizabeth happened to notice the dark green pickup behind them that she had seen before.

"I know that car." Glancing behind them only once, she fixed her eyes on the road ahead. "I think it's following us."

"The pickup?"

"Yes. I've seen it twice before."

Zach frowned as he looked in the mirror. "When?"

"He was back there the day I went to the newspaper office, so I drove on past the building. I went back to my office and walked over a little while later."

"Why didn't you tell me?"

"I just figured it was one of Carson's people trying to figure out what we were up to. I didn't really think it was important."

"Maybe it isn't, but I don't like it." They pulled into the hospital parking lot and the pickup drove past. Zach watched until the truck disappeared out of sight. "Big guy in a cowboy hat. Might be Les Stiles, my brother's number one flunkie. We'll keep an eye out for him from now on."

They went into the hospital and spent a

few minutes with Maria, who looked a little better than she had last night. But the doctor wanted her to rest so the nurse urged them to leave. Miguel was standing outside the door when they left the room.

Zach saw him and his jaw went hard. "We need to talk," he said darkly.

Miguel just nodded. He looked haggard, older than his twenty-nine years. His eyes were bloodshot, his face a little puffy, and Elizabeth wondered if might be suffering from a hangover.

Since the waiting room down the hall was full, Zach led the three of them out of the building. It was already heating up outside, which seemed to match Zach's mood. He didn't mince words with the handsome Hispanic.

"Your wife nearly died last night."

Miguel swallowed. "I know. I came home as soon as I got word."

"You mean as soon as you got home from the bar," Zach said.

Miguel glanced away.

"What's going on, Miguel?" Elizabeth asked. "You've never been much of a drinker. Lately it seems you're getting drunk all the time. If something's wrong, maybe we can help."

He shoved back his straight black hair. It

was unwashed and overly long, as if it hadn't been cut for some time. "I do not know what is wrong. Lately I just feel restless, you know? Maybe because of the baby. I get angry. I don't know why. Sometimes I just have to get away."

"Are you and Maria having problems?"

He shook his head. "I love my wife. I have loved her from the first time I saw her."

"What about the baby? How do you feel about having a child?"

"I want this baby. Already I love it. Maria lost a baby last year. Both of us want this one. I cannot wait to be a father."

"If that's the case," Zach put in, "then you won't try to stop Maria from moving out of the house."

Miguel stiffened. "What are you talking about?"

"She's frightened, Miguel," Elizabeth said. "I know you don't believe in ghosts, but I was there in the house last night. I saw the little girl — I saw the terrifying things that happened in that room. Maria can't stay there. She almost died. She will if she doesn't leave."

Miguel said nothing for the longest time. When he looked up there were tears in his eyes. "I am sorry. I will find her a place to stay."

"She can stay with me."

He shook his head. "She needs to be with her own kind. She can stay with Señora Lopez. She and her husband live in one of the other houses. They have an extra room and no kids. That way I will be close by if Maria needs me."

Elizabeth mulled that over, thinking it was a compromise Maria could probably live with. She cast a glance at Zach, whose jaw looked iron hard. He made a slight nod of his head.

"All right," Elizabeth said. "Once she's released from the hospital and out of danger, she can stay with Señora Lopez. But I want your word, Miguel. You won't do anything to upset her. And you'll stop drinking the way you have been."

He swallowed again, glanced away. "I give you my word."

"Thank you."

With Maria's immediate problems resolved and their bags in the trunk, they left the hospital and set off down the highway. Driving through Santa Clarita, they stopped at Red Lobster for lunch, then drove on down to Van Nuys, where the detective lived who had worked on the case of the missing child.

Ian Murphy had made the appointment

for three o'clock and they drove up in front of the small tract house in a subdivision just off the freeway with a few minutes to spare.

"You ready?" Zach asked as he unsnapped his seat belt. He was casually dressed in slacks, a short-sleeved shirt and loafers, and wearing his guarded expression. He had been all morning, and yet, again and again she could feel his eyes on her, the gold in them glittering like sparks that could blaze out of control any minute.

Elizabeth felt the same banked heat whenever she looked at him. She'd been attracted to Zach from the start. Knowing their relationship couldn't possibly work didn't change that. She wanted him, and it was obvious he wanted her.

Still, their first priority was Maria. Zach opened her car door onto an L.A. day far more pleasant than the one in San Pico. He helped her out on the sidewalk and they started toward the front door. A tall man in loose-fitting jeans and a faded old L.A. Rams T-shirt stepped out on the porch before they reached the bottom of the stairs.

"Zachary Harcourt?"

"That's right." Zach guided her up the steps. "And this is Elizabeth Conners."

"Liz," she corrected though she didn't know why, and extended a hand.

"I'm Danny McKay." McKay shook her hand and then Zach's. "I used to be a detective with the LAPD. I've been retired for almost eight years. Come on in." McKay looked to be pushing seventy, almost completely bald, with sparse gray hair around the shiny dome of his head. He held the screen door open and they walked past him into a living room with a white brick fireplace at one end.

"My wife passed away four years ago," McKay explained. "Place always looked real good when she was alive. I try, but I just can't seem to keep it the way she did." The house was built in the sixties, redone maybe late eighties. The light green carpet had begun to fade and the matching sofa and chair looked worn.

"We're just happy you took the time to see us," Zach said, all of them sitting down across from each other, Elizabeth next to Zach on the sofa.

"No problem. I don't get that many visitors these days. You want some coffee or something? I think there's some iced tea in the refrigerator."

Elizabeth glanced at Zach. "We're fine, thanks." She eased forward on the sofa. "What can you tell us about the missing girl, Mr. McKay?"

"It's just Danny. And I remember that case very well. I guess 'cause she was such a pretty little thing. Can't tell you much about it, though. That child just seemed to disappear."

Zach leaned forward. "According to what Ian said, she was taken right out of her own front yard."

McKay nodded, sunlight gleaming on his bald head. "Broke her parents' heart. 'Specially the mother. Only child, you know. Mother really loved that little girl."

Elizabeth felt a chill. According to Maria, the little girl had cried for her mother. *I want my mama,* she had pleaded.

"The papers said she was nine years old," Zach said, "with blond hair and blue eyes. From what Murphy told me, there wasn't much beyond that in the case reports. The files were thirty-six years old. Pages were missing. They didn't have everything on computer the way they do now."

"Unfortunately, that's true. It's a lot easier to track that kind of thing these days. And with the Amber Alerts and all the news on TV, we've got a better chance of stopping the abductor before it's too late."

"Any chance you remember what she was wearing the day she disappeared?" Zach asked.

"Crazy as it seems, I do. That day was her birthday, you see. She turned nine years old that day. The party was in full swing, the kids all out in the backyard. But according to her mother, her dog started barking — a little Pekingese — and Carrie ran after him, out to the front yard."

"Carrie?" Elizabeth asked.

"That was her name. Carrie Ann Whitt."

Elizabeth swallowed.

"Go on," Zach urged.

"At any rate, Carrie ran after the dog and I guess so much was going in the backyard with the party and all, no one missed her for a while. By the time, they did, Carrie Ann was gone."

Elizabeth didn't say anything more. Her throat was hurting. In the eye of her mind, she could see the little girl playing with her friends, all dressed up for her birthday party. The vision changed to the child at the foot of the bed dressed in her pretty pink pinafore, her blond hair freshly washed and gleaming. The ache in her throat grew more painful.

"Nobody saw anything?" Zach asked. "There weren't any witnesses?"

"When we were canvassing the area later that day, someone said they saw an old beat-up blue car in the neighborhood around the time Carrie Ann disappeared. But they couldn't give us the license plate number or anything more than a vague description of the vehicle."

"How many people were in it?" Zach asked.

"Two."

A muscle clenched in Zach's jaw.

"You don't seem surprised," the detective said, his eyes on Zach's face. "You see it in the files?"

He shook his head. "I haven't seen the files." Zach shot a glance at Elizabeth. "It's a long story."

"Yeah, well, I'd like to hear it."

Zach sighed. "All right. But before we start, maybe we'd better have that glass of iced tea."

Twenty-Six

"It's her, Zach. Carrie Ann Whitt. It has to be."

"Looks that way." They were driving down the freeway in Zach's car, the BMW snaking its way through the long lines of traffic.

"They kidnapped her, just like Holly Ives. They took her to the house they were living in at Harcourt Farms and they murdered her."

"Let's not jump to conclusions. We don't know for sure that's what happened."

"But she fits the description perfectly so there's a good chance that's exactly what happened."

"It could be. If the mother's home tomorrow, we'll see what she has to say."

"Are you sure we should? I mean, what can we really tell her?"

"We'll play it by ear. We don't want to hurt the woman any more than she's been hurt already."

Elizabeth sat back in her seat. She felt tired, exhausted clear to the bone. She was sure little Carrie Whitt had been murdered in the old gray house. She thought of Holly Ives and the torture she had suffered and her stomach rolled with nausea. She was just a child! Just a little girl!

Had Carrie Ann suffered that same terrible fate? More and more, Elizabeth was convinced that she had.

She fought to hold back tears. She was barely aware of her surroundings until she realized Zach had pulled the car off the freeway and they were heading toward the ocean.

His eyes found hers. "I know this is hard for you. I'm not liking it, myself. But we can't stop now. We have to find out what's going on."

She nodded, swallowed. "We have to know the truth. We can't stop until we do."

Zach navigated a turn in the road, taking the car along a highway running parallel to the sea. Beachfront homes lined the shore, and restaurants and boutiques popped up here and there on the opposite side of the highway.

"The afternoon's pretty well shot," Zach said. "I figure we might as well stay at my place tonight. We'll get settled in, then go get something to eat." He glanced at her, his hands still wrapped around the wheel, big dark hands, nicely shaped, the nails short and clean. Talented hands.

She remembered those hands moving over her body and felt a tremor of desire she didn't want to feel. "Maybe I should get a room."

"You don't have to do that. My apartment's got two bedrooms, you'll even have your own bath. You can have all the privacy you need." But his eyes said, *How much do you really want?*

Desire slipped through her as she thought of the last time they had made love, how hot she had been, how incredible the pleasure. A single glance at the beautifully sculpted angles of his face, the sensual curve of his lips, made the heat tug low in her belly.

As he turned up a narrow road that wound its way toward a cliff above the sea, she realized she was staring at his mouth, thinking of the way he had kissed her, the way his lips slid over hers, how soft but firm they were, how determined. Zach cast her a long, heated glance, and erotic images danced in her head.

The tires whined on the cement driveway leading down to the underground parking garage, then the car pulled into a space marked with Zach's apartment number, 3A. Rounding the car, he opened her door, then went back and popped the trunk, took out their bags, and they headed for the elevator.

The building was white stucco, four stories high, sitting on pillars that dug into the side of the mountain. The elevator moaned and lifted upward, carrying them toward the top floor of the building. The doors slid open and they walked out into the corridor. Zach set their bags down outside his apartment door, pulled out his keys, and opened the lock.

She kept telling herself it didn't matter that she was spending the night in his home. Nothing was going to happen. She wasn't going to give into her desire for him again.

With renewed resolve, she stepped into the marble-floored entry and came to a sudden stop, unable to look away from the breathtaking view. The sea and coastline, curving miles to the north and south, stretched in front of the floor-to-ceiling windows in the elegant living room.

"Like it?"

"Oh, Zach, it's beautiful."

His eyes moved over her face. "So are you," he said softly. He was standing so close she could feel the heat of his body, smell his expensive cologne, and a curl of heat slid into her stomach.

"Zach . . ."

He cleared his throat, looked away, took a deep breath. "I'll show you your room. You can get settled in. In the meantime, I'll pour you a glass of wine. You look like you could use it."

She sighed wearily. "Definitely." He led her down a hall carpeted in the same cream shade as the living room, which was done in cream and black with bright pieces of oversize artwork, and an interesting array of sculpted glass that added color wherever it was needed.

The guest room was lovely, very chic, with smooth dark furniture and a single chair upholstered in burgundy to match the comforter on the bed and the drapes at the windows, modern yet welcoming.

Setting her bag on the chair, she took out her cosmetic kit, comb and brush, then went into the luxurious bathroom. The black granite countertop over the sink reflected the lights above the mirror, and a single bud vase with a purple-throated white silk orchid looked so real, she reached out to touch it.

She studied the face in the mirror, saw the fatigue in her eyes. With a sigh of resignation, she ran the brush and comb through her hair, fluffing the dark strands around her shoulders as best she could, then put on a dash of coral lipstick and returned to the living room, feeling a little better.

As good as his word, Zach held out a glass of chilled white wine. The eyes that met hers were dark and intense, and though he wore his guarded expression, she could see the faint trace of hunger he couldn't quite hide. Their fingers brushed as she took hold of the glass and a tendril of heat slid through her. She took a sip of wine and realized her hand was shaking.

Afraid he would notice, she set the wineglass down on the black, marble-topped coffee table and moved off toward the window, her gaze fixed on the magnificent view of the sea. She heard Zach's footfalls as he moved up behind her, close but not quite touching. Just the thought of him standing so near made her breath hitch.

"I don't know if I can do this, Zach."

"What? Stay here with me?"

"Stay away from you. Be able to keep things objective." She turned to face him. "This is more difficult than I ever imagined."

His hand came up to her cheek. "In case you haven't noticed, I'm going a little crazy here, too, Liz. When I'm with you, half the time I feel like running for my car, driving off and never looking back. The rest of the time . . ." He caught her shoulders and gently drew her toward him. "The rest of the time I want you so much it's nearly impossible to think of anything else."

And then he bent his head and very softly kissed her.

She was surprised by the tenderness, the control she knew he exerted. Surprised at the force of her own desire. For an instant, she stiffened, determined not to give into her feelings for him again.

Then her eyes closed on a wave of need. She slid her arms up around his neck and kissed him back, wanting him as much as he wanted her.

Zach deepened the kiss and all gentleness fled. The kiss went deeper, turned wild and hungry. His lips were hot and fierce, his kiss fraught with emotion, the turbulence inside him he couldn't seem to put into words.

Don't do this again, a little voice warned.

But he was already unbuttoning her blouse, easing it off her shoulders, his long tapered fingers encircling her breasts. He kneaded and caressed them, replaced his hands with his mouth. Elizabeth moaned and clung to him, knowing she should push him away and completely unable to do so.

More kisses followed, deep, erotic kisses that left her breathless. Dark, seductive kisses that made her hungry for more. Her skin seemed to burn. Her nipples throbbed, and an ache began to pulse between her legs.

They were standing in front of the windows, but the apartment sat high on the hill and jutted out toward the water so that no one could see. She made no move to stop him when he began to strip away her clothes. The sandals came off, her blouse and slacks, her lacy push-up bra. She wore blue lace thong panties, just a scrap of fabric that teased her sex as he palmed her, slid his fingers inside the lace to tease and caress her.

Her head fell back as he kissed the side of her neck, and she thought how much she wanted him, how she craved this, craved him in a way she never could have imagined.

He left her only a moment, long enough to strip away his clothes. Elizabeth watched in fascination, his shoulders so broad, his flat belly ridged with muscle, his chest wide and hard, the muscles flexing as he moved. His legs were long and sinewy, his biceps and forearms muscular and tanned from his work in the sun.

She got wet just watching him, imagining the feel of him pressing her down on the mattress, sliding his hardness inside her. He must have read her thoughts for he simply shook his head.

"Not yet. I promised you once the things we would do. I think its time I kept my word." Moving closer, he slid his hands into her hair and drew her against the naked length of his body, began a slow seduction of her mouth.

Long wet kisses turned her knees to jelly; hot, wild kisses made her ache inside. A little mewling sound came from her throat as he began a slow, determined assault on her neck and shoulders, then he took her breast into his mouth. She trembled at the feel of his tongue ringing her navel, sliding across the flat plane below.

She shivered.

"It's all right, love, relax. There's nothing to be afraid of." Kneeling in front of her, he pressed his mouth against the tiny swatch of lace over her sex, dampening the fabric, then his tongue slipped beneath the lace.

"Zachary . . ."

"Easy." He slid the panties down her legs and urged her to step out of them, then returned to his task as if he had never stopped. His tongue slid wetly over her flesh, an erotic imitation of the act to come, and her body clenched with need. Her fingers slipped through the dark silk of his hair and she bit her lip to stifle a moan. Using his mouth and hands, he brought her to climax, an earth-shattering rush of pleasure that hit her so hard her knees buckled beneath her.

Zach caught her up in his arms. Long strides carried him across the living room, down the hall, into his bedroom. Tossing back the gray satin comforter, he settled her among the clean white sheets and came down on top of her, his mouth claiming hers once more.

"I want to be inside you," he said between deep, erotic assaults on her mouth. "I want to get so close I can't tell where your body ends and mine begins."

Elizabeth moaned, wanting exactly the same. The pleasure was incredible, but she wanted even more. She wanted to be joined with him, so close they were no longer two people but one single soul.

As if he read her thoughts, he eased himself inside her, his dark eyes fixed on her face. He held himself in check for several long moments, letting her body grow accustomed to his size, the heavy length and weight of him, then slowly he began to move.

He was big and hard and he filled her completely. Elizabeth clung to his shoulders, absorbing his heat, the power of his long, hard-muscled body, feeling the need build inside her. She arched her hips, taking him deeper still, and heard Zach groan.

His movements grew faster, deeper, harder. He thrust into her again and again and the need inside her built.

"Come for me," he whispered, his deep voice a command, and Elizabeth let herself go. Her body tightened, broke free. She felt as if she were soaring, as if time stood still. She cried out Zach's name, and the muscles in his powerful body went rigid as he followed her to release.

For seconds neither of them moved. He pressed a last gentle kiss on the side of her neck then lifted himself away and lay down close beside her.

Outside the window, she could hear the waves breaking on the shore at the bottom of the hill. The sound mingled with the beating of her heart and the turbulence of her emotions. She was in love with him. Running away from the fact wasn't going to change that.

Dear God, what should she do?

Zach trailed a finger along her arm. "That was amazing," he said softly. "I never knew it could be that way."

She turned a little so she could see his face. "You've been with dozens of women, Zach. How can this be any different?"

His eyes found hers. "It's different . . . because I never loved any of those women." He said the words as if they explained everything, and Elizabeth's world turned upside down.

They left the bed, went into the shower and made love in the hot, misty spray. They went out to dinner, then later that night slept together in Zach's big king-size bed. But he never brought up the subject of love or anything to do with his feelings for her.

Elizabeth said nothing, either. She had begun to wonder if she had actually heard him correctly, wondered, as she had before, even if it were true, what would it change? Zach was Zach and always would be. Whatever he felt for her, he would not stay.

As the hours slipped past, even curled up beside him, Elizabeth couldn't fall asleep. Her thoughts kept shifting from Zach and her love for him to Maria and the fear she felt for her friends.

Miguel still lived in the house. What

unseen danger did he face?

She wondered what they might discover tomorrow during the meeting Ian Murphy had arranged with Carrie Whitt's mother. And if they learned something important, what should they do with the information? Lying there in the darkness, staring up at the ceiling, Elizabeth thought of the little girl who had appeared at the foot of Maria's bed, warning her of the danger in the house.

Elizabeth closed her eyes and prayed nothing terrible would happen before they got back.

The home Paula Whitt Simmons lived in with her second husband was much like the one owned by Detective McKay, a San Fernando Valley tract house, this one in a subdivision of small, boxy stucco houses in Sherman Oaks. Paula, now sixty-five years old, had been twenty-nine when her nine-year-old daughter, Carrie Ann, disappeared.

"It was a terrible time," she said as they sat at the kitchen table drinking lukewarm cups of coffee. "It seemed like it would never end, and instead of getting better it got worse." Paula Simmons had short gray hair and the wrinkled face of a much older woman. As she lit up her third cigarette in

446

the short time since their arrival, Elizabeth understood why.

"How did it get worse?" Zach asked.

"My first husband left me eighteen months after Carrie Ann disappeared."

"I'm sorry." Elizabeth thought how hard it must have been to lose both a daughter and a husband.

"The divorce wasn't his fault. I couldn't seem to pull myself together. George wanted a wife and all I could be was a grieving mother."

"Divorce is fairly common when the loss of a child occurs in a family," Elizabeth told her.

"I read that later, in one of those self-help books. Didn't do much good by then. Lucky for me, eight years after Carrie Ann disappeared, I met Marty. He helped me get on with my life."

"Some people aren't that lucky," Elizabeth said.

Paula nodded and took a long draw on her half-smoked cigarette. Some of the ashes fell onto the table and Elizabeth realized the woman's hand was shaking.

"If this is too hard —"

"It's all right. It happened a long time ago. I've had two girls with Marty. Raising them helped me come to terms with what happened to Carrie Ann."

"And what do you think that was?" Zach asked gently.

"I think my little girl is dead. I think some monster took her away from me and killed her."

Elizabeth ignored the tightening in her chest and the shiver that slipped down her spine. "Can you tell us a little about her?"

For the next half hour, Paula Simmons talked about the child she had lost. She told them how pretty she was, how people said she looked just like an angel. How smart she was, that she was in the gifted children's program at school.

"She loved children," Paula said. "Especially babies. She wanted a little sister or brother so badly."

Elizabeth looked at Zach, whose jaw tightened though his gaze remained fixed on the woman's face.

"What did she call you?" Zach asked. "Did she say Mother or Mommy?"

"She called me 'Mama.' I guess because I always called my own mother that." Paula's eyes filled with tears. "I'm sorry. This just brings all of it back."

Elizabeth had heard enough. She had begun to feel as if she knew the little blue-eyed girl who had been so beloved by her mother, and it made her ache inside to think what might have happened to her.

With a glance at Zach, she shoved back her chair and rose to her feet, and Zach did the same. "We're sorry to have bothered you, Mrs. Simmons. But we really appreciate your help in this."

Paula made a jerky nod of her head. "On the phone, Mr. Murphy said that you wanted to talk to me about Carrie Ann. I figure you were with the police or something. But you aren't, are you?"

"No, we aren't," Zach said. "We're just trying to solve a mystery. It may have nothing to do with your daughter. But I promise you, if it does, we'll be sure to let you know."

"You don't think she might still be alive, do you?"

Elizabeth's chest squeezed hard. "We have no way of knowing for sure, but we don't think so."

"I don't think so, either," Paula said. "If she was, I think I'd feel it right here." She pressed a fist over her heart.

Elizabeth could feel the woman's pain, even after all these years. "I think maybe you would, too," she said softly, a thick ache swelling in her throat. She and Zach said goodbye, thanking the woman again for taking the time to talk to them.

They left the house and Zach aimed the car toward San Pico. He had decided to drive his Jeep today and as the vehicle rolled along the freeway, Elizabeth thought of Paula Whitt and turned her face to the window, unable to hold back tears, hoping Zach wouldn't see that she was crying. She didn't realize he had pulled off the freeway into the parking lot of a supermarket until her car door opened and Zach hauled her out of the car and straight into his arms.

"It's all right," he said. "Just let it go."

Locking her arms around his neck, she started crying in earnest, great heaving sobs that shook her whole body. Zach just held on to her. He didn't speak, didn't try to make her stop, just held her and let her cry. She wished she could stay in his arms for-ever.

"Better?" he asked as her tears began to ease.

Elizabeth nodded but didn't let him go.

"In time this will all be over and your life can return to normal."

She dragged in a shaky breath, eased a little away but remained in the circle of his arms. "I'm not sure that's possible anymore. Everything I thought was real has changed."

He held her a moment more, then let her go. Elizabeth climbed back inside the car and they rode in silence for a while, Zach's gaze focused on the road. They were driving through the mountains, the hills dry and brown, the valley still some distance away.

"That little girl I saw in the house . . ." Elizabeth said, "it's Carrie Ann, Zach. I know it. Those monsters murdered her and now her spirit is trapped in the house. She's been trying to protect Maria, trying to save the baby. We have to find out where she is, Zach. We have to set her free." Her eyes welled again and she glanced away.

"We'll find her," Zach said gruffly.

"We need to dig . . ." She swallowed. "We need to dig under the house. The Martinezes buried Holly Ives in the basement. If they murdered Carrie Ann, there's a chance they disposed of her body the same way. Since the new house is built where the old one stood before . . ."

"I know. It's the logical assumption." He released a tired breath. "If Carrie Ann *was* murdered, that might explain why her spirit's still there, even if her body isn't. There are acres of open fields around the house. They could have buried her anywhere."

She swallowed. "I suppose that's true, but

I still think we should look under the house."

"So do I."

She turned in her seat. "Maybe after Carson hears what we've found out, he'll let us search."

"I doubt it. Not without a warrant."

"Can we get one?"

"I'm not real popular in San Pico, and even if I were, I doubt any judge is going to sign a warrant based on the appearance of a ghost."

"Then we're stuck with having to go to Carson."

"I guess."

"But you don't think it will do any good."

"My brother can be a real bastard at times. He's determined in this, so, no, I don't think it will do any good."

"Then let's talk to the police."

Zach cast her a glance. "Maybe we should just get a couple of shovels."

Elizabeth didn't smile. "Maybe we should."

Twenty-Seven

They reached San Pico as the sun was just setting Sunday night. Zach drove the car directly to the hospital to check on Maria.

They found her propped against a stack of pillows, looking a little less pale, a little stronger, even with her belly a huge mound beneath the white sheet and some kind of drip running into her arm. Still, Zach could read the young woman's exhaustion, see her worry in the purple smudges beneath her eyes.

"How are you feeling?" Liz asked as she approached the bed.

Maria managed to smile. "I am much better. Miguel says I will be able to go home in a couple of days." She looked over at Zach. "It is good to see you, Señor Harcourt. Did you find out anything about the ghost?"

"We may have." Zach glanced at Liz, not quite certain how much he should say, worried that he might upset Maria. He decided to leave out as much as he could, yet try to reassure her that they were moving forward to solve the problem. "We think the child you saw may be a little girl named Carrie Ann Whitt. She disappeared from her parents' home in September of 1969."

"Did she die in the house?"

"There's a chance she died in the old house that used to be there before. We don't know yet for certain. In the meantime, Miguel says you're going to stay with Señora Lopez until the baby comes."

She nodded.

"I think that's a good idea," Liz said, holding on to her hand. "I told Miguel you're welcome to stay at my apartment if you'd rather."

"I want to stay close to my husband and my home."

"I can understand that." Elizabeth managed a smile. "In the meantime, we're going to keep working to figure things out."

They talked a while longer, Maria a little more relaxed, since she wouldn't be returning to the house. As they left the room, Zach spotted Miguel walking down the corridor, carrying a foam cup of coffee in his hand. He looked even more haggard than he had the last time they had seen him — his hair standing up in places, his clothes wrinkled.

He saw them and came to a stop outside the door.

"They are keeping her a few more days," he said. "Then she will be able to go home." His eyes were red and they darted nervously back and forth between Zach and Liz.

Liz gave him a smile. "Maria looks much better."

"*Sí,* I think so, too. The doctor says she is going to be fine."

"And she will be." Zach's words held a note of warning. "As long as you keep her away from the house."

"She does not wish to stay there . . . not until after the baby comes."

Probably not even then, Zach figured, thinking of Carrie Ann and the murderers who had once lived in the house.

Miguel returned to Maria's room, and Zach saw Raul walking toward them down the hall, striding along beside Sam Marston, who waved a greeting.

"Hey, Zach!"

"Good to see you, Sam. You, too, Raul." Raul shook his hand and so did Sam.

The boy tipped his head respectfully. "Hello, Ms. Conners." The earring was gone from his ear, though the tattoo below it remained, along with the one of a skull on the back of his hand.

Elizabeth gave him a smile. "Hello, Raul."

"My sister . . . she is going to be okay. And she is moving out of the house."

"We know," Zach said. "We're damned glad to hear it."

Raul just nodded. "Thank you both for all you have done."

"This isn't over yet, Raul. But we're hoping it soon will be. In the meantime, you keep up the good work you're doing at Teen Vision."

Sam slapped a hand on the strapping youth's shoulder. "He's doing great, just one more exam and he'll have his GED. Passed the last four with flying colors."

"That's terrific, Raul," Liz said.

He flushed a little at the praise, tilted his head toward the door to his sister's room. "I better go in."

"You go ahead," Sam said. "I'll wait for you out here."

Raul disappeared into Maria's room, and Zach turned to Sam. "I imagine you've heard about Maria's ghost."

"Raul told me his sister says there's one in her house. Says she's seen it."

"I know it's hard to believe," Liz told him, "but I saw it, too, Sam." She went on to tell him about the night she and Zach had spent in the house, then the night she had seen the ghostly apparition of the little girl in her party dress and the events that had wound up putting Maria Santiago in the hospital.

Sam scratched his hairless head. "That's a pretty incredible story."

"Totally unbelievable," Zach agreed. "Which means there's no way we can get a warrant to dig under the house."

"No kidding. You don't think Carson will give you permission?"

"Not likely."

Sam glanced both ways down the hall to be sure no one could hear. "Maybe you should just go under the house and start digging, see what turns up."

"So far that appears to be our only option," Liz said.

"I hate to do it," Zach said. "I don't like the idea of digging up a possible forensic site without someone in authority being present."

"So what will you do?"

"I'm not sure. Carson has control of the farm, but technically the property belongs to my father. I could probably gain legal access through the courts, but after what happened to Maria, time is a major problem. We don't want anything bad happening to her husband."

"You don't actually think he might be in danger."

Elizabeth looked at Sam. "You weren't there, Sam. Whatever is happening in that house, the forces unleashed are incredible. No one should have to stay in an evil place like that."

Sam ran a hand over his shiny dome. "This all sounds pretty far-fetched, you know."

"Never were truer words spoken," Zach said.

Sam flashed a grin. "Let me know if there's anything I can do to help."

It was dark by the time they drove out of the hospital parking lot. Both of them were tired from the exhausting weekend and fighting the Sunday night L.A. traffic all the way back to the San Joaquin Valley.

"I've got to go into the office for a while in the morning," Liz said. "I've got three appointments and a bunch of paperwork to do. I can probably take the afternoon off. Maybe we can figure out where to go from here."

Zach just nodded. Whatever they decided, two people telling the same insane story had to be better than one. He could just imagine the look on Sgt. Drury's face if they told him they were after a warrant to search for the body of a ghost. Smiling at the thought, Zach turned the corner onto Cherry Avenue, then drove down the alley into one of the guest parking spaces behind Liz's building.

"Are you spending the night?" Liz asked, her pretty blue eyes on his face.

His gaze moved over the fullness of her breasts and a shot of lust slid into his groin. He couldn't remember wanting a woman the way he did Liz. "You all right with that?"

She gave him a tentative smile. "I must be. I'm already starting to miss you and you haven't even left."

He returned the smile, knowing exactly what she meant. When he was without her, he felt as if something were missing. It was a feeling he had never known before. He hadn't forgotten the comment he had made when they were in bed. He was in love with her. He knew that for certain.

He just wasn't sure what to do about it. And he wasn't sure the feeling was returned.

Parking the Jeep in one of the empty spaces in the near-empty lot behind her apartment, he helped Liz out of the car then went to the back, lifted the rear door, and grabbed their bags. As he closed the door, he noticed the big overhead light that usually lit the parking spaces had burned out. He would have ignored it, except for the faint tickle of awareness raising the hair on the nape of his neck.

"Let's go," he said and started walking, crossing the empty parking lot in as little time as possible, herding Liz ahead of him. The sixth sense he had developed as a punk who ran in bad company was kicking in big time, and he had learned way back then to trust it.

They had almost made it past the tenants' parking garage when the shadowy figure of a man stepped out in front of them. He was dressed in jeans and a black T-shirt, dark-skinned, average height, a woman's nylon stocking pulled over his head. Liz gave a startled gasp as a second man, his appearance much the same, fell in behind them, and another appeared from out of nowhere to join the other two.

Everything happened at once. The first man swung a punch. Zach ducked, then swung a blow that connected with his assailant's jaw, knocking him backward, at the same time kicking out at the second man, slamming his foot hard into the man's left knee. The man went down, sprawling onto the walkway.

"Run!" Zach shouted to Liz, then turned

to see her swinging her white leather bag like a shotput at the third man's head. The blow smashed into his temple, careening him backward several paces.

"Bitch!" the man roared in a heavy Spanish accent, rushing toward her. Zach drove forward to intervene, but the first man hit him a crushing blow to the jaw that knocked him sideways. From the corner of his eye, he saw Liz's attacker grab the front of her blouse and jerk her toward him, saw him slap her roughly across the face.

Fury engulfed him. With a guttural growl, he charged his opponent, driving him backward into the side of the tenants' garage so hard his head snapped back, crashing into the wall and knocking him unconscious. Turning to fight the tallest of the three, he threw a hard punch to the man's face, and a shower of blood erupted from his nose. Zach kicked him in the stomach, doubling him over, then whirled toward the man attacking Liz.

He never saw the length of pipe swinging toward the back of his head, never heard Elizabeth's scream. Instead, a wall of pain hit him, driving him to his knees, and darkness whirled at the edge of his vision. He saw Liz struggling, heard her shout his name and tried to reach her. Instead, a deep black pit opened up and swallowed him, and the world around him disappeared.

Night sounds roused him: the distant whine of a car, the breeze rattling the leaves on the trees next to the building. He stirred and groaned as his memory returned and he saw that Elizabeth leaned over him. Her blouse was ripped open, her slacks streaked with dirt, and there was blood on her face.

"Zach! Zach! Are you all right?"

He groaned again and sat up on the cement walkway holding the side of his head against the pounding in his temple. "I'm all right." He looked up at her, reached out and touched her face, came away with a smear of blood on his fingers.

"What about you?" He rolled to his feet and a wave of dizziness hit him. Fighting to steady himself, he reached a shaky hand into his pants pocket to pull out his cell phone. "You're bleeding. I'm calling an ambulance."

"I — I'm all right, just . . . just shaken up a little. Oh, Zach. Those three men — I think your brother must have sent them."

He stiffened, swayed at a fresh round of dizziness. "What are you talking about?"

"One of them said . . ." She swallowed. "He said this was only a warning. He said we had better stay out of other people's business. If we didn't . . . this was only a sample of what would . . . what would happen to us."

Then she passed out cold, and Zach caught her up in his arms.

Zach drove to the hospital like a madman, squealing the tires around corners, roaring through intersections, ignoring stop signs, picking up a police car in the process, which turned on its siren, commanding him to stop.

He didn't, of course. For the second time in the past few days, he felt frantic, desperate in a way he hadn't been in years.

First Maria, now Liz.

He tilted the mirror to look at the woman lying unconscious in the backseat of his car. Outlined in the moonlight, her face looked deathly pale, and his heart squeezed hard. He pressed down on the accelerator and the Jeep squealed around a corner. If Carson was responsible . . .

He clamped down on the thought. From what Liz said, it couldn't be anyone else. The three men were all Hispanic. Migratory workers, no doubt, men Carson could pay and send on their way and no one would ever miss them. He wondered at his brother's motive. Surely the lawsuit he had begun wasn't enough to warrant this kind of response.

Behind him, the police siren roared. Zach spotted the two-story brick building up ahead, San Pico Community Hospital, and his heartbeat quickened. He had used his cell to phone ahead, told them what had happened, and that he was bringing in an unconscious woman. Two men in white coats were waiting as he drove up in front of the emergency entrance, jammed on his brakes, shoved the car into Park and threw open the door.

One of the attendants was already opening the back door on the opposite side.

"We'll take it from here," he said, eyeing the blood on Zach's clothes and the corner of his mouth. "What's her name?"

"Elizabeth Conners." He looked down at her pale, still form. "I call her Liz."

"Listen, Liz is going to be okay. We'll take care of her. They're going to need you to fill out some paperwork inside. In the meantime, the best thing you can do for her is just keep out of our way."

He nodded, stepped back as someone wheeled up a gurney and they began to lift her out of the car. From the corner of his eye, he saw the police car pull over and park, but the cop seemed to be waiting for the attendants to finish their work before he approached. As the two men settled Elizabeth on the gurney, her face emerged from the shadows and he saw her swollen bottom lip, the purple bruise beside her eye, and rage filled him. If Carson was responsible, the son of a bitch was going to pay.

Zach watched as the attendants wheeled her away, her thick dark hair curling wildly around her shoulders. She looked even paler than she had before and it occurred to him that she might be hurt really badly, that she might actually die.

His stomach clenched and the bile rose in his throat. For the first time he realized what losing her would mean. What if she died? He thought of her beautiful smile and lovely blue eyes, her long legs and the sexy way she moved. He thought of her intelligence and determination. He thought of her loyalty and how much she cared about others, and the knot in his stomach went tighter.

All his life, he had taught himself never to allow his emotions to rule him, never to let himself love anyone too much. It was simply too painful to lose them.

But Zach had broken his lifelong rule. He had fallen in love with Liz.

And now he might lose her.

Zach watched the white-coated attendants wheel her through the emergency room doors, watched her disappear inside, and knew a desolation worse even than the day his mother had given him away.

Zach turned as a wave of nausea hit him and threw up in the bushes outside the hospital door.

Zach wiped his mouth with his handkerchief and shoved the square of white cotton into the back pocket of his navy blue slacks. He turned and saw that the officer had stepped out of the car and was approaching him.

"All right, buddy. Put your hands behind your back. There are speed limits, my friend, and you broke just about every one of them."

"Look, officer, I had to get to the emergency room. I didn't have time to stop and explain." He thought of Elizabeth lying pale and unconscious in a cubicle alone, hurt, maybe even dying, and started walking toward the door.

"She's unconscious. I don't know how badly she's hurt. I had to get her here quickly. If it was your . . . friend, I think you'd do the same." He'd started to say wife, just to be sure he could see her, then caught himself. It was time to face the truth. He couldn't deal with the kind of emotional attachment he felt for Liz. He'd seen that clearly tonight. He had to detach himself, bring some control back into his life.

As soon as all of this was over, he was leaving. And he wouldn't be coming back to San Pico for Liz.

"What happened?" the officer asked, falling in step beside him, apparently deciding to let the matter of the broken speed limits drop.

"We were attacked by three men behind my friend's apartment. One of them hit me over the head with a piece of pipe. One of the others hit my friend."

"You sure she isn't more than just a friend? From the blood on your face, looks to me like maybe the two of you had a fight. Maybe you're the one who hit her. Maybe you're the guy who put her in the hospital."

"I didn't touch her. I told you we were attacked by three men. The lady's name is Elizabeth Conners. She's a family counselor here in Sam Pico." He started walking faster, anxious to find out what was happening, afraid to think how badly Liz might be hurt. Whatever happened between them, he still loved her. Nothing could change that.

He didn't think anything ever would.

They shoved through the glass doors into the emergency room, which was overflowing with humanity, a large percentage of the group Hispanic.

"Elizabeth Conners," he said to a nurse who passed through the room. "Where is she?"

"In cubicle B. You'll need to fill out some paperwork."

"Is she . . . is she going to be all right?"

"You'll have to ask the doctor. She took a pretty bad blow to the side of the head. She must have landed hard, too. Dr. Lopez says she's got a concussion."

A concussion. Damn. Couldn't something like that be deadly? "Is she awake?"

"I think so." The nurse walked off and left him standing there. Zach tore after her, leaving the policeman behind. He poked his head through one of the curtains, saw a white-haired old woman lying on a gurney, searched behind another curtain and saw Liz lying in one of the narrow, sheet-draped beds. He stepped inside, letting the curtain fall behind him, fighting the fear and the lump that was building in his throat.

For several seconds he just watched her, silently praying, as he hadn't done in years. Then she opened her eyes and looked at him, and a wave of relief hit him so hard his knees nearly buckled beneath him.

"Hi . . ."

He sat down in the chair next to her bed, reached out and took hold of her hand. "God, I was so worried. Are you all right? How are you feeling?"

It took an effort for her to swallow. "I'm a little . . . rocky. The doctor wants to run a couple of tests . . . but he thinks I'm going to be all right."

His hand shook as he reached up and touched her face. "I've never been so scared in my life."

"I was scared, too, Zach. When I saw that man coming at you with the pipe . . . I thought he was going to kill you."

He managed to muster a smile. He ought to be the one with the concussion, but apparently he got lucky. "I'm tougher than I look."

"There's blood on your face. Are you . . . sure you're okay?"

"I'm fine." His jaw went hard. "Tomorrow I'm going out to see Carson."

Her fingers tightened on his. "Maybe you shouldn't. Maybe you should just . . . go to the police, tell them what happened."

"We don't have any proof that my brother was involved. We have no idea who those men were and by now they're probably long gone. Carson has an endless supply of people ready to do his dirty work if the price is right."

Liz closed her eyes. "This is all so mixed up. I can't make sense of any of it."

"I know what you mean." He bent and pressed a kiss on her forehead. "Get some rest. Maybe tomorrow things will look better."

Liz nodded, but neither of them believed it.

TWENTY-EIGHT

Elizabeth slept lightly off and on. Dr. Lopez had ordered an overnight stay for observation and scheduled a CAT scan procedure in the morning to be sure there were no serious injuries. Sometime during the night, she'd been moved into a hospital room shared by an older woman asleep in the other bed. One of the nurses gave her some Tylenol for her seemingly endless headache and the general soreness she felt all over.

Just before dawn, she awakened and was surprised to find Zach sitting in the chair, asleep next to her bed.

He was still in the chair when she awakened several hours later, his dark eyes watching her, his expression full of worry and fatigue. A rough shadow of beard outlined his jaw and his dark hair was mussed, making him look dangerous and even sexier than he usually did. If her lip hadn't hurt, she might have smiled.

Instead, she reached over and caught his hand, gave it a reassuring squeeze. "Good morning." The words came out thick and husky, as if her voice didn't work quite right.

He smiled, but his eyes still looked tired, and it was obvious that he was worried about her. "How are you feeling?"

She managed a smile. "Like I've been run over by a truck."

"You were — three of them, as I recall."

"What about you?"

"A little stiff, is all. It's been a while since I've been in a street fight."

"I think you would have taken care of all three of them if it hadn't been for that pipe."

The edge of his mouth faintly curved. "I would have done my best."

A uniformed nurse came in just then and Zach stood up from his chair. His pants were wrinkled, his shirt torn and spotted with dried blood.

"We need to get those tests underway," the nurse said to him kindly. "You can wait in the room down the hall."

Zach just nodded. Reaching toward where she lay against the pillow, he gently traced a knuckle over her cheek. "I'll be here when you're finished."

Elizabeth just nodded. Her heart was squeezing, reminding her how much she loved him. Telling her that here was a man unlike any she had ever known, would ever know again. He had once said that he loved her. When she thought of the way he had looked at her last night, the worry she had seen in his eyes, she found herself believing it might be true.

But this was Zachary Harcourt, the Lone Wolf, and she thought that even if he loved her it might not be enough.

Sitting in the small waiting room down the hall from where the CAT scan was being done, Zach thumbed through the pages of a *Time* magazine, unable to concentrate on the printed words. He couldn't relax until he knew for sure Liz was going to be all right. He tossed the magazine aside and began to pace the near-empty room, his worry mixed with a simmering anger.

What the hell was the matter with Carson? He was bound to be upset about the lawsuit, a petition that asked the court to appoint someone who would agree to the surgery his father so desperately needed. But this kind of response was way out of line.

Damn him!

The fact was, Zach had underestimated

his half brother once again. It had never occurred to him that Carson would actually go as far as hiring a pack of thugs to attack them, that he would order his men to physically attack a defenseless woman.

Tamping down a fresh shot of fury, Zach mulled that over and tried to make himself think like his brother. If the surgery was approved and actually succeeded in restoring Fletcher Harcourt's mental capabilities, Carson might no longer be running Harcourt Farms. He would lose the power he coveted so greatly, the prestige in the community that seemed so important. It might even affect his lofty political ambitions.

Whatever his brother's motives, his men could have killed Elizabeth Conners and Zach wasn't about to let that pass.

The doctor was smiling as he approached where Zach stood next to the coffeepot, and seeing that smile, some of his tension eased.

"The tests came out negative," the doctor said. "There doesn't appear to be any unseen damage. We still have some paperwork to complete before she's released. She'll need time to dress and get ready. Why don't you come back in a couple of hours?"

Zach nodded. "All right. Thanks, Doc, for everything."

While Liz was completing the checkout

process, Zach went back to her apartment to shower and change, then drove out to Harcourt Farms. Unfortunately, when he pulled up in front of the house that had once been his home, he was met by Les Stiles and two of Les's goons.

Obviously they'd been expecting him.

Zach cracked his car door open into the morning heat and stepped out of the car, and Stiles and his cronies came down off the porch. At first, Zach thought the dark-skinned men flanking Les on each side were the guys who had attacked him last night, but during the brawl, he'd landed a few good punches, and these two didn't have a scratch.

Stiles stepped forward. "Where do you think you're going?" His big, meaty hands were wrapped around a baseball bat.

"I'm here to see my brother. Get out of my way, Stiles."

Stiles didn't move. Beneath his battered straw hat, his eyes looked hard. "You're not welcome here, Zach. Not anymore. Your brother wants you off Harcourt property."

"This property belongs to my father, not Carson — no matter what he believes. I'll come here whenever I damn well please."

"Carson runs this place, and as far as he's concerned, you're trespassing." Stiles moved closer, slapping the bat against the palm of his hand, his men staying abreast of him, one on each side. Both were young, hard-muscled, and itching for a fight. Zach's hands unconsciously fisted, every nerve in his body urging him to give them one.

"You're a troublemaker, Zach," Stiles said. "You always have been. You come here looking for trouble and you're gonna find it."

"You mean like last night?"

Stiles just smiled. "All you have to do is mind your own business. You do that, there won't be a problem."

A muscle bunched in Zach's jaw. He forcibly clamped down on his anger. Stiles was as tough as he looked. Even if Zach took down the other two, odds were, against all three of them, he'd come out the loser. He couldn't help his father or anyone else if he wound up like Liz, in some damned hospital bed.

"You tell Carson anything else happens to Liz Conners, he's gonna answer to me, and hiring all the muscle in the world isn't going to help him." Turning away, Zach stalked back to his car and climbed in, his jaw clenched so hard a stab of pain ran up the back of his neck.

Whatever the hell Carson was trying to do, he wasn't going to succeed.

Zach wasn't going to let him.

When it was time to leave the hospital, Elizabeth found Zach waiting for her at the end of the hall.

"You ready?" he asked as the nurse wheeled her up in a wheelchair. His hair was still damp from the shower he had taken and he was wearing clean clothes.

"Believe me, I'm more than ready."

His mouth edged up, drawing her attention to the cut on his cheekbone and the bruise along his jaw, reminding her she wasn't the only one who'd been hurt last night. She wanted to reach out and touch him, make sure that he was all right.

Instead, she leaned back in the wheelchair and let him roll her down the hall to the door.

"I stopped in to see Maria," she told him along the way. "She's going home on Wednesday."

He brought the wheelchair to a halt. "She hasn't changed her mind? She's not planning to go back to the house?"

Elizabeth shook her head. "She's staying with Señora Garcia."

"Thank God for that."

"A couple of policemen paid me a visit. I guess they talked to you last night."

"One of them did."

"I assured them you were not the guy who beat me up."

Zach's lips twitched. "Then I guess I don't have to worry about going back to jail."

She cast him a glance. "At least not for that."

Zach actually grinned.

Outside the hospital, he helped her out of the chair and down the wide front steps, then carefully loaded her into his car as if she were made of glass.

"I'm okay, Zach, really."

Zach nodded and continued to fuss over her all the way back home. He carried her into the apartment, settled her on a stack of pillows on the sofa, and insisted she rest for the day.

Elizabeth didn't argue. Her head ached as if someone were playing pool in the back of her skull, and though she had slept some during the night, she was exhausted.

Zach plumped her pillows for the third time since they got home then grabbed the remote and turned on the TV. He made her some soup, using some dry pasta noodles he found in the pantry along with leftover chicken, a meal far better than her usual Campbell's out-of-a-can fare.

As she ate the soup, he sat down in the

chair next to the sofa, but he didn't stay seated long. He seemed restless, uneasy. Just watching him made her uneasy, too.

Elizabeth used the tuner to mute the sound on the television show that neither of them was watching and propped herself into a sitting position on the sofa, ignoring the stab of pain that shot into her head.

"You're worried, aren't you? You're thinking about the house and what might be happening to Miguel."

Those intense brown eyes fixed on her face. "Among other things, yes."

"What are we going to do, Zach? Maria's still in the hospital. We can't just stop looking for answers, not after we've gone this far."

"No one said we were going to stop."

"Maybe we should go to the police, tell them our suspicions, see if they'd be willing to help."

"They won't believe us. Even I don't believe it half the time."

"We have to try. We have to find out if Carrie Ann Whitt was murdered in that house. We have to see if we can find her body."

"We can't go to the cops without proof." His gaze grew more intense. "Then again, if Carrie Ann is there and we can find her body — we'll have all the proof we need."

Her eyes widened. "Are you saying we're going to search for her ourselves?"

Zach raked a hand through his wavy dark hair. "I've given this a lot of thought, and I don't see any other way."

"Do you really think we can do this on our own?"

"Maybe I can find us some help."

She sat up a little straighter. "Who are you thinking of?"

"Sam offered," Zach said. "Let's see if he meant it."

Zach picked up the telephone, began to punch in the numbers to reach Sam Marston out at Teen Vision. As soon as Sam answered, Zach briefly explained what had happened on the way home from the hospital after their visit with Maria.

"Damn, Zach. Is Elizabeth okay?"

He glanced at her over his shoulder, saw her sitting there propped up on the sofa. Every time he noticed her shattered lip and black eye, he felt a fresh surge of fury at his brother.

"They knocked the hell out of her, Sam. She spent the night at Community, but the doc says in a few days she'll be good as new. The reason I called, I was hoping . . . If I remember right, you have a friend, a guy who took early retirement from the sheriff's department. I think his name is Donahue?"

"That's right, Ben Donahue. Took a bullet during a robbery at one of the local minimarts. Tall blond guy. You met him out at the farm once or twice. He works with the kids in his spare time."

"Yeah, I remember. Seemed like a decent sort. I was hoping maybe you could get him to listen to what we have to say, maybe go in with us when we dig. Then if we find anything, Donahue can bring in the authorities. The house is in the county. That means it's the sheriff's jurisdiction. Ben's word is bound to hold more weight than mine."

"Won't you be trespassing? I don't think he'd go for that."

"Legally, the farm belongs to my father. Carson's the conservator, which gives him control, but it's a very fine line. If we had more time, I could get some kind of access through the court, but time isn't something we have."

"Carson's a powerful man in San Pico. You sure you want to take him on?"

An image of Liz's battered face returned to mind and his hand tightened around the phone. "I've been butting heads with Carson since I was eight years old. Besides, this isn't about my brother. It's about what's happening in that house. Maria Santiago's lying in a hospital bed because of that place. Her husband has been acting more and more strangely. I have no idea what might happen to him if he stays there much longer. Do you think Donahue might agree to at least hear us out?"

"Ben's a good guy. And I've got to admit this whole thing is damned intriguing. I'll call him, see what he has to say."

"Thanks, Sam." Zach hung up the phone and turned to find Liz smiling at him. There was something in her eyes that made his chest feel tight.

"You're amazing, you know that? I bet you really are an incredible lawyer."

Zach smiled, too. "I'm good. No doubt about it."

"But we don't have time to do this by the book."

"Not if we're worried that something might happen to Miguel."

Liz shifted one of the pillows behind her back. "I'm worried about him, Zach. He's been acting strange for weeks, more so lately. I'm convinced that whatever's in that house has incredible power. And I sure as hell wouldn't want to be living there. When do we do this?"

"Wait a minute! You aren't going — you just had your head bashed in. You've got to take it easy."

She pinned him with a glare. "I'm going. You might as well accept it. There is no way in hell you're keeping me away."

Zach almost smiled. He looked at her and thought how beautiful she looked even with her bruised face and cut lip. If he closed his eyes, he could still see her lying there on that gurney, still recall the way he felt when he thought she might die. Now he knew the gut-wrenching pain he would feel if he lost her.

Better to leave now, before he fell for her any harder, before the pain of losing her became too much to bear.

Zach turned away from those beautiful blue eyes that seemed to look inside him. He felt like running, felt like getting in his car and driving away without looking back. He couldn't. Not yet.

"All right, fine, you can go."

"When?"

"The sooner the better."

Elizabeth passed the rest of the day sleeping lightly off and on. She was stiff and sore all over, her body battered and bruised. She was taking some sort of pain medication for the soreness but it made her drowsy. She wasn't taking it tomorrow. She had too much work to do.

She looked over at Zach, who got up to pace off and on, restless in a way she'd never seen him. Since he'd brought her home, he'd been even more distant than he had been before. She knew he was worried. She told herself it was nothing more, but deep down she was afraid it had something to do with her.

It was early that evening that Sam Marston phoned the apartment. Elizabeth answered and handed the phone to Zach.

"That's great," he said, nodding though Sam couldn't see. "So we'll talk to him tomorrow evening."

Sam said something else she couldn't hear.

"All right. Thanks, Sam." Zach hung up the phone and Elizabeth waited anxiously to find out what had been said.

"Donahue's agreed to hear us out. He and Sam are coming over at seven o'clock Monday evening. If we can convince him we're not just a couple of kooks, he'll go in with us Tuesday night."

Tuesday night? Elizabeth bit her lip, then winced at the soreness. "You don't think we could go in during the day?"

"If Carson sees us, he'll sic his two-legged

484

rottweilers on us."

"Even with an ex-cop there?"

"I hate to chance it. I'm not sure how far he's willing to go."

Elizabeth sighed. "I don't get this. Why is your brother so dead-set on keeping us away from the house?"

"I don't know. Maybe it's just a power trip. I know he wants that lawsuit dropped. He's got a lot to lose if the surgery works and my father gets well. I knew running the farm was important to him. I never thought he'd put Dad's health second to his own greedy ambition."

"You always seem to give him the benefit of the doubt."

Zach glanced away. "Maybe I keep wishing he would turn out to be different than he is."

"Maybe you keep wishing he was the brother you never really had."

Zach turned toward her. "Whatever happens, we're going to dig Tuesday night."

"With or without Donahue?"

He nodded.

"We've got to talk to Miguel, convince him not to interfere."

"After what happened to his wife, convincing him shouldn't be a problem."

■ ■ ■ ■

Elizabeth spent all day Monday at her office. Except for a persistent dull headache and a few aches and pains, she felt passably good. She told Michael and Terry she'd been mugged in the alley behind her house but left out her certainty that Carson Harcourt was responsible for the attack, since she didn't really have any proof.

Both of her friends urged her to go to the police and she told them that she had given a report to a pair of uniformed officers at the hospital. Thinking of the plans she and Zach had for tomorrow night, she figured they both might be speaking to the cops in the near future — whether they wanted to or not.

Refilling her coffee mug, she returned to her office and sat down at her desk. Carol Hickman, the twelve-year-old who thought every date should end in the backseat of some boy's car, showed up right on time. They spent the hour talking, making at least some progress with the young girl's self-esteem, Elizabeth thought, the real heart of the problem.

Next she was scheduled to meet with Emilio Mendoza, head of the Mendoza clan, as part of the family's counseling program.

Over the weekend, Richard Long, she discovered, had been tossed into jail for spousal abuse. He'd been released on bail, but didn't show up for his scheduled Monday morning counseling session. She shouldn't have felt any satisfaction in finding out his wife had finally had the courage to press charges, but she did.

While Elizabeth worked at the office, Zach worked long-distance out of her apartment. He represented a number of clients in the firm's Themoziamine class action suit and he liked to stay in touch with them. He had a list of calls to make, including a couple of conference calls with his partner, Jon Noble, and members of the opposing law firm.

"Plenty to do to keep me busy till ex-deputy Donahue arrives for our meeting tonight," he had told her as he walked her to her car. "Are you sure you're feeling well enough to work? Maybe you ought to stay home another day."

"I'm fine, Zach. Just a little headache. Other than that I'm okay."

He gently touched her cheek, his eyes on her face, then he turned away. "Call me if anything comes up," he said over his shoulder. "I'll see you when you get home."

She started the engine of her car, but didn't drive away until he'd walked back inside the apartment. Something was wrong.

Her stomach knotted at the thought of what it might be.

She was late getting home that night. The lunch hour had passed and she hadn't had time to eat. With Sam and Ben Donahue arriving at seven they wouldn't have time to cook dinner. Deciding to stop by the Chinese takeout, she pulled into her open parking garage at just before six that night.

Zach was waiting when she walked though the back door, pacing restlessly in front of the kitchen table, his face a mask of worry. His expression relaxed into one of relief, quickly followed by tight lines of anger.

"Where the hell have you been?"

Surprised at his tone, she held the paper bag she carried out to show him. "I stopped to get some Chinese food, something easy for supper since the men will be here at seven."

He took the bag out of her hand and set it down on the kitchen table. "Why the hell didn't you answer your cell phone? I thought . . . I was afraid . . . I was worried something had happened to you."

She would have been angry if she hadn't

noticed the edge in his voice, the unmistakable trace of fear. He had been frightened, afraid she might have been hurt.

"I'm all right," she said. "I would have called if I'd known you would worry. I don't know how I missed your call. I didn't hear the phone ring."

She slid the strap of her white leather bag off her shoulder and set the purse down on the table. Digging out her cell phone, she flipped it open and checked the dial. "I guess the battery is low."

Zach's gaze found hers, locked and held. She recognized the concern, and something more, something much deeper that made her heart pound with hope. Zach caught her shoulders, drew her against his chest, and very thoroughly kissed her.

"Don't scare me that way again."

Elizabeth went up on her toes and kissed him back. "I won't. I promise."

Zach looked away. He paced over to the window and stared out toward the parking garage. "I don't know, Liz. I don't think I can do this."

"Do what?"

He slowly turned to face her. "Love someone this way. Care this much. It's just not the way I am."

She walked up in front of him, cupped his

cheek with her hand. "I think it's exactly the way you are. I think that's what scares you so much."

When Zach made no reply, she kissed him again and he kissed her back. She could feel his hunger, his growing need, feel his heavy arousal pressing urgently against her.

Then the phone rang and the moment was lost.

Zach gave her a last long glance, then turned and walked over to pick up the phone. Apparently it was Sam, calling to confirm their meeting. Elizabeth busied herself setting out the Chinese food she had bought for the two of them, though she was no longer hungry.

Instead, she thought of Zach and the uncertainty in his voice, and fear of losing him made her stomach churn.

She was in love with him. She believed that he loved her. The question remained, did it matter? And how bad would it hurt if he chose to return to his solitary existence instead of choosing a life with her?

True to his word, Sam Marston arrived with Ben Donahue at seven o'clock. Zach shook hands with both men and Sam introduced Elizabeth to Ben.

"Why don't we go into the kitchen?"

Elizabeth suggested. "There's a table we can use, and we can all have something cold to drink."

"Sam's told me a little about your situation," Donahue said as they made their way into the kitchen and Elizabeth poured frosty glasses of iced tea and set them down on the table in front of the men.

Ben opted for a beer, twisting the top off a Bud Lite Elizabeth gave him, then taking a long, refreshing swallow.

"I gotta say this all sounds completely insane," he said, "but I have to admit, I'm intrigued." He was tall, lean, blond and fair, a good-looking guy in his mid-thirties, single, according to Sam.

Ben had only been in San Pico for about three years, two before he'd been injured on the job and forced to retire, which, Zach had earlier proclaimed, was probably the reason he'd agreed to talk to them.

"He doesn't know much about me or my brother. So far, he's still got an open mind."

Which Donahue proved by listening to the wildest tale any two people ever told. Together Elizabeth and Zach explained, step by step, how they had come to the conclusion that nine-year-old Carrie Ann Whitt might be buried under the little yellow house at Harcourt Farms.

"We worked backward," Zach told him. "We figured, if there really was a ghost like Maria Santiago claimed — which, of course, neither of us actually believed — it must be someone who had died in the house. In this case a little girl, since that was the vision Maria described."

"We didn't find any children who had died," Elizabeth put in, "but we found out that thirty-some years ago, a married couple who had lived in the old house that existed on the very same spot had murdered a little girl up in Fresno a couple of years after they moved away."

"It was a really brutal murder," Zach added, "and both the husband and wife were convicted. In fact, the guy was executed for the crime."

"Wow . . ."

Elizabeth took a drink of her iced tea. "Unfortunately, the little girl in Fresno — Holly Ives — didn't match the description of the ghost in the house on the farm and of course Holly was killed a hundred miles away."

"But you still thought you were onto something," Ben said.

"Exactly." Zach took a drink from his tall, frosty glass. "After reading about the pair and talking to some of the people involved in the case, we got to thinking that maybe someone as evil as these two — maybe they had killed before. Maybe they killed another little girl while they were here in San Pico."

Donahue leaned forward in his chair. "A serial couple?"

"The cops we talked to all agreed they were likely candidates, but they were never able to link them to any other murders in the valley."

"Still, you figured it was worth checking out."

Zach nodded. "I hired a private detective named Ian Murphy to canvas the L.A. basin. We figured if they kidnapped another child and she wasn't from the valley, the next closest place was L.A."

Ben set his beer bottle down on the table. "Don't tell me Murphy actually found a victim who matched the description of the ghost?"

"Incredible, isn't it? And the girl disappeared during the years the Martinez couple lived in the house."

"I can't believe this."

Zach leaned back in his chair. "Who the hell in his right mind would?"

Elizabeth stared into Ben's face. "I saw her, too, Ben — just like Maria Santiago. The ghost of a little girl."

Ben held up a hand. "Okay, okay. At this point you assume your ghost really was this little girl who went missing in L.A. What'd you do next?"

"We talked to the detective who worked on the abduction," Zach told him. "He's retired now, a guy named Danny McKay. McKay remembered Carrie Ann Whitt. He even recalled what she was wearing the day she disappeared."

"Good memory. So what did she have on?"

"A party dress," Elizabeth answered. "A pink pinafore, just like the one the little girl who appeared in the house was wearing. You see, the day she disappeared was Carrie Ann's birthday. That's why he remembered."

Donahue pushed up from his chair, beer bottle in hand. "This is nuts."

"You're telling us?" Elizabeth said.

"There are things going on in that house," Zach continued. "Dangerous things. We need to find out if she's there, if that's what all this is about."

"Why are you so convinced you'll find her there? Even if these people actually murdered the girl, they could have buried her anywhere around here."

"True enough." Zach finished his iced tea

and set the glass back down on the table. "But the Martinezes buried Holly Ives in the basement of their house in Fresno. So . . ."

"Jesus!"

"Exactly," Zach said. "Holly was tortured, raped and strangled. It was a terrible, brutal murder, the kind of violent death that, according to what we've been reading, might result in the spirit remaining in the house."

"But you said yourself Holly wasn't killed in San Pico."

"No, but we think Carrie Ann Whitt might have been," Elizabeth said. "That's why we need your help."

Ben sank back down in his chair. The knuckles wrapped around his beer bottle looked pale. "Who the hell would believe a wild-ass story like this?"

"I don't even believe it," Zach grumbled.

Elizabeth reached over and touched Ben's hand. "We have to find out if it's true, Ben."

He looked at her and then at Zach. "Crazy as it sounds, I'm beginning to see why you think it might be."

"So you'll help us?"

"Like Sam said, you sure can't go to the police. Which means you got no choice but to look for her yourself."

"No choice at all," Zach said.

Ben began a slow grin. "In that case, I guess we're going to have to dig."

Sam grinned, too.

The corner of Zach's lips barely lifted.

Elizabeth thought of the little blond girl who looked like an angel and what might have happened to her and didn't smile at all.

TWENTY-NINE

Elizabeth went into the office early Tuesday morning while Zach stayed home and made calls from her apartment. He was growing more and more distant, as though he had never been frightened for her, as though they had never talked about love, as though they were friends and nothing more.

They hadn't made love last night, though she had hoped they would. Zach had hardly touched her since the attack. She told herself he was waiting for her to heal, but she knew it wasn't the truth. He was afraid of his feelings for her.

Afraid of what might happen if he gave in to them.

She was determined to talk to him, to get things out in the open, but couldn't seem to find the right time. When the phone on her desk rang just before noon, she was surprised to hear Zach's deep voice on the line. It rolled over her like a caress, sent her nerve endings into high gear, and she thought again how much she had come to love him.

Lately, she'd had plenty of time to think and whenever she did, she remembered the look on Zach's face when she had opened her eyes in the emergency room and seen him standing there in the room.

He had told her that he loved her. When she thought of that moment, she believed him. She had seen it, written so clearly on his face. He loved her and she loved him.

And in these past few days, she had come to a decision. No matter how hard he tried to convince himself it couldn't work, she wasn't giving up on them.

Not without a fight.

"I just got a call from my office," he said into the phone. "Apparently Dr. Marvin went to see the judge assigned to my father's case. He told the judge it was urgent that Dad's operation take place as soon as possible, that the chances for success went down with every day they waited. The judge has agreed to a hearing Thursday morning."

There was something in his voice, a note of optimism that hadn't been there in days.

"You're smiling, I can tell. What is it?"

"The judge . . . his name is Hank Alexander. He was my father's best friend."

"Oh, my God." She shifted the phone

against her ear. "Isn't he supposed to re-cuse himself or something, since he knows one of the parties so well?"

"I don't think he will. If he knows my father as well as I think he does, he knows Fletcher Harcourt would want this surgery as much as I want it for him. I think he'll hear the case himself."

"Oh, Zach, I hope so. I really do."

He cleared his throat. "Listen, I've got to go. I'm working on a brief I need to finish. And I've got a couple of things to do before Donahue and Sam show up."

"All right, I'll see you at the apartment."

"Yeah . . ." he said softly. "I'll see you tonight."

Elizabeth hung up, wondering what she had heard in his voice. Yearning, she thought. Maybe he heard it, too. Maybe he would realize how much he cared and decide their relationship could work. Maybe he would decide he loved her enough to stay.

If he did — if he ever really made that kind of commitment — Elizabeth had come to believe he would keep it. She was con-vinced he was that kind of man.

Zach wasn't at the apartment when she got home. Elizabeth changed into jeans and a sleeveless white blouse meant for the Salvation Army bag, tied the tails up around her waist, and went into fix herself a glass of iced tea.

Zach arrived a few minutes later, carrying a small paper sack, which he set down of the table beside her glass. "I brought you a sandwich. I didn't think you'd want to cook."

She opened the bag and peered down at the crusty slices of bread.

"Turkey and cheese. I hope that's okay."

She nodded, but she wasn't hungry. Just thinking of the night ahead made her stomach roll. She looked down at the bag. "Where's yours?"

"Not hungry. Maybe I'll catch something later."

She rolled the sack closed and set the sandwich aside. "I think I will, too."

At ten after seven, Ben Donahue arrived. Sam walked in behind him.

"Thanks for coming," Zach said, shaking both men's hands. He led them into the kitchen and Elizabeth poured them a glass of iced tea. She offered Ben a beer but he declined with a grin.

"Tonight I think I'd better have my wits about me."

Sitting around the kitchen table, they talked about the house and the best way to approach the search. Zach showed them a grid he had made on the computer to use as a way of keeping track of their progress and mentioned the access hole on the side where they could go in.

"I bought some lights at Wal-Mart I think will work pretty well. It's going to be dark down there. We'll need as much light as we can get to see what we're doing."

"I've got a couple of short-handled shovels in my car," Ben said.

"We'll have plenty then. I bought some when I got the lights." Zach drained the last of his tea. "Along with a couple of buckets if we need to move the dirt around."

"I brought something I thought might help," Sam said. "A metal detector. I borrowed it from a friend."

"Great," Zach said. "Maybe it'll pick up something useful."

They went over a few last details and by the time they finished, it was getting dark.

"Time to go," Zach said, rolling up the grid he had printed out, wrapping a rubber band around it. "We've got to talk to Miguel before we start digging. I thought about going over there last night, but I didn't want him to have time to change his mind or maybe say something to Carson."

"What if he won't agree?" Ben asked.

Zach's jaw hardened. "He'll agree. I'm not

giving him a choice."

The night was dark, only a fingernail moon, the little house rising up out of an inky blackness. Though it looked no different than a thousand other houses, Elizabeth shivered.

"Maybe he's not home," she said, looking toward the windows of a darkened living room.

"He damned well better be. I called him. I told him we'd be coming over. I told him we needed to talk to him."

"He goes to work early. Maybe he's already in bed."

Sam and Ben stood next to them in the driveway. "You think he's in there?" Ben asked. They had all come in Zach's Jeep, which he'd parked next to the garage until they could unload their gear.

"You guys stay here and I'll go see."

"I'll go with you." Heading for the front porch, Elizabeth walked next to Zach up the porch stairs. Zach cast a glance her way, then knocked on the door. Inside the house, Elizabeth heard muttered curses, someone stumbling around inside, moving toward them across the living room, then the porch light went on and the door swung open.

Miguel Santiago stood in the threshold,

though for a moment, she didn't recognize him. His clothes were wrinkled and dirty, his black hair a long, tangled nest around his head, and his eyes were hollow and sunken in. In the faint light inside the house, she could see the odd, waxiness of his skin, the way his nostrils flared when he realized who stood on his doorstep.

"Sorry if I woke you," Zach said, stepping protectively in front of her. Seeing the wild look in Miguel's eyes, she was grateful. She backed a little farther away.

"I was not asleep." No, he just looked like he'd been sleeping in his clothes for a couple of days.

"We need to talk to you, Miguel."

"Why?"

Zach moved forward, forcing Miguel back inside the house, flicking on the lamp near the sofa. Elizabeth followed them in, turning off the porch light and closing the door behind them.

"We need to search for something," Zach said. "We've come to do that tonight."

Miguel frowned and shook his head as if he tried to clear his thoughts. "I do not understand."

For the next few minutes, Zach patiently explained about the murder they believed might have taken place in the old house that used to sit on the spot where Miguel's newer house now sat. Zach told them how they had searched and found a child who had disappeared, a little girl who looked like the ghost Maria had seen in the house, and that a couple who lived in the old house might have killed her. He explained that they believed they might find her body buried in the ground underneath.

"Things are happening here, Miguel," Elizabeth said gently. "Things that can't be explained. Surely you have felt these things. Surely you have noticed there is something wrong in here."

Miguel glanced away. "I have never seen a ghost."

"We think she comes to Maria because of the baby," Zach said.

"The ghost is trying to warn her that your baby is in danger," Elizabeth added.

Miguel seemed to be having trouble sorting all of this out.

Elizabeth reached over and caught his hand. "Look at you, Miguel. You aren't yourself lately. You haven't been for some time. You're angry. You've been drinking way too much. It's the house, Miguel. Whatever is here is making you act this way. We have to find a way to stop it. We have to look for the little girl. If we find her, maybe all of this will end."

For the first time, Miguel seemed to understand. "My wife believes there is a ghost. And I am not myself at all." He looked down at his wrinkled, dirty clothes as if seeing them for the first time. "Do what you must."

"Thank you," Elizabeth said.

While Zach went to the door and motioned for the men to unload their gear and move the car out of sight down the road, Elizabeth said a few more quiet words to Miguel.

"Everything is going to be all right, Miguel. We just need to find out the truth."

He nodded, seemed resigned, perhaps even relieved. "How will you do it?"

Zach walked up just then. "We'll go under the house through the access in the side. We've got lights so we can see and shovels to dig. We'll follow a pattern. That way we'll be sure to cover all of the ground. It may take more than one night."

"There is a way in through a hole in the floor of the bedroom closet," he said. "I will show you."

"Great."

They used both entrances, bringing in the lighting gear and a number of long, heavy-duty extension cords. A big piece of cardboard was used to cover the access hole at the side of the house so the lights couldn't be seen. Then they lowered the shovels and buckets and Sam's metal detector through the hole in the floor.

Zach took the grid sheet and dropped down through the access hole beneath the closet floor, followed by Sam and Ben.

"I'm coming with you," Elizabeth said. "I know you have plenty of shovels." Dropping down behind the men, bending over to fit beneath the floor, she picked up one of the shovels. The shorter handle made it lighter, she was happy to see, easier to use.

"You don't have to do this," Zach said. "I kind of figured you could just keep tabs on Miguel."

"I'm fine. I want to help."

He started to argue, but her warning look told him not to.

"Not much headroom under here," Ben grumbled. "Good thing the house isn't very big."

Using his flashlight, Zach panned the area under the house. Being just four years old, its condition wasn't too bad — only a few spiderwebs clinging to the floor joists and a cluster of bugs here and there, scurrying off into the shadows.

Elizabeth pulled up the collar of her

blouse and refused to think what else might be lurking in the darkness. "It's damp down here," she said, noticing the moist earth beneath them for the first time. "How can that be?"

Zach shined the flashlight on the garden hose stuck in through the side access. He grinned. In the harsh light and dark shadows, his features were distorted, making him look like a demon.

"I came by early yesterday and started the water while Miguel was at work. Earlier today I moved the hose around so it covered a different area. I just turned it off. I figured the ground would be a whole lot easier to dig."

Ben smiled. "Good thinking."

Sam turned on his metal detector, whose handle barely cleared the floor joists. Bent over, moving crablike, he began to make a sweep of the area under the house.

They had decided to dig down a couple of feet in each grid square, then run the metal detector again in that particular location. If they didn't find anything, and since there wasn't much room to stack the dirt, they would refill the square and dig the next. Sam finished his cursory sweep with the metal detector, turning up a few rusty nails and a quarter that read 1947 in the bank of lights that blazed under the house, then they started to dig.

Trying to decipher the placement of a possible grave, Ben and Sam worked the grid starting in the middle of the southwest quarter of the house, working outward, while Zach and Elizabeth started in the middle on the southeast quarter and did the same.

They'd only been digging for a very few minutes when Miguel jumped down through the opening. "I have decided to help. If there is a body, I will help you find it."

He seemed a little more himself, a little less distracted. He had even combed his wild mane of hair.

"Great." Zach handed him a shovel. "We can use all the help we can get."

And it didn't take long to discover how true those words were. Elizabeth's back ached from working in the awkward bent position and her hands were already getting sore. Zach laid out the grid pattern with string, covering the ground inside the square concrete foundation of the house.

He fanned one of the lights around the perimeter of cement, lighting the area.

"Looks like they actually used the old foundation instead of pouring a new one —

at least wherever they could. The old house was a little bigger, though, which means there's a chance the gravesite might actually be outside the existing house. But this would have been the main section for both. For now, let's hope we're in the right place."

Though it was cooler under the house than it was outside, it didn't take long for all of them to break out in a sweat. Moving the damp soil around was extremely hard work, but everyone was determined.

They took a break after an hour, climbing out through the hole in the closet floor, making their way straight to the ice chest filled with soft drinks Elizabeth had fortunately thought to bring.

Gatorade and Diet Cokes, all she'd had in the fridge.

"Man, I'm glad you thought of this," Sam said, guzzling half a bottle of Gatorade, wiping his shaved head with the cold moisture off the bottle. Zach popped the top on a Diet Coke and held the can out to Elizabeth, who took a good long drink and passed it back.

Zach finished the can. "How are your hands holding up?"

She looked down at them and winced, noticing the first sign of blisters. "Not as good as I'd hoped."

"The rest of us all brought gloves. Maybe Miguel has an extra pair around somewhere."

"*Sí,* I have some gardening gloves that Maria likes to wear. She loves to garden. I will get them for you." There was such a wistful note in the younger man's voice, a lump rose in Elizabeth's throat. This entire family needed help. She prayed that tonight they would get it.

Miguel returned with the gloves and they all went back to work. She and Zach had just cleared another square in the grid — without any luck — when a deep voice reached them from above.

Raul Santiago dropped down through the access hole. "Do not be angry. Pete and I came to help . . . if Sam says it's okay."

Hunched over, Sam duck-walked forward to where the two boys crouched. "Dammit, how did you know about this?"

"I heard you talking to Zach on the phone. We will go back if that is what you want, but this is my sister's house. We both have strong backs and we would like to help."

Sam sighed, but without any real rancor, and perhaps a hint of relief. It was really hard work. The more help the better.

"I'll call the farm," he said, "tell them you're with me and Zach." Sam passed over his shovel. "Here. You want to work. Get to it."

Raul grinned, making another ugly face in the eerie lights. "Thanks, Sam."

"I'd save my thanks until later," Sam warned as he hoisted himself up through the floor.

Zach took Elizabeth's shovel out of her hand. "Take a break. Let Pete dig for a while."

Pete smiled as he gripped the shovel. He was Raul's best friend, shorter than the beefy young Hispanic, thinner, a wiry youth with dark eyes and friendly smile. His black hair was short, flat on the top and combed upward, not radically, which wasn't allowed at Teen Vision, but neat and stylish.

As the shovel left her fingers, Elizabeth couldn't help an inward sigh of relief. Her hands were hurting and sweat trickled between her breasts. She wasn't used to manual labor. And she could start digging again a little later.

They traded off after that, four men on, working two grid squares, the others resting or getting something cold to drink. When the cold drinks ran out, they switched to water, which tasted delicious after the dirty, backbreaking labor.

By midnight they were all getting discouraged.

They had covered nearly the entire top half of the grid, but found nothing of interest. Each time a grid square was exposed, Sam ran the detector over it, hoping to pick up a clue of some kind. So far, there hadn't been any new sounds, nothing but a few more nails that had worked their way deeper into the soil.

Of all the men, Miguel seemed to be working the hardest. He refused to trade off with anyone and simply continued to dig, working like a madman.

The thought made Elizabeth uneasy. She kept seeing an image of Jack Nicholson in *The Shining.* Any minute she expected Miguel to grin and leer, "Heeere's Johnnie."

Instead he just kept digging.

"You need to take a break," Zach said to him, having a similar thought.

"Not yet." Miguel tossed out another shovelful of dirt, then plunged his shovel into the ground for another. When the square was complete, Sam ran the metal detector over the dirt and this time picked up a pinging sound from the machine. It came from the far left corner of the square and everyone's attention focused there.

"I'll get the hand rake and trowel." Zach went for the tools, then returned and jumped into the hole. Bending down, he carefully raked the dirt away from whatever it was they had found. It was buried deep. He used the trowel to dig down, then used the rake again. Something clinked. He pulled up a piece of metal, but couldn't make out what it was.

Moving over to the bank of lights, he held it out in his palm. "It looks like some kind of medallion, maybe a military medal of some kind."

"Can you make out the writing?" Sam asked.

"Looks like some other language."

Ben came over to look. "I think it's military, all right. You said the old house was built here during the war."

"That's right."

Whatever it was, it didn't look like a clue to finding the body they were searching for. Setting the rusty old medal aside, tired and discouraged, everyone went back to work.

THIRTY

The heat and the closed-in space finally got to him. Zach gave up and took off his shirt. His back ached from the bent-over working position and sweat covered his face, neck and torso. He'd known it was a crazy idea, finding the body of a ghost, but over the course of the past few weeks, he had actually come to believe they would find the little girl, Carrie Ann Whitt, buried under the house.

Inwardly, he cursed, called himself an idiot and a fool. There were no such things as ghosts. This was all just some crazy series of coincidences. He had half a dozen people down here breaking their backs and for what?

A big fat zero, no doubt.

He hefted another shovelful of dirt. With so many people working, they had covered more than three quarters of the grid squares on his printed plan. Everyone was hot and sweaty, tired and wishing this was over. But no one was willing to quit until they had covered every inch of ground under the house.

He was working again with Liz, though he had argued with her about it. He didn't want her down here busting her ass for nothing. He couldn't believe he had actually convinced himself they were going to find a body down here.

"Hey, Zach. What's that god-awful smell?" It was Sam, glancing around and oddly sniffing the air.

For the first time he noticed it. Not the foul, unmistakable odor of a rotting body. A thirty-six-year-old corpse would be decayed well past that stage. Instead the odor was heavy, cloying. Such a nauseating smell it made the bile rise up in his throat.

"Roses . . ." Liz said, looking across at him, a trace of fear creeping into her eyes.

"Smells awful," Ben said. "Like a decaying compost pile, only worse. And kind of sickening-sweet."

Miguel made a kind of hissing sound in his throat. "I have smelled it before."

So had Zach. The night he had come with Liz to the house.

"Maybe they're doing something to get ready for the Rose Festival," Sam said hopefully. "It starts next week."

Liz looked at Sam and shook her head. "She's here . . ." Her gaze darted around the tight space beneath the house. "The smell comes . . . whenever she appears."

Ignoring the nauseating odor and the conviction he heard in her voice, Zach jammed his shovel into the dirt, more irritated than ever. But instead of the blade sinking in, he felt a sharp jolt of resistance.

He tried again, more gently this time, felt an object beneath the blade.

"You find something?" Sam moved toward him beneath the floor joists as Zach jumped the two feet down into the square they had nearly finished digging.

"Hand me the hand rake and trowel." Kneeling in the dirt, he took the garden tools Sam handed him while the others moved toward him, forming a group around the edge of the hole. Liz stood above him, her face gone pale in the eerie glow of the lights.

Raul moved one of the light poles into a better position, fully illuminating the grid square, while Zach carefully began using the trowel, digging around the area where the shovel had hit, then using the rake to clear some of the dirt away.

"This is weird," Ben said, glancing around.

"How can it be getting cold in here?"

Goose bumps rose across Zach's bare chest. *How, indeed?* he thought, remembering the night he had spent in the house, remembering what he'd read about cold spots and beginning to feel as uneasy as Liz. Around the hole, it wasn't just cold, it was freezing. Zach ignored it and continued to dig.

"Can you tell what it is?" Raul asked, leaning over the hole, looking a little uneasy himself.

"Can't tell yet." But little by little, the object began to appear, something dark that looked like a piece of rotten leather. There was something underneath it. "Toss me the brush."

Pete went to get it, brought it back and handed it to Zach. Clustered around the square on their hands and knees, everyone watched as Zach used the trowel, rake and brush to uncover more and more of what lay buried in the earth.

"What is it?" Ben asked.

Ignoring the freezing temperature and the sight of his breath in the lights, Zach dug a little more, brushed the dirt away, and uncovered a square piece of metal that rose above what appeared to be a hunk of rotten black leather.

"It looks like a buckle of some kind."

Liz made a sound in her throat. "Oh, God, it's a little shoe buckle." Her gaze was riveted on the rusted chunk of metal, and he knew in an instant what they had found.

"The day she disappeared . . ." Liz said, "Carrie Ann was wearing . . ." She swallowed. "She was wearing a pair of black patent leather shoes. I think that's what that bit of leather is, and that's the buckle that must have been on top of her shoe."

He dug a little more, revealing bit by bit what they now all believed lay beneath the dirt. The shoe was mostly gone, eaten away by time and insects, but there was enough of it to recognize what it had been. He brushed away more dirt, exposing the first glimpse of bone, and heard Liz's sharp intake of breath.

Undisturbed for all these years, protected beneath the house from animals and weather, the body would remain pretty much the way it had been placed in the homemade grave. Though most of the clothes would have rotted away and the flesh would be gone, the bones would remain in the position they had been in from the start.

The moment the anklebone appeared,

Zach stopped digging. He carefully removed a little more dirt from the area and saw that a shinbone followed. Smaller than those of an adult, they could only be the bones of a child.

"Time to call the sheriff. Wouldn't you say so, Ben?"

Ben nodded gravely. Like everyone under the house, he was eager to leave. "I'll make the call right now." Moving toward the access hole in the closet, Ben hauled himself up and hurried off to use the phone.

They left the site exactly as it was. Crouching low, Raul and Pete followed Ben. They had almost reached the exit when Raul paused.

"That sounds like a train."

"Can't be," Sam said. "Track was abandoned years ago. The tracks aren't even there anymore."

The flashlight in Miguel's hand began to tremble. "It comes some nights . . . about this time. It comes down the track that is not there."

"I'm getting out of here," Pete said, scrambling toward the exit, Raul close on his heels. Following the boys, Zach grabbed his shirt and pulled it on over his head, noticing for the first time that the temperature had returned to normal. He reached for Liz's hand to help her out through the hole, and realized she was trembling. He looked over to see tears in her eyes.

"Time to go, love," he said gently, not wanting to be down there anymore than the boys.

Liz looked back at the shallow grave. "I knew she would be here . . . I knew it . . . but I prayed I'd be wrong."

Zach squeezed her hand. "It's all right, baby. If it's Carrie Ann, she'll finally be able to go home."

Liz nodded and the tears in her eyes ran down her cheeks. Zach helped her out of the opening into the house and climbed out behind her.

As much as he ached for the dead child and its mother, at the moment all he could think of was how the hell they were going to explain all this to the police.

THIRTY-ONE

The ten-minute wait for the cops to arrive seemed like hours. Elizabeth paced the small, sparsely furnished living room listening to the distant sound of sirens. A little while later, three sheriff's department patrol cars rolled up in front of the house. As Zach and Ben let the group of uniformed deputies into the living room, Elizabeth waited anxiously by the door.

"Thanks for coming," Ben said to Bill Morgan, the county sheriff. Morgan was tall, his blond hair streaked with silver, making it even paler than Ben's, a big, husky man who looked as if his ancestors could have been Vikings.

"They called me at home," Morgan said. "Figured I'd better get out here."

"Sorry about that," Ben said.

"Hey, that's what I'm paid for."

It was agreed Ben would talk to the sheriff first. He was a former deputy in the district, and Elizabeth and Zach both hoped that with Ben reporting the discovery, the insane story would sound more believable.

"Let's go into the kitchen," Morgan said to Ben. He cast a look at Zach. "I'll talk to you two in a minute." Morgan had recently been elected sheriff of San Pico County and so far had a good reputation.

Still, when he returned to the living room it was obvious he'd had a hard time believing Ben's story.

He fixed his attention on Zach. "Donahue's told me some of this. I'd say it's down right crazy, but since it seems there's a body under the house —" For confirmation, he glanced over at a deputy who had just returned from a trip below.

"They got a body, all right. Too small to be an adult, but it's definitely human. Been there a good long while, I'd say."

Morgan nodded, pulled a small notepad out of his light tan shirt pocket and flipped it open, then returned his attention to Zach. "Looks like Ben was right. Sooo . . . I guess I've got to listen to what you have to say."

Zach looked at Elizabeth as if he didn't quite know where to begin, then plunged in. "First of all, as your deputy said, I think you're going to find out the body has been down there for years, possibly since the sixties. I presume Ben mentioned the Martinezes, the husband and wife who murdered a young girl in Fresno?"

"He did. Apparently he thinks they may have been a serial couple who killed the victim you found under the house."

"According to what we've discovered, I think it's highly possible. As you follow up on this, Sheriff, chances are you're going to find out the victim was abducted in 1969 from her parents' home in Sherman Oaks. Her name is Carrie Ann Whitt."

The sheriff made notes in his pad.

"The year Carrie Ann disappeared, the Martinezes were living in the old gray house that sat on this spot way back then. By the way, if it turns out the body's that old, it means none of us could have had anything to do with the crime, since we weren't even born then."

"That's right, Sheriff," Elizabeth added. "We only got involved in this when Señora Santiago began having trouble."

"Any chance the Santiagos are related in some way to the Martinezes? Maybe their parents knew them, might have somehow found out about the body and told them about it?"

"They've only got a few distant relatives who live up north," Elizabeth said, "and their parents weren't even living in this country back then."

The sheriff pinned her with a doubtful stare. "So the way you figured all of this out is that the lady who lives here has been seeing a ghost."

"I know it's hard to believe," Elizabeth told him. "At first we didn't believe it, either. Then we started doing some research. This is where it led us."

Morgan scratched his big silver-blond head. He started to say something else, but a commotion at the door drew his attention as the county coroner and his men walked in, carrying their equipment.

"Body's under the house," he told them. "There's an access through the closet in the bedroom, another outside on the north side of the residence." Morgan pointed toward the bedroom and the men clopped off that way.

He returned his attention to her and Zach. "If what you say pans out and the girl really is Carrie Ann Whitt, we're talking about kidnapping. That means we'll be calling in the feds."

Zach nodded.

"I need you to write all this down . . . how you figured this out, who you talked to, everything that happened up until tonight.

In the meantime, I don't want any of you leaving town."

Zach flicked a glance at Elizabeth, who wished she weren't so glad he would have to stay. Of course, the hearing for his father's operation was set for Thursday, so even if he went back to L.A., he would have to return.

"You finished with us?" Zach asked.

"I'll need to talk to the others, get their take on all this. As soon as I'm done, you can all go home. But like I said, I need you to stay in the area. There's bound to be more questions."

Watching the sheriff, trying not to think what those questions might be, Zach nodded. He rested a hand at Liz's waist and guided her over to the sofa to wait while the sheriff spoke to Raul, Pete, Sam and Miguel.

They had just sat down when the front door slammed open and Carson came bursting into the house. He spotted Zach and stopped dead still in front of the sofa, his blue eyes iron hard.

"What the hell's going on here?"

Sheriff Morgan turned away from the discussion he was having with Miguel. "Evenin', Carson. I guess you heard the sirens. I'm glad you're here."

Carson's face was a mottled shade of red. His goons had failed to keep them away. Carson didn't like failure. "What's happening, Bill? This is Harcourt Farms property. I have a right to know."

"I was planning to stop by first thing in the morning. As you say, this is your property so you need to know that as of now, this place is a crime scene."

"A crime scene? Santiago do something to his wife?"

Zach couldn't help wondering if Carson had noticed the changes in his overseer's behavior in the past few weeks, though it was doubtful he would involve himself that closely with one of his workers.

"It's nothing like that. Your brother and his friends found a body under the house."

Carson's face went bone-white. "Someone . . . someone's been murdered?"

"Take it easy. From the way it looks, it happened a long time ago. At least thirty or forty years, maybe more. According to your brother and Ms. Conners, there's a good chance the people who did it have already been dealt with."

Some of the color washed back into Carson's face, though he still looked visibly shaken. "I see."

"We'll expect your full cooperation."

"Of course. That goes without saying." He didn't look at Zach or Liz but it was clear he wasn't pleased. His kingdom had been breached. His hired thugs hadn't been able to keep them away from the house. Now he was forced to deal with the consequences.

Zach thought he looked ready to explode.

"The Santiagos will need a place to stay until this is resolved," the sheriff said.

Carson's jaw moved back and forth. "The Easy 8 Motel is the closest. They can stay there until you're finished with the house. Harcourt Farms will take care of the expense."

Liz surged to her feet. "They'll need to stay until the baby comes. Maria can't deal with this right now, she's too close to her delivery date."

Carson gritted his teeth. "Fine. They can stay until she has the baby."

Barely able to hide his fury, Carson talked to the sheriff a moment more, then said goodbye to Morgan and left without a word to either Zach or Liz.

"My brother doesn't look like a happy man," Zach said.

"That's an understatement," Liz agreed.

Sam, Raul and Pete finished answering the sheriff's questions and all of them were finally able to leave. The deputies drove Sam and the boys the short distance back to Teen Vision, and Zach and Liz drove Ben back to his car which was parked at her apartment.

At last they were home and alone.

Zach watched Liz walk over to the sofa and wearily sink down. "I still can't quite believe it," she said. "Carrie Ann was there, just like we thought."

She'd been a real trouper tonight, he thought, demanding to do her share of the work even when she was so tired she could barely stand. And finding those little bones . . . knowing they had to belong to a child. It was obvious how badly she had been shaken.

"The whole damned night was surreal," he said. "The train whistle, that awful rose smell. Finding the body of a ghost. I don't think the Santiagos should ever move back in."

"Neither do I." She looked away from him toward the window, though the curtains were closed and it was too dark to see. When she turned, he caught the sheen of tears.

"I keep thinking about Paula Whitt. I can't imagine how she's going to feel when she finds out her little girl was murdered, maybe even tortured and raped."

Zach sat down next to her and gathered her into his arms. She looked so damned tired, so emotionally drained. He wished he hadn't let her go with them. Then again, she wouldn't have had it any other way.

"We still can't be certain it's her," he said. "Not yet. We don't even know for sure the child is a girl or that she was actually the victim of a crime and didn't die some other way. They'll have to get a DNA sample from the mother and try to match it to the body. It could take months for that to happen. Unless they run across some other clue, that's the only way to know for sure it's Carrie Ann."

"It's her," she said, leaning into his shoulder. "I know it is."

Zach just held her. He could feel her shaking as she silently wept and he didn't try to stop her. He had a feeling she was right, that all the weird coincidences they had stumbled onto weren't coincidences at all. That the DNA would prove the child was Carrie Ann Whitt.

He lifted her chin, forcing her to look at him. "If it's her, if it's really Carrie Ann, then she'll finally be at peace. And after all the years of wondering, her mother will be able to put this behind her and get on with the life she's worked to make for herself."

Liz nodded, pressed her cheek to his, and he could feel the soft brush of her glorious dark hair. Her breasts pressed into his chest and he felt the lush fullness. For days he had wanted her. Tonight, sex was the last thing on his mind.

"It's been a long night," he said. "Why don't you go in and take a shower? We're both sweaty and dirty. I'll take one when you get out."

She nodded, wearily stood up from the sofa. She started to walk away, then turned back and reached for his hand. "Come with me." She looked up at him, her eyes on his, the most beautiful shade of blue he'd ever seen. "I need you tonight, Zach. Make love to me."

He wasn't thinking about sex. But he hadn't stopped thinking of making love to her since they had walked into the apartment. She needed him, she said. Not as much as he needed her.

Sliding a hand into her hair, he ran his thumb along her jaw and gently tipped her head back to receive his kiss. Their mouths met and held. He felt her soft lips tremble under his and for a moment he deepened the kiss.

When he eased away, he saw that there were tears on her cheeks. She didn't say anything, just led him into the bedroom and began to remove her clothes. Zach did the same and they headed for the bathroom. The shower went on, warmed to a soft spray that rushed over his skin as he followed Liz into the water.

Wordlessly, they soaped each other down, then rinsed in the spray and soaped again. He loved her body, the full breasts and slender waist, the pretty legs and patch of dark curls between them. He was hard. He kissed her deeply, kissed her breasts, began to stroke her. He might have made love to her there in the shower if the water hadn't started getting cold.

Instead, they stepped out and dried each other off, and he carried her into the bedroom. They made love slowly, determined to bring each other pleasure, giving and taking until each of them reached a powerful release. Then he curled her against him in the middle of the bed, smoothed her glossy dark hair away from her face, and watched as she closed her eyes and drifted off to sleep.

I love her, he thought, as he had before. He loved her and wondered if she loved him.

Every day, his feelings for her continued to deepen. The longer he stayed, the risk of losing himself became greater.

He wondered if he could find the courage to leave.

THIRTY-TWO

There were questions, more and more questions. The FBI wouldn't be called in, the sheriff said, until all of the facts had been gathered and assessed, and they matched the story Elizabeth and Zach had told him.

But the body had been excavated from beneath the house and found to be that of a child, as they had believed. A sample of DNA had been taken from Paula Whitt Simmons. Now they waited for the lab to compare it with the sample that had been taken from the remains of the child. Unfortunately, the way the labs were backed up, it could take weeks, even months before the results came back.

In a twist Elizabeth hadn't expected, Sheriff Morgan had decided to have the coroner bring in an infrared camera for a more thorough search of the area beneath the house.

"We know the Martinezes killed a child in

Fresno," Bill Morgan said. "If they murdered the victim you found under the house, maybe there are other victims buried down there."

The thought made Elizabeth shudder.

Still, she couldn't help thinking that if they'd had a similar device, their efforts would have been a whole lot easier. According to the sheriff, the infrared camera could pick up the location of a decomposed body up to one hundred seventy years old!

Wednesday morning, she went to see Maria, who had left the hospital and was staying in the Easy 8 Motel.

"How are you feeling?" she asked.

Lying in bed in a small but clean motel room, Maria plumped the pillow behind her head and sat up a little straighter. "Much better. The doctor says I am to have complete bed rest until the baby comes, so I guess it doesn't matter that we have to stay in a motel room."

"I'm glad you're here. I think it's better if you don't go back to the house . . . at least until after the baby comes."

"I know what happened last night — I know you found her. Miguel told me all about it on the way home from the hospital. He said you found the little girl who came to warn me."

"We found her. The police aren't certain yet, but we think her name is Carrie Ann Whitt. She was kidnapped in 1969. We spoke to her mother while we were doing research on the house." She managed to smile, but thinking of the small bones lying in the grave beneath the house, it wasn't easy. "Her mother said she loved children, especially babies."

And Consuela Martinez had lost her unborn child in prison. Perhaps she wanted to replace that child with the one Maria carried. After what had happened, anything seemed possible.

"She was an angel," Maria said, "returned to earth to protect me." Tears welled in her eyes. "It makes me so sad to think what those terrible people did to her, to think that they killed such a beautiful little girl."

Elizabeth's own eyes started to burn. "I can't imagine how anyone could do something so awful to a child." She took a calming breath, let it out slowly. "Of course there's a chance it might not be her. We probably won't know for some time. I'll let you know what the sheriff finds out."

Maria's dark eyes came to rest on Elizabeth's face. "Do you think . . . now that you have found her . . . do you think she will be at peace?"

Elizabeth reached for Maria's hand, gripped it firmly. "Yes, I do. Once she goes home where she belongs, I think she'll find her way to heaven."

"*Sí,* I think so, too. I hope so very much."

"So do I," Elizabeth said softly. Glancing away, she swallowed past the painful lump in her throat.

On Thursday morning, as evidence was collected and the extended search got underway, Zach went to the hearing that had been set to determine whether his father would get the surgery he so desperately needed. He had hired a local attorney, a man named Luis Montez he highly respected, but he would also be there himself.

"Why don't I go with you?" Elizabeth suggested. "Maybe I could testify on your father's behalf."

Zach shook his head. "Thanks for offering, but you only met him a couple of times and I don't think it would do any good. You've got work to do at your office, and besides, this is my problem, mine and my dad's."

But Zach's problems had become her problems, too. If only she could make him understand that. "Are you taking him with you to the hearing?"

"The judge requested he be there. I have a hunch Dr. Marvin suggested it. If we're lucky, Judge Alexander will see the man my father is today and be reminded of the man he was before — the man he could be again."

"Good luck, Zach. I really hope this works."

Zach leaned down and very softly kissed her. "Thanks, love. I hope so, too."

Elizabeth went to work, but it was difficult to concentrate. Instead, she anxiously waited for the phone to ring, for the call that would tell her the outcome of the hearing. But each time a call came in, it was a client or some other work-related problem.

By eleven o'clock, when she still had received no word, she grabbed her purse off the credenza behind her desk and headed for her car, figuring the proceedings would be stopped for lunch and she would have a chance to talk to Zach when he came out of the courtroom.

If things didn't go the way he so desperately hoped they would, she wanted to be there for him. She headed for the door at a run.

"Where are you going?" Terry came up from her chair behind the receptionist's desk.

"Mason. I'll be back after lunch."

"Don't forget, you've got a new client in at two, Angel Sanduski, the woman with the five kids the court took away from her."

"I remember. I'll be back by then."

She was gone before Terry could say more, racing for her Acura. It was a thirty-mile drive to the county courthouse in Mason and she would have to find a place to park.

The car was roasting inside, even with all four windows cracked and a silver reflective sun shield across the front window. It was still hot in San Pico the first part of September, with a predicted high today of ninety-eight degrees, and it took a while for the air conditioner to cool down the interior.

Once she reached Mason, she spotted a parking place near the entrance to the courthouse — thank you, God — pulled in and turned off the engine. The courthouse was modern in design, flat-topped and square, built after an earthquake damaged a large portion of town in the nineteen fifties.

Elizabeth pushed through the glass front doors, asked the information desk the location of the hearing being conducted by Judge Alexander, and headed up the stairs to a room on the second floor. Hurrying past several people walking along the corridor in front of her, she finally found the room and sat down on a long wooden bench beside the door.

At ten till noon, the doors swung open and a man walked out, tall and blond, attractive except for the ruddy tint of anger in his face. She recognized Carson in an instant, followed by a guy in a three-piece suit carrying an expensive belted leather briefcase, apparently Carson's attorney. The man caught up with him; Carson called him an incompetent fool, and the two men disappeared down the stairs.

Elizabeth smiled. Obviously things weren't going the way Carson had expected. Which could only be good news for Zach.

Finally Zach walked out of the courtroom, pushing his father in a wheelchair in front of him. She saw the brilliant smile on his face and there was no doubt the proceedings were going his way.

"Zach!" She waved at him and he started toward her, leaving his father with the Hispanic man in the dark suit, who she guessed was his lawyer, Luis Montez.

"Hey!" He caught her against him, gave her a welcoming hug. "What are you doing here? You didn't have to drive over."

"I wanted to be here . . . in case things didn't work out."

"Yeah, well, you could have saved yourself

a trip." He grinned. "The judge granted our petition. He appointed an attorney here in Mason, a guy named Maurice Whitman, to act as conservator in matters of my father's health. Judge Alexander instructed him to make the arrangements for the surgery."

"Oh, Zach that's wonderful!"

He looked down at her and something moved across his features. "Thanks for coming. I appreciate it, Liz." He introduced her to Montez, who wheeled Fletcher Harcourt up beside them.

"Dad, do you remember Ms. Conners? You met her out at Willow Glen."

The older man stared at her and frowned. "You come down here to . . . bail him out? Won't do any good. Damned kid's always . . . in trouble. I'm sick and tired of sitting in courtrooms. Time he grew up . . . learned to behave himself. Maybe spending a few years in jail will do him some good."

Zach flushed, a hint of red creeping under the high bones in his cheeks. "She didn't have to bail me, Dad. Not this time. You and I are here to get some business matters settled, remember?"

Fletcher Harcourt just looked confused. It was then that Dr. Marvin walked up, hair neatly combed, expression warm and smiling. It was obvious he was happy with the outcome of the hearing.

"Hello, Elizabeth."

"It's nice to see you, Dr. Marvin."

"I gather you've heard the news."

"Yes, I have. Congratulations."

He turned his attention to Zach. "As I told Judge Alexander, I think we should proceed as quickly as possible with this. Dr. Steiner has tentatively scheduled the surgery for Monday morning. That will give you time to get your father checked into the hospital."

"They're going to do the surgery at the UCLA Medical Center," Zach told her. "It's one of the best facilities in the country. It's also fairly close to my apartment so I can be close by while Dad's recovering."

"That's great." And it was, but Elizabeth couldn't help thinking how much she was going to miss Zach when he went back home. Though he had seemed glad to see her, she wasn't really sure. There was a growing reserve in his manner that didn't bode well. She felt a pang in her chest. She wondered if this was the beginning of the end and found herself praying it wasn't.

They left the courthouse and Zach drove his father back to Willow Glen while Elizabeth returned to her office. The afternoon was slipping past. She had just finished her initial interview with Angela Sandini, the woman whose alcohol and drug abuse had cost her the custody of her five young children, when Terry buzzed her on the intercom.

"Sheriff Morgan is here to see you," she said, but Elizabeth had only risen out of her chair when the door swung open and the tall, blond sheriff walked in.

"I need to talk to you."

She noticed his grim expression and her eyes went wide. "Oh, my God — you didn't find the body of another child?"

"No, we didn't. We found the body of a man — and the corpse isn't all that old."

THIRTY-THREE

The questions began anew. It was a totally different ball game now, since the victim had apparently died sometime within the past five years. The sheriff questioned Elizabeth, Miguel, Sam, Ben and the boys. Zach came under close scrutiny because of his criminal record and the fact that his family owned the property. Even Carson was questioned.

"I wish I could have seen the look on my brother's face," Zach said. "One body wasn't bad enough — now they've got two. This ought to be great for his aspiring political ambitions."

"I guess that's what he was worried about."

"I guess. Makes you wonder though."

"About what?"

"If he somehow knew we'd find something down there. If that was the reason he was so hell-bent on keeping us away."

Elizabeth stared out the window of her apartment. "I can't believe any of this."

"Neither can I," Zach said.

Though it would take weeks for a DNA match, by Friday afternoon, they knew the child they had found was Carrie Ann Whitt. With the help of Carrie Ann's mother, the sheriff had discovered the family dentist was still in practice and they had been able to locate the little girl's dental records.

Paula Whitt Simmons had been notified of the results. The child they had found was indeed Paula's daughter.

As soon as they received the news, Zach phoned to express his sympathy and so did Elizabeth.

"I'm really sorry, Paula," she said. "I can't even imagine how you must feel."

There was aching weariness and bone-deep grief in the woman's voice. "At least I know what happened to her. As terrible as it is, it's over. Once Carrie Ann is back home, once she's buried where she belongs, she'll be at peace."

"That's what Zach said. How about you, Paula? Will you be able to put this behind you?"

"I'll rest easier, that's for sure. I tried not to let my husband or my children know, but there was never a day went by I didn't think of her, wonder where she was — pray that she was okay. Now she'll be at rest and I'll always know where to find her."

Elizabeth spoke past the tightness in her throat. "Take care of yourself, Paula."

"Thank you for everything."

It was over. Carrie Ann had been found and soon would be laid to rest. Elizabeth believed that the mystery they had solved would end the problems in the house. But now there was another mystery to solve.

It appeared that forty years later there had been a second murder. She wondered who the man was that had been found beneath the house.

The weekend came and went. It was early Sunday morning. Zach's suitcase was already packed and sitting beside the door. All weekend he had been restless and edgy, anxious to pick up his father and get on the road to L.A. He was growing more and more distant, backing away from her as he had before. Last night they hadn't even made love.

"Well, I guess I'd better get going," Zach said, glancing toward the door like a rabbit about to bolt.

"I guess you had."

He reached down and plucked his car keys

off the coffee table.

"Listen Zach, I'd really like to be there tomorrow. It's not that far a drive and I don't want you to have to go through this alone."

He tossed the keys up and down, rattling them in his hand. "I'll be fine. I'll call you as soon as my father gets out of surgery."

"Are you sure you don't want me to go?"

"Like I said, I'll be fine."

"You won't forget to call?"

He walked over to where she stood, bent his head and absently brushed her lips with a kiss. "I'll call. I promise."

She hated that he was so eager to leave — and so opposed to her coming down to wait with him during the surgery. It was obvious he didn't want her there and she knew why.

He's running, she thought. *He can't handle the closeness.* Her heart squeezed as he picked up his overnight bag and opened the door.

"I guess I'll see you around," she said far too brightly.

Zach merely nodded. "Like I said, I'll call you as soon as he's out of surgery."

She tried to smile but failed. Her eyes were burning. Damn, she didn't want him to see her cry. He opened the door, but didn't walk out, just stood there for several long seconds staring out toward the street. Then his jaw subtly firmed. He walked out and closed the door.

Elizabeth stood there in the silence, staring at the place he had been. Her heart was hurting. A painful knot burned in her chest. She loved him so much. She had known it was a mistake to get involved with him, but like the moth to the flame, she hadn't been able to resist.

She took a shuddering breath and turned away from the door, ignored the sound of his Jeep firing up, the whine of the engine growing more and more distant as he drove away. It made her ache to think of losing him, losing the special something she had never felt for any other man.

But one thing she had learned — if Zach didn't want her, she didn't want him. She didn't want a man who couldn't totally commit, didn't want someone she couldn't trust to be there when she needed him. She had married a man like that. She was better off by herself.

Still, she wished she could be there tomorrow. There was a chance something might happen during the surgery, and Zach would be devastated if it did. But if Zach didn't want her there, she wasn't about to go where she wasn't wanted. He was pulling away. She told herself it was better it happened now than later.

But she couldn't quite make herself believe it.

With his father carefully strapped into the passenger seat, the wheelchair loaded in the back, Zach drove straight to the UCLA Medical Center in Westwood. Before Fletcher Harcourt could be admitted, there were forms to fill out, then a number of tests to be completed before the surgery was performed.

Zach had spoken to Sheriff Morgan on Saturday about the operation scheduled for Monday morning, and Morgan had agreed to let Zach return to L.A.

"I'll either be at the hospital, my office or my apartment," Zach promised. "And I always carry my cell phone."

"Just make sure you're reachable," Sheriff Morgan said.

Zach didn't blame him for keep close tabs. There were two bodies under the Santiago house — buried over thirty years apart. The fact itself was amazing. That one was a child, the other a large adult male, made the happenstance even stranger. But like Carrie Ann, according to the coroner, the death of the second victim had definitely been a result of foul play.

"There was a bullet hole in the skull," Morgan told him. "There was also a depression in the skull that looks like it came from a blunt instrument."

Zach mulled that over. "So you think maybe someone hit this guy over the head, then finished him off with a bullet?"

"At this point, it's still anyone's guess, but that would be my take."

"Any chance you can narrow the date of death down a little?"

Morgan's silver-blond eyebrows pulled down in suspicion. "Why is that important?"

"The current house wasn't built until four years ago. If I remember right, it was under construction for about eight months. The old house was completely gone by then. The area inside the foundation would have been easy to access and no one would have thought much about it if the ground in the construction site was disturbed. Might have been a good place to hide a body."

"Interesting thought. I'll look into it. When will you be back in San Pico?"

The question made him uneasy. Once his father was stable enough to be moved, he would be transported home by ambulance, but after he got there, Zach would want to be close by for a while. On the other hand, his return to L.A. gave him the perfect opportunity to ease into his break with Elizabeth.

His chest tightened at the thought. *It's gotta happen sooner or later,* he told himself. It wasn't fair to either one of them to go on this way, as if their relationship might actually turn into something more, might even end up in marriage. He wasn't the type to make that kind of commitment. He'd only been fooling himself. It was time to give her up and get his life back on track.

He recited the litany all the way back to L.A., determined to convince himself, trying to ignore the churning in his stomach.

It was Sunday afternoon. Zach was gone, on his way back to Los Angeles, taking his father with him, and the annual San Pico Rose Festival was in progress.

Though Elizabeth had always looked forward to the yearly event, this year she didn't want to go. Though no one had said as much, she had an odd suspicion that little Carrie Ann Whitt had been murdered during the Rose Festival. It was the only explanation Elizabeth could come up with for the overwhelming rose scent that accompanied the young girl's apparition whenever she appeared.

Though they would probably never know, and even if it weren't true, somehow she simply couldn't bear to go this year. Instead, she spent her day off catching up on paperwork, trying not to think of Zach.

Zach didn't call that night. She didn't think he would.

On Monday she went to the office and tried not to think about the surgery. But she was worried about Fletcher Harcourt, worried the operation might not succeed, worried about what would happen to Zach if the surgery failed — or worse. Zach might be able to turn his emotions off and on, but Elizabeth wasn't that way.

Seated behind her desk, she tensed when Terry finally buzzed to announce Zach's call, took a deep breath, and picked up the phone.

"Liz? It's Zach."

"I've been worried. How's it going?"

"Dad's out of surgery. He's in I.C.U. and so far he's doing great." She could hear the relief in his voice. Though he'd never said so, she knew he was terrified that his father would die and he would be to blame.

"That's great news, Zach."

"Doctor Steiner says he isn't out of the

woods yet, but the surgery went exactly as planned. They won't know for several weeks how effective it was, but they're hopeful that little by little his motor functions and memory will start to return."

"When will he be able to leave the hospital?"

"Not for at least ten days. Then he'll go back out to Willow Glen until he's fully recovered."

She wanted to ask him if he would be coming back with his dad, but she didn't want to hear the hesitation in his voice. She didn't want to feel the sharp stab of pain that moment would bring.

"Well, I'm really glad everything's going so well," she said with false brightness. "I'll be keeping your dad in my prayers."

There was a long pause on the line. Zach didn't say when he'd see her, didn't tell her he missed her. "Thanks, Liz," he said softly. "I'd appreciate that." He rang off the line and Elizabeth was left with the receiver pressed against her ear.

Her hand trembled as she set the phone back down in its cradle. Her chest was aching and there was a painful lump in her throat.

You have to let him go, she told herself. He didn't want a life with her. He didn't need her. He simply wasn't the kind of man to settle down.

It wasn't as if she hadn't known that from the start, hadn't told herself this was bound to happen with a guy like Zach. Still, she was glad her office door was closed, that she could put her head down on the desk and let go of her tears.

She didn't hear the quiet knock on the door, didn't hear her friend walk in.

"Liz? Oh, honey, come on, don't cry."

Elizabeth's head jerked up. Petite and red-haired, Gwen Petersen stood on the opposite side of the desk, a worried look on her face.

"Come on," she said. "It can't be that bad. Why don't you tell me what's the matter?"

Elizabeth took a shaky breath and slowly released it, worked to pull herself together. She was glad her visitor was only Gwen and not a client who had somehow gotten past Terry.

"It's nothing you didn't warn me about," she said. "Zach is pushing me away. I think he wants to end our relationship. I let myself get in too deep and now I'm paying the price."

Gwen reached across the desk and caught her hand. "Hey, everyone has a weakness for something sinful. I like Häagen-Dazs ice cream. You're a sucker for tall, dark and handsome."

She managed a smile, pulled a Kleenex out of her drawer and wiped her eyes. "It's not only Zach, it's everything that's been going on. It's just been so crazy lately."

"Yeah, I read about some of it in the newspaper. That's the reason I stopped by. What a story. The paper was pretty vague about the little girl you and Zach found under the house . . . something about she'd been missing for thirty-odd years. I gather the police think the couple who did it killed another child several years later."

"That's pretty much it."

"What about this other thing? The paper said a second body was found in the same location two days later. That's incredible."

"Yeah. Weirder yet, they were murdered more than thirty years apart. Of course, after spending a night in that house, it isn't that hard to believe."

"What do you mean? You think the house itself had something to do with it?"

"A month ago I would have laughed at the notion. Now? I tell you, Gwen, that place is downright evil."

Gwen shivered. "I never believed in ghosts, but what do I know, anyway?"

"They haven't identified the second body.

Whoever it is doesn't fit the description of anyone who's been reported missing in the area over the past few years. Sheriff Morgan says there's a chance they'll never find out who it is."

"Sounds like he's been keeping you pretty well informed."

"I'm sure he isn't telling me everything, but I guess he figures Zach and I have a right to know."

"You don't think he suspects Zach, do you? I mean he does have a criminal record and he was raised out there on the farm."

"Zach was living in L.A. when the man was killed. And I doubt that if he really had murdered the man, he would lead the police to the place he had buried the body."

"Good point. Carson's been making all kinds of statements. His picture's all over the front page of the paper."

"Carson's a guy who could turn rotten lemons into lemonade. He's actually making political hay out of this."

Gwen gave her a reassuring smile, reached over and squeezed her hand. "You'll get past this Zach thing. It'll just take a little time."

"I know. I'll recover. I got over Brian and now I'm glad to be rid of him." Only she didn't think she would ever feel that way about Zach. She didn't think she would ever find a man who suited her the way he did, a man who just felt so right.

"Well, I gotta run. I just wanted to make sure you were okay."

"I'm fine. Mostly it's just a reaction to all the stuff that's been happening. Thanks for stopping by. You're a good friend, Gwen."

Gwen waved away the words, though they were completely true. "Call me if you get to feeling depressed."

"I will."

"Take care of yourself, Liz."

She nodded, knowing she would. She would get over Zachary Harcourt. Someday.

Just not all that soon.

THIRTY-FOUR

Fletcher Harcourt was released from the UCLA Medical Center ten days after his surgery. They were the longest days of Zach's life. Though his father was improving daily, Zach was becoming more and more depressed.

Whenever he was in his apartment — the place he had loved and considered his own personal retreat — it now felt empty and cold. He thought of the day he had brought Liz home with him, remembered how she had looked standing in front of the living room window, how he loved having her sleeping next to him in his king-size bed.

Every night he slept alone, aching to have her beside him. In the mornings, he looked for her as he walked into the kitchen, though he knew she couldn't possibly be there. Even in his office, he thought of her, had to forcibly make himself refrain from picking up the phone.

I'm in love with her. Desperate, crazy in love.

And he was coming to believe it was the kind of love that didn't happen to a man more than once.

As the days crept past and as his life resumed its same familiar patterns, he found himself more and more dissatisfied. The women who flirted with him in Mickey's Sports Bar after work held no appeal. He took his new sailboat, *Devil May Care,* out into the harbor, hoping it would help, but the warm, sunny day only made him wish he had someone to share it with, and not just anyone would do.

Even his work didn't seem as interesting as it had before.

In the days after his return to L.A., he replayed over and over all that had happened in San Pico. He thought of little Carrie Ann Whitt, dead at nine years old, thought of the man who had been murdered and buried under the house, and it occurred to him how very short life could be.

He found himself asking, *Do you really want to live the years ahead alone?* Before he'd met Liz, the answer would have been yes. He'd been comfortable in his aloneness.

Now he knew what he had been missing.

The thought nagged him, wouldn't leave him be.

Still, the question remained, if he pursued a different sort of life, if he made the one hundred percent commitment it would take, could he keep it?

Searching for an answer, he drove absently around the city, the black BMW eventually turning with almost a mind of its own, onto the off-ramp that would take him to his mother's apartment in Culver City.

He was halfway up the stairs to her second floor apartment when he realized he hadn't brought her a present, as was his routine. Still, he knocked on the door and surprisingly found her there.

"Zachary! Come on in!" Wearing tight black ankle-length stretch pants and a low-cut blouse, clothes that did nothing for her robust figure, she led him into the kitchen where she had a cigarette burning in the ashtray, and they both sat down at the table.

"So how's your father doing?" She frowned. "You're not here because something's happened? He's okay, isn't he?"

"Dad's doing great. He's going to be released in a couple of days."

She reached for her half-burned cigarette, dotted the ashes and took a long drag. "I wasn't all that worried. The old bird's too tough to croak." Zach had called to tell her about the surgery, then kept her posted during the recovery period.

She flicked him a speculative glance. "You didn't bring me any coffee? Not even a box of chocolates? Okay, tell your mama what's wrong."

Zach leaned back heavily in his chair. "You want to know what's wrong? I'm in love, that's what's wrong. I'm in love and it's killing me."

Teresa's black eyebrows shot up, then she laughed, a raspy, deep, cigarette smoker's rumble in her very substantial chest.

"Who's the lucky girl?" she asked. "And why aren't you happy? It's taken you years to find someone." Her dark eyes widened. "Don't tell me she doesn't love you? No woman with half a brain would —"

"I don't know if she loves me or not. I haven't asked. I'm tying to end our relationship."

"What? She cheat on you? If she did —"

"She didn't cheat. She's not that kind of girl. Liz is special. She's smart and fun to be with. She's loyal and brave. She's sexy as hell and I'm crazy about her. But I . . ."

"You what, Zach?"

"She's the kind of girl you marry and I don't think I can do that."

"Why not?" Teresa asked gently, reaching over to take hold of his hand. "You know, Zach, you've been a loner all your life and I've never really understood why. You get along with people. You seem to like them and they like you. But in the end, you always pull away. You were a lonely little boy, Zach. There's no reason for you to spend your whole life that way."

He glanced out the window, saw only the wall of the building next door. "Maybe not. I don't know."

"You need to ask yourself what it is you really want out of life and if the answer is that you want to be with this girl, then go for it. You're not like your father — or me, for that matter. If you give your heart to a woman, you won't betray her. That's one thing I know for sure."

A corner of his mouth edged up. "How could you possibly know that?"

"Because I'm your mother. I never was much of a one, but I know if you make a promise, you keep it. And I think you would make some woman a damned fine husband."

Zach looked at her hard, seeing something in her eyes he had only begun to notice. In her own strange way, Teresa loved him.

He shoved back his chair and stood up.

"Sometimes you amaze me . . . Mother." Catching her chin, he bent and gave her a soft kiss on the cheek. "I'll think about what you said."

But he didn't really have to think anymore. He'd been back in L.A. for two weeks, fourteen long, restless nights, searching for the answer that suddenly seemed so clear. He knew what he wanted, had known for sometime but was afraid to admit it.

Unfortunately, before he had come to that conclusion, he had made a miserable mess of things.

Now the question was, *What the hell should he do?*

The office was just about to close for the day. Elizabeth still sat working behind her desk when a phone call came through from Miguel. He sounded frantic, yet more like his old self than he'd been in some time.

"Elizabeth. It is Miguel Santiago. I am calling from the hospital. Maria . . . she is having the baby!"

Elizabeth grinned. "That's wonderful, Miguel! I'm just leaving work. I'll be there as quickly as I can."

"Oh, no, you do not have to come. You have done enough already. And Señora Garcia, she is here with me."

"I'm coming. I'll be there as soon as I can get there."

She didn't miss the relief in his voice. "*Gracias*. That would be very good. I know Maria will be happy to know you are coming."

She hung up the phone and grabbed her purse. Terry was on the phone when she walked up to the desk. She ended the call and looked up. "You're smiling. What's up?"

"I'm off to the County Hospital in Mason. Maria Santiago is having her baby."

Dr. James emerged from his office just then. "So the big day has finally arrived."

Elizabeth grinned, excited and wildly relieved. "Looks that way."

"I guess I owe her an apology . . . though I still have a tough time believing in ghosts. I'm glad you stuck with her through all of this."

"I have to say, there were times I thought I was going a little crazy myself."

"By the way, Babs and I are finally getting married. Funny thing is, after all the indecision, I'm really excited about it."

Elizabeth thought of Zach and ignored a stab of pain. "Congratulations. I guess when you finally figure out what you want, everything falls into place."

"Yes, I think it does."

Pasting a smile on her face, pushing thoughts of Zach away, Elizabeth waved a quick goodbye and dashed out the back door to her car.

The roads were a little bit busy this time of day, but she made the trip to the Mason hospital in record time. Once inside, she headed for the maternity ward and found Miguel pacing the floor of the waiting room. The man looked completely different from the last time she had seen him, his dark hair neatly trimmed, shirt and trousers spotlessly clean.

"Elizabeth! Thank you so much for coming."

"I wouldn't have missed it for the world. Where is she?"

"She is in the labor room."

"Aren't you going in with her?"

Miguel's dark face turned pale. "I would rather wait out here."

Elizabeth bit back a smile. In Miguel's mind, having a baby was a woman's job. It was the man's job to wait and worry.

"This is Señora Garcia," he said, introducing her to a heavyset woman sitting in one of the chairs.

"Con mucho gusto, Señora," Elizabeth said.

"It is good to meet you, too. Maria has spoken of you often." She had snow-white hair and very dark, very weathered skin. She wore a flowered housedress and serviceable brown leather shoes with the stockings rolled down around her ankles.

"How is she doing?" Elizabeth asked.

"She is a little nervous, but then this is her first."

For the next three hours, they waited, drinking cups of thick black coffee.

Then a green-gowned nurse appeared in the door of the waiting room. "Mr. Santiago?"

Miguel shot to his feet. "*Sí*, that is me."

A grin spread across the nurse's face. "It's a boy! You have a son, Mr. Santiago. A seven pound, twelve ounce baby boy."

Miguel let out a whoop of glee.

"Congratulations," Elizabeth said, grinning nearly as wide as the nurse.

"When can I see her?" Miguel asked.

"Give us a few minutes to get her cleaned up and I'll come get you."

By the time visitors were allowed into the room, Maria was propped up in the bed, proudly holding her bundled-up son in her arms. Everyone *oohed* and *aahed* over the tiny black-haired infant and said what a beautiful child he was — which indeed he was.

Then Maria fixed her attention on Elizabeth and her wide smile softened. "I owe my son's life to you. To you and to Mr. Zach."

"I'm glad we were able to help."

"No one believed me. No one but the two of you." Maria's dark eyes welled with tears. "My son might not be here if it hadn't been for you. I will never forget what you did for all of us."

Elizabeth reached out and caught her hand. "The important thing is that you have a fine, healthy boy."

Maria nodded and wiped at the wetness, turned back to her husband before more tears could form.

Elizabeth stayed a few minutes more, then the nurse returned and the group was asked to leave so the new mother and child could get some sleep.

As she left the hospital, Elizabeth remembered Maria's words, *my son might not be here if it hadn't been for you.* She thought of the evil force that dwelled inside the house and couldn't help wondering if Maria's grim words might not be true.

Zach drove up to San Pico late in the afternoon of the following day. His father had arrived back in town the week before, released into the care of Dr. Marvin, Dr. Kenner and the nursing staff at Willow Glen. According to the daily reports Zach had been receiving, Fletcher Harcourt was doing very well, but Zach wanted to see for himself the progress his father was making.

And he wanted to talk to Liz.

His stomach tightened. He'd had days to think about her, consider his future, a future he was now certain he wanted to share with the woman he loved. He wanted to marry her, have kids with her. Be a husband and father.

He wanted the family that he had never had.

He was in love with Liz, but was Liz in love with him? And even if she were, after her disastrous marriage and the way he had ignored her for the past two weeks, would she have the courage to take a chance on a guy like him?

It was early evening when he pulled the BMW into the parking lot at Willow Glen and turned off the engine. Tomorrow — if he could work up the nerve — he'd go see Liz. By then, maybe he could figure out what to say, find the words that would convince her to forgive him for running away.

At the time, it had seemed the best way.

In the old days, it would have been.

But Zach wasn't the same man he had been before. The trick was to convince Liz of that. How could he make her believe, if she agreed to marry him, she would never regret it?

Tomorrow, he told himself. A little more time was what he needed. In the meantime, he had his father to think of, and so he pushed through the front doors of Willow Glen, into the reception area, signed in with Renee, the young woman on duty at the desk, and headed down the hall.

He was amazed to see his father sitting in a wheelchair in front of the TV. He was a big man, barrel-chested and thick through the shoulders, yet before the surgery, he had seemed fragile, even frail. Now he sat up straighter in the chair, his impressive shoulders no longer slumped, his entire body appearing stronger. When he turned, Zach saw that his face was clean-shaven, his silver, once-blond hair short and neatly combed.

"Hey, Dad. It's good to see you. How are you feeling?"

His father smiled. "Pretty damn good . . . considering."

"I'm sorry I didn't get up here sooner."

His father shook his head. "You don't have

a damned thing to apologize for. Doc Marvin says if it weren't for you, I wouldn't have been able to have the surgery. I'm grateful, Zach. You'll never know how much."

He held out one of his hands. It looked steady, not shaky as it had before. "See that?"

"Yeah. That's great, Dad."

"I'm still pretty weak. Sometimes I get kinda dizzy. At this age, it takes a while for a guy to get back on his feet. I start physical therapy on Monday. The doc thinks in time, I'll be able to walk on my own."

Zach just nodded, fighting the lump in his throat. Dr. Marvin had told him how much progress his father had been making, though they weren't completely sure how fast the recovery would be. Fletcher had been confused off and on the first few days after surgery, but the doctor had said that was normal.

"Memory any better?" He hated to ask and it didn't really matter. As far as Zach was concerned, the operation had been a phenomenal success.

"Some better. Doc says before the operation I got the past mixed up with the present. I don't seem to do that now."

"That's good, Dad."

"Still can't remember much for the past

couple of years, just flashes here and there. I don't remember the accident, but Doc says that's pretty common with such a bad head injury. He says I probably won't ever remember what happened that night."

Zach looked at his father, saw the intelligence in his gold-flecked brown eyes that had seemed so much dimmer before. "I'm glad things are going so well, Dad."

"I want to go home, Zach."

Zach frowned. He'd figured this moment would come, but not for some time yet. He didn't want the old man leaving before he was ready.

"What about your therapy? You'll need to be here for that. What does Dr. Marvin say about you leaving so soon?"

"Haven't asked him yet. I figured maybe I could hire a driver. He could take me down to therapy every day. I could get the house fixed up a little, you know — get some of that handicap stuff in the bathroom. I could hire some of those nurses who work in people's homes — just till I can get back on my feet."

It was exactly what Zach had wanted to do after the accident. He had known his father would hate being in a rest home, no matter how nice it was.

"That sounds good. I could do the legwork, get it all lined up for you, and God knows you can afford it. Carson's taken good care of the farm for you. I'm not sure how he's gonna like being tossed out of the house."

The old man frowned. For a moment his mind seemed to wander.

"What is it?"

He shook his head. "Nothing. Sometimes my brain's still a little muzzy. I'll give this place a little more time, but I don't want to stay here any longer than I have to."

"I don't blame you. Have you talked to Carson about moving home? Dr. Marvin says he's been in to see you every day."

"He's been here. He says he's sorry he tried to block the surgery. Says he was just worried about the outcome."

"I'm sure he was concerned that something might happen to you."

"I haven't mentioned leaving. I figured I'd talk to you first."

Zach just nodded. Carson was going to pitch a fit.

Zach's jaw tightened. It didn't matter. Carson wasn't calling the shots the way he had been before. If Fletcher Harcourt wanted to go home, Zach was going to see that it happened — whether Carson liked it or not.

In the meantime, Zach was tired. He'd been up since 5:00 a.m., and the nerve-wracking drive through traffic up to the valley always wore him out. He wanted to get back to his room at the Holiday Inn and climb into bed.

He told himself he'd head there now, go straight to bed and try to get some badly needed sleep. But the car seemed to have a mind all its own and he found himself heading in a different direction.

Elizabeth stood at the sink in the bathroom, her face freshly scrubbed, auburn hair pulled into a ponytail on top of her head, her short blue terrycloth robe belted around her waist as she prepared herself for bed.

She almost didn't hear the doorbell ringing. Grumbling about who could be calling this late at night, she tightened the sash on the robe and headed for the door.

Her eyes widened as she peered through the peephole and recognized the man standing on the opposite side of the door. After two weeks of crying, two weeks of trying to get over him, for a moment she considered pretending she wasn't at home.

Still, she had to face him sooner or later. Ignoring the unwanted clatter of her heart, she blew out a breath, turned the deadbolt and pulled open the door.

"Hello, Liz." He looked unbelievably handsome, even with his hair a little mussed and his slacks slightly wrinkled.

"Hi." She didn't invite him in. She wasn't about to do that. He wasn't going to con her into the same routine he'd had with Lisa Doyle, sleeping with her whenever he needed a little sexual relief then heading back to a life without her. "Listen, Zach, I was just about to go to bed. Was there something you wanted?"

His gaze ran over her, searching her face, trying to read her thoughts, just as she tried to read his. "I need to talk to you. Can I come in?"

Her fingers tightened around the doorknob. "I don't think it's a good idea. I think we both know what's going on here and I'm not about to continue where we left off. Now, if there's something you want —"

"Actually there is. It would be better if you would let me in."

She didn't want to. She didn't want to see him. She had been hurting for the past two weeks. She didn't want any more heartache and she knew if he walked through that door there would be.

"Please, Zach . . ."

"It's important, Liz."

She took a deep breath and stepped back from the door, pressing her hands against her robe so he wouldn't notice that they trembled. He walked past her into the living room, his legs looking longer, his shoulders broader, even more attractive than she had first thought. God, Gwen was right. She was a sucker for tall, dark and handsome.

"So what is it?" She told herself to ignore the way he kept looking at her, as if he simply could not stop.

"You aren't going to make this easy, are you?"

"Why should I? I know why you're here."

"Do you?"

"All right, fine I'll say it, then you won't have to. 'I'm sorry I left the way I did. I'd still like to see you on weekends — you know, whenever I'm in town.' The answer is I'm not interested. Now I'd like to get some sleep."

He looked at her and simply shook his head. "That's not what I came to say. I came to tell you that I love you. I want to know if you love me."

The words sent her reeling. It was the last thing she had expected him to say. "Wh-what?"

"I said I love you. The question is, do you love me?"

He loved her? He had said those words before, and once she had even believed them. But even if they were true, it hadn't kept him from leaving. What amazed her was that he didn't seem to know that she loved him.

Elizabeth felt the unwanted sting of tears. "I love you, Zach. I love you very much. It doesn't change anything."

"Maybe it does. Maybe it changes everything." He led her over to the sofa and both of them sat down. "I screwed up, leaving the way I did. I couldn't think straight. Everything just seemed so confused. To tell you the truth, I was flat-out scared. But those two weeks I was gone gave me time to figure things out."

Her heart was pounding. She could see how nervous he was, how important this was to him. Maybe he really did love her in his own way. It wasn't enough for her. Not anymore.

"Please, Zach. Don't do this to me again."

"I'm in love with you, Liz. Crazy in love. The forever kind of love. I want to marry you. I want to have kids with you. I want us to be together for the rest of our lives."

Her throat closed up. She had imagined him saying those words but never really believed it would happen. The tears she'd been holding back welled in her eyes. "Zach . . ."

He reached out and cupped her cheek. "You said that you loved me. What I need to know is if you love me enough to forgive me. I know I hurt you. I need to know if you love me enough to look inside my heart and know with absolute certainty that you can trust me never to hurt you again."

Her chest was aching. The tears in her eyes spilled onto her cheeks. Did she love him enough? She loved him so much she would die for him. But trusting him so completely . . . that was a far different thing.

Zach moved off the sofa, went down on one knee, caught her hand in both of his. "Marry me, Liz. If you say yes, I promise you'll never be sorry."

Elizabeth shook her head and more tears ran down her cheeks. "Are you sure this is what you want?"

"I've never been more certain of anything in my life."

A huge smile broke over her face. "Then I'll marry you. You must have thought this through or you wouldn't be here. You wouldn't ask if you had the slightest doubt. I'll marry you, Zachary Harcourt — and I promise you'll never be sorry."

THIRTY-FIVE

Elizabeth decided to play hooky from work and she and Zach spent the day in bed. They were in love. At last, their feelings were out in the open and the knowledge set them free.

"I can't wait to tell my father," Zach said. He glanced at the clock. "It's only five. Let's go over to Willow Glen and tell him the news."

"Are you sure?"

"Damned sure." He cast her a glance. "Today's Friday. If we stop at the store for groceries, we won't have to leave the house all weekend."

She smiled at the warmth in his eyes, the desire mixed with love. She thought that sometime during the past two weeks, he had discovered what he really wanted in life and apparently he wanted her.

She felt like the luckiest woman on earth.

It was nearly six o'clock by the time they

reached Willow Glen. Walking along the corridor holding hands, they paused outside Fletcher Harcourt's room. The door was open and Zach went in to announce their arrival. When Elizabeth joined them, she found the older man sitting in his wheelchair watching TV, a different man than he had been before.

"Dad, do you remember Liz?"

He studied her a moment, looking thoughtful. Then he smiled. "You were at the courthouse." He was a handsome man, as she had noticed the first time she met him, but now she sensed the powerful presence he had once been.

"It's nice to see you again, Mr. Harcourt."

Zach reached down and took hold of her hand, and his father's silver eyebrows went up.

"I take it you two have known each other for a while."

"Liz is a family counselor. We met out at Teen Vision several months ago, but I think I've been waiting for her all my life."

"That sounds promising. Don't tell me the Lone Wolf is finally thinking of settling down?"

Zach raised their linked hands to his lips. "We're getting married, Dad. Liz was crazy enough to say yes and I'm not letting her out of it."

His father's smile was wide and sincere. "Congratulations. When's the wedding?"

"Tomorrow isn't soon enough for me, but Liz wants something a little more personal than a trip to the courthouse."

"Just something small and private," she said. "And we want you to be there."

Fletcher reached out a steady hand and Zach clasped it. "I couldn't be happier for you, son."

"We're still talking about where we're going to live. I'm not one of those guys who believes in long-distance marriages. I was thinking maybe I'd take Jon Noble up on his offer and accept that job running our new branch in San Francisco. I don't think Liz would have much of a problem finding work up there, either. At least until we start raising kids."

His father nodded, looked absurdly pleased. "You couldn't have brought me better news. Now I've got something to look forward to. An even better reason to get well enough to get out of here."

A shadow appeared in the doorway. "What's that? You're not thinking of leaving Willow Glen, are you? It's far too soon for you to consider something like that."

Zach looked over at his brother. "Hello, Carson. You're just in time to hear the news."

"Really? And what news is that?"

"Liz and I are getting married."

Carson's lips flattened out. "Now that is news." He flashed Elizabeth a cool, knowing smile. "Exactly how long do you expect him to stick around after the wedding? Surely you don't think this is going to last more than a year."

Instead of the uncertainty Carson had hoped for, Elizabeth felt a shot of anger. "You don't know your brother, Carson. You never have."

Listening to his oldest son, Fletcher Harcourt's face turned red. "You've been jealous of your brother all your life. I kept hoping you'd grow out of it, but you never did." He glared at Carson and began to frown. Something shifted in his dark eyes, moved over his strong features.

"What is it, Dad?" Zach asked.

"I don't know. There's something in the back of my mind . . . It's right there but I can't seem to . . ." He shook his head as if he were trying to clear it, to catch hold of a distant memory. "I think it's something important but I can't quite latch on to it."

"It's okay, Dad," Zach said. "Eventually,

it'll come back to you."

Fletcher continued to struggle, to wrestle with some hidden thought that refused to surface.

"Take it easy," Carson said. "What's happened in the past isn't important. Better you think about the future."

Fletcher looked up at his fair-haired son and his eyes widened in shock. "My God — I remember! I remember what happened the night of the accident!" He came half out of his chair, staring at Carson as if he were seeing a ghost. "I heard you — that night on the phone. We were both upstairs in our rooms. I didn't know the line was busy. When I picked up the receiver, I heard Jake Benson's voice coming over the wire."

Carson glared. "You can't possibly remember that. The doctor said with the kind of head trauma you suffered, the odds would be a thousand to one that you would recall anything at all about the incident."

"That so? Well, I remember Jake asking you for money, saying if you didn't pay him, he'd tell me the truth about the car wreck that sent Zach to prison. He said if you didn't come up with another fifty grand, he'd tell me what really happened — that it was you who was driving the car that night. You who swerved into the oncoming lane.

You killed that man, Carson. You! Not Zach!"

Zach's gaze swung to his brother, whose face had gone bone-white. "You were driving that night? You were the one who killed that guy?"

"You can't listen to him. He doesn't know what he's saying. H-he's still recovering from the surgery."

"Bullshit! He knows exactly what he's saying."

"That's right," Fletcher said. "You told Benson to come over to the house and you'd give him the money." Fletcher rose completely out of his chair, his legs shaking as he pointed wildly at Carson. "He had just walked through the front door when I confronted you about what I'd heard. Jake was standing in the entry when you pushed me down the stairs!"

In an instant, all of the pieces rolling around in Zach's head came together. Why Carson hadn't wanted their father to have the surgery — he was afraid Fletcher might remember what had happened the night he had nearly died.

Zach looked at Carson and another piece of the puzzle fell into place. "Son of a bitch — you killed him! You murdered Jake Benson and buried him under that house!"

"You're insane! You're as crazy as that old man."

"You lied all those years ago, and you're lying now. The night of the car wreck, you hadn't even been drinking. The law would have seen it as an accident and that would have been the end of it, but you would rather send an innocent man to jail than see your spotless reputation tarnished."

"None of that is true!"

"Isn't it? You sent me off to prison, but it wasn't over, was it? Jake knew what happened that night and he started milking you for money. I wonder how much you paid him before you finally killed him four years ago."

"I didn't pay him anything! You're talking nonsense."

"That's the reason you didn't want us hanging around the Santiago house. You were afraid someone might stumble onto Jake's corpse and that's exactly what happened."

"Benson left on his own. He got a job somewhere else."

"Where, exactly?"

"I don't know."

"You know exactly where Jake is because you put him there. You knew he wouldn't be missed. He had no family. He was just a working man, a guy who moved from job to job. Better to have him dead than have him tell the truth about the wreck and what you did that night to Dad. Better he be dead than blackmailing you for even more money."

Carson's eyes darted wildly from Zach to his father then back again. He started to say something but no words came out. Instead he turned and started running, his feet pounding off down the hall.

Zach tore after him, reaching him just as he turned the corner, tackling him and bringing him crashing to the ground.

"Get off me!" Carson rolled onto his back, trying to get away, but Zach grabbed the front of his shirt and hauled him up. Carson began to struggle and Zach drew back his fist, aiming it at his brother's face.

"Give it up, Carson. The game is over." His fist tightened in warning. "I'm better at this than you are. You might as well face it. You aren't going to win this one."

Carson hesitated a moment, then his head fell back against the carpet. Zach relaxed his grip on the front of his brother's shirt and slowly rose to his feet.

"Call 911," he instructed the receptionist who was standing wide-eyed at the end of the hall. "Tell the sheriff that Carson Harcourt wants to talk to him." He looked down at his brother. "Isn't that right, Carson?"

Carson nodded, and Zach backed a couple of feet away. Even if Carson tried to run, there was really no place to go, and when Zach looked at him, he could almost see the wheels turning in his brother's head, planning his strategy, figuring the best way out.

"I'll let you handle this," Zach said to him. "Good luck."

Carson struggled to his feet, brushing off his sport coat, straightening the front of his shirt. "This isn't over," he said darkly.

"Actually, Carson, it is." Turning, Zach started walking. Down the hall, Elizabeth raced toward him. Zach met her halfway and pulled her straight into his arms.

EPILOGUE

Fletcher Harcourt sat at the desk in his study. He was still using his wheelchair to get around, but during therapy he was able to walk on of those aluminum walkers. His body was taking its own sweet time to heal, but his brain seemed to be working. He still couldn't remember everything that had happened in the years since the accident. But oddly, his strongest memory was of the night he'd been pushed down the stairs.

Fletcher pulled his mind away from thoughts of his son and the ugly moment that would be forever burned into his brain. He leaned back in his old oak swivel chair, pulled out of storage in the barn. Damn, it felt good to be home, to be sitting at the rolltop desk he had worked at for more than forty years.

The house was different now. Carson had redecorated the whole damned place, but Fletcher had to admit he'd done a good job, and though it was more formal than he liked, the rooms were comfortable and he was getting used to the changes.

There were going to be a whole lot more of them.

Since his return to the house, he'd had time to do some thinking. He went over the life he'd led, how selfish he had been through the years, never really thinking of his sons or his wife, always doing exactly what he wanted, no matter who he hurt.

Constance had been dead for more than a decade. There was nothing he could do for her. Teresa was happily married, and she had Zach to look out for her. And Carson would be spending the next few years in jail, though not as long as he undoubtedly deserved.

His son had pled guilty to manslaughter, said that he and Jake Benson had gotten into a fight the night Jake was killed, said Jake had pulled a gun and Carson had turned it against him and shot him in self-defense.

Afterward, he'd been scared, he said, so he buried the body inside the foundation of the overseer's cottage that was under construction on the farm.

Both Zach and Fletcher had refused to testify against him, or mention anything about the wreck that Zach had spent time for in prison. Blood was blood, and both of them would probably have perjured themselves if they'd been subpoenaed. But Carson had always been a smooth talker.

Fletcher had hired his son one of those fancy, overpriced criminal lawyers from L.A., and together they'd negotiated a reduction of the charges. With good behavior, Carson would probably be out in a couple of years.

It didn't seem quite right, yet Fletcher wouldn't have it any other way. The man was, after all, still his son.

"Hey, Dad."

He looked up to see his younger son standing in the doorway, an arm around the little gal he was marrying next Sunday afternoon. She was a pretty thing, he thought, with her heavy auburn hair and blue eyes. Fletcher believed his son had finally found a woman who would make him happy. And the girl was getting a damned fine man in the bargain.

"You said you wanted to see us," Zach said, looking a little concerned.

"That's right, come on in."

Zach ushered Liz through the door then fell in behind her. He dragged over a chair and she sat down, then Zach sat down in the chair next to Fletcher's desk.

"I asked you to come because there's something I want to show you. You got that medal I asked you to bring? The one you said you found under the house?"

"I brought it." Zach pulled the old rusted piece of medal out of his pocket and laid it down on Fletcher's desk.

Fletcher picked it up and examined it. "See this writing on the front?"

"We tried to read it the night we found it but we couldn't make out what it said."

"That's because the letters are in German."

"German?" Liz picked up the medal, studied the printed letters. "Ben Donahue said it looked like something that came from the military. We thought maybe someone brought it back from the war."

"Well, in a way, that's what happened." Reaching down, he pulled open the bottom drawer of his desk. He'd had Isabel, the housekeeper, dig around in his old room upstairs until she found the box he was looking for. He was living in a bedroom downstairs now and she'd helped him collect his things.

Nice girl, Isabel. He'd asked her to stay on and she'd agreed. It was good to have someone else in the house.

Fletcher lifted the metal box, set it on the table, and lifted the lid. Inside was a stack of old, dog-eared, time-yellowed newspaper clippings.

He lifted them out of the box and set them down on top of his desk. "I been doing some thinking. Mostly about that house over there and this one, too. You see, I did a little research on that couple who killed those little girls. Sheriff Morgan says before they kidnapped that child, they were model citizens. Not so much as a parking ticket. Then they moved into the old gray house."

"What are you getting at, Dad?" Zach asked.

"You told me about Miguel Santiago, how the house seemed to change him."

"That's right," Liz said. "He was different before things started happening in the house. He's different now. Thank you for giving them another place to live."

He waved away the thanks. The couple was afraid to live in the house, and after finding two dead bodies underneath, he didn't blame them.

"I started thinking about Carson . . . about how a boy I raised could kill a man the way he did. I still have trouble imagining it. Which got me to thinking even more." He shoved the stack of clippings toward Zach, motioned for Liz to come round where she could read them.

Zach picked up a page of yellowed newsprint. "These came out of the San Pico *Newspress.* Looks like they were printed during World War II. They're all dated in the 1940s."

"That's right. I don't know if you remember me ever mentioning it. It was so far back . . . I was just a kid at the time. I don't remember much about the war, but my dad would sometimes talk about it."

Zach and Liz both started reading the articles, skimming the pages, picking up the next article in the stack.

Zach finished first. "It says that between 1941 and 1945, the government set up prisoner of war camps all along the San Joaquin Valley." Zach tapped the yellowed page. "It says one of them was right here in San Pico."

"That's right. In fact, the camp was right here on this property. It was a farm labor camp even back then. The government needed a safe place to keep German prisoners until the war was over."

"I think my high school history teacher mentioned the camp," Liz said. "It seemed so long ago I never gave it much thought."

"Being patriotic, my old man agreed to let

the government use the land. Unfortunately, according to what my dad told me years later, he wound up with the worst prisoners of the lot. The captured German soldiers were Gestapo and Nazi S.S. Really bad men. Some of them were responsible for the massacre in Warsaw in 1941."

Zach shook his head. "I'm afraid my history's not that good."

"I read up on it. Happened in a little town called Jedwabne. Nazis forced sixteen hundred people into a barn and set it on fire."

He looked over at Liz, saw the color wash out of her face. "Sorry, but that's what happened. That's the kind of men these were. Evil men, according to my dad. When the war was over, they shipped the soldiers back to Germany. I have no idea what happened to them. My father tore down the temporary buildings and tents that housed them and in their place, built the old gray house."

Liz leaned toward him. "Are you . . . are you thinking that maybe that's where all this began?"

"That's about it. I guess you could say I've been thinking a lot about evil. About the nature of the beast, if there is such a thing. Seems to me a lot of bad stuff has gone on around here since the war. Maybe . . . well, maybe if the evil is strong enough, it stays on after the carrier is gone."

"That's pretty far-fetched," Zach said.

"Maybe. But considering what's happened out here —"

"Good point."

"At any rate, I've decided to close this section of the ranch, move the workers to another part of the property. The overseers' houses are old and in need of repair. I'm gonna tear 'em down and rebuild in a new location."

Zach just stared.

"I guess you think I'm crazy. Maybe you'll start believing your brother was right about me, all along."

Liz reached over and caught his hand. "I don't think you're crazy. I was in that house. I felt the evil that lives there. I think it's a good idea."

"So do I," Zach said softly.

Fletcher Harcourt just nodded. Perhaps men of strong will weren't affected by the forces of evil, or perhaps they were able to overcome them. Maybe that was the reason he had lost only one son and not both.

Or perhaps it was all just a big pile of bull.

He looked at his younger son and the woman who would soon be his daughter. He thought about the spirit of the little girl who had come to warn Maria Santiago of the evil that still existed in the house years after the child was gone.

Whatever the truth, they were all starting over.

Fletcher figured it was long overdue.

AUTHOR'S NOTE

Though both the characters and story are purely fiction, this tale is based on an incident that actually happened in the summer of 1995 in a small town in the San Joaquin Valley. During that summer, a Hispanic couple repeatedly saw the ghost of a little girl at the foot of their bed. It was later discovered that, in 1961, a child who had lived in the house had been abducted by a man and his pregnant wife, raped and brutally murdered.

The apparition appearing to the young woman warned that her unborn baby would die if she didn't move out of the house. The couple, unable to relocate, remained in the house and the baby did die, strangled by its own umbilical cord.

During World War II, the spot had been a Nazi prisoner of war camp.

ABOUT THE AUTHOR

Kat Martin is the *New York Times* bestselling author of over 30 historical and contemporary romance novels. To date, she has nine million copies of her books in print and has been published in 17 foreign countries, including Sweden, China, Korea, Russia, South Africa, Argentina and Greece. Kat and her husband, author Larry Jay Martin, live on their ranch in Missoula, Montana. Visit her Web site at www.kat books.com.

The employees of Thorndike Press hope you have enjoyed this Large Print book. All our Thorndike and Wheeler Large Print titles are designed for easy reading, and all our books are made to last. Other Thorndike Press Large Print books are available at your library, through selected bookstores, or directly from us.

For information about titles, please call:
  (800) 223-1244

or visit our Web site at:
  www.gale.com/thorndike
  www.gale.com/wheeler

To share your comments, please write:
  Publisher
  Thorndike Press
  295 Kennedy Memorial Drive
  Waterville, ME 04901